CHILDREN,
MY CHILDREN

CHILDREN, MY CHILDREN

A NOVEL

CELESTINE SIBLEY

HARPER & ROW, PUBLISHERS, New York
Cambridge, Philadelphia, San Francisco,
London, Mexico City, São Paulo, Sydney

1817

To my daughters,
Susan and Mary

ACKNOWLEDGMENTS

I'd like to especially thank Forrest and Catherine Granger for their help with West Florida life and lore.

FIRST EDITION

Designer: C. Linda Dingler

Library of Congress Cataloging in Publication Data

Sibley, Celestine.
   Children, my children.

   I. Title.
PS3569.I256C47   1981   813'.54   80–8231
ISBN 0–06–014872–1   AACR2

81 82 83 84 85 10 9 8 7 6 5 4 3 2 1

FALL 1976

The bench outside the telephone booth was wet with spray blown by the west wind. Sally sat on it anyhow, feeling the cold concrete through her jeans. With the wind whistling around the tin roof of the combination marina-launderette, and the choppy river water rocking the boats in the slips, it was hard enough to hear. When the phone rang she wanted to be there to grab it.

She used her foot to nudge the plastic basket, with her sheets and towels and work jeans still warm from the dryer, closer to the building and tucked the plastic garbage bag covering it snugger. As much as she hated plastic, it would be impossible to live on an island and make frequent, sometimes daily, trips across the wide waters of the Sound without plastic to keep things dry. Even the olive-drab poncho she wore over her pea jacket had the slippery touch, the petroleum smell of plastic instead of the silky feel of the old oilskins she remembered from childhood.

She pulled the drawstring in the hood tighter and fished in her pocket for a handkerchief to blow her nose. The two-lane highway that ran along the coast was quiet tonight. She hadn't seen more than half a dozen cars pass since Sarge locked up the marina hours ago and told her to slam the door to the launderette when she finished drying her last load. The street lights of the little town of Lucina did not begin for another quarter of a mile; from where she sat, she could see not the lights themselves but only the faint rose flush they made against the gray sky. The little floodlight over the dock wore an aureole of mist. By contrast, the lighted drink machine beyond the locked doors of Miss Peachy's grocery next door looked warm and dry as a crackling fire.

Sally thought longingly of the fire laid in the fireplace in her little house across the Sound and then of the rough, wet trip that lay between her and it. She could hear the bell buoy rocking with the swelling waves down at the mouth of the river, bonging dolefully, more like a country church bell calling the sinful to repentance than a marine bell warning oystermen and other small boatmen of the treacherous spit of sand that the tides had thrown up between them and the harbor.

Most of the fleet of small fishing vessels was already tied up downstream. Earlier, Sally had seen their lights and heard an occasional burst of laughter, as some crewmen returned from a beer at Lucina's one bar, or a blast of music as somebody turned up a radio overly loud to get a weather forecast. Now they were quiet. Sally guessed it must be close to midnight. She considered getting up and looking at the big neon-framed clock on the water side of the building, handily placed for the convenience of boatmen rather than for women using the washing facilities of the laundry room or for traffic on the highway.

Suddenly the telephone in the glass booth shrilled.

In her haste to get to it, Sally stumbled and then wrestled for a moment with the folding glass door, which had been ajar, closing it instead of opening it. She fumbled for the telephone and spoke into it.

"Mama?" It was Leslie's voice, husky and breathless as it had been when she was a little girl, but now trembling. "Mama, I've found the children. They're here. But Mama—they don't want to come . . . with me!"

"What?" cried Sally. "What did you say? They don't want—"

"Talk to them, Mama, talk to them! Here's Bunny."

Bunny was crying. She seemed to be having trouble holding on to the telephone at the other end. Sally's heart lurched, and she gripped the receiver in her own hand all the harder, as if it would give the little girl, her granddaughter, strength.

"Bunny . . . honey . . . are you there?"

"Gran," said Bunny, "have you and Mama stopped loving us?"

2

"Ah, Bunny, baby," crooned Sally, "of course we haven't stopped loving you! Come on home with your mother. We love you and miss you."

"We can't," whimpered Bunny. "Not till after court. Daddy says we can see you all after court."

"Bun—" Sally began but the girl, her voice fading away, was saying, "Here's Bunk."

Bunk's voice, young and brash and a little smart-alecky, was in her ear. "Hello-o, there!"

Bunk, the one who had nearly died, the one whose baby arms she could still feel clinging to her at any time of parting, now spoke peremptorily, a brisk and competent thirteen-year-old.

"I can't talk but a minute, Gran," he said. "We're not coming with *her*. We'll see you after court."

"But Christmas, Bunk," began Sally, now near tears herself. "Don't you want to come home for Christmas? We miss you and we've all been so worried about you. Come home for Christmas. Get your daddy to come too."

"We've already got plans for Christmas—just we three," Bunk said.

"Three?" Sally whispered. "You mean, not your mother too?"

"Nope, just we three," said Bunk. "I got to hang up now. My father may be trying to call me."

The phone went dead.

The rain was now sluicing down the side of the glass telephone booth. Sally stood a minute in the lighted cubicle, looking dazedly at the telephone's blank face and the senseless graffiti on the little sheet of instructions above it. Where were they? Where had Leslie found them? She hadn't asked the name of the motel and now she couldn't call back.

Panic threatened her. You couldn't pick up the phone and call out into the cold and rainy night, "Operator, get me New Orleans. Get me my grandchildren."

Somewhere out there were three of the people she loved best in the world. Two of them were crying, and one, with teenage bravado, was trying to cope with a tangle of adult problems. His briskness—ruthlessness?—was somehow more terrible than Bunny's tears.

Her fingers curled around the telephone and she reached for the little directory. The town of Lucina, maybe 500 numbers, and the neighboring towns of Shell Cove and Hammerhead, maybe 500 more. There was no help there. She couldn't say to that languid voice who would answer "Information," "Tell me where they are. Find that faraway phone for me, please!"

She leaned against the glass wall and opened the folding door a little to cut off the overhead light. There was no use standing there like a guppy in a goldfish bowl for Harvey Benton, the town policeman, to see when he made his rounds to check on Lucina's lawless element, teenage kids who might be stealing gasoline from boats and cars. No use having him ask what she was doing away from Point Esperance at that hour of the night and lecture her against crossing the Sound in the turbulent weather. She had to go; she wanted to go to be in her own house to examine this new dilemma.

Hal had not only taken the children, he had somehow made them like it, made them want to be there with him, without their mother!

Sally edged out of the phone booth and walked down to the bollard where she had tied the bowline of the little runabout, called *Wild Jelly* after an ill-fated excursion she and her mother, Angie, had made into the business world. Angie, who had had to laugh at failure a lot, had insisted on naming the boat for their latest venture, partly in fun, partly as a thumb-to-nose gesture at fate. Rainwater had darkened the canvas top over the small cockpit and accumulated in the bottom, enough to slosh around the fat red gas tank and the battery, which looked like a huge lump of sugar in the open stern. Was it enough to bail, or should she just wait and run it out when she got to the mouth of the river and could up the throttle? She stood a moment, distractedly trying to wrench her mind from the telephone booth and fix it on the practical matter of navigating seven stormy miles of churning water in the darkness.

She could do it, of course. She was reared on the wooded curve of that little island out there. She knew every capricious season and tide-changing facet of St. Dominique Sound and had taught them to her children and grandchildren, especially the twins, Bunny and Bunk, who had lived with her every summer and for other random months here and there, when their parents were on the road or unemployed, temporarily homeless.

Oh, Bunny and Bunk, she thought with an ache, Bunny and Bunk—ridiculous jazz-musician names for babies! Twins but dissimilar, except for their father's sun-bleached silver-blond hair and nearly matching eyes. Tall for their age and good children, competent, helpful. Now Bunk is being cool and crisp with his grandmother—wants Christmas without his mother!

Oh, find him, find him, Sally prayed to the squally night. And Bunny, sweet Bunny, solemn and loving and patient. She was the one who had said, "I know one thing, Gran, my mom will never divorce my dad. I made her promise that."

Look who's asking for a divorce now, look who took the children away and told them about *court*. "We'll see you after court" indeed.

Sally sat back down on the concrete bench. She had not wanted Leslie to go to New Orleans. She had not believed for a moment that Hal intended to keep the children. It was some idiotic game compounded of extramarital sex and marijuana, she was convinced. Why should he want to keep Bunk and Bunny now when he had never been able to take care of them when they were all together?

Sally had thought it strange that he asked to have them sent to him in New Orleans, and even stranger that Leslie would comply. She had learned by plowing through some very shoaly water as a mother-in-law to keep her mouth shut, but she did ask the question: Why send the children ahead if Leslie herself planned to join Hal in New Orleans at Christmastime?

"Oh, Mama!" Leslie had said impatiently. "Hal misses the children. He says there's a good school near the place where he's staying, and he can get them started there, and then I'll drive down with all our things."

"But they're in school here," Sally pointed out.

How well she knew they were in school. She and the *Wild Jelly* had been chiefly responsible for taking them to school and picking them up daily since they all came home to Esperance last summer, after Angie died.

It had suited Hal fine to leave his family there while he took a playing job at a summer hotel in Virginia Beach. And when the job ended on Labor Day he had wanted them to stay on while he presumably found another in New Orleans.

The children always loved being on the island. It was the closest thing they had ever known to a permanent home, and

5

they had joyfully participated when Sally fixed up an old summer cottage on the bayside for them. She would have loved
having them with her at the point—and the children were
there much of the time—but the mother-in-law thing intimi-
dated her. She didn't want to destroy their privacy by having
them in the same house with her. She didn't want Hal to think
she was interfering. Once, years before, when she had given
Leslie some grocery money, he had said sullenly, "I want you
to stop that. I'm responsible for my family."

"I'm sorry," Sally had said humbly. "I just thought you might
need a little help right now."

"I can take care of my family," Hal had said stubbornly.

Since when? Sally had wanted to ask. But maybe he *would*
support them. She had very little money herself, Angie had
had even less, and it would be a little easier if they didn't
have to spread it out to help Hal's family. But he was young,
and a musician's jobs were not dependable, and they were
always being evicted from one dingy apartment or another
or the utilities were cut off or one of them got sick and there
was no money for medicine or the doctor. So Sally had adopted
the system of sharing what she had with Leslie *secretly*. It
saved face for Hal and eased her own fear that they might
be hungry and homeless.

Then, the summer just past, Hal had worked steadily and
sent money weekly for two or three months. Leslie had been
ecstatic, going on flings at the grocery store, inviting old friends
from town to come to the beach and cook steaks, promising
the twins they would buy a boat of their own and maybe a
horse to pasture on the grassy end of the island where goats
and wild hogs roamed.

Late summer had come, and a hurricane which bypassed
Florida hit the Virginia coast. Leslie, worried over Hal, had
borrowed the boat and gone to Lucina to call the hotel where
he played. She made a funny story about it when she reported
to Sally.

"The phone rang and rang, Mama, and I was about to give
up when a girl answered. You know, all low-voiced and husky
and sleepy-sexy sounding. I lost my cool. You know what I
thought. I yelled, 'Is that Hal Ellis's room?' She gave the phone
to Hal, and I said, 'Who is *that girl?*' He started laughing and
said, 'Shook you up, didn't I?' Mama, it turned out they were

6

having a hurricane party in Hal's room and a lot of members of the band were there. The girl had gone to sleep next to the telephone."

Sally had laughed with her, but from time to time she wondered if Leslie had really believed in the hurricane party. Her daughter's buoyant delight in having the little beach house, which she named "Rent Free," seemed to have staled. She watched morosely for the mail and talked uncertainly about starting the children in school in Lucina. She had always liked to drink, and now, Sally worried, she seemed to be doing a lot of it.

"We'll probably be in New Orleans," she kept saying. "No use starting them here."

Labor Day came, Hal flew down to Tallahassee, and a jubilant Leslie and Bunk and Bunny met him. Leslie had swept and garnished the little beach house and prepared all Hal's favorite things for supper. She planned to ask a few friends from the mainland over the next night for a cookout, but Hal didn't stay. There was a man he needed to see about a job in New Orleans, he told Leslie, and because he wanted to get there in a hurry he planned to fly. A frugal eight-hour bus trip wasn't Hal's speed, not if he had any money.

Leslie had walked over to her mother's house while Hal and the children played in the surf. "Mama, can you lend me fifty dollars?" she asked apologetically. "I need it so Hal can buy his airplane ticket tonight. You see"—she flushed guilti-ly—"he thinks from that hundred a week he's been sending that I have saved up some money."

Sally shook her head in mystification at the ignorance of men of such mundane matters as the high cost of food and utilities and school shoes and dental bills, and went to get her pocketbook. "Lend" was, both she and Leslie recognized, a face-saving euphemism, but she was glad she had the money to give the girl.

Hal had not come by to see her before they left for the airport, but she had not really expected it. He had not been there for Angie's funeral, or even tried to express sympathy, but she had put it down to shyness. She had Leslie's word that he had loved his wife's grandmother and was really numb with grief at her death.

Leslie had gone back to watching for the mail. She put the

twins in school in Lucina. Bunny had made friends immediately, but Bunk was having rough sailing. He had a friend or two from the summer—a shrimper's son and the son of a mechanic who worked on cars. But when he got to school and made friends with two black boys who were being bused in from a farming community up the road, his white friends ostracized him. Hurt and baffled, the little boy had become a loner except when he could fall back on the society of his sister and his grandmother. Even his mother, who had been ever ready for games and projects, seemed worried and short-tempered these days. The checks were not coming regularly from Hal. He had not been able to get a regular job, he wrote, but only occasional gigs.

Sally had noticed that when Leslie did get money she usually brought home a bottle of cheap wine. She talked constantly of when they would join Hal in New Orleans, but he had not been able to find a place and suggested that she get a job in Lucina. So she had found a job clerking at a new Junior Food Store which was opening up on the highway at the edge of town, and for several weeks she and the children went to and from the mainland together every day. She was good-humored and efficient, and it pleased her to be able to write Hal not to worry that he couldn't send much money now. Her salary, supplemented by free seafood and access to Sally's store of home-canned vegetables, was sufficient to feed them.

He was to save up for an apartment, she wrote, and she would try to put something by to move them to New Orleans when he gave the word. She hoped it would be soon, because Bunk was not flourishing in school in Lucina and both the children missed their father. She missed him so much herself, she had confided to her sister, Sarah, that she had to slug herself with sherry at bedtime to keep from crying herself to sleep.

Sarah and her two children had come down from Tallahassee for a brilliant Thanksgiving weekend when the beach goldenrod turned the dunes and woodland paths on the island into a billowing sea of gold. She and Sally had sat on the dock watching Bunk and Bunny and their cousins, Hank and Say-Say, combing the tideline for sand dollars. Their great-grandmother Angie had had a go at selling seashells—this after the wild-jelly-making enterprise failed—and all the children had a commercial, rather than esthetic, interest in shells. In common with Angie, they looked on what the tide brought in as a bonanza from a kind providence which intended them to convert everything into picture and mirror frames and shell-covered boxes and plaques, and, as the baby Say-Say put it, "May monee." Sally had not had much faith in that make-money enterprise of her mother's, but she had welcomed shelling as an occupation for the children and as an opportunity for them to learn to identify and appreciate the delicate and intricately patterned sea life.

That afternoon Sally had watched the children with pleasure, their jeans rolled up, the white-foamed surf curling around their ankles, their young bodies caught and held in attitudes of singular grace and beauty by the bronze light of the setting sun.

"You know she's going to have to give up that job at the Junior." Sarah had picked up the thread of their conversation, mostly about Leslie.

"Why?" Sally had asked, pulling her attention from the children. "Give it up? Sarah, she needs it—terribly. It feeds them."

"Mother, did you know they make all their employees take lie-detector tests, and Leslie's is coming up."

Sally had been confused. "It's an awful thing to do," she murmured, "but Sarah, I don't see why Leslie can't take it. She *needs* the job. It's not as if she could make an issue of her rights—"

"Mother-r!" Sarah said. "It's not a question of *rights* this time; I think Les is too beat and too tired to protest anything any more. But they'll find out she's been in jail and they'll fire her and it'll be all over Lucina and the children are having it rough anyhow."

Sally had taken a deep breath and let it out slowly. A wave knocked Say-Say down and the other three children went to the rescue, using it as an excuse to get wet themselves. Sarah, who had lived inland long enough to worry about wet clothes and twilight chill, slid off the dock and went to herd the children to the house.

Sally sat on. It was too much, too much that a Texas jail and a charge of possessing marijuana should now rise up and swat down poor Leslie and the children, years after they had thought that particular trauma was behind them. Hadn't it been enough, the sleepless nights, the stark terror of having

9

the two young parents in jail, the teacher's warning that the children would be taken into custody by juvenile authorities if Sally didn't get them out of Dallas immediately? Wasn't it enough that she had had to sell her car to raise plane fare to get the twins home and to pay bail and a lawyer's fee for Leslie and Hal. It was the first and last new car she would ever own.

Angie had watched it go with tears in her eyes. "I'm sorry I don't have sapphires and rubies we could sell instead," she had said. "There *was* my engagement ring—"

"I know," Sally had said. "It went for Sarah's braces. This is all right, Ma. I'm just glad we had *something* we could turn into money. This old clunker will do me the few times I'm ashore and need to drive around. Lucky we didn't have to sell the boat."

"Yep, lucky," Angie had said briskly. "But you would have sold that too, if the kids needed it. You would have sold it and bought us two pairs of water wings."

They had laughed together and coaxed the old jalopy to make the trip to Tallahassee to meet Bunk and Bunny.

Blessed babies, Sally had thought that afternoon on the dock, her eyes following them as they straggled up the path to the house behind Sarah. They had never had it easy and it seemed they never would. Now their mother was going to lose her little job, the only toehold she had on independence.

Leslie had quit the job two days after Thanksgiving, just before the man with the lie-detector machine arrived. And a few days later there had been a letter from Hal with two airplane tickets in it.

"Just two tickets?" Sally had asked.

"He wants me to send the children on ahead," Leslie had explained. "He has a furnished room now, but by Christmas he is getting a nice apartment and he'll be ready for me to drive over and bring all our stuff. Mama, isn't it wonderful? The children are so excited!"

Sally hadn't thought it was wonderful. She had thought it extravagant and capricious of Hal to spend money for airplane tickets for the children when he couldn't afford an apartment. And there was something else, some deep foreboding which she carefully hid from Leslie. She met the twins after school and took them shopping for new shoes and raincoats. Bunny had wandered off to look at a cream-colored wool coat with a hood and Sally saw the longing in her eyes.

"Try it on," she suggested and then looked at the price tag. It was $75! "Oh, baby," she said, dismayed. "We can't get it now. Maybe by Christmas. . . ."

"I don't want a coat for Christmas," Bunny said decisively. "Other girls get coats just because they *need* them, not for Christmas presents."

"I know." Sally had sighed. "I used to hate clothes for Christmas when I was your age. But you need so many other things right now, honey. Underwear and a sweater and socks. Your father may not have a good way to keep your clothes clean."

"Some lady who is a friend of his is going to meet us at the airport," Bunny said. "Daddy will be playing at a club and can't come himself."

Sally wondered privately about the lady who was a friend of Daddy's but she said nothing, concentrating on the selection of socks to match the skirts she had made for Bunny.

"Are you glad to be going?" she asked as Bunny hovered at her elbow.

"I'll be glad to see Daddy," the little girl said. "But I don't want to stay. I want to come back here until Mom's ready to go. She needs me."

Sally put her arm around her granddaughter and hugged her. "We all need you," she said. "But this may be a wonderful new life for you all in a new and exciting place."

Bunny, the impressionable one, reflected optimism. "Yes!" she said eagerly. "Daddy will be so glad to have us and he'll take us shopping. You know how fathers are about their daughters."

Sally was puzzled. The words were vaguely familiar, but she hadn't remembered that Hal had any special caring way with his daughter. Then she remembered. Sarah's husband, Henry, so glad to have a little girl after ten boisterous-boy years with Hank, spoiled the baby Say-Say terribly, buying her any trinkets her velvety brown eyes fell upon.

"We'll go in a store," Bunny planned, "and Daddy and Bunk will go look at records and sporting goods and leave me to shop for myself. Daddy will say get anything I want. I may get a coat with a hood."

"Ah," Sally said approvingly. "That will be lovely." Then, as an afterthought, "Did your daddy ever take you shopping?"

Bunny's blue eyes clouded, but she rallied. "Once," she said.

"And what did he buy you?"

Bunny faltered. "I think . . . I think . . . I remember, it was a pair of socks."

Sally had turned away to hide the tears in her eyes. Fantasy, pure fantasy, she thought. Hal never could have bought her a pair of socks. She was ashamed that she had crowded the child into reducing her dream to socks size.

Leslie had taken them to the airport and spent the night in Tallahassee with Sarah so Hal could call her and tell her the twins had arrived safely.

Sarah had reported Leslie's end of that conversation on one of her visits to the island.

"Oh, they're there!" Leslie had cried gaily. "Honey, hug them for me. It's awful without *all* of you. I miss you terribly, but maybe it won't be long now till we're all together. Let me speak to B and B."

Sarah had started to walk from the room when she heard Leslie gasp and saw her face go white.

"What did you say?" she had whispered into the phone.

"Mother, it was like seeing somebody stabbed to death," Sarah told Sally later. "She was choking and speechless with pain and that funny kind of surprise. You know, like it had to be happening to somebody else, not her."

What Hal had said, as Sally was later to determine from the garbled report of a drunken, sobbing Leslie, was that she not only couldn't speak to the children but she wouldn't see them again. He had them, and he was filing suit for divorce. He did not, of course, want her to come to New Orleans for Christmas or at any other time.

But Leslie had gone.

Now, waiting by the telephone booth, Sally marveled that Leslie knew to do it. If she had listened to me, Sally thought tiredly, she would be here waiting it out, waiting for Hal's little charade of independence and decisiveness to dissolve.

"You know he won't get a divorce," she had told Sarah. "He can't even exert himself to carry a driver's license."

It was true he had received more than one ticket for forgetting his driver's license. Sally had paid one whopping fine for him.

But Leslie had believed him. She got some clothes and went back to Sarah's to be near the telephone, which did not ring for her until her mother called from Lucina in a couple of days to say that she was there with the boat and to urge her to come on back home.

"I'm going to New Orleans, Mama," Leslie had said. "I've got to look for Bunk and Bunny."

"Oh, Les." Sally had sighed. "You can't go now. You haven't any money. You can't drive your old car, and mine is no better. Where will you stay? You don't even know where to look."

"I know where Hal was playing," Leslie had said. "I'll go see him and talk to him. I think if I tell him I'll give him a divorce—I think he has a girl—that might be all he wants." Her voice broke.

"Oh, baby," Sally had murmured helplessly. It was so terrible to be young and vulnerable to the whims of a callow boy husband. "Wait."

"I can't," Leslie had said, her voice stronger now. "I have a tank of gas and I bought a secondhand tire that will do for a spare. Sarah lent me fifty dollars. I can manage. I've got to get my children, Mama. You know that."

"Yes," Sally had said resignedly. "Well, come by the marina. I'll cash a check. And, honey, tell Sarah to give you Angie's good coat. It's in her cedar closet in the guest room. You'll need it."

Cashing a check had been slower than usual. All the young tellers were helping to decorate the big Christmas tree in the center of the little bank lobby. By the time Sally got outside, the wind was blowing colder and the rain felt sleety. She stood in front of the marina launderette stuffing her checkbook back in her purse and looking at the five $20 bills she had to give Leslie. A measly $100—more than she could spare, really, with taxes on the island facing her. If she only had $1,000, she could buy Leslie an airplane ticket and some other clothes besides too-tight jeans and chunky backless sandals, which were all she owned, and be sure that she was safe in a decent hotel.

She had picked the old car out of the line of traffic coming toward her on Main Street by the cloud of evil-smelling blue smoke following it. Leslie turned into the parking lot and rolled down the window. She was smiling valiantly.

"Don't look so worried, Mama," she had said determinedly, falsely cheerful. "I'll probably be back tomorrow with those terrible twins."

Sally made herself smile and held out the money. "Be careful," she said. "Let me know."

"I'll call Sarah when I get there," Leslie promised. "She can relay to you. Don't worry."

With a wave and a roar of the ailing muffler she was gone.

If you get there, Sally had said to herself as she went to call Sarah. "Sis," she began when her other daughter answered, "Leslie—"

"Did she get off?" Sarah asked. "Well, Mother, don't worry about her. She's traveled around the country in old junky cars with no money before. She'll manage."

"I should have gone with her," Sally had said.

"Not you," Sarah said. "Me. Hal would hate it if you were with her—probably if I was with her, too. He hates both of us."

"Oh, I don't believe that," Sally had said. "Why would he? We've always treated him well. We don't hate *him.*"

"*Ma-ma,*" Sarah had said with exaggerated patience. "Of course he hates us. He loathed every bite of food you put in his mouth. You can play that he's-my-child-too game if you want to, but I won't. I think he's taken those children off to some dump where he's probably giving them pot to smoke instead of food to eat, just to spite Les."

"I should have gone," Sally said again.

"Well, Mother," Sarah said, laughing a little but with a catch in her voice, "now that I've cheered you up, why don't you come up here and have supper and spend the night with us? Hank and Say-Say are still around."

Sally had thought of the two grandchildren who were safe and noisily visible two counties away and was tempted. To see and touch them, Hank, just a few months older than the twins, and Sarah IV, the funny, sweet baby of the family, would have cheered and comforted her. She had looked at the sky and thought of Leslie, alone and doggedly pushing the old car westward.

"I better go home," she said. "Leslie will probably call you.

Tell her the phone on the island is working now and to call me there."

"Well, if you change your mind, come on," Sarah said. "And, Mother . . . don't worry."

Sally smiled. It was what her children always said. Don't worry. They vacillated between regarding her as an insane optimist, eternally riding for a fall, and a doomsday worrier. She sometimes wondered how they could have it both ways. But she really knew. She did it both ways, seesawing between aching anxiety and the witless conviction that everything was going to be all right. As she walked toward the *Wild Jelly* that afternoon she had wryly paraphrased Churchill. *We have a great deal to be anxious about.*

The marine telephone in Sally's kitchen was a new acquisition, and she neither trusted it nor liked it. She expected it to go out of service when the wind blew, and when it was in service she had a feeling that operators and random shortwavers all the way to the call's point of origin were listening in. But she blessed it that night when it started clattering and Leslie's voice came through.

"Mama, I'm here. Over," Leslie said in the ridiculous patois of shortwave communication.

"You made it," Sally said, reaching for and sagging into a kitchen chair with such relief she forgot to say "Over."

"Yes, ma'am. The car didn't give me a speck of trouble. I've got a room at the St. Claude Hotel. It's a little hotel not too far from the French Quarter. Cheap but it's pretty clean and safe, I think. The kind of place where Japanese students and schoolteachers stay."

"You sure?" Sally said. "I never heard of it."

"Pretty sure," Leslie said. "Anyhow, it's only six dollars a day and there's a good lock on the door. The phone is in the hall. I'll give you the number. I've called the club and left a message for Hal to call me here. They said they *thought* he was playing tonight. Like they didn't *know!*"

"Do you think he'll call you?" Sally asked.

"I hope so," Leslie said. "He might be over whatever was bugging him by now and want to get back together."

"Don't say 'bugging,' it's a terrible word," Sally said, reverting to her scolding-mother role now that she knew Leslie was safe and had hopes of getting the children.

Leslie giggled. "I'm going to clean up and wait by the phone. I'll call you when I have some news."

But there had been no news that night or the next. Leslie had sat in the bare, musty little hall until close to dawn, after she knew the club would be closed but hoped that Hal would come by to see her. At daybreak she had fallen into bed, weeping and exhausted. She slept and awakened and spent the morning driving aimlessly about cheap neighborhoods, the kind where she and Hal had always lived, looking for some sign of him or the children. It occurred to her that he might have put the children in school, and she parked near a close-to-town junior high school and got out and walked. Twice she had seen the backs of children who looked like either Bunk or Bunny—never twins—and had run after them, calling out, only to have strange blank young faces turned her way. The second night she had again left messages for Hal at the club.

She told Sally about it over the phone, forcing hope she couldn't have felt into her voice.

"I think he may have been off last night," she told her mother. "He probably didn't get my message. The person I talked to tonight said he would be sure Hal knew I was here and waiting to hear from him. So I'm going to stay by the phone."

"I don't suppose you'd want to go to that nightclub," Sally had offered tentatively.

"Oh, Hal would hate me for that," Leslie said. "I haven't anything to wear but bluejeans, and I'm so fat and tacky. He wouldn't want me to come there."

"Is it cold there?" Sally asked. "Are you warm enough."

"It's cold and raining," Leslie said. "But I have Angie's good cashmere coat and I'm all right. If everything else I have looked as good as her coat, I wouldn't hesitate to go strutting into that club and walk straight up to the bandstand."

"Oh, baby," sighed Sally. "I wish you had some decent clothes. I wish—"

"Don't worry, Mama," Leslie had said briskly. "If I find Bunk and Bunny I won't need a thing. I'm sure I'll hear from Hal tonight."

But she hadn't heard from Hal that night, and she spent another day wandering through the rainy streets of New Orleans, searching. The third night she pinned her long light-brown hair into a chignon, rummaged through her suitcase for a clean blouse, applied a faint touch of lipstick to her pale mouth (Hal hated for her to wear makeup), bundled into her grandmother's coat, and went out. The rain still fell and her sandals, the only shoes she owned, were a pulpy mess. Her bravely pinned-up hair got wet and drooped on her collar. The lights in the French Quarter were bright but there were pockets of darkness in doorways and courtyards, and as she hurried past them a man called out to her. She ran until she reached the lights of the Club Avignon.

Through the window she saw Hal on the bandstand lifting his trombone to play a solo. He looked handsome and dear to her, and she swallowed hard and pushed ineffectually at her sopping hair.

He saw her and waved and smiled, and her heart lifted. He would come out to see her when he had a break, she thought. She huddled under the awning and waited, blowing on her gloveless hands, fumbling for a handkerchief for the cold she was taking.

Hal finished his solo with a flourish and returned to his seat. The band swung into an old Dixieland melody, and Leslie smiled in appreciation. It was a piece Hal had always liked. She could hear his trombone in the background picking at the theme and then latching on to it and soaring. Ah, he was good, she thought, he was so good.

The band didn't take a break and she couldn't see Hal on the stand. It was getting late, toward closing time, and she edged into the doorway, shivering from the cold. The door opened and a man in a tuxedo said, "Did you want something, lady?"

Leslie smiled. "I'm waiting for Hal Ellis. I'm his wife."

The man smiled maliciously. "He's gone," he said with satisfaction. *"Been* gone."

"How? When?" Leslie asked desperately.

The man shrugged. The band was packing up, and he called out, "Ain't that right, boys? Ain't Hal Ellis gone?"

"Been gone," somebody echoed.

"Good night, chick," the man said spitefully and closed the door.

Leslie, telling her mother about it over the phone, had broken down and cried.

"He knew I was there, Mama, and he let me stand in the rain and wait! Everybody there knew it!"

It was a trivial piece of cruelty compared to the taking of the children, but it seemed to be the final straw to break Leslie's heart.

"Come on home, honey," Sally had urged. "Give it up and come on home. Have you got any money left?"

"I've got enough," Leslie said. "I'm going to spend some on phone calls and try to see people we've known here. I haven't wanted to call on anybody who was Hal's friend too. I thought they wouldn't want to get in our hassle. But now I'll try anything."

For three days Leslie's calls had been bleak. Her cold was worse and then better. The friends she had found either knew nothing about the children or would tell her nothing. One couple said firmly they did not intend to become "involved" and showed her to the door. On the fourth day she said she was checking out of the hotel and coming home. She had $10 for the trip.

"Stay there until I can wire you some money," Sally had urged. "Go to Western Union and wait. You can't get home on ten dollars."

The money order was slow to arrive, and Leslie had sat and waited in a coffee shop. It was there she met an old musician friend from their days in Denton. He had been fired by the Club Avignon, blown his last paycheck on an evening in the French Quarter, and was now waiting for his wife to send him bus fare home. He knew where Hal and the children were living.

"Mama, it's that horrible old motel on the Airline Highway," Leslie told her over the phone, practically singing out the words. "You know, where we stayed when the children and I came over here before?"

Sally smiled to herself and wanted to say, Yes, but you didn't say it was horrible then. It had ever been Leslie's way to make whatever place Hal put them sound delightful. When she told her mother they were living in a cheap motel, waiting to find an apartment, she emphasized the fact that it had a swimming pool for Bunk and Bunny to enjoy. No kitchen, only one room, but a swimming pool. The children had later told their grandmother that they hated the place, even scorning the dirty swimming pool.

Now Leslie was high with hope. She meant to wait until

after eight o'clock, when she expected Hal would have gone to the nightclub. She would go straight there and pick up the children and head for home.

But they had not wanted to come. They had hung up the phone on their grandmother. What on earth had happened to them?

The phone rang again and Sally walked shakily to answer it. Leslie was weeping uncontrollably now.

"He came, Mama!" she cried. "Hal came and they ran out and got in his car. Mama, he knocked me down and tore Angie's coat! He threw me out on the floor in the hall."

"Oh, Leslie!" Sally gasped. "Are you hurt?"

"I don't think so." Leslie was calmer now. "But Angie's good coat, Mama, it's ruined. And I dropped my pocketbook in the room when he pushed me and now I can't get it. He slammed the door and told the man at the desk to *call the police on me*, Mama!"

The expression "call the police on me" was one from their childhood, hers and Hal's, and Sally almost smiled at it.

"Well, come on home, honey," she said.

"I can't!" Leslie wailed. "My pocketbook, my keys! The man at the desk won't let me in. He say's it's not my room and he can't do it."

"Let me talk to him," Sally said.

An officious young male voice said hello.

"This is Mrs. McMillan in Florida," Sally said. "I'm Mrs. Ellis's mother. As you can see, she is having difficulty with her husband and is upset. I wouldn't like for her to have to wait there until our attorney arrives. If you will just let her have her pocketbook and car keys, I'll be much obliged."

"I'm sorry, ma'am, I don't have the authority to let someone into a guest's room." He was going to be stubborn, Sally thought bleakly, feeling cold water trickling off her poncho into her knee-length rubber boots.

"Oh, of course not," Sally said, as if he had imparted fresh and imperishable truth. "Of course you can't. I hadn't thought of that. Well, suppose *you* go in yourself. You will see her pocketbook, the one she brought in when you directed her to the room, and if you'll just return it to her, she can leave. We certainly don't want to give you any trouble."

"We-ell. . . ." The young man was reluctant.

19

"Ah, thank you!" said Sally warmly. "I'll just hold the line while you get it."

The telephone was set down slowly, as if the young man were still not certain that he was going to do as she asked. But then she heard voices moving away and knew he was going with Leslie away from the desk, presumably toward the room lately occupied by Hal and those blessed, uprooted, turned-around children, Bunk and Bunny.

I think I might cry, she thought, reaching for her handkerchief with her free hand and blowing her nose. I'm either going to cry or I'm taking a terrible cold.

The wind was blowing the rain against the outside of the glass wall harder now, and her breath had fogged up the inside so she couldn't see the drink box in Miss Peachy's grocery. She wiped at the grayness halfheartedly, absently, while she listened for Leslie's return.

"I've got it, Mama, I'm leaving now," Leslie said in a little while.

"Wait, honey," Sally said quickly. "Get away from there but don't try to travel too far tonight. Wait and get an early start in the morning. Do you have any money?"

"Yes, ma'am, I've still got what you sent. Oh, Mama, you should have seen that room! Liquor bottles everywhere—garbage—this man says if I want him to testify in court for me, he'll be glad to."

"That's fine," said Sally automatically, relieved that Leslie could now think ahead to court—beyond the torn coat, the lost pocketbook, the rejection by her husband and children, the rattletrap car, and the unfriendly big city. "Maybe you should leave that old car and catch a bus home," she suggested.

"No, ma'am, it'll bring me home all right," Leslie said. "I want to keep it. It's all I have. . . ."

Oh, baby, Sally thought wearily. To be down to that junky old car is poverty indeed. "Well, cheer up," she said briskly. "We haven't begun to fight."

√ Sally had slogged tiredly toward the slip and her little boat and was squatting in the stern pumping the black rubber bulb that would send gasoline coursing toward the engine when she remembered the basket of laundry. She stumbled scrambling up to the dock and dragged one rubber-shod foot in the water.

"Damn Hal," she mumbled to herself. "He knows we're scuttled. He's just a rat leaving a sinking ship. If we weren't in a bad way as a family I'd have a working washer and dryer on the point. I'd have a marine telephone I could count on and wouldn't have to hang around a pay station half the night. I'd have a bigger boat. I wouldn't even be on the point. I'd be in a warm condominium in St. Petersburg!"

The last came out in a half sob, and Sally realized she was crying. Well, tears have their use, she thought staunchly, but there's no place for them on a dark and stormy night in a small boat at sea. To firm up her resolve she stomped up the creaking wharf to retrieve the plastic basket and said aloud to the rainy night and a dark car slithering along on Highway 98, " 'I am the sea and not the shooting star, the vice and not the rapier. I come. . . .' "

She couldn't think of the rest of it, so she sniffed and wiped her eyes with one slippery poncho-covered arm and stuffed the clothes basket into the boat's one dry spot under the bow. Slipping off the stern and bow lines, she slid into the damp seat under the wheel, adjusted the spark, and turned the key to the starter. Benét was for those who could remember him; what did he know about trouble, anyway? she thought irritably. Suddenly the lines came to her: " 'I come building on the wrecks of ruined dreams because I have the labor and the skill. . . .' "

The engine coughed and caught and Sally shouted the last line above the wind and the voice of the water: " 'Now, in God's name, let them go forth to sea!' "

Remembering cheered her so she jabbed the throttle to reverse and thrust the boat neatly from its mooring without touching a single barnacled post or giving way to the pummeling of waves which could have canted the *Wild Jelly* crosswise in the slip. Free, Sally eased the throttle forward, and then, because it was late and there were no small boats in the harbor to be swamped by the wake, she jabbed it firmly toward wide open. The Marine Patrol boat was tied up at the Department of Natural Resources dock, and there were lights on in the office. For luck Sally picked up the mike of her small CB radio and said cheerfully, "Hello, Marine Patrol! This is Sally McMillan on the *Wild Jelly*. Do you read me? Over."

"Marine Patrol to *Wild Jelly*—go ahead," a warm, dry masculine voice said.

"We're off to the point. Over."

Sally hung the mike back on its hook and turned down the volume so she couldn't hear the warning and admonition which had started crackling out. They would be telling her not to attempt the crossing, but if she didn't read them it wasn't defiance. Joe Worthy, on duty there, would know she was out and would be alert to send help if she ran into trouble. She heard the bell buoy over the noise of the motor and swung wide out of the mouth of the river and into the Sound, checked the lighted compass on the dash, and concentrated on quartering the waves, which were now coming at her like great gray elephants bent on stomping the little white boat to death.

"Damn Hal!" she muttered between clenched teeth. "I told Leslie not to go—and I was wrong!"

Forty minutes later, Sally had the light on the Esperance dock in sight. Although drenched and shivering, she somehow felt warmer and safer. Esperance, refuge of women and children, she thought. Angie used to tell the children that French explorers called this point of land out in the Gulf of Mexico Esperance because they couldn't pronounce the word *Hope.* One at a time, as they grew older, they arrived at the conclusion that anybody who could say "esperance" could say "hope."

Angie had been unfailingly surprised at that discovery as each child made it in turn. "That's right!" she would cry delightedly. "I wonder why they didn't see that? Anyhow, it's all the same. Hope means esperance and vice versa."

It had meant hope to their family for three generations. The island had been theirs since before the Civil War and had, from time to time, looked like prime resort property, which would make them rich when all else failed. It had not made them rich, but it had been a refuge for most of them when, as in the case of both Angie and her daughter, Sally, and Sally's daughter Leslie, they had no other place to go.

Joseph Sellars, Sally's grandfather, was the first to visualize the little gulf island as "the Newport of the South." Excursion trains had started bringing visitors from afar to the Coast, and he saw no reason why they shouldn't proceed by steamer to Point Esperance, the high wooded promontory which the little island thrust out into the blue-green waters of the Gulf of Mexico. Except for dunes and patches of pine woods, the rest of the island was low-lying, running to marsh and brackish ponds, and Grandpa had been content to sell a few lots on it for $25 and $50 apiece, mostly to fishermen who cautiously put up gray shacks on stilts on the Sound side. He had loftier hopes for the beautiful point and built a big brown-shingled three-story hotel there, which flourished for a time. The dining room was celebrated for its seafood. The big ballroom, with floor-to-ceiling windows open to what Grandpa called "tropical zephyrs," became the scene of weekly dances which drew husband-hunting mamas and their marriageable daughters from such inland cities as Montgomery, Tallahassee, and faraway Memphis.

Angie had married a handsome young naval aviator from Pensacola in the ballroom, with masses of smilax and palmetto fronds making of it a green bower and a string ensemble imported from Tallahassee to play the wedding march and tunes for dancing. The young naval officer crashed his plane into a swamp one night and Angie came home, bringing baby Sally with her. She had a natural talent and enthusiasm for hospitality, and she darted about the big hotel like a bright-winged shorebird, organizing meals, setting light bread to rise, checking the water bowls and pitchers on the guest-room washstands to make sure they were immaculately clean and fresh-filled, mending the worn linen napkins, arranging the flowers, and then donning a dinner dress at night and mingling with the guests.

"Miss Angeline," the gentlemen always said, "made" the Esperance the best place to stay on the coast. It was a good thing, Angie had said, because her father had needed the insurance money the Navy paid her to repair the storm-damaged dock where the steamer landed and to put a new roof on the hotel. She and Sally had no other place to go.

Because Sally was considered a smart child, an easy learner, and because her mother was considered a "brainy" woman, who ordered boxloads of books from Atlanta and New York and memorized poetry for her own pleasure, Grandpa decided that Angie should teach the child herself. Angie did read omnivorously, but apparently not the things they were teaching in grammar and high school, because Sally went off to college ill-prepared. She left in her sophomore year to marry a newspaperman who rushed her into marriage because he was going to Washington to work and was afraid of being lonesome. Sally

23

had been glad enough to go with him. She hated half the subjects facing her in college and she could get a job with a congressman whose politics her grandfather and mother considered dangerously liberal. Her sole inclination and opportunity to rebel against her family, it was short-lived because she soon had to give up her job to take care of the babies, first Sarah, named for herself, who was named for her grandmother Sellars, and two years later Leslie, named because it sounded British and she was crazy about anything British, starting with Leslie Howard and including the conduct of the war, which was in progress. Bob McMillan had liked the British too and had wanted to fight on their side, but the United States wasn't taking married men with young babies then. He was on his way to Canada to offer himself to the Canadian Royal Air Force when he was killed in an automobile accident.

They brought him back to Point Esperance for burial. His parents were dead and he had no other relatives that Sally knew of. Sally had cried to see his body borne across the Sound in a coffin, covered with flowers and resting in the stern of a shrimp boat.

Later she had wondered if it had been the utter picturesqueness of it that had affected her, since she barely knew Bob McMillan and had certainly not inspired such fealty in him that he hadn't been able to leave her for a war his own country wasn't begging him to fight.

Sometimes, looking back, she had marveled at how quickly she had been able to forget her young husband and go on to other things, but in her absence the war had unexpectedly reached Esperance. The old hotel was perfect for quartering troops who came to the island to learn the operation of amphibious landing equipment, so the government divested her and Angie and the children of their home.

Taking Ladneer, a black woman who had served the family since Angie's youth, Sally and Angie moved to a rented house in Lucina and got jobs in a shipyard which had opened up down the coast. Then the war ended, the government money for the hotel ran out, and so did the jobs at the shipyard. They were planning on moving back to the point and reopening the hotel when a hurricane swept that prospect—and the hotel—out of their hands.

"What have we got and what can we do with it?" Angie

had asked as they sat over the kitchen table one night, looking over bills.

"Well, the island," Sally had said. "Maybe we could sell some lots."

"Not likely. Not as remote as it is," Angie had said. "If there's ever a bridge or a ferry over there, we'll be rich."

"Until then, I don't know," Sally had said, getting up to put on the coffeepot. "I suppose we'll have to live on sand and south wind. And"—her eye fell on jars of wild mayhaw jelly they had put up that afternoon—"mayhaw jelly."

"That's an idea," said Angie. "We could make jams and jellies and sell them. The woods are full of wild fruits nobody knows about or gathers. I can think of a dozen offhand."

Sally had not been optimistic, but her mother's optimism and enthusiasm were enough to carry them for the two years that Wild Jelly, Inc., lasted. They roamed the swamps and pine barrens, hauling the children and Ladneer, with them and recruiting young pickers along the way, gathering all the wild fruits the Florida earth offered in season—blackberries and huckleberries, haws and gooseberries and the bitter wild orange. Their nights had been spent over the fragrant steaming kettles in the hot kitchen. Sally had thought they might branch out, hiring a building somewhere with a big, better equipped kitchen.

"Not yet," Angie had said cautiously. "To be good, jelly has to be made in small batches. Let's stay where we are for now."

The wild jelly sold well. It was Angie's idea to put it in small jars and pack them in nests of gray Spanish moss or greenish reindeer moss for shipping. Tourists were beginning to find north Florida, and Angie and the two little girls rode up and down the coast, putting wild jelly on consignment in the souvenir stands, restaurants, and motels that were beginning to open. Their product sold so rapidly and so well the time came when another building and a good kitchen were essential.

"We'll get a loan from the bank," Angie planned. "Let's dress up and go in together and take Herb Wilcox a box of jellies so he can sample them and see what we're doing. He'll lend us the money."

But Herb Wilcox ate the jelly and refused the loan, taking the line to which the other bankers up and down that part of the coast would hew: two women with their little homey kitchen project were charming—really terrific cooks—but amateurs in a league already dominated by the big food-processing plants. They were not good risks, particularly since their only collateral was a sandbar littered with the rubble of an old hotel out in the gulf.

"Besides, Angeline," Wilcox had added insult to injury, as they were leaving. "Ain't you a little old for starting a business? I figure you're about my age, and I'm fixing to retire."

"More fool you!" Angie had snapped and slammed the little gate that separated the bank president from the rest of the employees.

They moved back to Point Esperance, into one of the few remaining buildings in the cluster that had surrounded the old hotel. The long rectangular brown-shingled dormitory, where girls from Lucina had stayed when they came to work as waitresses and chambermaids at the hotel, was little damaged, and the two women found that there was driftwood enough to shore it up and partition off a living room and kitchen. For the time being they shared a common bedroom with the children and Ladneer, but Angie launched her shell business and Sally opened a little real-estate office on the main highway into Lucina and eventually they had money enough to add more rooms and screened porches, which stuck out like the opaque wings of flying fishes in all directions. Ballast rock which sailing ships had dumped on the island was hauled up and used to make a big fireplace to supplement the old woodstove that was their main source of heat.

Sally's first thought, as always when she rounded the point of land and saw that light, was one of thankfulness that the old generator still functioned. There were long periods of time, usually in the summer when she needed electricity the most, that it quit. Angie, with her special talent for things mechanical, had been able to coax it back into action when it stalled, but Sally had never mastered the ancient machine and now usually had to wait until a mechanic from Lucina would favor it with his attention.

Tonight the generator lived and breathed and shed its light on the wind- and rain-whipped dock, and Sally gratefully guided the little boat into its niche between the dark warped pilings with their padding of old tires to protect the precious fiberglass hulls of the few craft that tied up there. They were mostly real-estate just-looking-thanks people that Sally enticed that way, hoping to sell them waterfront lots and beach home building sites.

Tying up the boat, Sally glanced upward toward the rocky point and long low cottage that lay just beyond the crest of the hill. A refuge for women and children, she thought again, wryly. Before Ladneer died, a few months after Angie, she had admonished Sally to get a husband or a man of *some* kind to live on the point.

"Ain't nothin' but a monotony of women and chillun here," she said mournfully. "A pure monotony."

"And I am old and it is late," Sally said to herself as she secured the *Wild Jelly* to the dock and picked up the plastic laundry basket for the climb up the cliff: fifty-five years old and never pretty. Even when the vaunted bloom of youth had been on her, she had been tall and angular and freckled on those portions of her anatomy which didn't blister and peel under the sun's hot rays. The last just-looking-thanks couple she had brought to the island had paid more attention to Sally's complexion than to the waterfront lots.

"Honey, this place has ruined your skin," the wife had cried. "You've got crow's feet like I never saw before. You know you can get creams now that screen out the sun's most damaging rays."

"You can?" Sally had been determined to sound more interested than she was.

Usually prospective real-estate customers looked at the rest of the island and then tried to persuade her to sell the high wooded point, but this pair, a middle-aged couple from Tennessee, had hit a day very like this night—windy and cold. The woman, plump and smooth-faced, had worn her fur coat against her husband's advice. When he worried that spray on the crossing would wet it, she had answered smugly, "Don't you suppose it got wet when the *minks* wore it?"

Shivering in the minks' rainwear, she had stood on the dock waiting to board the boat for the trip ashore and worrying about Sally's sun-dried and wrinkled skin.

"I bet it's nice here in summer," the husband had ventured, "and probably the fishing is always good."

"You're not bringing me here," the woman had said, looking

27

at Point Esperance with loathing. "This is the most godforsaken place I've ever seen in my life."

Sally had laughed that day, relieved that they hadn't wanted to buy the point because, broke as she was, she might have been tempted. Tonight she didn't laugh. It did seem godforsaken—lonely and far away from all the people she loved, particularly Bunk and Bunny, particularly Leslie, hurt, bereft, and broke in New Orleans.

The tide was high and the waves seemed to batter the beach relentlessly. She stood a moment on the step listening before she opened the screened door and pushed through the small-paned French doors into the living room. The familiar smell of wet ashes and old seashells, dry and chalky but still faintly fishy from the creatures that had inhabited them, rose to meet her. She knew she wouldn't bother with a fire or even much lamplight tonight. Things would look a lot better in the morning.

Even as she stood there, Hal and the twins might have come back to Leslie. They all might be sitting in some warm and bright restaurant eating good New Orleans gumbo and laughing at the confusion of that little self-saving motel desk clerk.

The next day the sun was shining and Leslie came home. Sally had not recognized her when the oyster boat on which she had hitched a ride put in at the point. She had seen only a lumpish figure in the stern, of vaguely familiar cinnamon color. As the boat drew closer she saw it was Leslie in her grandmother's coat, hunched over to hug her knees and rest her face in her lap. She straightened up when the boat bumped the little dock's piling and, seeing her mother, smiled and waved, suddenly cheerful.

Sally went to meet her, thanking the oystermen and inviting them up to the house for a cup of hot coffee against the chill of the afternoon.

"Much obliged, Miz Mac," the one at the wheel said. "We got our coffee with us. We just wanted to bring your young'un home."

They were young themselves; Sally recognized them as boys who had been around the point off and on for years, Sarah's age about, now married with houses full of children.

"I appreciate it," Sally said, putting an arm around Leslie.

28

"I didn't know she was back from her travels or I'd have been at the marina to get her. Where'd you pick her up?"

"Aw, I was walking the waves and hitching out about St. Dom's light, wasn't I?" Leslie joked, grinning at the two young fellows in the boat. "Just lifted my thumb as they came to a screeching halt." She reached for the battered old suitcase. "I do thank you, Jody. Maybe I can return the favor someday when I get delivery on my yacht."

They laughed and waved and shoved off, and Sally, studying Leslie's face anxiously, saw she had been crying. A brave attempt at mascara ended in black smudges halfway down her cheeks.

She hugged her daughter again and reached for the suitcase. She didn't know what to say, what to ask. All she could do was wait for Leslie to tell it all again, the hideous thing that had happened to her in the seedy New Orleans motel.

"You hungry, honey?" she asked. "I made a pot of vegetable soup."

"Yes, ma'am," Leslie said. "Hungry and sleepy. I drove straight through, just stopping for gas."

She walked ahead, and Sally saw a great diagonal tear across the back of the cashmere coat.

"How on earth did he manage to tear a good coat like that?" she asked.

"Oh, Mama, I don't know." Leslie sighed. "I'm sorry. I meant to hide it until I could get it rewoven or something. But I was so shocked at the way he started knocking me around. Not even speaking, just hitting me. I told you about the coat without even thinking, and then I had to wear it home. I think he must have been holding on to the coat and hitting me when I fell. I can get it rewoven. . . ." Her voice dwindled off in apology and pain and futility.

"Don't worry about it," Sally said. "It's just a coat. Come on in the house and let's get some food in you. Why don't you take a hot shower while I set us up some trays by the fireplace? Then you can take a nap."

Leslie emerged from the shower, her snub-nosed freckled face scrubbed and shining, her wet brown hair bundled into a towel wound turbanlike around her head. Sally's old terrycloth robe hid the heavy planes of hips and bosom which had thickened, Sally thought, from childbearing and a diet of peanut butter on which the young family had subsisted from time to time. Swathed in terry, Leslie looked childlike and vulnerable. She wandered restlessly around the room, opening cupboard doors and closing them as Sally set out soup bowls and made toast.

"Mama, could we have a drink?" she asked at last.

"Oh, yes, if you want one," Sally said, surprised. "There's a bottle of sherry somewhere. Will that do?"

"It'll help," Leslie said shakily.

She needs it, she needs a drink, Sally decided, again surprised. She brought out the bottle and two wine glasses thoughtfully.

While her mother stirred the soup and sipped her wine, Leslie had two glasses of sherry. She poured herself a third, which she sipped as she ate. It will help her sleep, Sally thought, poking the fire, which had languished but was now mended with chunks of driftwood burning blue and green from salt soaked into its grain.

Once Leslie looked up from her plate and gazed into her mother's eyes, her own wide with pain. "It was unreal, Mama," she said, choking.

"I know," Sally said for lack of anything else to say. "But don't worry, honey. It'll all come straight."

Leslie toiled up from the cushions of the rocker where she sat and headed toward the little guest room. She turned at the door and faced her mother. "You know . . . you know, it may be all my fault. I'm not a good person."

"Silly!" said Sally briskly. "Of course you're a good person. Don't you dare start feeling guilty about this. Get some sleep, and you'll be able to think about it more clearly."

Sally pulled the old down comforter up from the foot of the bed and tucked it around Leslie's shoulders and then went out and closed the door. Unreal, she thought, it's their word for everything. But this *is* unreal. Leslie, the most loving of mothers and wives, rejected and repudiated by her husband and children.

She took the soup bowls and cups to the kitchen and washed them, and then she returned to the living room and saw the torn coat where Leslie had thrown it across the chair.

Angie's coat, the one she had been so proud of, the one they gave her on the last birthday before her death. She had kept it in a special cedar box, since they lacked a cedar closet like Sarah's, and had only taken it out on Sundays for church. A coat's nothing, just a piece of cloth, Sally thought, putting it on a hanger. Only Angie, who had been poor most of her life, thought the cinnamon cashmere something special. She had "saved it for good," but she would have been glad for Leslie to have it. Leslie had not owned a good coat since her marriage to Hal but had made do with hand-me-downs from her mother and sister.

Suddenly Sally leaned into the closet and buried her face in the cinnamon fabric. "Oh, Angie," she whispered. "Oh, God, help us, help us!"

1961

Angie was charmed with Hal when Leslie first brought him to the house, a high-school boy with his trombone case always in his hand as if it were a living, growing, connected part of his body. Although the hotel was no more, summer activity on the island seemed to be reviving. Sally had sold a few lots for beach cottages, and some of the original fishing shacks on the Sound had been replaced with more substantial houses, running heavily to concrete blocks painted coral and aqua like the Mediterranean houses some of the veterans of World War II had seen in Italy.

The Willard family from Tallahassee owned one of these, and that summer they rented it for a month to some Tallahassee neighbors, Mr. and Mrs. Ellis and their son, Hal.

Driving her ancient, salt-scarred, and rusting Army surplus jeep, Sally crossed the island one morning to meet the visitors and offer them anything they might need—groceries, fishing gear, trips ashore. Hal had not been at the house at the time, and later Sally told Angie she could see why he might want to stay away.

"We're really here for spiritual rest and refreshment," Dorinda Ellis told Sally, meeting her at the door but not asking her in. She was very short, but slim and fair, with a bundle of curls pulled into a cluster on top of her head by a blue ribbon. "Hubert," she whispered, glancing over her shoulder, "is in prayer at this hour."

"Oh," said Sally uncertainly. "That's nice." She had had in mind asking them to the point for a drink. Now she didn't know. "Well, if you need anything," she said, turning to go.

Mrs. Ellis followed her out, pulling a blue satin robe closer over the rose satin nightgown she wore beneath it. Satin, Sally had thought, in this heat. The woman needs a cotton shift.

"You were nice to come," Mrs. Ellis said. "Weren't you Sarah Marlowe, and didn't you go to Florida State?"

Sally slipped under the steering wheel of the jeep and turned to face her. "Yes," she said. "I was there briefly. I dropped out to get married."

"Ah-h," sighed Mrs. Ellis. "So did I. I was a tri-Delt and in the May court. And you?"

"Neither," said Sally, feeling unaccountably apologetic as she started the jeep. "Do come and see us if you feel like it or if you need anything."

Angie, utilizing the morning cool to set her bread to rise, had not gone with her and, of course, had the isolated islander's curiosity about the visitors.

"She's an ex-Cute Girl," Sally said flippantly. "Curls, sorority, May court. I didn't see him—or the boy. The boy wasn't there and *he* was praying, she said."

Angie looked shocked. A devout Methodist herself, she considered prayer something like a bathroom function, a personal, private daily necessity but not something you talked about. "Did you ask them up for a drink?"

Sally shook her head. "She said they were here for spiritual rest and refreshment, and I didn't think that would include boozing it up with you."

Angie tossed her head. She looked forward to her afternoon dram of bourbon and to any random summer visitors who dropped by to drink with her. "They could do worse," she said airily. "Anyhow, that old Cute Girl has a nice son. While you were over there, he came over here with Leslie and Sarah. Plays trombone—well, I think."

Hal did play well. Sally grew accustomed to seeing him around the house, a slight boy with blond hair, which the summer sun bleached to off-white, even as his thin shoulders and slender arms and legs slowly darkened. He always had his trombone with him, and to Sally that seemed a phenomenal attachment. She had bought piano lessons for both Sarah and Leslie, and although they could play simple tunes on Angie's old upright in the living room, they had no love of the instrument.

Hal, unable to detach himself from the trombone, was always pleased when Angie would head for the piano and invite him to play. "Come on, Hal," she would say. "Let's give them 'Red Wing.'"

She would tromp down on the loud pedal and for a little while drown out the tentative, note-seeking doodlings of the trombone. Then Hal, his sleepy silver eyes alive with mischief, would tilt the instrument ceilingward and give it its head, sending the high sweet music pouring out in a reaching, climbing, falling torrent of sound. Angie would pound the keyboard, striving to overtake him, but more often she stopped and listened, awed and admiring. Once, to Sally's amusement, she said. "All right, Hal, you cut me."

"Mama, what a thing to say!" Sally said.

"Musician talk," Angie said smugly.

Part of Angie's pleasure in Hal was that she could teach him the old blues songs she had known in her youth. He was an eager learner, and sometimes Sally was amused to hear her seventy-year-old mother faking a hoarse, sexy contralto in a Helen Humes song while the boy did an imitation of Jack Teagarden.

"'I'm a big fat mama with the meat shaking on my bones!'" Angie sang. "'I'm a big fat mama with the meat shaking on my bones! And every time I shake it some skinny woman loses her home!'"

His eyes shining, Hal would take the song from there, playing circles around his mentor while she shook her shoulders and snapped her fingers and tossed her head under its knot of crisp gray hair.

What they didn't count on was that the end of summer would bring the departure of the Ellises but that Hal would return.

"Mama, he has to stay with us awhile," Leslie said, the day Sally went to the marina to pick the girls up after school and saw Hal lounging around the dock, his trombone case in hand.

"With *us?*" Sally said. "Where are his parents?"

"They've thrown him out of the house, and he's come here to get a night job and finish up school in Lucina."

33

"Oh, parents don't throw children out of the house," Sally protested. "It's something else. Let me call his mother."

"Mama, don't," Sarah whispered, following Sally up to the pay station in front of the marina. "He hasn't any place to go tonight. But tomorrow Les says he's going to get the Willards' key and sort of camp out there on the island. He says he's never felt so much at home as he does here."

"Nuts," said Sally. "I'm calling his mother. I'd want her to call me, if it were you or Leslie."

But Dorinda Ellis seemed only mildly interested. "Is that where he is?" she said. "Heavens, I didn't know. But the Willards won't mind if he uses their cottage. Hubert and I found it a sweet retreat suited to prayer and meditation. I hope he will find himself there."

Sally hung up the phone and called to Hal, who was waiting outside the booth. "Come on, honey! Angie will be glad to see you."

Angie agreed with Sally that Hal's mother sounded strange and did her best to welcome and comfort the boy by filling him with fish chowder and crisp corn cakes. He slept on the sofa that night, and the next day he moved into the Willards' house and got a job on a shrimp boat, going back and forth with another shrimper who had a small boat and lived on the island.

"He's not going to school?" Sally asked Leslie.

"Oh, he was failing anyhow," Leslie said. "His parents were going to send him to Juilliard, but then they got mad at him and said he'll have to earn any more education he gets."

"Why did they get mad at him?" Sally asked.

"Mama, you won't believe this," Leslie said. "He was playing at a night spot with a band that had a black musician in it. They're very racist. Hal told them he was going to hitch a ride to Selma and join Martin Luther King—just for spite. So they threw him out."

Sally said no more, but Hal's presence on the island made her uneasy. He was not one of the ones who followed her around the house and sprawled across the foot of her bed to talk to her. There were other shy ones. Henry Parker, a chubby university student, came often to see them, and he was shy. But there was warmth and humor in him, and even when he said nothing, Sally could sometimes catch his eyes across the room and feel a momentary flash of communication.

Hal, usually neatly groomed and carrying his trombone case, seemed remote and oddly secretive. She tried to talk about him to Angie, but her mother had discovered the theory that there is no error in the young. Everything wrong with them could be blamed on their parents. She tried it on Sally.

"Well, with Cute Girl and Holy Hubert—"

"Now, Angie, we don't really know them," Sally protested.

"He does. And he's here."

Sally privately hoped that he was by himself. She worried that Leslie was seeing too much of him, and when they left the house together she wasn't absolutely certain they were beachcombing or setting traps in the pinewoods to catch the little beach doves for Hal's supper.

"How old is Hal?" she asked her mother.

"Sixteen, seventeen," Angie said. "Whatever Leslie is. A few months' difference, I forget how much. But they're close."

"Too close," Sally muttered and privately resolved to make Leslie spend more time in the house studying.

But before she could put the resolution into practice, Leslie and Hal disappeared.

He came by the school at the lunchtime recess, Sarah told her mother, and Leslie had been standing by the parking lot back of the building talking with him when the bell rang for classes to resume. Sarah said she waved at them and went in, and she hadn't seen her younger sister the rest of the afternoon.

Sally drove around the town of Lucina looking for them, asking at the drugstore soda fountain, peering in stores, stopping high-school friends of the girls to ask about them. Toward dusk she and Sarah were checking the boats tied up at the shrimp dock when Boots Bacci, skipper of the *Caledonia*, where Hal had worked, called out to her.

"I got a note for you, Sally. I was gon' bring it to the point on our way out tonight. I see you here, not there."

"A note? Who from?" Sally asked, standing on the dock and straining to reach the line that would draw the *Caledonia* close enough for boarding.

"Your girl was here with Hal Ellis when he come to draw his pay, and she asked me to give you this," Boots said.

On a piece of blue-lined school notebook paper, Leslie had written, *Dear Mama, I am going to New Orleans with Hal. Back soon. Don't worry. Love you all. Leslie.*

Sally was frantic with anxiety. She cried and cursed herself for not having known her child well enough to have foreseen and protected her from this senseless caper. Then, fighting panic, she called the Ellises in Tallahassee. "They've gone *where?*" Dorinda Ellis asked.

"Leslie's note said New Orleans," Sally told her. "I don't know anybody to call there. Have you any friends or relatives they might get in touch with?"

"An aunt and some cousins," Dorinda said. "But I don't think Hal would call *my* family. He hates anybody related to me. And I certainly wouldn't want to embarrass myself by calling *them.*"

"Well, I'm going to New Orleans to look for them," Sally said. "I thought you and Mr. Ellis might want to go too."

"Tell me," said Dorinda. "Is your daughter pregnant?"

"Pregnant?" Sally faltered at the word. She had not considered pregnancy as something already accomplished. She was thinking that if she went to New Orleans she might circumvent that.

"I—I don't know," she said weakly.

"Well, I should certainly think you *would* know," Mrs. Ellis snapped. "What kind of place do you run there on the island anyhow?"

"Run?" Sally was caught off guard. "I don't *run* anything," she said, suddenly awed at the truth she recognized in that statement. She didn't run a thing, even her own life. Here she was in the preposterous, pitiable role of mother of a runaway daughter. How had it come about? She shook herself and summoned the strength to say, "What about New Orleans, do you all want to go?"

"Let me ask Hubert," Dorinda said.

Sally waited. The long-distance operator asked for more money, and Sally fished it out of her skirt pocket and put it in the coin box. After a long time Mrs. Ellis was back.

"I asked Hubert to write down his feelings about this matter," she said primly. "I wouldn't want to misquote him, so I am going to read what he wrote."

"Go ahead," said Sally.

"Here it is, just as Hubert wrote it, and I quote: 'I cannot condone immorality.'"

"What?" gasped Sally.

"I'll read it again," Dorinda said obligingly. "Quote: 'I cannot condone immorality.' Unquote."

Sally deplored obscenities and never used them. She used one now.

"Shit," she said and hung up the phone.

Angie had a heart attack during the night, and Sally had to call the Marine Patrol to come and transport her to the doctor in Lucina, who examined her and sent her on to the hospital in Tallahassee. Two days later, looking pale and depleted but spunky, Angie sat up in bed and said, "Go on to New Orleans, Sally. Go find those children. I'll be back home at the point to greet you all when you get back."

Sally went to settle Sarah with a friend in Lucina and to swap the stained and worn slacks she wore for some town-going clothes. She was tying up the *Wild Jelly* at the marina when she heard Leslie's voice calling her.

Leslie and Hal had stepped off the Trailways bus at Miss Peachy's store and were running hand in hand toward her.

"Mama," said Leslie breathlessly, "guess what? We're married and we're going to have a baby!"

Sally stood with a line in her hand, looking from one to the other. Hal's silver eyes flicked over her face and flicked away. He said nothing. Sally enveloped Leslie in her arms and started crying. "Go call your parents, Hal," she said.

FALL 1976

It was funny about the world, Sally thought, standing up and moving toward the bedroom door where Leslie slept. You think the world is coming to an end and brace yourself for it, and it never obliges you. There's more, always more. She opened the door a crack and saw that Leslie was burrowed into the covers, face down, the way she had slept as a little girl. The sherry bottle stood on the floor beside the bed—empty.

She hadn't seen Leslie take that to bed with her, she thought, easing the door shut. It didn't matter. Or did it? It wasn't much, but how much did Leslie need to drink? She heard again her young voice, husky and weary. "It may be all my fault. I'm not a good person."

Fresh air was what she needed, Sally decided. She took her windbreaker and knitted cap off a hook by the kitchen door and reached for the little pruning clippers. She would take the path away from the beach to the sand hills, where the beach cedar grew like the boxwood of some ordered cavalier garden in Virginia, and fill a basket to make Christmas wreaths.

1962

Angie's heart seemed to be behaving, and sometimes Sally thought she was actually glad that Leslie and Hal were married. Between them she and Sally managed money for an apartment for the young couple in Lucina. It had been the servants' quarters of a sea captain's once-grand house, tucked into the basement with an outside entrance and a tiny terrace from which they could see the harbor. They furnished it with things from the house on the island, and Leslie glowed with pleasure and pride at being mistress of her own place. She hung around Angie, getting lessons in cooking, and squandered some of her precious grocery money to buy wool for a carriage robe she meant to knit for the baby but never finished.

"To think," she marveled to Sally, "I was about to give this baby away! We went to the Florence Crittendon home in New Orleans with that in mind. But, Mama, I couldn't do it. Hal didn't like it either. He said we'd get married and I was glad. So glad. Oh, Mama, I do love him!"

Hal took his trombone and went up and down the coast looking for gigs in night spots. He played for a week once at a joint outside an Air Force base, and the proprietor paid him off with a bottle of vodka.

"I'm going to have that man arrested!" Sally cried when she heard it. "Giving vodka to a boy! That's contributing to the delinquency of a minor. Besides, Hal has a family to support, and he needs money."

"Better stay out of it, Mother," Sarah said. "If that man knew how young Hal is he wouldn't let him in there anyhow. Besides," she said, mocking Sally, "Hal *likes* vodka."

Sally couldn't really take the time to worry about Hal and vodka because she was so worried about Leslie and food. Except for the bulge of the baby, the girl was thin and gaunt, and when Sally went by the apartment with loaves of fresh-made bread or a meat pie Angie had sent, she saw little evidence of any other food in the house. There would be beer bottles but no milk bottles. She was paying the rent and utilities, and she assumed she would pay the family doctor Leslie was seeing.

She decided to have a talk with Hal about finding a job that didn't involve his trombone.

"Listen, Sally." He used her name so rarely it seemed awkward to them both when he did. "I'm a musician. I tried that shrimp-boat hassle, and there's not enough money in it to bother with."

"Honey, a lot of men and boys in Lucina make a living shrimping," Sally said patiently. "I know you're a musician, but you have Leslie now and a baby coming and you're going to have to take care of them. Angie and I will help all we can, but it's not going to be enough. There's the hospital, you know, and when the baby gets here there'll be all kinds of expenses."

Hal looked at something past her, not meeting her eyes. Sally, studying his face, saw that it was thinner, too, and the broad shoulders drooped under the cloth of his old jacket. So young, she thought, with all the pathos inherent in the boy child. He needs a mother, not a wife.

"Do you hear from your parents?" she asked tentatively.

He laughed, and it was a harsh sound. "I called them, like you said to. They told me my cat had died—of a broken heart."

"Of *what?*" Sally wondered if she had heard him.

He grinned at her, the silver-blue eyes bleak and unamused. "Habersham, my old cat I'd had since I was little. He was nine years old. But they said he died of a broken heart when he heard I'd gone." He turned away and then turned back to her. "Oh, yes. There was one thing more. They will pray for me."

39

Appalled, Sally stood by her car, unable to move until the figure of the boy, head down, hands jammed in his pockets, had moved out of sight around the corner of the house. Then she went inside and gave Leslie $25 for groceries.

For one week Hal was soloist with a jazz group playing in Pensacola, and Leslie was so pleased and proud she urged her family to make the trip over there to hear him. Sally had thought Angie would not want to make the long drive, but when she walked into the kitchen and found her mother pressing an old dinner dress of rose lace, she knew better.

"You want to go?" she asked needlessly.

"Certainly," said Angie. "I'm even going to wear my dyed-to-match slippers, as much as they hurt."

In the darkness of the club, with the spotlight trained on the bandstand, Sally got a new and totally surprising view of Hal. He wore a white dinner jacket, undoubtedly borrowed, and as he moved to the microphone he seemed of a piece with the golden instrument in his hands—Apollo, god of light, of poetry, of music. No longer a displaced kid, awkward and ill at ease, he was master of the moment, confident, smiling, a bestower of great riches. Deep, throbbing, sexy sounds poured out of the gleaming bell, and Hal closed his silver eyes and swayed lightly to the throb of the music his mouth was making.

"Charlie Big Green," Angie whispered.

"Who?" Sally asked.

"I know," Leslie said, nodding and smiling. "Accompanied Bessie Smith. She sang a song about him."

" 'Oh, Charlie, play that thing!' " Angie quoted. " 'I mean that slide trombone. You'd even make a king jump down off his throne!' "

Leslie nodded happily, quoting another line: " 'Nobody can do his stuff 'cause he won't teach 'em how.' "

The solo ended. Applause swept the crowded room, and there was a keening in the air Sally couldn't identify. She turned in her chair to see a table full of young girls squealing ecstatically.

"Sillies," Leslie said complacently. "They'll be swooning next."

Instead, they crowded to the edge of the bandstand at intermission, calling out to Hal. "Take a break and dance with us, hear?" one of them said boldly.

Lordly, superbly confident, Hal gave them a sleepy smile and shook his head. "My wife and her entire family are *watching!*" he said dramatically.

The girls retreated, giggling, and Leslie blew him a kiss.

In June, Sarah was graduated from high school and Henry Parker from the university, with a good job offer in Tallahassee. They wanted to be married on the island, and Sally, too tired and too worried to fight for more time, more education for Sarah, capitulated and planned the wedding.

"Ah, I wish we had a gazebo with roses on it for the ceremony," Angie said wistfully as she whipped lace and seed pearls on the bodice of the wedding dress.

"And a ballroom and an orchestra and champagne," said Sally. "We'll be lucky to have magnolias in front of the fireplace and peanut butter and jelly sandwiches on the screened porch."

But to please Angie, who was looking older and frailer these days, she did get a carpenter to nail together a little arched trellis and set it on a point of land, with the blue waters of the Gulf behind it and the brilliant patchwork of wild orange and brown gaillardia daisies in front of it. With no time to grow roses, she hauled smilax from the woods and made a green bower of the trellis. The morning of the wedding she went back to the woods and brought masses of fragrant golden-hearted Cherokee roses, packed them in damp moss to keep them fresh, and tucked them in the smilax so skilfully that Angie, standing back to admire, said, "They look just exactly like they're growing there! I'm going to get you to decorate for my next wedding."

Leslie said Hal would get some musicians for the wedding, and although he looked uncertain and noncommittal about it when Sally mentioned it to him, he showed up shortly before the ceremony with a trumpet player, a bass player, a drummer, and his own trombone, of course.

"Hot ziggity!" cried Angie. "We'll have some real music now. How would you like 'Because' in ragtime, Sarah?"

"I'll settle for 'Muskat Ramble' or 'Jelly Roll Blues,' Granny," Sarah said equably. She was so happy she seemed to move through the days in a dream, nodding and smiling at anything they suggested or tried to do for the wedding.

Leslie had arrived at the island ahead of the musicians, and Sally thought she looked a little forlorn.

"Peaked. Pregnant-peaked," Angie said, but Sally paused distractedly in the midst of the wedding preparations to walk to the back steps where Leslie sat, her arms hooked around her knees. At that moment Leslie's face was rosy and smiling.

Sally immediately saw why. Hal was on his knees on the ground writing in the sand with his forefinger. Even upside down, the big message was clear: I LOVE YOU. I LOVE YOU. I LOVE YOU.

He had drawn some music notes around it, so it was probably the lyrics of a song—possibly *their* song, Sally thought, surprised. She withdrew, closing the screened door softly. Love letters in the sand—symbolically impermanent but no less touching.

Sarah's happiness on that day was so great it might just be pointing up for Sally the things her younger daughter had missed. A wedding certainly wasn't essential, and yet the gathering of families and friends, the approval of the church, the gifts, the felicitations—any girl should have that. Not to mention a husband with a steady job.

Still, Sally thought, touching the centerpiece of white flowers she had put together for the table, still, love is what it's all about, and Leslie and Hal have that. She didn't share Angie's reverence for talent, but it *was* something of value. Even— and Sally hated herself for the thought—possibly future monetary value.

The wedding was so pretty both Angie and Leslie cried, but Sally, worried about the punch, was saved from emotion. Unable to afford champagne enough to go around, she had decided on champagne punch, a pallid substitute, she now realized, looking at the wedding guests who had gone to the trouble to cross the Sound to honor them with their presence. They deserved something better, Sally thought. Henry's family and friends would feel disgraced by their abstemious fare. But the Parkers were amiable people, obviously disposed to enjoy everything about the wedding and their son's new relatives. They loved the island and the house, they loved the punch, the cake, and the little sandwiches, they loved the music, and they loved Sarah.

The reception was ending, Sarah had changed to her linen going-away suit, and she and Henry were running toward the dock where a borrowed speedboat, flower-decked and strung with JUST MARRIED signs, waited to take them ashore, when Sally noticed a change in the music. Hal and his friends were playing the "Funeral March."

"Hal!" Leslie cried, stricken.

Sarah turned and looked back, a puzzled frown on her face, and then she laughed and took Henry's hand and ran on.

As the little boat roared away from the dock, the music of the combo died out except for the sobbing wail of the trombone moaning in the bright afternoon air. Suddenly it flatted out and died and Sally heard the disquieted voices of Hal's friends back of the palmettos. Someone spoke to her and she turned away, so she did not see the bass player and the drummer propelling Hal between them around the corner of the house toward the bedrooms. But later she found Leslie and Angie in the kitchen brewing coffee for her granddaughter's young husband.

"Drunk as a skunk," Angie said to Sally. And, to Leslie, "I don't know how he did it on that weak punch."

The baby, a little girl, was born in August. Sally drove Hal and Leslie up to Tallahassee the day Dr. West said it was due, and they sat around Sarah and Henry's apartment three days waiting. Hal checked the musician's union, borrowed money from Henry to join, and miraculously found somebody who had heard him play and got him a job subbing for a sick trombone player at one of the hotels.

He was working when Leslie's pains started, so Sally and Sarah took her to the hospital, dispatching Henry to the hotel to tell the expectant father.

"Oh, I hope he gets here," Leslie gasped between pains. "I want him with me."

"I know," Sally said, holding her arm and steering her toward the elevator. "He'll be here later. You just get along with your job and get me a grandchild born."

Over her pain Leslie grinned. "Mama, you're good."

Henry joined Sally and Sarah in the waiting room to say

that Hal would come when he got off work. It was near dawn when Hal arrived, and the baby, two hours old, had been cleaned and oiled and swathed in a pink blanket and tucked away in the nursery. Leslie had seen her and pronounced her name—Angeline Dorinda—and gone to sleep.

"Angie will be delighted to have a namesake," Sally said to Hal. "And I bet your mother will be pleased, too."

"Leslie's idea," Hal said. "One name is as good as another to me."

Henry was waiting to drive them back to the apartment, but Hal had vanished down the hall.

"Go on, get the car. I'll wait for him," Sally said.

He's looking in on Leslie, she thought, or peering again through the nursery glass at the pink bundle in the bassinet. But when he came he said offhandedly, "I called my parents."

"Oh, good," said Sally. "It's their first grandchild too. Were they happy? Is your mother pleased that you named her Dorinda?"

Hal shrugged and held the lobby door open for her. Sally noticed irrelevantly that the worn sleeve on the arm that held the door was too short.

"I'll tell you what they said," he offered in a louder voice than seemed warranted in the early morning quiet. "They said, 'Are you still a member of the Communist Party?'"

Sally took a deep breath and looked at the lightening sky. "It's going to be a nice day for a birthday," she said, reaching for his arm and holding it tight.

FALL 1976

Sally filled her basket with fragrant clippings of cedar, and now she found a log that had washed ashore in a hurricane many years ago and stayed, half embedded in sand, on the sunny side of a dune. She automatically checked it for snakes. Even in December they sometimes came out of their holes and stretched out to warm themselves in the sunshine. The log's bleached and ridged flank was clear except for a skittish, nearly transparent fiddler crab which disappeared as she approached. She sat down, putting her basket and clippers beside her.

For years she had thought about the baby Angeline Dorinda and that terrible time. It would lessen the pain to think about it and talk about it, she told Leslie, and she told herself the same thing, endlessly. If you tried to cram it back and forget it you were laying yourself out, exposed and defenseless, to the anguish which would rise up and engulf you when you least expected it.

"But babies die," Angie had said sadly. "Honey, we were lucky to have her for three months. In the old days mothers didn't expect to raise all their children. So many died in infancy. Try not to think about it."

"It's not the same," Sally had said angrily. "She was healthy. We had good doctors. She should be *alive!*" She choked on the word, and her throat ached from unshed tears.

But after ten years she had stopped talking about little Dodie to Leslie, unless her daughter brought it up herself. Sometimes, when they were involved in something together, Leslie would fall suddenly silent and then come up out of a miasma of pain and grief to ask piteously, "Mama, was I to blame? Did I kill her?"

For a long time Sally thought she actually physically felt the emptiness of the baby's going. Her arms ached for the weight and shape of that little body. She could feel the hollow between shoulder and breast where the bright little head had rested. She knew, as no one else knew, that the birth of the twins eased the pain but did not wipe out that void. As long as she and Leslie lived (she had not been sure about Hal), there would be a raw and jagged hole, a stretch of wasteland in their lives where there should have been Dodie. Not just a baby, not just a little girl, but Dodie, who was uniquely and exceptionally herself. The pitiful graves of newborn babies in old cemeteries, nameless little ones too weak to make it in a perilous time of typhoid and diphtheria and other mysterious untreated fevers of infancy, did not comfort her. They were babies expected to die. They were not Dodie.

Thinking about her now, Sally's lined, wind-reddened face crumpled but she did not cry. There had been so much to cry about in fourteen years.

Angeline Dorinda seemed to them all to be the prettiest, most charming baby in the world. Leslie came home to the island to regain her strength from a difficult birth, and Sally and Angie and even Sarah, who was now pregnant herself and could not stay away from the marvel of this new baby, fought for the privilege of rocking her and feeding her and walking with her on the beach at twilight when the house was hot and the baby was restless.

Hal came and stayed too, and Sally, watching him sprawl on Leslie's bed with a sandwich and a beer in his hand, found herself caught between delight in Dodie and irritation and impatience with Dodie's father. He didn't offer to help with tasks around the house, and one afternoon toward the end of Leslie's convalescence she came home from a wearying trip to take Angie to the doctor and found the kitchen piled high with their dirty dishes, the bathroom piled high with Dodie's dirty diapers, and garbage everywhere. Leslie and Dodie were sleeping, and Hal was smoking what to Sally and Angie looked like a funny homemade cigarette and dreamily watching television.

"Hal, this is the limit!" Sally cried in exasperation. "Get off your backside and clean up this mess! Angie and I are so tired we could drop, and there's not even a clear spot to start supper."

She started stacking dishes and picking up the litter and directing him to burn the paper and haul the bottles and cans to the ravine in the middle of the island which they called the Glory Hole and were filling in gradually with garbage.

Hal moved silently to obey, giving her a cool look from his light eyes as he went by. But the next day, before Sally was awake, he walked down to a little cove where shrimpers sometimes anchored to sleep in the early morning hours and hitched a ride back to Lucina for himself and Leslie and the baby.

Dismayed to see their belongings packed and on the porch, Sally dragged out Dodie's bath unnecessarily. "Are you sure you feel like taking care of her?" she asked Leslie.

"Mama, I'm fine," Leslie assured her. "We can manage by

ourselves now, I think. But Mama"—she made sure Hal was outside before she leaned her head against Sally's shoulder— "we really appreciate your help. I know the hospital bill must have hit you hard. When he gets a job, Hal is going to pay you back."

"That's all right," Sally said tiredly. "I'm glad I had the money."

She smiled at Dodie, whose rosy little body in the warm water almost floated above the hand and forearm her grandmother held beneath her for support. "This one is worth a house and a lot and a sackful of gold guineas," she said, wrapping the baby in a towel that had warmed by the kitchen stove and lifting her to her shoulder. "You look like a rose petal," she said, kissing the crease in the back of the little neck.

"Leslie!" Hal yelled from the yard. "You going to stay in there all day? Come on!"

They left, but that afternoon, egged on by Angie, who was worried too, Sally got in the boat and went to check on them. She found Leslie alone in the apartment trying to nurse the baby and near tears because the hungry, seeking little red mouth hurt her and apparently found no sustenance either.

"Didn't Dr. West say you would have to supplement her feeding?" Sally asked, taking Dodie in her arms.

"He did, Mama," Leslie said defensively, "but we're out of her milk. Hal's gone to see if he can borrow some money. He'll bring her some milk when he comes. But she keeps crying, and I thought maybe I might be able to nurse her."

Leslie looked wan and tired and the apartment was sunless and chilly. Sally bought a case of milk for the baby and arranged to have the little Lucina laundry's new diaper service keep Dodie supplied in clean lingerie. She bought a roast for Leslie and Hal's supper and fruit and milk and cookies and called Dr. West and made an appointment for the baby's first-month checkup. Then she stopped by Lucina's main store, a dry-goods emporium which sold everything from dress fabric and shoes to fishing tackle and compasses. Meg Stamps, who ran it, was a lifelong friend, and she told Sally that she would be glad to give Hal part-time work.

"He's a musician, you know," Sally said, uncertain now if this was an act of unforgivable effrontery. "If he gets a playing job he will naturally prefer that. But maybe he could play at night and sell shoes for you in the daytime?"

"Sure he can," said Meg. "He's young. It won't hurt him to take a double shift for a while."

But Hal hadn't taken the job in the store. He borrowed money and went to Tallahassee and looked for a job in a night club. He found one that lasted two weeks, and when he came back to Lucina he told Leslie he had talked to his parents and they wanted to see Dodie.

Sally dropped by the apartment to bring some little dresses she and Angie had made for the baby and found Leslie in the midst of bathing and dressing Dodie.

"She's going to see her other grandmother!" Leslie whispered excitedly.

"They're coming here?" Sally asked, glancing around the untidy apartment with half an idea of helping Leslie slick it up for her in-laws.

"Not here," Leslie said. She smiled around a big safety pin held in her mouth, the self-consciously insouciant smile of her childhood when she knew she was doing something her mother would not approve. "They want Hal to meet them at the Shell station with Dodie. They don't want to see me."

"Well, I'll be damned!" Sally said. "You're going to let them see your child when they don't want to see you?"

"Yes, I am, Mama," Leslie said firmly, using a damp brush to swirl Dodie's red-gold hair into a topknot. "It doesn't matter about me. Hal needs his parents. I have you and Angie and Sarah, but he hasn't anybody. If they like Dodie—"

"That's the nerviest thing I ever heard of!" Sally said furiously.

"Mama," Leslie pleaded, "please let me do it my way. I love Hal, and I want him to have his parents."

"Okay," Sally said, subsiding. "I think you're a fool, but it must be because you are a nicer, kinder, more generous person than I am. Do it your way."

She laid a cheek against the baby's head, patted Leslie's shoulder, and left.

Later, Sarah told her about the Ellises' meeting with the baby. "Don't tell Les you know," she begged. "She has to talk to somebody, but she'd never tell me anything if she knew I blabbed to you and Angie. She wants you to think well of Hal."

√ Hal had stood on the corner with Dodie, freshly bathed and powdered and curled for the occasion, in his arms. His father drove up to the curb and opened the back door where his mother sat. ("Like gangsters," Sarah said.) Hal and the baby got in beside his mother. She lifted the afghan Angie had made and peered into the baby's face and then silently held out her arms to take her.

Hubert Ellis drove aimlessly around town and down the coastal road for half an hour while Dorinda made chirping sea-gull sounds at the baby. He never once turned and looked at his granddaughter. When his wife had looked her fill, they dropped Hal and the baby off at the corner near the apartment.

"Well, I can't wait to find out if Dodie passed inspection," Sally snapped. "I do hope they found her acceptable."

Sarah giggled. "Peachy-dandy," she said. "They invited Hal to come and bring her to their house for Thanksgiving."

"Not Leslie?" Sally asked.

"Not Leslie," Sarah said.

Angie, ostensibly dozing in her rocker by the fire, lifted her head and very distinctly, in a tone of cold rage, said, "May the good Lord strike them dead!"

Hal went to his parents' house for Thanksgiving, but he hoped to get a playing job and did not take Dodie. Sally picked up the baby and Leslie and took them to the island for the wild duck dinner Angie prepared over coals in the fireplace. They drank white wine and admired Dodie, and it was the happiest time any of them remembered for many weeks.

Dodie was dead when Sally and Angie saw her again.

It never went away, the horror of that night. The Marine Patrol came and got her, and the sheriff, Winston Fume, an old friend of her grandfather's, met them at the dock in Lucina.

"Your little grandbaby is dead, Sally," he said. "Down at Dr. West's clinic. I'll take you there."

"Dodie? Dodie can't be dead!" Sally cried. "I saw her the other day. Thanksgiving. I saw her. She was fine."

The sheriff put an arm around her and guided her to his car. "I don't know what happened," he said. "Your girl and her husband are there. They'll tell you. It happened up the highway at Bucky's Playpen."

"That joint?" Sally said. "What was Dodie doing there? Was it an automobile accident?"

49

"No. They'll tell you."

They found Leslie standing under a tree in front of the little building where Dr. West had his office, weeping wildly. Sally jumped out of the car and ran to her. The face Leslie lifted to her was streaked with makeup and tears and contorted in agony.

"Mama, she's dead, she's dead, Dodie's dead!" the girl cried. "I killed her. Mama, I left her in the car and she froze to death!"

Clasping Leslie to her breast, Sally looked over her head at the sheriff. He shook his head.

"Couldn't have," he said. "It's not that cold. We're checking to see if it could have been carbon monoxide. I don't know."

"Come on," Sally said, pulling at Leslie's arm. "I want to see her. Maybe it's not true. They can do something. Artificial respiration. Dr. West can do something."

The sheriff shook his head again and stood aside to let them in the door. Hal sat slumped in the doctor's front office, his chin on his chest, his eyes red and wet. Sally went by him with Leslie to the little examining room where Dr. West and another doctor she didn't know stood over the quiet still little body of Dodie. The irrational hope she'd had that it had all been a mistake, that she could pick up the baby and her little body would be warm and animate against her heart, died immediately. Dodie was still, so still, the once-rosy little face pale and waxy.

The sound of Leslie's sobbing was the only sound in the room.

"How . . . how did it happen?" Sally faltered.

Dr. West glanced at Leslie, who was pacing the floor. "Hal was playing at that juke joint up the road," he said. "Bucky's Playpen, I think they call it. Leslie and a couple of their friends went to hear him. The baby was asleep in her basket on the back seat, so they left her there. When Leslie went out to check on her—"

He paused and Leslie stopped walking and faced her mother, her eyes unnaturally wide and bright, her mouth wobbling. "She was so still, Mama. I couldn't wake her up. I grabbed her and ran inside and told Hal and somebody called Dr. West. . . ."

The younger doctor spread a sheet over Dodie and walked

to the door of the front office. "We need to do an autopsy," he said. "I'll have to ask you to sign this consent form."

He handed a paper to Hal, who stared at it helplessly for a time and then obediently took the pen the doctor offered and wrote his name on it.

"I'll put in the date," the doctor said. "December first."

Sally looked at Hal's silver head bent over the form as he tried unnecessarily to read it again. Tomorrow he would be eighteen years old.

The autopsy revealed that Dodie had died of a staphylococcus infection which could have stricken her anywhere, but it did not comfort Leslie or Angie.

"It has nothing to do with her being in the car," Dr. West patiently explained to them. "It's called 'crib death.' We don't know why it seems to strike perfectly healthy babies, but it wasn't anything you did, Leslie. She was warm and all right in the car."

"Bucky's Playpen," Angie said scornfully. "Some place to take a baby! You should have stayed home with that child, Leslie."

Leslie was all too willing to indict herself. She reached for blame with a burning, ravaging greed. "I should go to jail. I'm a murderer. If I had been with her, if I'd had her in my arms, I might have known. But . . . I was so tired of staying in the apartment," she whimpered. "Rod and Adrian came by and said why didn't we go hear Hal play? We took turns sitting in the car with her for a while, but she seemed to be sleeping fine. I was only gone for Hal's solo."

Sally tried to comfort her. "It wouldn't have made any difference, honey. Dr. West told you that."

The next day when Sally went to the funeral director's office to make what they euphemistically called "the arrangements," Leslie and Hal met her on the front steps. Hal was silent, as always, but Leslie drew her aside and said softly, timidly, "Mama, Hal's parents are coming. They have a cemetery lot in Tallahassee they will let us use, and they want to pay for the funeral."

Sally never knew where her rage came from. She had not known that it was there waiting to erupt. She looked at Leslie and Hal with something close to hatred.

"I'll be goddamned!" she said through clenched teeth. "They never gave that baby a bottle of milk or a diaper, and they sure as hell aren't going to give her a hole in the ground to be buried in!"

Leslie went white and turned away. Hal walked to the other end of the porch.

The Ellises hired Lucina's water taxi to take them to the island the next day, and Leslie and Hal rode with them in the little procession of boats following the undertaker's launch bearing the small white coffin.

Sally, walking up the pine-clad hill to the family burying ground with Angie and Sarah and Henry, decided guiltily that she should invite the Ellises back to the house for coffee and sandwiches after the funeral.

"Of course you should," said Sarah, mimicking Leslie. "You know Hal *needs* his parents."

It was after Dodie's funeral that Leslie told them she was pregnant again.

FALL 1976

Leslie was up sitting by the fire drinking coffee when Sally walked in the house.

"Hi, Mama," she said, smiling wanly. "Where you been?"

Sally held out the basket. "Gathering beach cedar for a wreath."

"Wonderful," the girl said, standing up. "I've decided Bunk and Bunny will surely be home for Christmas, so let's decorate like crazy, hear? Let me put on my jeans and I'll start the wreaths. How many you gon' make?"

"I was thinking about just making one for the front door, but if you want to we'll do a lot. A big fat one for the door, smaller ones for each window, and what do you think about refurbishing that shell one Bunk and Bunny made for the mantel?"

Leslie bit her lip and took a time at the sink with her coffee cup. When she lifted her face, Sally saw that her eyelashes were wet. "I *know* they'll come," Leslie said. "They hate to be away from Esperance at Christmas. It's the most Christmasy place they've ever been."

Sarah and Henry and Hank and Say-Say were coming. Sally suspected they would rather have stayed in Tallahassee but were determined this year anyhow to preserve the custom of Esperance festivity because it would be the first Christmas without Angie—and now, the way things looked, without Bunk and Bunny too.

"We *want* to come, Mama," Sarah assured her over the marina phone. "Hank and Say-Say think Esperance is where Christmas started. You know the picture of the wise men riding over the desert? They think with all that sand it's got to be their island."

"Bless their hearts," Sally said, laughing. "I wish we had some wise men on hand."

"And Mama"—Sarah lowered her voice—"what would you say to having Henry's parents too? He doesn't know it yet, but his mother swore me to secrecy and told me they are giving us a boat, and I know they'd love to see it in the water!"

"A boat!" Sally yelped. "How perfectly marvelous! Do you know what kind? How big? Did they get a trailer too?"

"The works," said Sarah. "Down to life jackets for all hands and a CB radio and flares for emergencies. Mr. Parker told her it is a twenty-footer, but she thinks it's bigger. When I talked to her she was going to take her tape measure and check it out. They have it hidden in a neighbor's garage."

"Ah, they're nice people," Sally said, her eyes following Leslie, who was making trips between the launderette and *Wild Jelly*, her head down, her shoulders hunched. "By all means bring them. You want me to call them and make it official?"

"It would be nice," Sarah said. "They aren't picky. They'd take an invitation from me, but if you'd call them and go into your hospitality act, I'd appreciate it."

The Parkers were duly invited and duly accepted, and Leslie plunged in to help Sally give the house a thorough cleaning, with special attention to Angie's room, which would be assigned to Mr. and Mrs. Parker. A side screened porch where all the children slept in summer engrossed Leslie's attention for so long a time that Sally went to check on her. She was sitting on the lower bunk of the Army surplus double-decker that the twins claimed as their own, the broom idle in her hands.

"You think it will be too cold for them out here?" she asked, looking up.

"No . . . I don't know," Sally said, suddenly helpless before Leslie's stubborn dream. "If they come, wouldn't you want to go back to the cottage?"

"Not if I can help it!" Leslie said sharply. "I can't stand to see that place, Mama."

"Why? If they are there too? I thought you loved the cottage."

"I did . . . once," Leslie said, standing up and looking toward the path which led to the bay side of the island and the cottage she called "Rent Free"—which the children called "Raccoon Castle" because there were always coon tracks, five-fingered and shaped like a baby's hands, in the sand beneath the cottage. One time they had found a mother raccoon and a cluster of babies on the topmost branch of the wind-twisted live-oak tree behind the cottage.

"I loved it once—but not any more. It wasn't always a happy home."

She turned and gave Sally a crooked, forlorn smile. And then she shook her shoulders as if to dislodge a load resting on them and picked up the broom.

"We'll do whatever you think, Mama. If it's going to be crowded here, of course B and B and I will stay in the cottage."

"Oh, it won't be crowded," Sally said, wishing that it would, that there was a chance the phone would come to life in the kitchen and it would be the twins, or that a boat would put in to the dock and she would see Bunk, always so eager and helpful, leap to the dock, line in hand.

"It's never too crowded for family. If it's medium chilly we'll put up the canvas curtains and get out sleeping bags. If it's freezing cold, we'll bed the twins and Hank down on the living-room floor. Say-Say too, if they'll have her."

"And if Hal comes with them?"

"Then you all can have my room and I'll sleep on the sofa."

Leslie seemed relieved and tackled the sweeping and dusting with renewed vigor.

But Hal and the twins did not come.

Every time the marine telephone in the kitchen sputtered

and crackled, Leslie ran to it. A few days before Christmas, when they were in Lucina to shop, Leslie got up her courage, borrowed coins from her mother, and called the little town in Virginia to which Hubert and Dorinda Ellis had moved shortly after Dodie's death. A woman's voice answered the phone.

"Dorinda?" Leslie began uncertainly. "Is this Mrs. Ellis?"

"Yes, but I can't talk to you," Dorinda had answered and hung up.

"Mama, she hung up on me!" Leslie said, stricken.

"What did you expect from a fool?" Sally said savagely.

"Oh, Mama, they're there. I know they're there. I've got to go and get them!"

"Leslie." Sally had sagged on the concrete bench by the phone booth. "It would take the United States Marines to get Bunk and Bunny from those people. Think about it awhile."

1963–1964

There was a time, right after Dodie's death, when Sally hoped Hubert and Dorinda would be of some help and support.

Leslie couldn't bear to go back to the basement apartment after the funeral so Sally and Sarah went instead, packing up the baby's bed and all her clothes and the pitifully new and unused teddy bear and rag dolls Leslie had arranged around her crib. They returned the furniture to Point Esperance and packed dishes and clothes and sheet music in boxes to be moved to a new apartment if and when they got one.

The Ellises invited the children to Tallahassee to stay with them and Hal and Leslie went, only to find that their hosts were even then packing to move to Virginia.

"Mr. Ellis is going into a new business. Apple Orchards. Bought some land in Virginia, and now they're going down there to live." Leslie told her mother and Sarah when they met at the young Parkers' apartment one day to put the finishing touches to a nursery Sarah confidently expected to be occupied within a couple of weeks.

"Well, where will you all live when they move to Virginia?" she asked Leslie. "If Hal has work here, I don't suppose you want to come back to Point Esperance?"

"Hal is going on the road, we think," Leslie said. "And I'm getting a job. Dr. West has a friend here, an obstetrician, who needs a receptionist. He recommended me."

"Henry has a good idea for Hal," Sarah put in. "But I don't suppose he's interested, if he's going on the road."

"A job?" Sally asked, certain that Hal wouldn't be interested if it had nothing to do with playing the trombone.

"School," said Sarah. "The Marine Corps music school. Henry has talked to some men he knows in the service, and they say the services share a wonderful school up near Norfolk somewhere. If Hal enlists and gets in the school he'll be doing what he likes to do and getting paid for it. And"—she nodded significantly at Leslie's still slim waistline—"Les will get all kinds of free baby-having care."

Sally went home to tell Angie about it, hopeful but determined not to be too hopeful.

"What a wonderful opportunity for that boy!" Angie said. "John Philip Sousa all over again!"

"Put me down as 'cautiously optimistic,' " said Sally, using a business phrase which was just coming into style. "I can't see Hal playing 'Stars and Stripes Forever.' "

Hal couldn't see it himself. He hated the idea of the Marines and of the Marines' music. He brushed aside Henry's suggestion with a scornful "Man, you're jiving me." But his parents had gone, the road job did not materialize, and Leslie, already at work in Dr. Lamont's office, told him tearfully that the alternative was for her to quit her job and move back to Point Esperance. It would be weeks before she could save enough money to rent an apartment.

Glumly, gracelessly, Hal showed up at the Parkers' just as they were leaving for the hospital.

"That Marines gig you're so high on," he said to Henry, disregarding the fact that he was putting Sarah's suitcase in the car and Sarah, clutching her stomach with both hands, was lumbering out the front door.

"What about it?" Henry asked.

"If you'll give me the pitch I might look into it," Hal offered.

"Hal, for goodness' sake!" cried Sarah. "Don't slow us up.

You might have to help Henry deliver this baby on the sidewalk."

Hal had paled and backed away.

But Henry, who had an orderly mind and could handle one exigency while thinking about another, gave Hal the doorkey and said, "Go on in the house and get you some coffee, Hal. I'll call you there after I get Sarah to the hospital."

As a result, the afternoon little Hank was born, Hal enlisted in the Army with the promise that if he auditioned satisfactorily after basic training at Parris Island, South Carolina, he would be sent to the music school at Little Creek, Virginia.

Leslie moved in with a girl from Lucina who had just got a job and a new apartment and, except for long weekend bus trips to Parris Island to see Hal, she seemed settled. Hal hated the Marines she told Sally, and blamed Henry for getting him in, and she came back from every trip to see him feeling desperately sorry for him.

But he apparently did well enough to make the music school and they all relaxed when he was settled at Little Creek.

"It's not Juilliard," Angie said, "but it's music, and that boy has to have music to live. I think he's a genius."

They were all sitting around Sarah's living room admiring little Hank, who had discovered his feet and lay on a blanket on the floor with a pink bare foot in each hand.

"I think he is too," Leslie had said to her grandmother, her fond eyes on the baby. "I just know we're going to strike it rich when everybody sees how really great Hal is. You know, like Tommy Dorsey and Jack Teagarden and people like that. When he graduates and gets out of the Army we may even live in glamorous places like New York and Hollywood or Vegas. You know, a house in each place?"

"Ah-h *Vegas,*" Sarah repeated, emphasizing her sister's easy abbreviation of the name. "Meanwhile, Les, do you want to try on my old maternity clothes? They're pretty shot, but if you're going up there to wait out the baby near Hal, you'll need a lot of changes."

"Take what Sarah offers, honey," Sally had said, "and then we'll go and buy a couple of new things. I sold a lot on the beach last week and the money is burning a hole in my pocket."

They all went down to the railroad station to see Leslie off to Norfolk. She was obviously pregnant but "chic pregnant," as Sarah said, wearing a well-cut navy-blue maternity outfit they had "bought so new it wasn't even marked down." She had a new suitcase full of baby clothes, and she looked happy as she hugged and kissed them all three times each and promised to send her address the minute she knew where Hal was putting her.

Sarah was, as usual, the one who learned that Hal had not only not found a place for Leslie but had not even been at the station to meet her. She arrived early in the morning, after riding all night in the coach, and sat in the station waiting until afternoon, certain that every uniformed youth coming in the door would be Hal. At last she had timidly approached the USO desk and asked for help.

"I keep having to run to the bathroom," she confided to the girl at the desk. "I'm so afraid he came while I was in there."

"Oh, I'm sure he would have waited for you," the girl said, pulling up a chair for her and getting her a cup of coffee. "Let me see what we can do."

Hours later the Red Cross had found Hal in class at the base and sent him on his way, and by nightfall they had walked many blocks through the old, tired neighborhoods of Little Creek, lugging Leslie's suitcase and looking for a furnished room.

Leslie wrote glowingly of the old house where Hal settled her. A front room, she said, with windows looking out to sea. Shabby but with evidence that it had once been rather splendid. And so convenient—a big bed, a gas plate, a sink, and refrigerator all in one room. The base was close enough that Hal could come nearly every day and many weekends, and Leslie assured them all that she was safe and happy.

"I wonder why he didn't meet her?" Sally mused. "He knew exactly when she was getting there."

"Mama, you know Hal can't do things like that," Sarah said. "He probably was embarrassed to ask to get out of class."

"So young," said Angie, and they all nodded.

Real estate was enjoying a small boom on the coast, and Sally was beginning to make an occasional sale. Not many people had shown an interest in the island. It was too inaccessible, they said. But the boat business was good, and Sally could foresee a time when inlanders would be towing their boats to the coast every weekend for trips around the islands and down the inland waterway. Heartened by a little evidence of coming affluence, she opened a real-estate office on the main street in Lucina. It was a gala opening with great gaudy baskets and bowls of florist flowers from the bank and the politicians and some of their friends. Angie baked six dozen cookies and made cheese balls and chicken salad for an afternoon open house, and Sally bought a thirty-six-cup coffeepot and, boldly, daringly, at the last minute, invested in a case of champagne.

Sarah and Henry and little Hank came down for the festivities, and it was Henry who answered the phone when Leslie called from the hospital.

Over the noise of laughter and talk and the clink of the champagne glasses they heard him shout, "Baby—*babies?* *Twins?* My God, Leslie, what have you done? Well, congratulations, honey, it's terrific news. Here's your mother."

But it hadn't been altogether good news. Twins, a boy and a girl, two months early, weighing less than four pounds each, and in critical condition from respiratory difficulties.

Sally's questions were pouring out. Was Leslie herself all right? Had she known it was going to be twins? Why did they come early?

"Mama, I can't explain now," Leslie said. "Somebody is waiting to use the phone. I'm all right. Fine. I can go home tomorrow, but the babies have to stay in the incubators. Oh, Mama"— and she was crying—"suppose they die?"

"Hush, baby, hush," said Sally. "They'll make it. That's a wonderful hospital with the best doctors."

And then she remembered the Kennedy baby, Patrick, who had the same problem.

"Don't cry, Leslie, I'm coming. I'll have to take Angie back to the island and get some clothes, but I'll start tonight."

"No, Mama, wait till tomorrow," Leslie said. "I'll be at the room to meet you. I don't want you driving all that way at night. Alone. I'll worry."

"All right," Sally decided. "I'll need to get the car serviced and get some money. Maybe tomorrow would be better. And things will have improved there. The babies—how do they look, honey?"

Leslie was quiet a second, and Sally could hear her taking

a deep breath. "Beautiful. Perfect. But so little . . . so *little*, Mama, like baby birds."

Angie would not be left behind. She had her bag packed before Sally had stopped gazing distractedly at her own scant row of dresses in the closet. Then Angie turned her attention to food, packing a basket with jams and jellies and tomato sauce she had canned from last summer's garden.

"Now, Angie," Sally objected, "it's too long a trip for you. You know it is. I hadn't planned to stop for the night. I was going to drive straight through. It will take us twenty-four hours."

"Of course we're not stopping," Angie said. "I'll take a pillow and a blanket. You're not going a step without me."

They arrived in the middle of the night to find Leslie sitting on the front steps of the old rooming house, waiting for them. She came out to the curb, all smiles and kisses and offers to help bring their bags in. Hal, she said, was at school and they were to share her room. The landlady had provided a cot for her and it was all made up.

"Your babies not three days old and you running up and down stairs and kiting around the street," Angie said disapprovingly.

"This is the new way," Leslie said. "The Marines don't believe in all that bed rest you and Mama had. It's stop the plow in the furrow, have the baby, and pick up the plow and go on."

They smiled at the picture of young Leslie in the role of a pioneer woman and toiled up the stairs with their bags by the dim light of a weak and dusty bulb set in the belly of a brass replica of the Statue of Liberty on the newel post. The house smelled like all the rooming houses Sally had ever known, of mildew and old plumbing, of greasy cooking and a gas leak somewhere.

Leslie had seen the babies at eight o'clock for half an hour. She couldn't go beyond the glass wall of the nursery, but the nurses would wheel the incubators close enough for her to see the weak tiny beings inside, fighting for breath. The little girl was the stronger of the two, the little boy smaller and weaker.

"The names I gave them may be too heavy for them," Leslie said, turning back the spread on the double bed for her guests. "She's Hope Hamilton Ellis—Hope for Esperance, of course.

And he's—for Hal and Daddy—Harold Robert McMillan Ellis. How do you like them?"

"Heavy," said Angie.

"Grand," said Sally.

Leslie giggled. "Right away Hal decided on nicknames. Bunk for the boy after Bunk Johnson."

Angie nodded approvingly. "What a trumpet!"

"And Bunny for the little girl," Leslie went on.

"Bunny Berigan, of course," said Angie knowledgeably.

Leslie nodded. "Another trumpet player."

"What a trumpet player!" Angie said fervently.

Sally nodded and smiled at Angie's pleasure in the jazz-musician nicknames and privately hoped that they wouldn't irrevocably mark the children for careers in music. Her back ached miserably from the long hours at the wheel and she looked at the flimsy little cot fearfully. She would have to take it herself. Both Leslie's and Angie's need for a decent bed superseded hers. She made sure she would get the cot by falling asleep on it herself. The last she heard was her daughter offering supper to Angie. "Sure you don't want a peanut butter sandwich? I've got lots of peanut butter and bread."

It was the only food she did have, they were to learn later.

Sally and Angie stayed in Norfolk three days, spending the morning and evening half-hour intervals the hospital allowed in front of the nursery window beside Leslie, and the rest of the time shopping for bassinets and diapers and bottles. Hal came and went in the early evening each day, greeting them pleasantly but not lingering in the room or making the pilgrimage to the nursery window at the hospital with them.

"He can't bear to look at the babies," Sally said wonderingly.

"Well, Mama," Leslie began defensively. "Do you blame him? He's scared."

"I suppose," Sally agreed.

"Men are not strong about such things," Angie explained. "Little babies and hospitals scare them to death."

They scare us all, Sally thought, watching the rise and fall of the tiny chests in the incubators. The little boy came close to being a blue baby, the doctor had told her. He was losing weight and might not make it.

But in three days the babies were out of danger, and Sally

and Angie decided to leave. Bunk and Bunny (they were already becoming easy with the names, Sally realized) would have to stay in the hospital until they had gained back their birth weight and a pound or two more, but they were going to pull through and Leslie was delirious with relief and joy. She had arranged the bassinets near the window of her room, "so they will get some sun and have a view to look at."

It was still a mystery to Sally that Leslie had not known she was carrying twins. If Dr. Lamont, the obstetrician for whom she worked in Tallahassee, had not detected two heartbeats, surely the doctors at the Army's prenatal clinic should have known.

She attempted to question Leslie, but the girl was busy arranging rows of canned milk they had bought on the closet shelf above her clothes, and she changed the subject after saying lightly, "Doctors don't know everything."

Angie had shopped for groceries and made a big pot of vegetable soup to leave them. "I'd stay with Leslie and help her," she said to Sally, "but Hal wouldn't come home if I was here, would he?"

"I doubt it," Sally said. "He hasn't spent any time here during our visit."

"Well, she needs him with her," Angie said firmly. "So I'll go."

Bunk and Bunny were a month old when Leslie brought them home to Point Esperance. Hal had graduated from music school—at the top of his class—and was heading for Quantico, where he would play marching airs for the cadets and even more stirring martial music for the football team.

"Hates it, hates it all," said Leslie, grimacing. "But it won't be too long now."

She left the twins with her mother and grandmother while she went back to Quantico to apartment-hunt in the little towns nearby. Sally had never seen Angie so happy. She bathed and rocked and fed the babies, sometimes both at the same time because they were so small even her frail old arms and bony old lap could accommodate them.

"You little picked chickens," she would fuss. "Got to get some meat on your bones."

Remembering the radiant, healthy Dodie, Sally looked at these scrawny, bluish infants and wondered if they could live. And privately she wondered if she could love them as she had loved the lost Dodie.

But she found that they all loved Bunk and Bunny protectively, obsessively. The babies cried a lot and their milk disagreed with them, but there was always a pair of arms to hold them, always somebody listening, watching, vigilant that death, which had taken Dodie, would not take these two. Sarah brought Hank, now a husky six months old, and spent two weeks at the beach with them, taking a turn caring for the twins while Sally buckled Hank in his seat and rode around the island or played with him in the surf at the tide's edge.

One day, Sally was busy contriving a palmetto-frond shade over the blanket where the babies slept on the screened porch, filtering the sun so it would reach their crooked little legs but not touch the small faces and the still faintly lavender eyelids.

Sarah, sitting nearby in a canvas deck chair, watched her thoughtfully. "Mama," she said after a while, "did you ever ask Leslie why these babies came so early?"

"I don't think so," Sally said. "I just assumed, with twins. . . . You know, Sarah, I seem to have forgotten all I ever knew about baby-having. Why did these babies come prematurely?"

Sarah shook her head. "I don't know. I just wondered." She crinkled her blue-gray eyes at her mother and added mischievously, "Trying to get up some dirt on Hal, probably. I want to blame him for everything bad that happens to Les."

"You think he did to Leslie what Rhett Butler did to Scarlett, don't you? Knocked her down the stairs?"

"Well, Mama, it *is* one explanation," Sarah said. "But if Les doesn't tell us voluntarily, I don't suppose we should ask."

"Leslie doesn't tell much about Hal," Sally said, touching the twins' feet lightly to be sure they weren't cold. She scoffed at Angie's theory that cold feet gave babies colic, but Bunk and Bunny seemed to have a lot of colic and she wasn't disposed to take any risks, even to flying in the face of old wives' lore. "I'm really glad that she doesn't," Sally went on. "They should put in the marriage ceremony a promise that neither party will tell tales on the other as long as they live. Or at least, as long as they live with one another. Call it chivalry or noblesse oblige or whatever. Lawyers and doctors claim a confidential relationship with their clients and patients. Why shouldn't husbands and wives?"

"Yes, ma'am," said Sarah patiently, as one who had heard the exposition many times. "You and Angie always say that, and I guess Les really believes it. She's always covering for Hal. Not me. If Henry Parker should ever lay a finger on me in anger I'd come screaming my head off to you and Angie. I'd say, 'You better mind out, you Henry Parker, I'm gon' sic the mean old women in my family on you?'"

They laughed together.

"I can see Henry shivering and shaking now," Sally said. "But Hal? You know, Sarah, I don't believe he feels close to us, like a family member from whom we expect anything. And that's my fault. Angie really accepts and likes him. But I'm always seeing him in a poor light, when he's weak and failing."

One of the twins stirred and her eyes rested on them.

"Face it," said Sarah, "He's weak and failing most of the time."

"I suppose he does the best he can, considering that his only qualification for being a husband and a father is that he plays a mean trombone," Sally said.

"Mom, you're so nice," Sarah said, grinning. "It wasn't Hal's trombone that got Les pregnant and started all this."

"Oh, hush!" said Sally, embarrassed and annoyed to be showing it at her age. Any mention of sex in the presence of her daughters invariably turned her face bright red beneath the overlying patina of freckles. She considered herself sophisticated for a country woman. She saw some of the movies and read some of the books, and after all she had worked in wartime Washington for a while. As long as the subject was academic and impersonal, she could discuss it with a certain earnest dutifulness. But when it involved herself or her young daughters, sex was a matter so awkward and embarrassing as to render her tongue-tied. Dirty jokes, which had been the badge of sophistication among the newspaper crowd of her Washington days, made her acutely uncomfortable. She had often felt obliged to listen and to fake appreciation, but she had always been relieved when they were over. It was, she sometimes thought, a gap in her education caused by the fact that she had not lived in a sorority house and been privy to what other college girls talked about at midnight sessions.

Now she found herself unaccountably offended at the mention of sex in connection with Hal and Leslie. She threw Sarah a reproving look and said with simulated boredom, "Don't be biological, Sis, it's too hot. In fact, I think we can stop picking at Leslie and Hal's problems. They started too young but they're getting older every day, and it just may be that they're going to be able to cope. Hal certainly distinguished himself in music school, and that could mean a career for him when he gets out of the Marines."

"You're right," said Sarah, going to get Hank up from his nap. "This time next year Les may be the one doing the worrying—over you and me."

But it didn't work out that way. Leslie found a house trailer for rent outside Quantico, and the Ellises decided to give them their old car instead of trading it in when they bought a new one. It would enable Hal to get back and forth to Quantico. Sarah left Hank at Esperance with her mother and Angie and drove Leslie and the twins and all the paraphernalia the family had assembled back to Virginia. When she returned she reported that the trailer was old and shabby but surprisingly roomy, and all the little towns in that area, including Quantico, were very beautiful.

"Hal hates the Quant," Sarah said, "but Les thinks he might outgrow that. He's getting wonderful assignments. He was in the group chosen to go to Washington to play at the White House for some returning general."

"He *was!*" cried Angie, awed. "How wonderful! Now that boy's going to be getting the breaks, just you watch."

When Leslie wrote the following year that they were coming home, the family was surprised but delighted. She hadn't said it was a holiday visit but they assumed it was and so were not prepared, when they met them at the marina dock, for Hal's footlocker and the clutter of house plunder jammed in the car. For a time they were too caught up in delight over the twins even to notice. The babies, now nearly a year old, had filled out and, as Angie marveled, were "picturebook babies, as gorgeous as Ivory-soap ads."

She held one, Sally the other, and they gloried in the exquisite dilemma of wondering which was which.

"They're so alike" Sally said to Leslie over one twin's shock of straight white-gold hair.

"Like as two peas," Angie gloated. "Which one do I have?" she appealed to Hal.

"Beats me," he said, smiling down at her. "Either Bunk or Bunny."

"Aw, Hal!" scoffed Leslie. "You know you can tell them apart. I can. Easy. That one's Bunny, Granny."

"Then I have Bunk," said Sally, extending the armful of baby to get a better look at the sweetly molded arms and legs, the clear blue eyes, the shyly smiling mouth. "He's smiling at me!" she cried. "He's too young to know to smile at me!"

"He smiles a lot," said Leslie. "Bunny isn't so smiley. That's one way of telling them apart. I don't know why she's so glum."

Sally drew Bunk closer and was moved when he rested an arm around her neck and leaned his head against hers. It was a gesture of such baby trust she wanted to cry.

They loaded the boat with as much of the stuff from the car as it would take and arranged with Sarge at the marina to store the rest of it until they could either borrow a bigger boat or make a second and possibly third trip to transport it to Esperance.

"Hal's not going with us," Leslie said as Sally arranged the bags and boxes in the boat to leave seating for four adults and two armfuls of babies.

"He's not?" Sally asked. "Why not, Hal? We haven't seen you in so long. Aren't you coming for a visit?"

"Sure you are, Hal," put in Angie. "You and I are way behind on our duets."

"Sorry," the boy said with perfunctory courtesy. "I'm going back to Tallahassee and look for a job."

"A job?" Sally and Angie echoed together.

"What about the Marines?" said Sally.

"Mother, I'll tell you all about it," Leslie murmured hastily. "Don't you want to get going?"

"*She'll* tell you all about it," Hal said mockingly, waving a languid hand at Leslie. "Suffice it to say I am lucky enough to be *out* of the Marines."

"Oh, no," Sally said involuntarily, staring at him. You didn't just walk off from the Corps like it was a job in a filling station, did you? She stood rooted to the dock as Hal leaned down to kiss Leslie, who stood in the boat, patted the babies, and turned toward the car. He seemed older, broader, longer of arm, not quite the boy she had seen briefly at the old house in Little Creek, not quite a man.

"Well, Hal," she said, her hand on his arm, "You know what you have to do, but we'll be glad to have you whenever you can come. Just let us know, and somebody will come pick you up."

"It's like this," Hal said, doodling with a finger in the dust on top of the old Buick. "I mean, I got to work so I might as well get started, you know?"

"I thought you were going to be in the Marines another few years," she began.

"Lucked out there," Hal said briefly, getting in the car. "See you."

"Let us hear from you," Sally said ineffectually, as Hal started the old car and gunned it out of the parking lot.

They didn't try to talk over the sound of the boat's motor crossing the Sound, but Sally, at the wheel, kept looking back at the twins, one in Leslie's arms, the other in Angie's. She thought she could tell the difference now.

"Hi, babies!" she shouted over the noise and flapped a hand in the air.

The baby in Leslie's arms smiled at her. The one Angie held had the comic, undecided expression of a jowly country judge about to make a ruling.

"*That* one's Bunk!" she called to Leslie, pointing to the one in her arms.

Leslie smiled and nodded.

Oh, I love him, Sally thought to herself. He's going to be the one who laughs at my jokes.

When the boat was unloaded and supper was started, the women gathered on the screened porch to drink sherry and watch the twins in their fiddler-crab perambulations over the floor. They crawled at a fast clip, lopsidedly, with bottoms held high. Bunny seemed interested in getting to her feet, pausing when she came to a chair to reach for a hold and start to pull up. Watching her, Bunk would try the same.

"Monkey see, monkey do," said Angie, laughing.

They all gazed raptly at the two soft-boned, silk-skinned infants miraculously standing on oval-soled pink feet. Bunny toppled first. Bunk followed and they both howled, but it was a brief token protest and they were crawling again in an instant.

"You were going to tell us how Hal happened to get out of the service," Sally said after a while.

"Mama, it was so awful I didn't want you all to bug Hal about it," Leslie said. "He hated every minute of it, playing Sousa and marching and all. But then there was this sergeant who had it in for Hal. He was always talking about lazy, cowardly Southerners."

"The lowdown scoundrel!" cried Angie, looking at Sally. "I'm going to write Congressman Sikes!"

Sally shrugged. "I thought sergeants always talked mean and nobody expected anything else. But how did Hal get out?"

"Rashes," Leslie said. "They think it was something in the food, or maybe the weather. He started getting these big red blotches all over, and feeling achey in the joints. It was just awful. When it kept coming on, again and again, they said he could go—and here we are!"

Barefoot and in her frazzled cut-off jeans, Leslie looked so happy to be there Sally had not the heart to ask any more questions.

"You won't say anything to Hal about it, will you?" The girl looked anxiously from her mother's face to her grandmother's.

They shook their heads.

"There must be something we could do," Sally ventured. "I wouldn't think it good to have a medical discharge, or whatever they call it. If Hal could have stuck it out he might have been transferred, and I think there are all kinds of benefits, health and education and all, that he'd be entitled to."

"He'd rather skip all that and be free," Leslie said.

Angie nodded emphatically. "With a so-and-so like that talking about Southerners, I don't blame him. Didn't that sergeant ever hear of Andrew Jackson and Nathan Bedford Forrest and old Joe Johnson? Why, the bravest men in the world—"

Sally grinned at her and went to set the table for supper. By the time Angie finished her spiel on the valor of southern fighting men she would have convinced herself that, instead of being out of the Army on some kind of dubious discharge, Hal was Robert E. Lee himself, complete with his horse Traveler. If it cheered Angie and comforted Leslie, it was all right with her, Sally decided, as she got out the good plates to make it a more festive homecoming meal.

But it was Angie who found disturbing evidence that Hal might be a sick boy instead of just a disgruntled one. After supper she had the old gray dishpan set up on the kitchen table with a towel spread beside it and some of her special Castile soap at hand for the babies' baths.

"I'll take which ever one I can catch," she said to Sally. "You or Leslie can grab the other one."

"I've got Bunk," Leslie said. "I'll take him in the shower with me."

Angie sniffed.

Bathing *with* a baby instead of the tender, precise bath ritual she knew seemed unsanitary and even a little scandalous to her. But her protest was drowned out by the sound of running water and Bunk's squeals in the bathroom, so she concentrated on undressing Bunny and getting her in the big pan. Sally heard her gasp and turned to see her staring at Bunny's little buttocks.

"Lord God, what has happened to this baby?" she whispered.

Still clutching the plate she was drying, Sally rushed to see.

The skin on the little round bottom was drawn and puckered in an ugly scar as big as the veined old hand grasping the baby by the small of the back.

"Look!" Angie cried. "Look! This baby has been burned! Badly burned!"

The eyes she turned to Sally were filled with horror. "What on earth happened to her?"

Shocked, Sally reached for the naked baby and held her close to her breast. Her fingers found the uneven corrugated ridges in the soft flesh and she winced.

"Poor baby. No wonder she doesn't smile much."

But Bunny was happy now and tried to tip herself out of Sally's arms and reach the soap.

"It's healed," said Angie, "but she remembers."

She took Bunny back and lowered her gently into the warm water, but her hands trembled and she looked at Sally and shook her head helplessly.

"You'd better finish," the old woman said. "I can't."

However, she was strong enough to take up her post by

the bathroom door and wait for Leslie and Bunk to emerge. Bunk's white hair stood up in damp points, and he squealed and wriggled in the cocoon of bath towel his mother had wound around him.

"Let me have him," Angie directed. "You dress. I want to talk to you."

While Leslie went to put on something besides the towel she wore, the old woman carefully unwound the towel swaddling the baby boy and inspected his body.

"He's all right," she called to Sally in the kitchen. "Bunk's all right."

"Thank God," whispered Sally, lifting Bunny to her shoulder once more.

Both women were waiting on the porch when Leslie emerged from putting the twins to bed.

"Leslie, I want to know about Bunny's burn," Angie said directly. "How did it happen? Tell me the truth. Was it Hal?"

Leslie looked startled. "Gran, how—?" Recovering quickly, she said firmly, "It was an accident, just an accident! Bunny had diaper rash, and this neighbor we had in Virginia said if we put a sunlamp on it it would heal right up. She lent us hers, and Hal—we let it stay on her too long."

"Long enough to give her third-degree burns?" demanded Angie. "Wasn't she screaming with the pain?"

"Granny," Leslie said helplessly.

Sally started to say something but Angie threw her a look which reduced her to silence. "Tell the truth and shame the devil, Leslie," she said sternly. "I *will* know what happened."

"Yes'm," said Leslie, ducking her head. "I went to the store. I shouldn't have. I knew Hal was sleepy. He had to get up so early and I knew he was ready to doze off. I should have turned off the sunlamp before I left. So I took Bunk with me to get some groceries. When I got back I heard Bunny screaming. Hal had gone to sleep on the sofa in the front of the trailer. Oh, it was terrible! Her little skin scorched and the pain so bad! I woke him up and we took her to the hospital. There was a Navy doctor there and he made us leave her overnight. He was good to her but hateful to us. He said we were terrible, neglectful parents and what we had done could have killed

Bunny. Mama"—her eyes sought Sally—"I was so scared and ashamed. After Dodie . . . I couldn't have stood it if Bunny hadn't got well."

"Why didn't you let us know, honey?" Sally asked tiredly.

"I wanted to. I always want to scream for you and Angie when things are bad. But Hal said it would just worry you and there wasn't anything you could do. We had stuff the doctor gave us, and the pain wasn't bad after a while. She healed . . . you saw she healed up, Angie?"

Angie nodded and got to her feet. "Healed this time," she said and walked in the house.

"Mama, you know it was an accident. You know we didn't mean to hurt Bunny, don't you?" Leslie appealed to Sally.

Sally sighed and stood up. "You're going to have to remember this, Leslie. Remember. You can't take any risks with the babies."

She walked to Angie's door and looked in to see if her mother had gone to bed, but the old woman sat in the darkness by the window, her head bowed on her hands.

"Ma," Sally said, "you all right?"

Angie turned from the window, and light from the hall doorway fell on her face. The eyes back of the bifocals seemed unnaturally bright, and Sally couldn't decide if it was from pain, anger, or fear.

"*I'm* all right," Angie said, "but I'm somewhat worried about the rest of you."

"Me too," Sally said softly and walked away, closing the door behind her.

Sarah and Henry had bought a house, a little brick ranch house in a new subdivision, and Hal stayed with them while he looked for a job. A group he had played with was in town, and he sat in with them occasionally, but they already had a good trombone player and there didn't seem to be another job in town. Henry suggested that he try for something else and Hal agreed that he would have to. But after scanning the want ads at the breakfast table he usually went back to bed.

"You get him something," Sarah had urged. "I'm tired of trying to keep Hank quiet so he can sleep all day."

Henry was reluctant to push a job on Hal after the way

the Marine music school had turned out, but as the weeks passed he began to wonder if they had a permanent houseguest. The janitorial firm that cleaned Henry's building went out of business about that time and in the pinch clerks and salesmen and young executives like Henry pitched in to sweep and mop and scrub the washrooms. Henry thought of Hal.

"I can get you minimum wage," he said. "It's not much, but it's better than nothing."

"Janitor, huh?" said Hal.

"Yeah," said Henry. "Janitor. They have big outfits that do that work now. A real business. We'll sign one of them up sooner or later, but meanwhile—"

"Handy Hal," the boy said glumly.

"Well, you wouldn't do it forever," Henry said. "But it'll be a few bucks for you to travel on until something comes up."

"Night work?" Hal asked.

"That's right," said Henry. "And if something comes up in music you can quit, you know."

Hal took the job, but at the end of two weeks the office building contracted with a new janitorial service and he was unemployed again.

"You could probably get on with the new company," Henry said. "You're as good a clean-up man as they've got."

"Man, you're crazy," Hal said, and he took his trombone and went and stayed with a drummer and his mother, an old waitress, who had an apartment in a public housing project.

The high school in Lucina started night courses in vocational subjects. Sally saw the announcement on a flyer posted in the launderette, along with notices of lost dogs and offers of free kittens, boats for sale, and baby-sitting services. She pointed it out to Leslie, who was stuffing the twins' clothes in a washing machine.

"Shorthand and typing," she read. "Don't you want to take it?"

"Mama, could I?" Leslie said, brightening. "I used to hate it when you wanted me to take shorthand and typing in school, but now"—she leaned over to wipe the mush of wet vanilla wafers off the twins' chins—"now if I could just do *something*. I hate sponging on you and Angie and being separated from

Hal. But how would I get ashore every night and what about the twins?"

"We'll work out something," Sally promised. "Let's sign you up for the course and then see what we can do."

Registration took the $15 Sally had for groceries, but she didn't mention it to Leslie. She had prospects for the sale of some lots on the island, and if even one of them jelled they would be prosperous again. When they got back to the island, Angie was working in the small vegetable garden she always planted back of the house. Before they had climbed the hill, they saw the frayed sun hat and heard the wheeze of the pump in the well, trying to keep up with the sprinkler, which was watering beans and tomatoes.

"Hi, voyagers!" called Angie, waving a hoe at them. "Did you bring my grocery order?"

"Tell you about that," Sally said lightly. "Come sit in the shade and I'll fix us some tea."

Angie came, pulling off her hat and her work gloves and mopping her face with a sleeve of the smock she wore to protect her arms and neck from the hot sun.

"That stuff you wanted from the store," Sally said, "well, we're out of it. I saw this marvelous opportunity for our gal young'un here—"

"I know," said Angie. "You gambled away the grocery money again. Horses or slot machines?"

"Horses named Typing and Shorthand," said Leslie, grinning. "Mama wants me to be *employable.*"

They pulled folding aluminum chairs to the eastern side of the house, where there was shade and a good breeze from the Gulf, and talked about it. If the classes had been scheduled for daytime it would have been easier. Sally went over nearly every day to sit in her office in the hope of luring land buyers to the island. But none of them liked the idea of Leslie's making the trip across the Sound at night alone. And Sally didn't want to leave Angie by herself with the twins on the island, although she was apparently well now and had had no recurrence of the heart trouble.

"If I could get a job I'd move to Lucina," Leslie said wistfully. "Then Hal could come and maybe find something. You know he can teach music, if there are kids around who want to take trombone."

Sally was skeptical but her mother greeted the idea with enthusiasm. "Of course he can teach," she said. "I don't know why we didn't think of that before. Write him, Leslie. Meanwhile, Sally, I'm going to Lucina with you tomorrow and talk to that old fool Herb Wilcox about getting Leslie a job in the bank. He calls himself retired, but he can still tell them what to do. If Leslie has a daytime job she can afford an apartment and be on the spot for those night classes."

To Sally's surprise, Angie and Leslie between them worked it out. She kept the twins in the office while her mother and the girl, dressed in their best town-going clothes, visited the bank and talked to Herb Wilcox's son, Oliver, who now ran it. Then they called on an old friend of Angie's who owned the dime store on the main street, which ran along the river dock.

"Mama! Angie did it!" shouted Leslie, hanging her head out the car window as she parked in front of the office. "She's fixed everything!"

Sally held a finger to her lips and gestured, to warn them that the twins were asleep in their baskets under the electric fan, and then tiptoed out to meet them.

"I've got the job *and* a place to live!" Leslie crowed. "The most *charming* place! I can't wait for Hal to see it. It's upstairs over the dime store with a view of the whole waterfront. We can fix it up so cute."

Angie looked complacent. "You might think it's not the best place in the world for young folks with children," she said. "But there's next to no cheap rental property right in Lucina. I remembered that during the war the Nathans fixed housekeeping rooms over the dime store for some of their children. Full of junk now, stuff they store, but they are willing to clear it out and let Leslie and Hal have it."

"There's even a little scrap of yard where the stairs go down in the back," Leslie said. "We can fence it in to make a play yard for Bunk and Bunny."

And so it was arranged. Angie packed a picnic lunch and loaded a basket with cleaning materials and rags, and she and Sally went with Leslie and the twins to ready the new apartment.

To Sally, who had not seen it before, it seemed small and hot: one room with a toilet and a rusty shower back of a thin partition in the corner and a dingy kitchen with torn linoleum on the floor and rusty water dripping from a single faucet over a stained and cracked old sink. There was a two-burner hot plate and a tin oven that could be pressed into service over one of the burners if Leslie ever decided to bake, and an old white-enameled icebox with a drip pan under it, which couldn't quite hide the soft place in the floor where the overflow had rotted it.

Sally set down the playpen she had brought along to restrain the twins, while the cleaning was in progress, and looked around her, sighing.

"Now, don't droop, Mama," chided Leslie. "It's going to be darling. Look at the view."

She flung open the windows overlooking street and harbor.

"Just like Marseilles," said Angie. "I can see madame now shaking her bedding over the street every morning and calling out to the neighbors."

"And Hal—monsieur—riding up on his bicycle with fresh hot French bread," put in Leslie, who had seen the movies too.

In the face of their high spirits, Sally felt glum and graceless. The place *smelled* poor, she thought. The whole project of job and school and family togetherness seemed impossibly outsized and unmanageable with this bleak little base. She sighed again and went to fill the mop bucket she had brought from Esperance.

With the help of a shrimp-boat captain who hauled furniture from the island for them, they moved Leslie in. Pursuing the Marseilles theme, Angie wouldn't let them settle for a pull-out sofa bed in the one big room.

"That old iron bed from the hotel, that's what it needs," she said. "With curtains hanging from the ceiling like a tester and lots of pillows and flounces. I'll make 'em—with window curtains to match. It won't look living roomish but it will look French."

"Far out!" cried Leslie, delighted.

"I'll put a coat of red enamel on the kitchen floor," said Sally.

"Bright yellow curtains at the window over the sink," suggested Angie.

"Oh, yes!" said Leslie. "But won't it all cost a lot?"

"Dyed sheets everywhere," said Angie. "We've got some worn ones I can cut up, and dye is free if you make it yourself from weeds and roots."

It was a skill Angie had perfected for fun, and now she taught it to Leslie. Sally, feeding the twins and preparing to haul them, one on her hip, one in a pack on her back, to the beach to play in the waves, listened to Angie and Leslie chattering over the dye pot. They had bushels of leaves from the fragrant swamp myrtle steeping to make blue dye, and when it was done they meant to simmer the stems and leaves of a wild yellow daisy to color the kitchen curtains. Sally was warmed by their contentment.

Leslie began work at the bank on Monday morning and short-hand and typing classes Monday night. Bunk and Bunny were to stay on the island, but when the time came for Sally to embark for the mainland and her office she stood in the door, troubled and uneasy to be leaving Angie alone with them.

One would have been a handful for an old lady, but two, scampering about the floor on their hands and knees, bumping into things and crying and eating and wetting and needing to be lifted . . . it was going to be too much.

"I'm going to take them with me," she said.

"Aw, Sally, we'll be all right here," Angie protested. "How can you work with babies on your hands?"

"There doesn't seem to be a lot of work for me to do," Sally said. "If I get any nibbles on land I'll look around for a baby-sitter. There must be somebody in Lucina I could hire."

To be prepared, she started asking around and a friend at the fish house told her about Millie Staples, a black woman who had just got out of jail and started to work cleaning seafood.

"She's a good worker but she's allergic," he said. "Got three children of her own and needs a job, but every time she guts a fish seems like she breaks out."

Sally went to see Millie, who lived in a warren of apartments and rooms in a ramshackle house in the Negro section. Her own place was clean, and her pregnant teenage daughter and two younger sons were almost majestic in their courtesy.

"Your children have such nice manners," Sally said as she introduced herself to Millie.

"Yes'm," said Millie briefly, in a voice as deep and harsh as a man's, and she scowled at her children until they left the room.

Sally began talking of Leslie and the twins and the little apartment over the dime store and their need of help. Millie stood with her arms folded across her chest. A long scar ran across one cheek from mouth to ear, and Sally saw that her arms were ridged with similar scars.

A knife fighter, she thought, and wanted to stop talking and leave, but she couldn't seem to stem the flow of her own words, which clearly were crashing against a wall of silence and impenetrable hostility in Millie.

Finally, to get out of the house, she said, "The babies are asleep in the car. I'd better check on them."

"Yes'm," said Millie in her gruff baritone and followed her out the door.

Bunk awakened as they approached, and he began crying. Bunny, by some system of twin ESP, cried too without fully waking up.

Without a word Millie leaned into the back window and reached for Bunk, cradling him against her starched and ironed dress front. One hand checked his diaper and she said briefly. "He wet, lemme change him."

Sally fumbled for the diaper bag on the floor in the front of the car and handed it to her, watching helplessly, a mere bystander, while the big woman plumped Bunk down on the seat and expertly changed his diaper.

Millie's face appeared the same, closed and angry, but Bunk, drowsy and rumple-cheeked from sleeping face down, was smiling at her with a sunny radiance that lit up the car. Sally turned to Bunny and saw that she was awake; her usually solemn little face was transfixed by a smile also trained on Millie.

Still unsmiling, Millie balanced Bunk in one arm and with a powerful thrust of the other plucked Bunny from her basket and held her close.

Both babies gurgled delightedly, bouncing in the big arms.

Millie turned with them and walked toward her door. Oh, no, Sally thought, she's taking them inside. She turned quickly to follow, but Millie stopped at the door and said something in a low voice to her children, ending with, "I be back."

To Sally she said, "I go wid you."

And I'm glad, Sally thought wonderingly, as she started the

car. We haven't discussed references or hours or pay and especially what she was doing in jail and how she got those scars, but I'm glad. The babies know something about her that I don't.

Whatever the twins knew was right on target, it seemed. Millie came early, stayed until Leslie got home from the bank, went home to feed her own children, and returned and stayed with the twins until Leslie was home from her classes. Order emanated from her like the web from a spider's body. The little apartment was spotless, the babies the same.

She seemed to do all the laundry and housework while the twins slept, and the rest of the time was devoted to playing with them and taking them for walks in their double stroller. Sally and Angie arrived one day to find her sitting on the grass in the little back yard, holding her arms out to Bunny, who stood erect, swaying uncertainly.

"Loney, loney," Millie coaxed in her deep voice.

And Bunny seemed imbued with a steadiness, a baby resolve. Her blue eyes on Millie's face, her little hands reaching for the big dark hands, she took one step and then another before she fell into Millie's arms.

Millie said nothing but hugged the little girl to her before she set her back on the grass and said again, "Loney, loney."

"She'll have them walking in no time," Angie said.

And Millie did, Bunny first and then Bunk. She said nothing to indicate her pleasure in the accomplishment. She never smiled. But when Sally suggested that she bring the twins and her own children to spend a day now and then at Esperance, she was willing.

All five were always immaculately clean, and Millie's were so quiet and mannerly Sally worried that they weren't having a good time until she looked out on the beach and saw them frolicking in the surf. Millie sat with her skirt up to her waist and a twin on either side of her. The babies watched the incoming waves as if mesmerized, and when one wet their feet they fell into a convulsion of joy, wriggling and squealing.

Millie's pregnant daughter, Idella, and the little boys, Wayne and Jeffry, wore new bathing suits and had a big beach towel each with great many-rayed orange suns printed on them, along with the words FUN IN THE SUN.

"I told Millie the kids could wear cut-off jeans for swimming,"

Sally remarked to her mother as they prepared lunch. "All the kids who come to the beach seem to wear 'em now. I also told her we had plenty of old towels."

"She wanted them fixed up right," Angie said. "She's firm with those children, determined they are going to behave. But she wants them to have things. Millie's a proud woman."

Sally turned a piece of chicken she was frying and said thoughtfully, "I never did find out why Millie was in jail."

"Murder," Angie said promptly.

Shocked, Sally turned to her, tongs lifted, drumstick dangling.

"Her sorry husband. He got Idella pregnant. It was the last straw. He had been beating them and he cut Millie when she tried to protect them. So she bought a gun and shot him."

"Oh, Mama, how horrible!" Sally cried.

"He *needed* killing," Angie said as if that closed the subject. "The judge must have thought so too, because he let Millie out on probation after six months. It would have been justifiable homicide, I imagine, if Millie hadn't premeditated around. She bought the gun and waited for him in the bushes away from the house so the children wouldn't see him shot."

"Poor Millie," Sally said.

But she felt a sudden urge to hurry to the window and check on the children. Idella sat by her mother and watched while Wayne and Jeffry helped the twins dig holes in the sand for the waves to fill up.

Sometimes Sally feared that Millie might decide Hal "needed killing." She had seen the scars on Bunny's buttocks and heard Leslie's story about it, but when Hal came she barely spoke to him.

He came down from job-hunting in Tallahassee and seemed unable to find anything on the coast. The hoped-for trombone pupils did not materialize, and Hal prowled up and down the coast from Pensacola to Panacea, looking for spots where a trombone was needed. He rarely found more than a one-night or weekend gig.

Worried, Sally asked again around Lucina about part-time jobs for him and came up with two—mornings pumping gas at the Shell station and a day now and then at the marina when Sarge had a boat hull to clear of barnacles and repaint. Hal worked at both for a while.

Then one day the owner of the filling station called to ask Sally why her son-in-law had failed to show up.

"I had to go to Tallahassee, and I counted on the boy to open up for me," Joe Hyde said. "It's noon and he's not here yet. Do you think he's sick?"

Sally closed her office and drove over to the little apartment to see.

Millie and the twins were in the back yard, ostensibly watering six tomato plants Leslie and Millie had set out and called "the farm." The twins wore only their diapers, and for every drop that fell on the sandy ground around the tomatoes two arced through the air in a rainbow curve and fell on the sun-gilded heads of the squealing, dancing children.

When they saw Sally they rushed to her to be lifted and hugged and to press their wet bodies against her.

"Is Hal here?" Sally asked Millie, leaning around two armfuls of babies.

The big woman grunted. "Sleep."

"He's supposed to be at the filling station."

"Huh!" snorted Millie. "*She* woke him up before she left. I call him three times. He growl and go back to sleep."

"You should have dragged him out and got him on his feet," Sally said, putting the babies down and heading for the stairs.

"Ain't my business to try to make no man out of a growed-up boy," Millie said sourly. "Saying I *could* do it."

Hal had drawn Angie's bed draperies to shut out the light. It made a dim, smelly cave. Sally called first to awaken him. When there was no answer she pushed one of the curtains aside and touched his bare, sweat-glistening shoulder.

"Hal, Hal," she called. "Wake up."

He stirred and opened his eyes, glaring at her foggily for a minute before his silver eyes cleared and he groped for the sheet to cover his chest.

"What time is it?" he asked.

"It's past noon," Sally said, suddenly tired. Was there any point, she wondered, in waking him? The little job was probably gone anyhow, and he might as well stay submerged in that heavy young sleep which affected teenagers like a paralysis. She dropped the curtain and turned away, saying over her shoulder, "They called from the filling station."

"Jesus," he said, stirring and turning. "Will you tell old Hyde

I'll be right there? I'll take a shower. Tell him I was sick or something."

The filling station was only a few blocks from the apartment and he could walk it in a minute so Sally went ahead, stopping to give Joe Hyde the message.

"Sick, huh? Couldn't he have let me know? I depended on him, Sally. When I go off and leave my business I've got to have somebody I can depend on."

"I know," said Sally, nodding. "Tell him that. He's a good boy. He'll straighten up. He's just young."

But Hal did not return to the filling station. He was not well, Leslie said. The funk which hit him in the service had descended again and he couldn't bring himself to leave the apartment.

Sally stopped by to leave off Millie's pay and to deliver a box of groceries and found Leslie, between work and school, playing with the twins in the back yard.

"Is he strong enough to carry the groceries upstairs?" Sally asked sarcastically.

"Oh, Mama," Leslie said helplessly. "I'll take them up. I do thank you. We were out of nearly everything and my paycheck went for the rent and utilities."

She fingered the bills for Millie.

"I hate for you to keep paying this. Millie's wonderful but it's a lot of money. And while Hal's at home maybe he could look after Bunk and Bunny."

"No!" said Sally sharply, remembering the scar on Bunny's little bottom.

Leslie flushed.

Sally said hastily, "He'll never find a job if he has to stay home and baby-sit. Let's keep Millie for the time being anyhow. If you let her go, somebody else will grab her and the twins love her."

She couldn't tell the girl that she and Angie would never sleep at night if they thought the babies were alone with their father. Even as she handed the bags of food and the jugs of milk out of the car to Leslie, she worried that she had said too much.

"If Hal is sick," she said after a moment, "maybe you should let his parents know."

"I thought of that," Leslie said. "He really can't stand them, but they've been trying to be nice to us. Dorinda sent the children matching tricycles. They're too big for them now, but they'll grow to them and they're perfectly beautiful."

"That's nice," Sally murmured, turning away.

Leslie laughed. "I know what you're thinking. You pay Millie and feed us and pay for diapers and shoes and milk and they come through with tricycles."

Sally's grin admitted it.

"It's not their fault, Mama," Leslie said. "Hal won't write to let them know anything about us. I'd write but he thinks anything they know about us they'll use against him. That's why they don't even know how big they are. I can't tell them that without telling them other things about us."

Sally sighed. "I'm not telling you what to do. But if you think they care about their son at all, maybe you'd better tell them about his depression."

Leslie did write the Ellises and had a letter within a few days that they were planning a trip to Florida and would stop off in Lucina for a visit. Before they arrived, Hal disappeared, trombone case in hand. The old car was giving trouble, so he left it where it stood back of the dime store and struck off down the highway hitchhiking.

"He's gone to New York," Leslie said with defiant pride. "He has to find himself."

Angie nodded. "New York is the place for musicians nowadays. Is he going to Gotham?"

Sally smiled at the expression coming from her mother's lips so glibly, and Leslie nodded.

"I think so. He's going to let me know. A lot of musicians we know are there."

When she and her mother were alone, Sally said scornfully, "Hal's got to 'find himself'! Isn't that the most ridiculous thing you ever heard of?"

Angie looked thoughtful. "I don't know, honey. There is such a thing as a young person being lost and floundering and finally coming into his own. Maybe it will happen to that boy."

When the Ellises came, they took a room at a motel down the coast. They had been in and out of Lucina for a couple of days when Leslie and Millie brought the twins by Sally's office one afternoon. They were dressed alike in pretty blue sunsuits, and their white high-topped shoes gleamed with polish. They had come, Leslie said, to say goodbye. Mr. and Mrs. Ellis were going to take them home with them for a visit.

"It will give Millie some time off," Leslie said, smiling at the dark woman, who glowered back. "And I can catch up on stuff at school."

Bunk made it to Sally's arms first. They had grown so fast there was room for only one in her arms at a time, and they seemed to know it and were competitive about getting there first. She picked him up and he bumped her chin with his silky head, trying to get close.

"Kiss Gran goodbye," Leslie directed, and the little boy flung his arms around her neck and held on tight.

Bunny was pulling at her skirt, ready to offer her kiss, and Sally attempted to kiss Bunk and swap him for his sister. He clung tighter.

"Oh, babies." Sally sighed. "I hate for you to go away."

"That Bunk he don't want to go," Millie pointed out.

"Well, he's got to go, the Ellises are waiting," Leslie said, pulling the baby arms loose from her mother's neck and handing the little boy to Millie. Sally hugged Bunny and handed her to her mother and followed them to the door.

The Ellises waited down the street in their white Cadillac, the engine running, the air conditioner whirring. Dorinda waved gaily, and Sally waved back and turned again to the hot, close little office. It seemed bleak and empty, and she wanted to run out on the sun-baked sidewalk and cry "Don't go!" to the twins—but how dopey can you get? she asked herself. The Ellises had a right to see their grandchildren, she supposed, although she wasn't certain. The babies had a right to another set of grandparents—she was more certain of that. And it was nice that they drew a brace who were vacationing Cadillac owners and donors of pretty sunsuits.

Self-pity was closing in on her like a salt wave, Sally decided, and the only thing to do was to lock the door and get to the island.

Two weeks later she saw Angie's iron bed, which Leslie and Hal had been using, in front of the little secondhand furniture store Miss Esther Atkins ran on a back street.

She went to the apartment and found Leslie, barefoot with her long hair pinned on top of her head, busily conducting a sale. A young couple was tying one of the two baby beds on top of their station wagon, and a bearded young man was picking through the dishes and pots and pans which were stacked on the little pine table.

"No carnival glass?" he asked at last.

"No, but some of this is pretty old," Leslie told him. "My grandmother's stuff."

"And why are you selling it?" Sally demanded from the doorway.

"Oh, Mama, come in," Leslie said with fake cordiality. Sally knew the tone well. It had always masked Leslie's determination to have her way. "Hal wrote. He has a job playing at a club. He wants me to come to New York."

"What about the twins?" Sally asked.

"They're going to stay with the Ellises until we can get a place for them. That's what I'm going to do right away, get a job and an apartment."

The young man picked up four cups and saucers and reached for his wallet. Leslie happily pulled out newspapers to wrap his purchase, chatting gaily as she pocketed the bills he handed her.

"I've got nearly enough for an airplane ticket," she whispered to her mother. "The iron bed brought the most—fifty dollars. Can you imagine?"

"Yes," said Sally dryly, turning toward the door. "I can imagine. I saw one like it in a Tallahassee antiques shop for a hundred and fifty."

"Oh, Mom!" said Leslie, stricken. "I've messed up again, haven't I?"

Sally didn't have the heart to answer. She walked outside and sat down on the steps. She was glad about Hal's job. She thought Leslie should be with him. But it was all happening so fast. The things she and Angie had carefully and lovingly set up—the job, the school, the apartment, Millie for the babies—all heedlessly toppled and scattered like a tower made of babies' ABC blocks. Leslie, she thought, was still a heedless, impulsive child, as irresponsible in her way as Hal.

Her eyes rested on the valiant little row of tomato plants with fruit just beginning to color. It would be almost a relief, she thought, to have them gone, to have them faraway in New York. Even as she thought it, her mind pictured Bunk and

84

Bunny growing up in some distant place foreign to the beaches and the woods of Esperance, some place where she couldn't reach them, and an ache akin to homesickness spread through her. She called Sarah.

Sarah arrived with baby Hank and a selection of her own dresses and jeans and some false eyelashes for Leslie.

"I think it's perfectly wonderful that she's going to New York," she told her mother and Angie. "We're going to fix her up so she'll knock Hal dead with her looks and maybe get herself a job on the stage."

"Oh, Sis," said Leslie, "I'm so glad you came."

Together, the girls busied around, packing for Leslie and stowing the babies' things in Sarah's car to be sent from Tallahassee when a home was found in New York. Sarah was going to drive Leslie to the airport. Neither of them saw any point in Sally's making the trip, and she was relieved but anxious as she watched Leslie, slim and brown from weekends on the island, preening herself in the sleek green linen sheath Sarah had brought and applying false eyelashes.

"They get in my way," she admitted, "but I want to look super when I arrive in case Hal's at the airport to meet me."

"In case?" Sally said. "Won't he be there for sure?"

"Probably not," Leslie said easily. "He hates meeting and seeing off. I have the address where he's staying."

"You're going to need more money," Sally said, rummaging for her checkbook. "I'm pretty low right now, but I can scrounge up another twenty-five to get you a taxi and a meal or two. Send the address when you know it, and if that contract I wrote on a lot on the bay side goes through . . ."

The contract was rejected at the last minute by the prospective buyer, so Sally wasn't flush as she had hoped to be. She worried to Angie that Hal and Leslie might be hungry in New York, and then she was sorry when she saw her mother tucking $5 into a letter.

"It'll buy peanut butter and bread," Angie said defensively.

"It's all you have, isn't it?" Sally asked.

"Ask me no questions and I'll tell you no lies," Angie snapped. "Besides, they'll be rich one day and we'll all live on the fat of the land."

The money had run out, but Angie's resourcefulness had

not. Seeing her mother's light on late one night, Sally went to investigate and found Angie squatting on the floor beside a boxful of old Christmas cards.

"I just remembered somebody who might be able to help Leslie and Hal," she said. "Theresa Loring, whose folks used to spend every summer at the hotel, married a man who has something to do with Broadway. I had a Christmas card from her not too many years ago. If I can just find the address . . ."

Angie found the address and promptly wrote her friend. She hoped the husband, "who had something to do with Broadway," might find a job in the orchestra of one of the theaters for Hal. He had tried, setting up an audition for the young trombone player, but for some reason that Leslie's letters never explained, the job was not forthcoming. Nevertheless, the Lorings had not stinted in their kindness to Angie's granddaughter. They had moved the young couple from the cheap and dingy hotel where they were staying to a pleasant old-fashioned rooming house "with kitchen privileges" run by a friend of theirs and had found Leslie a job in a department store.

"I looked too tacky to apply even," Leslie wrote. "The good clothes Sarah brought me are suddenly too tight. All that peanut butter. I was sitting at the window worrying when I saw Theresa arrive with an armful of dresses. All beautiful, all big enough."

The job in the store's gift department was "fun but not easy," Leslie wrote, and Hal was getting regular work at some of the night spots in Greenwich Village. They would soon be able to rent a nice apartment they had found and send for the twins.

But before that happened, Dorinda Ellis called Sally at her office one day.

"Why does little Harold have those blackouts?" she asked. "And what do you do about them?"

"Blackouts?" cried Sally. "I never heard of such a thing! What happened?"

"He just topples over—out of it, like," Dorinda said. "They last a minute or two, and then he seems all right."

"I never heard of such a thing," Sally repeated, anxiety taking hold of her so her hand on the telephone trembled and she had trouble speaking.

"Hubert said you might know," Mrs. Ellis said uncertainly.

"I *don't* know," Sally said, "but I'll call our doctor right away and see what he has to say. He knows the twins. What about Bunny, does she have the same symptoms?"

"Oh, no," said Dorinda, "she's as right as rain."

To coin a phrase, Sally thought sourly. Aloud she said, "I'll call you right back."

Dr. West knew of no blackouts Bunk had ever had, but he took the report seriously.

"I'd get him to a neurologist right away, Sally. It could be a tumor or epilepsy. Don't waste any time, you hear?"

Sally called Mrs. Ellis and told her what Dr. West had said. "Do you have a neurologist there?" she asked.

"No," Dorinda said. "We just have a drugstore. There are doctors in Fredericksburg. Hubert has been saying he would take the twins to a pediatrician there soon."

"Dr. West said this could be urgent," Sally said. "I tell you what, I'll make an appointment with somebody in Tallahassee and fly up and get Bunk tomorrow. Can you meet me at the airport with him?"

"Will you bring him back?" Dorinda faltered.

"Well, sure," said Sally. "I hadn't thought of anything beyond getting him to a doctor."

"We've spent so much money on them," Dorinda said. "Their clothes have cost a fortune. I don't know what to do. Let me ask Hubert."

Sally clung to the phone with one hand and brushed the damp hair up off her neck with the other. The little office seemed unbearably hot and close in spite of the fan turning overhead. It had happened with the phone call—sticky, body-soaking fear which glued her clothes to her thighs and shoulders and back. Let him be all right, she prayed silently, let him be all right.

Dorinda came back on the line. "Hubert says not to come. He will take care of it. He will call a pediatrician in Fredericksburg soon."

"Not soon, *now!*" shouted Sally. "This could be serious!"

"Hubert says that you are overreacting. He will take care of the child."

"Listen," said Sally, struggling for control, "do it right away. And call me back. I'll be waiting here by the phone."

"Just a minute," Dorinda said and left the phone again.

Sally stood up, pacing the length of the phone cord.

"Sally." Dorinda was back. "Hubert says you'll have to leave everything to us and don't wait for a phone call. All this long-distance calling back and forth might upset the twins."

"What?" Sally gasped. "Upset—!"

But Dorinda had done one decisive thing. She had hung up.

The rest of the afternoon passed in a haze. A baby having blackouts. Sally had never heard of it before but, remembering Dodie, remembering the meager, bluish little body that had been Bunk in the incubator, she couldn't sit still and wait. She called Leslie at the store in New York.

"Blackouts?" Leslie said, puzzled. "He never had blackouts before! Mama, I want to come and get my babies!"

"I'm leaving for Tallahassee now to send you a ticket. It will be at the Delta counter at the La Guardia airport in three or four hours," Sally said.

Sally and Sarah met Leslie's plane. She walked into their arms, laughing and crying to see them.

"What have you heard from Virginia?" she asked as she hugged them.

"Nothing," said Sally. "Not since Hubert sent word that he didn't want me phoning."

"Hal called them," Leslie said. "They said you were over-reacting."

"I was. I am," Sally admitted. "I'm out-of-my-mind crazy. I won't be any better until we get Bunk to a doctor."

"We're going to do that right away," Sarah said firmly. "The Parkers are going to keep Hank for me, and I'm going to drive to Virginia with Les as soon as we can get out of the parking lot. It's all arranged."

"Yes," said Sally. "You all leave now. I'd go with you, but I hate to leave Angie that long."

"Ha!" Sarah hooted cheerfully. "You're just afraid Angie will kill those people."

Leslie grinned. "She would. Angie's tough. But the Ellises aren't really bad. They just don't know how scary it is for us, a sick baby."

Sally nodded and threw a warning glance at Sarah. It wouldn't help matters if her older daughter pointed out that it had been the Ellises' choice to remove themselves from contact with death and serious infant illness. And she knew that was what Sarah, the open, the forthright, intended to say.

Apparently Sarah thought better of it herself. "Let's get your bag and get going," she said. "We should be there by tomorrow afternoon. We'll call you, Mama, when we arrive and then when we get Bunk to a doctor."

Sally expected to keep vigil by the telephone alone, but Angie would not hear of it.

"I should have gone with the girls," the old woman said. "I'd like to get my hands on those idiot Ellises."

"Yes, ma'am, that's what we thought. That's why the girls are going alone. They don't trust you and me to behave."

"Well, I'm going with you to wait for word," Angie said. "I've got my knitting. I'll just sit in the office and work on that sweater and wait."

The first call came sooner than they expected. It was Sarah.

"Mother, the Ellises *are not going to let us have the twins!*"

Sally thought she had not heard aright. "What did you say, Sarah? Say that again!"

"It's true. We're about twenty miles from their little town. We called to tell them we were on the way so they could pack for the babies, and they said there was no use coming; they wouldn't let us have Bunk or Bunny."

"Did Leslie talk to them?"

"Leslie's the one who called them."

Angie, alert to new trouble, was at her shoulder. Sally relayed Sarah's words to her.

"Fools!" said Angie contemptuously. "Let me have the phone! Sarah," she said into the mouthpiece, "stay where you are until we can talk to a lawyer. Give us that number. We'll call you back."

Sally was already finding the number of the Tallahassee lawyer who had always done their legal work. It was late and he had gone home. She called him there and poured out the story of the blackouts, the refusal of the Ellises to have her come, and now their word to the twins' mother that she could not have her children.

"Obviously unusual," he said. "But you know, Sally, if we had to go to court in their little town we could lose. They're probably settled, respected citizens, and they might look better to a jury of their neighbors than an itinerant musician and his young wife."

"You mean any jury in the world would take those children from their mother?" gasped Sally.

"It's a chance we don't want to have to take," he said. "Tell the girls to get in there fast, grab up the babies, and get them across the state line before they stop. Let me know what happens."

Later, when he heard, he seemed less surprised at what happened than Sally and Angie were.

"We've got B and B and we're on our way home!" Sarah said jubilantly in a call that came close to midnight.

Sally sagged deeper into the old office chair and smiled at Angie, who had been dozing on the sofa but now sat upright and was listening attentively.

"Mama, they're so beautiful and are so glad to see me!" Leslie said over Sarah's shoulder. "Thank you, thank you!"

"What happened? Did the Ellises give you much trouble?"

"It was a breeze," said Sarah. "By the time we got there they had changed their minds and were packing the twins' clothes and toys. But they wouldn't let me in the house. They said Les could go in and get the babies, but I would have to wait outside."

"How funny," mumbled Sally.

"Not as funny as what they said about you," chuckled Sarah. "When they finally came out of the house and spoke to me, Dorinda said, 'Is your mother still a member of the Communist Party?' "

In relief, as much as shocked amusement, Sally started laughing, and she laughed until Angie caught the infection and began laughing too. With the phone back in the cradle and the dark night pressing against the windows, they sat in the little circle of light from the desk lamp and laughed and laughed, holding their sides and mopping their streaming eyes.

The next day they drove to Tallahassee to meet the girls and the twins and to set up an appointment with a neurologist for Bunk.

FALL 1976

There was no point in reminding Leslie twelve years later of what the Ellises were capable of doing. If they decided to keep Bunk and Bunny, they now had Hal to back them up. He had been absent, if not downright neutral, the last time. Now he had somehow maneuvered the children at the age of thirteen years to the same side: if not *for* the parents he had despised, at least *against* Leslie and Sally.

We've already got plans for Christmas—just we three. Sally could hear again the bumptious, satisfied voice of Bunk on that rainy night.

"Leslie," she said on impulse, "let's go get our hair done."

"Mama, you all right?" The girl had been folding towels as they came out of the dryer, and she looked at her mother in astonishment.

"No, I'm not all right and you're not either. We're depressed and we look depressing. Let's get curls and cuts and eyeshadow and stuff. Let's get something new to wear. Here it is practically Christmas, and we've decked everything but ourselves."

Later, when the Parkers, junior and senior, had arrived and the little house on the point whooshed in and out like an accordion with noise and movement and Christmas-dinner preparations, Sally and Sarah basted the turkey and agreed that Leslie had been markedly improved by their sortie into the beauty parlor and the dress shops.

"You know I never found that a new hair-do was anything but a new hair-do," Sally said. "It never lifted my spirits or rejuvenated the inner and outer woman like it's supposed to do. But I have to admit that I feel better just looking at Leslie."

"Me too," Sarah said. "She's really an awfully pretty girl. I forget how pretty until I see her fixed up a little."

They watched out the window as Leslie, holding Say-Say's hand, listened to something Mr. Parker was saying. Her face was rosy from the morning run to try out the new boat and luminous with a singular attentiveness that had ever been her special gift. She listens, Sally thought, really listens. And whatever Mr. Parker is saying, he thinks it's the wisdom of the ages because of Leslie's responsiveness. The long mane of straight brown hair had been shorn, and her head gleamed under a feathery pixie cut. She wore the new makeup and, although the day was bright and unusually warm for late December, she had on the fluffy yellow sweater and brown tweed slacks Sally bought her for Christmas.

"She doesn't even look fat when she has on clothes that fit her," Sarah said.

"She *is* fat," Sally said. "But she's determined to go on a diet so she'll look good when—"

"*If,*" Sarah said. "Do you think either Hal or the children will come today? Or ever? I have a terrible feeling that Hal wants those twins now. I don't think he ever wanted them before, but now that they're older, I don't know. I wish Henry and I could have kept them. Henry really loves those two."

Sarah and Henry had kept the twins for three months after the girls brought them back from the Ellises. Bunk's trips to the neurologist were going to be spread out over a period of weeks, and Leslie had agreed to let them stay while she went back to her job in New York and resumed the effort to get a place for them all to live.

The first diagnosis had been petit mal, and Sally, opening the refrigerator to check the ambrosia for Christmas dessert, smiled to remember the notes which Sarah had taped to her refrigerator in the little brick ranch house when it had seemed so full of babies. *Bunk's Medicine* the signs had reminded her and Millie, who had been dispatched by Sally to help.

"Don't need no letters to tell me to give that baby them pills," Millie had said gruffly. "I see *him,* I remembers."

But the baby tranquilizers had been administered only a short time, after all. Sarah's pediatrician, who took care of Hank, questioned the diagnosis of one neurologist and ultimately persuaded Sarah and Sally to take Bunk to Atlanta to see another who specialized in children.

They went prepared for a siege at the hospital with an overnight bag packed with Bunk's pajamas and toys and one for Sally, who was going to sleep on a cot beside his hospital crib. But Dr. Isaacs, the new doctor, had sent them home. Brain scans had been done and redone, and he studied those and read the report of the pediatrician. The next day he spent an hour talking with Sally and Sarah and casually playing ball with the patient.

"Catch it, Harold!" he would call, using Bunk's real name, and then he'd watch while the little boy scrambled to get the big red ball. "Now throw it back, throw it to me!"

Eagerly, his face screwed up with enthusiasm for the game, Bunk would grasp the ball, move his arm in a baby imitation of a pitcher's windup, and thrust it toward the waiting doctor. At first he had trouble letting the ball go.

Dr. Isaacs smiled. "That's the complicated part. They have to learn to let it go."

After half a dozen tries, Bunk almost mastered the trick and crowed with delight when he was able to send the ball close enough for Dr. Isaacs to catch it.

Laughing too, Dr. Isaacs picked him up and hugged him and handed him to Sally.

"I think your grandson's blackouts are psychological," he said. "Mrs. Parker tells me he has had only two since he's been at her house, and both of those were in moments of stress, once when she slapped his hand for something."

He turned to Sarah for confirmation.

She flushed guiltily. "That's right. He poured his milk on the floor and I hit him. He went out like a light."

"Oh, Sarah," Sally reproached her.

"I know. I felt like a monster. But you have to draw the line at some things."

"You do indeed," Dr. Isaacs had said. "Harold's trouble may have been that too many lines were drawn for him. Everybody in his world is bigger than he is, and when he can't cope, he withdraws. He blacks out."

"What do we do?" Sally had asked.

"What you're doing. Love him and let him know it. Discipline him when you have to."

Sarah had the turkey out of the oven and was scraping the roasting pan preparing to make gravy. Sally stood a moment with the salad plates in her hand, watching gratefully. She hadn't taught either of the girls to cook. There had never seemed to be time. What they knew they picked up by osmosis from Angie. Now, on this first Christmas Day without Angie, Sally more than ever appreciated Sarah's presence, Sarah's competence.

"Sis, you are an ever-fixed mark," Sally said lightly, but her face was solemn and loving. "You look on tempests and are never shaken."

"Don't tell me," she said sunnily. "Shakespeare. And I do thank you, Ma, but maybe we better put dinner on or we'll have a tempest that'll shake us all. Hank can stay away from the new boat just long enough to remind me every ten minutes that he's starving to death."

"I'll hurry," said Sally. But she hurried tranquilly, smoothing the good linen cloth with its wide hemstitched hem, pushing a sprig of cedar back into place in the green-encircled center-piece pyramid of fruit. They had no dining room, but the gateleg table from the kitchen, placed end to end with the dropleaf table, had extended it enough to accommodate them all. The day was too warm for a fire, but Sally refused to believe in a Christmas that didn't warrant at least one piece of drift-wood burning blue-green on the hearth, its smoke an incense of salt and beach sage.

The shabby room with its wall of books and its bay window looking out on the Gulf pleased her. The sofa needed a new cover, but with Angie's needlepoint and patchwork pillows artfully arranged, its stains and worn spots weren't noticeable. She smiled to see the last pillow Angie had made, with Bunny, an eager little acolyte, needle in hand, beside her. Shades of gold and Chancellorsville gray filled the background. White golden-hearted Cherokee roses twined around the border, and in the center in Angie's own Spencerian script was a quote from General Robert E. Lee: *Duty the Sublimest Word.*

"Not a fun quote for a little girl, is it?" Sally had asked as she watched Angie diagram the letters for stitching.

"Needlepoint is not a 'fun quote' medium," Angie had said severely. "Bunny will spill blood on this, learning to use a nee-dle, and I want it to be something she will remember and be guided by all her life."

Now, looking at it, Sally wondered what duty meant to her granddaughter and if it would conceivably encompass loyalty too—loyalty to all those people who had loved her and Bunk, and who had done for them all they could.

Standing there, her back to the fire, she thought fleetingly of moving the cushion so Leslie wouldn't see it and be saddened. Then she knew that would be a futile gesture. The little house was a catch-all of memories. Everything in it had known some previous life, had been made or used by hands now gone. They never bought new furniture. They used what they salvaged from the old hotel. Even the pictures on the wall represented Grandpa Sellars' taste, not hers, although the primitive painting of a three-masted schooner over the mantel suited her fine. It was painted by a German sea captain who had stayed at the hotel one summer and had given Grandpa his choice of his summer's work.

"Just be glad Father didn't choose the moose and the waterfall," Angie used to say in the day when primitives were considered the clumsy work of unskilled artists and had not achieved status in the art world. "At least, the old captain had *seen* a schooner and seawater, but he'd never clapped eyes on a moose."

Sally had loved the picture since her childhood and had resisted the efforts of her daughters to retire it to a back room and hang something "better" there. What was better than the known, the faithful friend of a lifetime?

Sarah came through the kitchen door, the turkey held before her on the old ironstone platter with the delicate pride of one bearing crown jewels on a velvet cushion.

"Call 'em in, Mother," she said. "We're ready. Henry, pour the wine."

Henry's father, the senior male present, asked the blessing. A bit of old-fashioned chauvinism, Sally admitted to herself, her head bowed. But didn't the masculine voice lifted in prayer sound fine? He had offered a standard from the Episcopal prayer book. Angie, a Methodist, would have improvised, not settling for thanks for the food and "its use to our bodies and us to Thy Service." She would have ticked off the names of those present for special blessing and then mentioned the "absent ones."

Ah, the absent ones. Sally looked at Leslie, who sat between Hank and Say-Say, her face remote and sad until one of them spoke to her. Then she smiled and attended to their needs, cutting Say-Say's turkey for her, serving Hank more cranberry sauce. Hank had been especially dear to her all his life. His birth had helped to ease the aching emptiness caused by Dodie's death. He looked like a teddy bear when he was little, a huggable fellow with caramel-colored hair and eyes as shiny as glass buttons.

And he still looked like a teddy bear, except that his huggable chunkiness was lengthening out. At almost fourteen he was taller than his mother and his aunt, almost as tall as his grandmother. His hair and his eyebrows were still caramel-colored, his eyes glinted like amber glass, and he had acquired a talent which was his father's. Straight-faced and solemn, he could lift one eyebrow in a quirky arc of delicious amusement or appreciation, an accomplishment which delighted his aunt.

"Look at this idiot child," Leslie would cry. "He's laughing at me without laughing!"

Pleased himself, Hank would engage in a running battle of insults with her which often ended with their ducking one another in the water or wrestling on the floor. Today, Sally thought, looking at them, Hank seemed unnaturally polite, unnaturally careful with his aunt.

Say-Say was too young to be careful. In the silence that fell on the table when all the plates were served, she said loudly, "Aunt Les, I'm glad Bunk and Bunny *aren't* here. We'd have to eat at a *children's* table. I hate the children's table."

Sally and Sarah exchanged quick anguished looks, but Leslie laughed and gave the little girl a quick hug. "Me too, Say-Say. I like to eat with the grown-ups myself. But you can't spill at the big table, remember. And you have to be careful not to talk when other people are talking."

"You *are* grown up, Aunt Les," Say-Say said implacably.

Leslie looked at her mother, her eyes suddenly misty, her smile lopsided. "Almost," she said.

Good girl, Sally thought. She's trying, really trying not to put a pall on Christmas with a walking-wounded act. She's got guts; my child's got guts. She looked around the table, grateful for those who were there—a gratitude she recognized as illogically accentuated by the absence of the twins. They had not always been at Esperance at Christmas. There had been a few other Christmases when they were not able to come. But this time they had *wanted* to be elsewhere.

Her eyes rested on Sarah, gray-eyed instead of blue-eyed today, her face peach-pink from the heat of the oven. Tendrils of her light hair had escaped from her smooth ponytail and curled moistly around her face. Her gaze was watchful of her family. Henry's plate—did he get some of the sweet potato soufflé?—Hank's manners, Say-Say's appetite. The little girl played with her food, never eating more than a bite or two at mealtime and an hour later a wailing victim of harrowing, wrenching starvation.

Bless Sarah, Sally thought, Angie's own, created in her grandmother's image, caring for us all, ever-present in time of trouble.

Henry moved around the table pouring more wine. Sally lifted her face and smiled at him—chunky, capable Henry, his square freckled hands nicked and burned from handling the lines of his new boat today. He loved Sarah and their children but, more than that, Sally thought, he *cares* for them. He works and pays bills: insurance, braces for Hank's teeth, dancing class for Say-Say, and hospitals and doctors when they need them. Sarah had a secondhand station wagon but it ran. Sarah had a good winter coat. The children had shoes. Love, thought Sally, is cheap and easy, but care is beyond pearls.

She looked at Warren Parker, Henry's father, who sat opposite her at what would have been the head of the table, if it had been one table instead of a makeshift arrangement of two. Owner of his own small business, Kiwanis instead of Rotary, a warden in the old and stylish Episcopal church but so simple and good himself he was unaware that churches were fashionable or unfashionable. Taller than his only child, Henry, and rail-thin, Warren had a long, bony, humorous face, bright bird-dog eyes, and a big nose that had been broken when he played football at the university.

He was listening to something his wife, Ann, was saying, and Sally let her attention follow his. Ann Parker at fiftyish was an easy, uncomplicated woman, apparently well content with her life and with the people who dwelt within its boundaries. She loved Warren, Sally felt sure. A couple who, after thirty-odd years of marriage, could listen so attentively, so appreciatively to one another, must be in love.

Small, with a head full of tousled curls, which had been red and were now diluted by gray into an orangey pink, Ann looked on husband, son, daughter-in-law, and grandchildren with brown eyes which alternately twinkled with enjoyment and grew pansy-wide and velvety with tenderness. Now she was talking to Leslie about the twins' nicknames. She couldn't remember what Bunk and Bunny stood for.

"Harold and Hope. Hope, of course, for this place, Esperance," Leslie said, sipping her wine and ignoring her plate of turkey and dressing. "I would love to have called her Esperance, but Hal thought that was tacky and pretentious. He nicknamed Harold Bunk for Bunk Johnson, one of the original New Orleans jazzmen. He was a toothless old man working in a Louisiana rice field when they found him back in the 1930s and had a big Bunk Johnson revival. And Bunny—well, you know, another jazz musician, a trumpet player, Bunny Berigan."

"Oh, sure, I remember Bunny's 'I Can't Get Started with You.'" Ann Parker nodded enthusiastically. "Those are nicknames that mean something. I had one"—she giggled—"that didn't mean a thing. Sax."

"Sax!" exclaimed Leslie. "Didn't they change it to Sex on you?"

"That was the general idea," Ann said demurely. "I gave it to myself when I went off to boarding school, thinking it would make me more interesting. My roommates loved it, but I didn't notice that it made me more popular with the boys at the military academy across town. I think it embarrassed them."

"Sax," repeated Sally. "Does anybody call you that now?"

Ann shook her head vehemently. "I'd kill them. Saxon is my middle name and I use it on legal papers occasionally, but Sax fell by the wayside, thank heaven."

They all laughed and Leslie sipped her wine. There had been drinks before dinner, and Sally noticed that while she and Sarah asked for white wine and then forgot to drink it in their absorption in preparations for dinner, Leslie kept pace with Warren Parker, who was drinking bourbon and water.

Sally didn't want to be in the position of counting drinks on anybody, particularly Leslie, who was already split into halves, one part of her at the table being pleasant to the company, one part of her glued to the telephone in the kitchen. If anybody *needed* a drink, she thought—and yet there was the persistent, nagging worry that Leslie was not only drinking too much but that she might have *been* drinking too much. There was literally no reason anybody of any age was justified in turning against his parents, Sally thought. But if there should be a reason, alcoholism came close.

She couldn't visualize Leslie as a drunk—a bitter, abusive person who did hurtful things to others. But she occasionally found herself wondering if anger and resentment might be less tedious than self-flagellation, the tireless, soft-voiced analyzing and blame-receiving. Too much to drink makes bores out of the best of us, Sally told herself philosophically, rising to go to the kitchen for more hot rolls. But she found the feather-cushion softness Leslie had displayed recently more distasteful than anger. Not softness, she corrected herself, opening the oven, not mushiness, but a sort of sponginess, soaking up pain and blame and enveloping us all.

Her conscience smote her when dinner was over and Leslie insisted that she and Sarah leave the dishes to her and go on out to ride with all the Parkers in the new boat.

"We'll do them together and then we'll all be free," Sally said.

"I want to stay here anyway, Mama," Leslie said. "The children might try to call."

Free was the wrong word, Sally acknowledged to herself, picking up a sweater and a scarf. Who is free when they have children? As she walked through the living room her eyes fell on the only unopened packages under the tree, gifts they had all wrapped for Bunk and Bunny.

"Wherever they are," said Sarah, reading her mind, "I hope they got *something* for Christmas."

It was Henry who suggested that Leslie go back to Tallahassee with them and get a job. He had a friend whose secretary was taking a three-month maternity leave, and he would recommend Leslie as a replacement.

"Three months," Leslie said, her eyes brightening. "That's fine. I wouldn't want anything permanent until I get the twins and we can settle down. Do you suppose he would let me have time off if I have to go and see about them?"

"I'll ask him to," Henry said.

Leslie's eyes sought her mother's. "Mama, you think I should?"

"I think it's the best thing you can do," Sally said firmly. "A job will keep you busy and you'll have some money when you need it. But clothes—oh, honey, you'll need something to wear to work every day!"

"I'll share," put in Sarah. "I've got a coat that will fit her, and we can whip up some skirts."

"I suppose I should go back to 'Rent Free' and check over the stuff there," Leslie began uncertainly.

"You go ahead with Sarah and Henry," Sally said. "I'll go over to the cottage tomorrow, and if there's anything that looks possible I'll bring or mail it to Sarah's."

The sun was still shining when the Parkers finished loading their Christmas gifts and overnight bags into the new boat and boarded it for the mainland. Sally stood on the dock and waved them off. And then, because it was still light and she felt restless and the beginning of an unaccustomed loneliness, she decided to take a walk over to Angie's rental cottage and check it for any of Leslie's belongings that might be useful.

An old turpentine road led through the reaches of white sand curving through pine, cedar, and palmetto thickets to the bay side of the island. Sally took one of the wagon ruts and skirted a small pond where water flowed sweet and coffee-colored from tannin-seasoned springs beneath the cypress trees. A frog leaped from the bank into a stand of cattails, sending ripples lapping against the marsh grasses, now winter-brown. A little branch flowed from the pond to the bay, cutting across the road. Sally would have waded it in summer, but now because the December wind was freshening and she wore loafers instead of sneakers, she leaped from tuffet of marsh grass to hummocks of laurel to keep her feet dry and searched the bank of the little stream for remnants of watercress that she and Angie had planted there.

She always stopped and looked, although the cress had disappeared almost immediately after they set it out, either swept out to the salt water by summer rains or shriveled by the heat. Angie had predicted that the island climate was too warm for cress and the water probably brackish and they could continue to make do with the succulent, peppery beach greens that sprang up along the tide line in the spring. But every time she passed that way Sally looked for it nevertheless.

"Rent Free" stood as Leslie had left it only a few weeks ago, all the doors and two or three of the windows open. No matter, she thought, the cottage was an old Florida shack with deep cypress eaves beneath its salt-scarred and rusting tin roof, and after the torrential rains of the fall there was seldom a shower that penetrated beyond the windows.

Kicking the steps to knock the sand off her loafers, Sally entered the front door and stood a moment on the little screened porch. The air was so clear she thought she could see the new boat loaded with her children and grandchildren rounding the point headed for St. Dominique light. Automatically she lifted her hand to wave and then realized that they couldn't see her back of the screen, even if they happened to be looking that way. Feeling unaccountably alone, she turned to the living-room door.

The house was a shambles: beds unmade, sink full of dirty dishes, clothes and books and papers strewn everywhere. For an instant Sally thought thieves or vandals had been there, but she knew better. Leslie, never a meticulous housekeeper, had been in a hurry to get the twins off to New Orleans and had let everything slide. She had not returned to the cottage since Hal's catastrophic call.

Sally began picking up. An old sneaker of Bunk's under the fake maple sofa, a blouse of Bunny's on the mantel over the cold fireplace, half a glass of milk, now green-molded, on the coffee table. Some wind of the last two weeks had blown papers over the floor, and Sally leaned over to pick them up.

At the top of a blue-lined leaf from a school notebook, numbered Page 2 and written in Leslie's childish scrawl were the words *my lovers.*

Lovers? Leslie?

Caught between shock and amusement, Sally read the rest: *I don't want to deal but if I have to I will. I love you, miss you. Find a place for us SOON! Your Leslie.*

Deal? Deal what?

Sally scrabbled through the other pages looking for the letter's beginning. Not marijuana, surely. Not after what happened to them in Texas. Frantically she searched through the papers for the letter's beginning. It was not to be found. There were spelling papers belonging to the twins and one letter in Bunny's handwriting: *Dear Daddy we miss you. please come. Mama is mean to us. I think it is because you don't come. I'm saving up to buy a horse. Bunk's scab on his knee fell off. Love, your dauter Bunny.*

Sally sat down on the battered and threadbare old hassock,

more because her legs were suddenly too weak to bear her weight than because she wanted to sit. *Lovers? Deal? Mean to us?* What on earth was it all about?

It was pointless to try to make something out of these fragments of handwriting, Sally knew. She would not let herself read miserable meanings into a few random words taken out of context. But she was disturbed and suddenly so tired she felt heavy-limbed and inert. She sat on, looking wearily around the cottage. It was a shack, nothing more, but it had served beachcombers for thirty years, bringing in a few hundred dollars each summer until the one just past when Leslie and the children needed it. It needed fixing up badly, Sally thought with part of her mind, seeing the frayed straw rug, the dilapidated pseudo-maple "suite," the starfish and shell mobiles which every batch of renters—and non-renters like Leslie and the children—added to the decor. Now a dozen of them, swinging from the rafters, danced senselessly in the chill breeze from the open door.

They're hysterical, Sally thought, eyeing the spinning shells. And so am I.

She stood up. A little neatening and then she'd look for Leslie's clothes. She would tackle the kitchen first. Angie had always held that a sink full of dirty dishes advertised a sloven. Wash 'em or hide 'em, she said. If the sink and tabletops were clear, your slovenliness was your own secret.

She put on a kettle of water. (The electric water heater was off again.) Then she began scraping and stacking plates. A clutch of little slips of paper flapping on a nail over the sink drew her attention. She squinted and saw that they were from one of Miss Peachy's charge books, the little rough paper notebooks she kept in pigeonholes by the cash register to enter the purchases of her credit customers. Sally and Angie had charged groceries at Miss Peachy's from time to time, and apparently Leslie had too. The top paper had the sum of $102.58 encircled in red ink and a note obviously from Miss Peachy herself: *Leslie, please take care of this.*

Sally sighed and reached for the other slips. They were lists of things Leslie or, in some instances, the children had bought: Eggs, bacon, bread, milk, hamburger meat, tomatoes, spaghetti, steak once or twice. In every case one of them, either Leslie or one of the twins, had signed at the bottom of the page, attesting to the fact that they had indeed received the groceries. These were carbons. Miss Peachy had the originals.

Sally sighed and folded the little slips of paper together and tucked them in her sweater pocket. If Leslie had not paid—and she felt sure she hadn't—Sally would have to take care of Miss Peachy's bill immediately. She was an old lady, a long-time friend, whose little business, assailed by competition from the new Junior Food and IGA markets, was already shaky if not expiring. It wasn't fair to make her wait for her money.

The kettle hissed and Sally shook liquid soap into the sink and tackled the dishes. When they were done and the sink scrubbed, she washed out the dish towels and went to hang them on the line on the back porch. The little porch was screened for use as a dining room in the summer, but now it had caught the flotsam and jetsam of the Ellises' living—drink bottles stacked and others not stacked but loose on the floor everywhere, brown paper bags swollen and stained with garbage, dirty clothes, a grits pot soaking sourly, the table loaded with shells, some sorted and cleaned and stored in milk cartons, most of them spread out on the table beside a picture frame and a bottle of glue. The twins, Sally thought wistfully, had been making a shell frame for somebody for Christmas.

Sally looked at the mess of bottles and garbage and knew it would have to wait until she could bring the jeep over in the morning and collect it. The garbage she would bury or burn, the bottles return to Miss Peachy for credit on the bill, except . . . she looked again. They were mostly beer bottles, and Miss Peachy didn't sell beer.

Bunk's bed was an army cot on the porch, screened from the weather by a length of canvas and made winter-warm by an electric blanket. Sally decided to strip the bed and roll the mattress over the head rail to air. The bed was warm to the touch. In the twilight area on the floor beneath the spread Sally saw the steady, unwinking eye of the blanket control.

It had been on for two weeks!

She had thought electric blankets so neglected burned themselves out or set the house on fire. Leslie, in her carelessness, could be very educational. She unplugged the blanket, folded it and the spread, and gathered up the sheets and pillowcases and dumped them on the pile to be washed the next day.

Inside she entered Bunny's room first. The little girl had

left her iron bed under its flouncy white spread smooth and neat. Sally's hand caressed the eyelet flounces. Leslie had been so pleased when they had found the spread and matching curtains at a thrift store in Tallahassee. They were in perfect condition and priced cheap, and Leslie had fingered them covetously.

"Sissified—little-girlish. Just what Bunny loves," she had said. "I wonder if they would let me put them on the layaway."

Putting secondhand thrift-store finds on the layaway struck Sally as so pitifully poverty-stricken she winced and made up the $3 Leslie needed for the purchase price. They had hauled the spread and curtains home and washed and starched them afresh. Bunny had been pleased with them and had been meticulous about keeping her room in order.

Sally's eyes traveled over the scaling, white-painted dresser, veteran of many years of renters' use and renters' abuse but neat under the embroidered scarf that Bunny had made under Angie's direction. A sheaf of hair ribbons hung from one corner of the mirror, a little jewelry box containing what Bunny had once regarded as precious jewels was set precisely stage center. Sally lifted the lid and saw Bunny's Brownie pin, a tangle of dime-store beads and pins, and, wrapped in a bit of tissue with a card still attached, a slender gold bracelet Leslie had bought her only weeks ago. Bunny had been trying out for a play at Lucina school and Leslie was almost certain she wouldn't make it.

"She'll be so disappointed if she's not chosen," she had said to Sally. "I'm going to buy her a little surprise to cheer her up in case she misses."

The consolation bracelet was doubly dear to Bunny because she *did* get the part and she didn't need it. But she had left it behind.

Sally closed the lid.

A blue bottle, salt- and sand-pocked, held a sea fan and a stalk of sea oats. And the scruffy lamp table by the bed held *Little Women*, Sally's own copy, which she had brought out and read aloud to the twins through the many summer evenings when they were with her and Angie. Bunk had loved the book as much as Bunny had and played at being Laurie to Bunny's Jo when they dressed her dolls and re-enacted the old story. They were younger then, and Bunk didn't mind playing girls' games. Now . . . oh, *now,* she thought, what do I know about them now?

She picked up the book and opened it to the flyleaf.

Sarah Marlowe. Happy birthday 1929. Love, Ma. And, beneath it: *Happy* un*birthday to Hope Ellis, my blessed Bunny. Love, Gran.* She closed the book and put it back. It would be there when Bunny returned.

Leslie's bedroom, the bigger of the two, had twin beds pushed together with a foam-rubber splicer unit in them. Both were unmade, and a tangle of clothes was snarled with the covers. Methodically, Sally began sorting and folding: a gingham shirt she thought Leslie might use, bras and underpants she would take to the launderette, a faded and dingy nightgown with its lace yoke ripped, jeans, and one sock.

Sally pulled back the covers, searching idly, without hope, for the second sock. You never could find the second sock, she knew from experience. But she looked. At the bottom of the bed where the tucked sheets held it was a pair of men's jockey shorts. Hal's, Sally thought, aghast. Left there last fall. It was preposterous for even a housekeeper like Leslie. As sloppy as she was, she loved to wash clothes. Sometimes Sally told her she ruined clothes by washing them too much.

Gingerly, she held the shorts up by one finger. Size 38. Too big for Hal, a skinny 30. Lover?

Oh, God, Sally cried soundlessly and burst into tears.

Dark was settling in when Sally finally closed the windows, pulled the doors to, and left the cottage. She stood a moment on the front porch, looking over the Sound and listening to the waves lapping on the beach. Wind-twisted and sand-stunted little oak trees grew on the dunes between the porch and the beach, framing the view like bonsai trees. Only she had never seen a water tank in a Japanese painting, Sally thought wryly, and Lucina's new shiny silver water tank, lights winking on its summit, dominated the horizon across the Sound when all else was blurred by gathering darkness. Tomorrow she would go there and begin tidying up other disorders in Leslie's life. Leslie's? Hers. For whatever was wrong with her children, Sally recognized bleakly, scrubbing at the tear-scalded skin of her face with her hand, was wrong with her.

She walked down the steps. Eavesdroppers never hear anything good about themselves, she thought, and snoopy mothers poking around the wreckage of their children's marriages never find happiness. She wished she had left the cottage to its squalor. The clothes she found that Leslie might wear to her new job were so few they hardly warranted postage to mail them. Poor child, she thought. If there was anything left in her bank account after she paid Miss Peachy, she would buy a few new things to send Leslie.

Leslie got the job with Henry's friend and worked so hard she had no time to come to Esperance for weekends.

"Mother, it's wonderful for her," Sarah reported over the phone. "She has starved down to a size eight, looks bone-beautiful, and is talking about getting an apartment with a girl from her office. We hate for her to spend the money, but she says Henry and I don't need in-laws in the house, and I guess it's true. She shares Say-Say's room and that can't be too easy on her. Say-Say still wets the bed some, and she always abandons the wet one and climbs into the dry one with Aunt Les when that happens."

Sally laughed. "I'm sure Leslie loves it. What about the twins? Has she heard anything?"

"Nothing," said Sarah. "I think she writes to them every day. A friend of Hank's, a kid who works in the office after school, told us the last thing he does every day is to mail a letter Leslie has written to her children."

"Where does she send it?" Sally asked.

"In care of those Ellises, of course, plainly marked *Please forward*. You remember how Hal used to say his mother believed she had a right to read any mail that came into her house, no matter to whom it was addressed? Les thinks they read, she just doesn't know if they forward."

"Sarah," Sally began hesitantly, "do you think Leslie was ever . . . unfaithful to Hal?"

Sarah laughed. "Mother, do you have any idea how quaint you sound?"

"Yes," Sally admitted humbly. "But it might explain why Hal decided to leave her and take the children."

"Aw, Mother!" Sarah scoffed. "Do you think Hal wasn't 'unfaithful,' as you put it?"

Sally found herself wincing but she persisted. "How about Leslie?"

Sarah sighed. "I don't know. She may have dabbled a little just to show him, make him jealous or something. But I believe she loved Hal—still loves him—too much to do anything serious."

Sally thought of the size 38 shorts between the sheets of Leslie's bed, the letter with the words "my lovers." It seemed serious to her, very serious. She felt reluctant to mention it even to Sarah, but if it was the reason Bunk and Bunny wanted to stay with their father she had to know. She took the plunge.

"Poor Mama," Sarah said when she heard the account. "You've been taking it hard, haven't you?"

"Stop poor-mothering me, Sarah," Sally said sharply, "and tell me what is going on."

"Well, all I know is that some musician friend of Hal's— bass player, guitar player, somebody—showed up on his way somewhere and needed a place to spend the night. Leslie had your boat and she took him to the cottage. She said she gave him her room and slept with Bunny. The reason she told me about it was that she and the fellow had a few drinks and he got a little amorous, and she was worried that the twins might have seen him kissing her."

"He kissed her?" Sally hated herself for sounding offended.

"That's all, Les says—and I believe her. A little tacky alcoholic kitchen smooching. Nothing more."

Sally sighed, surprised that it was not a sigh of relief but one of distress. A little tacky alcoholic kitchen smooching was nothing, of course, but if the twins saw it and were frightened or hurt by it . . .

"When did it happen?" she asked.

"Oh, a few days before the twins went to New Orleans. I'm not sure. Don't worry about it. If Hal wants to use something like that for a divorce, Les has plenty to counter with, I'm sure."

"I was thinking about the children, not court," Sally said slowly. "But I'll let you go now. Your phone bill must be a sight."

"Gon' make Henry get me a WATS line," Sarah said cheerfully, and they hung up.

A few days later Leslie called from the office.

"Mama," she said shakily, "a man just served me with a divorce paper!"

"Oh, honey," Sally said helplessly. "What does it say—what does he want?"

Leslie read: a standard no-fault petition, but it asked custody of the children.

"He flew into town and went to some old lawyer who is a friend of his family's," Leslie said. "Do I have to get a lawyer?"

"What do you want? Do you want to give him a divorce and the children?"

Leslie was quiet for a moment, and Sally heard the quivering intake of breath, the catch of a stifled sob. "Mama, he can have a divorce if he wants it: I hate him, I hate him, I hate him!" She was weeping audibly now.

"Oh, baby," Sally murmured, waiting. "Don't cry. It'll work out. What about the children?"

"I can't give Bunk and Bunny away!" Leslie's voice was strong now in outrage and anger. "He's crazy if he thinks he's going to get custody of my children!"

"All right," said Sally. "Dry your eyes and get back to work. I'm coming to Tallahassee and we'll see a lawyer."

Elbert White, who handled land transactions and wrote their wills for them, did not take divorce cases, he told Sally, but there was a young woman in his office who was an able domestic-relations attorney.

He called her in, a tall tanned girl with a curly crop of prematurely gray hair and matching gray eyes framed by black eyebrows and thick black eyelashes. She was stunning, Sally thought, approving her tailored gray skirt and a heavy silk blouse which exactly matched it. It had long sleeves, and she wore a silver chain around her neck.

Her name was Lee Lambert, and she smiled at them reassuringly as she led them to her smaller office down the hall. Leslie handed her the paper that had been served on her by a deputy sheriff, but before she read it she poured coffee for them and pushed a box of Kleenex closer to Leslie, whose hand on the coffee cup shook and whose eyes were brimming with unshed tears.

"You don't want this divorce, do you?" Miss Lambert said, looking up from the petition.

Leslie looked at her mother. "I never thought I'd have a

divorce," she faltered. "I wouldn't have got one. But if Hal wants it . . . I think there is somebody he likes better than me. . . ." She gulped and ducked her head. "The children always made us promise we'd never be divorced like the parents of some of their friends. I would have kept the promise. Now . . ."

She was silent.

Miss Lambert waited.

"It's the children," Sally said. "She wants the children."

"Complete custody or joint custody?" the lawyer asked Leslie.

"Oh, I wouldn't ever keep Hal from seeing them!" Leslie said. "But I won't give them up either. Could you arrange it so I have them and let him visit or something?" Her tone was piteous, and Sally reached out and put her hand on the girl's arm.

"We'll try," Miss Lambert said, reaching for the phone. "Get me Mr. Anton Lofton," she said to a secretary. "He's a retired attorney, I think, maybe works from his home."

She refilled the coffee cups from a carafe on the window ledge behind her and the phone rang.

"Hello, Mr. Lofton!" she said cordially. "Lee Lambert of White, Cook and Erickson here. . . . Oh, you've heard of us!" She laughed. "Well, thank you. I haven't been with the firm long but I'm impressed too."

Sally winked at Leslie, and the girl managed a smile. Lawyers playing scratch-back, she thought, while the customer waits and hurts.

But Lee Lambert was brief and brisk. "I represent Mrs. Ellis—Leslie McMillan Ellis," she added, glancing at the paper before her. "She has been served with your client Harold Ellis's petition. Yes, well, we are amenable to a no-fault divorce, but . . ."

We, thought Sally sourly. What does this chic, thriving, on-top-of-it girl have to do with the death and destruction of a marriage? She doesn't hurt, but my child is falling apart. She looks like a petcock has been opened in her somewhere and all the blood drained out.

". . . children," Miss Lambert was saying. "Yes, naturally we'll have to oppose you on that. Mrs. Ellis will want custody— with suitable visitation rights for Mr. Ellis, of course."

She listened and smiled and made a little face at Sally and Leslie.

"I certainly understand your position," she cooed, nodding vigorously. "Oh, good talking to you, too."

She hung up, grinning.

"I don't think Mr. Lofton meant to get into a fight. He says he filed that petition out of friendship for your husband's father. He thought it would be unopposed. He's going to call them, and if they want to contend further he'll suggest another lawyer."

Leslie looked dazed. "Is that good?"

"It could be," said Lee Lambert. "Maybe they won't want to proceed."

Back at Sarah's they sat by the living-roon fire, drank more coffee, and tried to assess the situation.

"What do you think, Les?" Sarah asked. "Will Hal really fight you?"

"I don't think it's Hal," Leslie said, brooding. "I think his parents are doing it for him."

"Of course they are!" Sarah said with dawning understanding. "*They* got the lawyer, their old friend."

"Well, I got the lawyer for Leslie," Sally put in. "Same thing."

"No, it isn't, Mama," Leslie said. "You didn't instigate the divorce. You're just helping me defend it so I won't lose Bunk and Bunny. Mr. Ellis—and maybe Mrs. Ellis too, although I don't think so—would be pleased to have Hal divorce me."

"Oh, honey, why would they? What do they care? You've always been nicer to them than Hal has, haven't you?"

Leslie nodded. "I really like them. At least her. She's kind of funny and nice sometimes, and bright, I think. But I know he hates me."

"Let's not be paranoid, Les," Sarah said equably. "They're different from us, we all know that. But you haven't any reason to believe you're on their hate list."

"Okay," said Leslie, "I'll tell you what happened. Do you know when we were in jail in Texas, Mama? We asked the Ellises for help the same time we called you. I made Hal call them. I knew they could afford it easier than you could, but Hal didn't want to ask them. For a good reason, too. Mr. Ellis told him he would pay *his* bond and *his* fine but not mine.

He would pay the lawyer for him but not for me, and on condition that Hal left me."

"But they did send some money?" Sally said.

"Two hundred dollars—a loan. *After* Hal told them to go to hell, he wouldn't leave me, and that you had sold your car and were sending us four thousand dollars!"

Sally stood up. "I got to go."

"I'm sorry, Mama," Leslie said. "I'm running you off by talking about that old trouble. I'm always upsetting you."

"That's right," Sally said, grinning weakly. "You always are. No, I got to get across the Sound before dark."

But after the girls had walked her to the door and waved her to her car, Sally sat a moment behind the steering wheel, immobilized by shock. Was it true? Could Leslie be telling the truth? Could any parent, *anybody*, anywhere in the world bribe a son or daughter to break up a marriage? It was too melodramatic, too corny, like the classic line from all the plays about rich boys marrying chorus girls. She said it aloud, mimicking Lilyan Tashman or Kay Francis or Joan Blondell, the Ziegfeld girls of the 30s: "I don't want your money, sir, I love your son." Could even the anti-Communist Ellises have offered to get Hal out of jail if he would leave Leslie there to rot?

Sally leaned forward and turned the key to start the car. Somehow, she believed they would.

1966–1968

Sally could never bear to think of Texas. She always came back to the horror of the marijuana in the crayon box. She always remembered that she had sent Bunk and Bunny into the mess. They hadn't especially wanted to go. They would have been content at Esperance, but she had thought they should spend Christmas with their parents. My fault, she had mourned for years. If they locked people up for sloppy sentimentality as they did for possession of marijuana, she would be serving a life sentence.

Leslie and Hal and the twins had come home from New

111

York two years earlier with the wonderful idea of returning to school. Hal was tired of playing in seedy night spots, Leslie said. He hated wearing a cowboy hat and ringing cowbells almost as much as he hated the yeah-yeah-yeah yapping that went with rock and roll.

"Oh, that boy's coming of age," Angie said approvingly. "He's a musician, not a clown. I'm so glad he's serious about it. Where are you all going?"

There was a college in north Texas famous for its music. Hal could get government money under the GI bill.

"He *can*?" Sally and Angie had asked together.

"With that early discharge, they'll still pay for his education?" Sally went on.

Leslie nodded. "His father looked into it for him, and he's applied. I think he's getting it. I'm going to find a job and maybe take some courses at the college. There's a fine Montessori school there, and if it isn't too expensive we'll send Bunk and Bunny."

"Let me know how expensive it is," Sally said. "Maybe I can do it."

Hal and Leslie had gone ahead to find a place to live, and Leslie had come back to get the children and their things. They had rented a big old house in a close-to-town neighborhood, shabby but cheap, Leslie explained happily.

"Furniture. You'll need furniture," Angie said.

"We always do," Leslie agreed, grinning. "We had pretty good stuff in New York, which we sold or gave away when we decided to come home. Now we start over again."

Angie hummed "River Stay 'Way from My Door." " 'Leave my bed and my fire, they all I own,' " she sang. "That's all you need for a start. Beds and a stove. Let's assemble some stuff, Sally, and rent a trailer."

It had been a memorable trip, pulling a trailer loaded with mattresses and springs, a table and chairs, and an old gas stove from Florida to Texas. Sally's little Volkswagen labored under the load, struggling up hills and caroming down hills. Leslie drove much of the way, singing happily or playing Count-the-Cows with the twins. Traffic piled up behind them, and when a driver, seeing an opportunity to pass, gnashed his teeth and swerved around them, Leslie would call after him reprovingly, "Speed demon! Road hog!"

Angie had packed them a picnic, and they stopped to eat at a roadside table beside a golden, slow-moving stream. The twins, barefoot and in their underpants, waded in the water, and Sally and Leslie shed their sandals and joined them.

The second day, as the sun was setting, Leslie, her eyes checking the loaded trailer in the rearview mirror, said thoughtfully, "I hope Hal remembered to get the gas and lights turned on. Water is furnished."

Hal either had not remembered or had not had the money for deposits. They pulled up to the old house under ancient shade trees, and he came down the steps to meet them.

"You're late," he said. "I've been worried."

"Us too," Leslie said, smiling, as she stepped out of the car and stretched her arms and legs and leaned forward to kiss him. "There were times when we thought we might not make it. Mama needs a truck instead of a Volkswagen, if we're going to keep giving her our moving business."

The house wasn't totally dark. A street light on the corner sent enough light through the branches of the big oak trees to define the walls and doors of the rooms. Leslie took her on a tour before they started unloading. Sally remembered her flashlight in the glove compartment, and the three of them dragged in mattresses and springs and set up beds before awakening the twins, who sprawled together like sleeping puppies on the back seat.

"I've got sheets, lots of sheets," Leslie said happily. "Angie made us a dozen, honey. Unbleached sheeting, bought by the bolt, hemmed and hand-bleached in Esperance sun by my granny. We're going to sleep as pretty as in a motel tonight."

Sally peered through the dusty windows of the room she was going to share with the twins and saw lights in the house next door.

"Let's use some of your granny's sheets for curtains," she suggested.

"Far out," Leslie approved. "Hal, help us."

Together they draped the sheets over curtain rods some previous tenant had left behind, shutting out not only the eyes of the neighbors but the vagrant brightness which had made it possible to get around the rooms as well. Bunk stirred on the other twin bed, where he and Bunny had been put, feet to feet.

"Mommy, I'm hungry," he said.

"Honey, did you . . . ?" Leslie turned to Hal, her tone apologetic.

"How could I?" Hal said irritably. "I didn't know when you were getting here. No stove, no refrigerator. What do you want me to do, build a bonfire and cook supper in the yard? I ate a hamburger at school."

Sally had started to undress, but she pulled her blouse back on and stepped into her shoes.

"We had stuff left from our picnic," she said. "Let's get the basket."

Hal went for it, and they sat on the beds and dined by flashlight on crackers and cheese, apples, and lemonade from the thermos jug. The twins went back to sleep, but Sally lay awake a long time, her eyes now adjusted to the darkness, looking at the old-fashioned flowered wallpaper, the dark woodwork, the yellow-tiled fireplace set in the corner of the room.

"Bless this house," she prayed silently. "Bless my children. Let it be a good place for them."

From Leslie's letters, Denton, Texas, had been a halcyon place—joyful and carefree and accomplishing. "She always writes this way," Sally said to Angie, trying to make a realistic evaluation of Leslie's latest report of how Hal and the children were thriving in their respective schools and how much she loved her job as assistant to a social worker in the Head Start program.

"Yes, but this time she sent a clipping," Angie said triumphantly, passing over a newspaper tearsheet containing a story about the town's symphony orchestra and, specifically, its newest trombone player. There was a small inset photograph of Hal, smiling, trombone lifted, ready to play.

"My, he photographs like a movie star," Sally said.

"He's a good-looking boy," Angie agreed smugly. "I'm surprised Hollywood hasn't discovered him. They did the Benny Goodman story and the Glenn Miller story and 'Young Man with a Horn,' with Kirk Douglas playing Bix Beiderbecke. They'll get around to Jack Teagarden yet, and Hal should play him."

"But he's gone serious now," Sally said, reading the story. "First trombone in the Denton symphony."

"In the Goodman tradition," Angie pointed out. "Good jazz musician, good classical musician. Both are *serious*, Sally."

114

Sally grinned at the rebuke and wasn't surprised a few days later when Angie announced she was going to visit Leslie and Hal and the children. Leslie had said in one of her letters that she was eager to learn to "cook cheap but good," and her grandmother was the world's authority on the subject.

Angie made lists and shopped for presents for them all and took along bedroom slippers and a jacket to cover herself for overnight sleeping on the Greyhound bus when the air conditioning chilled her bones and her feet and ankles swelled.

Sally gave her $50 to spend and was pleased when they sent her a postcard signed by all of them, saying, *Turnip greens, sweet-potato pone tonight. Oxtail soup tomorrow. Thinking of you.*

Angie had gone to a symphony concert to hear Hal, and then they had taken her to a roadside dive where he also played one night a week.

"He has to," Angie told Sally. "Work with the symphony is more prestige than money. Good exposure but no good for groceries. They pay him well at those juke joints. I wish the boy could give them up and concentrate on his studies, but they have to eat. Leslie's pay is small, their expenses high."

Angie had gone to Sears and charged a washing machine for them, and she had shopped carefully for groceries with Leslie, bearing down on the advantages of vegetables ("cheap and nourishing") and dried beans and peas ("cheap and filling"). Hot biscuits and cornbread made a feast out of plain fare, she told her granddaughter, showing her how to run her fingers through home-ground meal to determine its quality, standing beside her and teaching her how to dip biscuits in melted butter to give their feather-light interior a crisp and golden crust.

"One night," Angie was to confess to Sally with an embarrassed, slightly defiant laugh, "we got drunk."

"*You* got drunk?" Sally said.

Her mother nodded. "Hal said we should have some wine with all those good meals I was engineering, and I agreed with him. I'd buy, I said, and we went out and bought a gallon of the best red wine. Then I looked in my purse, and I didn't have enough money left for groceries. They didn't have a dime to their names. So we fed the twins milk and cereal, and the three of us drank the wine."

"You enjoy it?" Sally asked.

"I had the time of my life," Angie said, bobbing her gray head. "After the children were in bed we sat on that nice old porch in some chairs somebody gave Leslie, and we talked and laughed and drank until after midnight."

"Hal too?"

"Especially Hal," Angie said. "He's good company if you give him a chance. Funny and, of course, full of music. We started some songs; he knows everything I ever heard of, including some from my childhood a hundred years ago."

Angie didn't mention it and Sally didn't find out until after her death that Angie had given Hal her father's gold watch that night. It wasn't the kind of thing Angie would report, although she talked often about her trip to Denton and her time with the young Ellises. Sometimes Sally knew she thought about them, especially at mealtime, hating to enjoy food herself when she knew they might be hungry.

"You know," she remarked once, apparently apropos of nothing, "you can't thin the grits with butter and milk if you don't have the butter and can't spare the milk."

Sally had smiled understandingly and said quietly, "No, Ma, you can't. And it's not the same if you stir in water, is it?"

Because they were already in Texas, Houston was perhaps the natural next step, but Sally and Angie were unprepared for it when Leslie called Sarah one day and said they were moving. Hal had quit school and gone on to Houston, and Leslie wanted to send the twins home to stay until they were settled. Sarah wired tickets and was at the airport with Hank to meet them.

Sally and her mother were overjoyed to see the children when Sarah arrived at the island with them but full of questions. Why had Hal left school short of graduation? What was he going to do in Houston? What about their house and belongings in Denton?

Sarah gave them a wait-a-minute look and went on stuffing the three children into slickers and boots for a trip outside. The day was rainy and cold, but they had a secret tunnel they wanted to build. Bunk had learned about secret tunnels in Texas, and Hank, impressed, wanted to start one immediately in the front yard at Esperance.

"Hank thinks Bunk knows everything because he has been to Texas and *says* he knows a cowboy," Sarah said fondly. "Even if he is six months older, Hank defers to the twins in everything. Bunny told him being a twin is magic, and he believes that too."

Leslie, Sally thought. Leslie has always seen a lot of magic floating around. Aloud she said, "Now tell us what is going on."

"We-ell," said Sarah, "you know Les doesn't tell me everything. Make that anything. But she was upset enough this time—and needed help bad enough, I guess—to tell me that Hal flew the coop again. He's been unhappy at school, failing some subjects. Not musical ones," she said quickly to her grandmother, "but history and English, I guess. Anyhow, one of his depressions has been on him, and Les came home one day to find a note. He'd gone to Houston with somebody, some musician friend, probably. He didn't say that he had a job, but he didn't say he didn't. Might be he's gone to 'find' himself again. He promised to call her but, as luck would have it, the day he departed the telephone did too. Disconnected. So she was going to look for him."

"Has she given up their house?" Angie asked.

"She's about to *have* to," Sarah said. "The rent is past due, and the landlord is threatening. I would have sent her some money, but the airplane tickets for the twins depleted my allowance for months and I hated to ask Henry for more. I suppose I will, though."

"No," said Sally. "I'll give you some to wire her when you get back to Tallahassee."

She stood up to poke the fire and put another piece of wood on it and saw that the rain had stopped and the sun was weakly trying for a comeback. The children had hit a snag in their tunnel. The soft sand caved in around every hole they dug.

"It needs to be wet," they heard Bunk say.

The three stood with the slickers sliding off their shoulders, inspecting the sky critically.

"I'll make it rain some more," Bunk said.

"Aw, you can't make it rain," Hank said.

"Sure I can," said Bunk.

"Sure he can," said Bunny. "I can too, a little bit."

"That Bunny," said Sarah, shaking her head. "She builds Bunk up all the time. You'd think twins would at least be equal, but Bunny puts Bunk ahead of herself in everything."

117

"I've noticed that," Angie said. "Maybe we've talked too much about how we nearly lost him when they were born."

"Well, I don't think the quantity of rain is going to be a measure of his superiority, little or lot," said Sally, smiling at the three golden-slickered children. They looked like lemon lollipops, she thought, sugar-coated with sand. "Bun might as well make the big unlimited claim for herself, for all the rain Bunkum is producing."

But Bunk was glowering at the sky commandingly. "Rain!" he cried. "Rain!" He swept his arm in a vast circle to include sky and earth and sea. *"Rain!"*

Hank and Bunny watched respectfully.

Island weather is ever capricious, and within seconds the thin sunlight evaporated and a slow, drizzly rain began to fall. The twins nodded to one another complacently and resumed their digging. Hank rushed into the house, breathing hard, unable to speak for a moment in his excitement.

"Gran." He finally settled on Sally as the one who might have the information. "How long has Bunk been able to make it rain?"

"Why, Hanky-Panky," said Sally, reaching down to hug the little boy. "I didn't even know Bunk had that gift."

"He has," said Hank solemnly, wriggling out of her embrace. "I'm gon' find out how he does it." And he was gone again.

The twins elected to stay on the island because Hank was going to a kindergarten in Tallahassee and would not be around to play with them much of the day if they went home with Sarah.

"We want to be with you, Gran," Bunk whispered to Sally when he heard the grown-ups discussing it after lunch. He stood by her chair and leaned his head against her shoulder.

Bunny, seeing him, took possession of her other side.

"Can we stay with you?" she asked. "Of course you can," Sally said huskily, hugging them together. "I wouldn't have it any other way. Angie's got a lot of work around here, and she needs some strong children to help her."

"We very strong," Bunny assured her gravely. And then, characteristically, "Bunk's the strongest boy in the world."

"I am pretty strong," Bunk said casually.

Angie delighted in their presence. Winter gales churned up

the Gulf and caused it to deposit a dark rich border of sea kelp along the beach like a black ruching. Kelp was the staff of life to Angie's garden. She could not have beans and tomatoes, corn and potatoes and the tender salad greens if she did not nourish the soil with fish heads and entrails and shrimp and crab shells and mulch it with kelp, which she piled up and composted all winter. The house sheltered the garden from the strong Gulf winds, and a fence strung with Spanish moss protected it from the depredations of deer, wild hogs, raccoons, and rabbits.

Angie's system was to rake the kelp into piles and wait until Sally was there to pull a trailer along the tide line with the jeep and collect it. Sometimes days went by before Sally had time to perform this chore, and a new storm would wash the kelp back out to sea before she got there.

"I got a idea, Gran," Bunk said at supper one night. "If we could make or buy a wagon, me and Bunny could bring that kelp straight up here."

"Bless your hearts," Sally said, looking at their scrubbed little faces, earnestly intent on her answer. "We'll go shopping for a wagon tomorrow. You and Angie will have to help pick it out."

Shopping for a wagon at the hardware stores up and down the coast was the subject of amiable squabbling between the children and Angie. They wanted the biggest wagon available. She held out for a wooden one to defeat rust. Big wooden wagons seemed in short supply. Finally they found one with a wooden body and a big plastic insert which would triple its hauling capacity. Triumphantly the twins pulled it down the dock and Sally fitted it in the stern of the boat. Thereafter, on fair days and windy cold ones, Bunk and Bunny, often accompanied by Angie, combed the beaches and wore sandy ruts up the hill, hauling kelp, seashells, driftwood, and other treasures home.

Except for snakes, which were sluggish and not much in evidence in the winter months, the women didn't feel that there was anything on the island to hurt the children and allowed them to roam freely. They had known since infancy the rule against going in the water without an adult present and had never been known to question or break it.

One morning, in a hurry to leave for the mainland to meet

a prospective real-estate customer, Sally forgot to tell the children that Angie was going with her and so, of course, must they. She had dressed and accompanied Angie to the dock to board the boat before looking around for Bunk and Bunny.

"Do you reckon they're kelping?" she asked her mother.

"No, the wagon's in the yard," Angie said. She climbed off the boat and stood on the dock, shading her eyes with her hand and examining the point.

"Don't worry," said Sally. "I'll find them. Get aboard and get comfortable. They can't be far." But for twenty minutes she trudged up the hill and along the woods paths nearest the house, calling their names. Finally, beginning to worry, she went back and got the jeep.

A day or so before, Bunk had talked of fishing, and she had promised him that if the surf did not calm down she would take him to one of the two freshwater ponds near the center of the island to try his luck for bream and catfish. Cursing herself for being fast to offer them an outing and slow to deliver, Sally stomped down on the accelerator and ground the four-wheel-drive through the sand to first one pond and then the other. There was no sign of the blue jackets and red knit caps around the ponds, no small Ked tracks in the sandy road leading to them.

Sally turned back and went to the dock for her mother. "How about staying at the house so somebody will be there if they come," she said. "They might be frightened if they think they're alone. I'm going to drive around the island."

She had gone less than a mile when she saw two small figures, red-capped, blue-jacketed, on top of a sand dune. Blowing the rusty, squawky horn, she raced the jeep toward them. They slid down the side of the dune and came toward her, hand in hand. Bunny was crying.

"Oh, baby, what's the matter?" cried Sally, getting out of the jeep and kneeling in the sand and taking Bunny in her arms.

"She was scared," Bunk explained. "We went to the graveyard to see our sister's grave, and then we decided to take a shortcut. I got kind of turned around."

"And Bunny was afraid," crooned Sally, wiping the little girl's tears away and kissing her on the forehead.

"I don't know why she was scared," Bunk said. "I *told* her I'd take care of her."

Sally put out a hand and drew him close too. A little boy but already taking responsibility.

"You did just right," she said. "You climbed the highest dune you could find so you could see and be seen when I came looking for you. You're a good boy."

Christmas was coming, and the children warmed Angie's heart with their pleasure in carols. They both had true sweet voices and they loved to sing, knowing the words to almost every song in Angie's piano repertoire.

Every night after supper they all moved to the piano in the living room, and while Angie played they sang "Come Let Us Adore Him," "Hark the Herald Angels Sing," and "Silent Night." One of Angie's favorites, the spiritual "Go Tell It on the Mountain," was also theirs, and they sang it with fervor.

One night Bunk said, "Angie, do you know 'Once in Royal David's City'?"

"Now that's a tough one," said Angie, leafing through her hymnal. "We don't sing it at the Methodist church. Where on earth did you learn it, at school?"

"Our father taught us all our songs," Bunny said proudly. "He's very musical."

"I know he is!" Angie said warmly. "And there's nothing better to share with his children than music. Now let's see. How does this go?"

" 'Once in royal David's city,' " they sang together, " 'stood a lowly castle shed.' "

Angie picked up the melody, and they carried it along together. Sally, watching them from her chair by the fireplace, reread a letter that had come that day from Leslie. She was in Houston with Hal. He had a job with a group playing in a club, but he had not been paid yet so they had no place to live. They were sleeping on the sofa in another band member's apartment. They would love to come for Christmas, but unless something broke for them they wouldn't be able to afford the fare.

Sally looked at the little Scotch-pine Christmas tree she and the twins had hauled home from the woods and set up in the bay window. Bunk had tried to hammer a stand together for it, but even after Angie took a hand it had a distinct list to starboard. She had brought out all their old ornaments, many of them homemade, and they had worked along together, attaching them to the stubby green branches. When it was done Sally and Angie exchanged looks.

"The usual," Angie said in a low voice so the children wouldn't hear her. "The family's usual tacky Christmas tree. A sentimental catastrophe."

Sally nodded. "I love it."

But Bunny stood at a distance looking at it critically. "It needs *something*," she said in a grown-up voice. "This girl I knew in Denton, she had bubbling Christmas lights on her tree."

"Bubbling?" Angie and Sally said together.

Bunny bobbed her head enthusiastically. "That's what they did. Bubbled in all colors. Could we get some like that, Gran?"

Sally looked at her mother, who looked back threateningly. She thinks I'm going to say bubbling lights are tacky and she'll kill me, Sally thought, amused.

"We'll look in the stores tomorrow, baby," she said.

Before they went shopping the next day, Leslie called Sally collect at her office. "I just wanted to hear your voice," she said wistfully. "I don't suppose the twins are there?"

"They sure are," Sally said. "Here, talk to them."

"Mom!" the twins cried together, putting an ear each to the receiver. "When are you coming? How's Daddy?"

While they talked, Sally picked up a pencil and figured Houston to Tallahassee air fare for two. She had sold an old summer house on the mainland, and she planned to send Leslie and Hal plane tickets home for Christmas. It came to over $400. And if they took the twins back with them it would be more. She stared wanly at her worn pocketbook hanging on its hook by her coat. Flabby old thing, she thought. Good leather in its day, but eight years old and showing every minute of it. It had never held cash that she could spend for something nonessential and needful only to herself. Now she was going to subsidize an airline and, for good measure, squander the rest of the money she had on a new car for herself and Angie.

"Let me speak to your mother," she said, taking the phone from the twins, who were now having a fit of the sillies and babbling nonsense.

"Mama, they sound so beautiful," Leslie said, tears in her voice.

"I've been thinking," Sally said. "Would you rather I sent the twins to you for Christmas and gave you the $400 extra I was going to spend on yours and Hal's tickets here to rent an apartment?"

"Oh, Mama, can you? Oh-h, that would be so wonderful! But all that money—" Leslie was crying happily now.

"It's only money," said Sally giddily. "You can take care of me in my old age."

She crossed her eyes and poked out her tongue at the twins, who whooped and fell on the office couch in a convulsion of amusement.

"I hear them," Leslie said. "Hug 'em for me and tell them they're coming soon. I'm going to call Hal."

Sally loaded Angie and the twins in the car and drove to the city to draw the money out of her savings account, so fluid it often evaporated, and send it before the impact of her spendthrift folly could hit her. Children and their parents should be together at Christmas. Leslie and Hal had to have a place to stay.

Later she marveled at the impulse she had followed so blithely. The children were not enthusiastic about leaving Esperance for Christmas. They had found the bubbly tree lights and put them on the tree, and they were reluctant to go off and leave them. Knowing that they were going to a strange place and uncertain how they were facing it in their young minds, Sally spent the day of their departure in a whirl of festivity for them, taking them to lunch with Hank, seeing Santa Claus at a Tallahassee department store, and helping them pick out and wrap presents for their parents and Hank and Angie.

At the airport they looked young and vulnerable and uneasy about where they were going, but they clung to each other's hand and said nothing about it if they were frightened.

"Mom will meet us, won't she?" Bunk asked once.

Sally had reassured them. One or both of their parents would be at the Houston airport. But if for any reason their parents were not at the airport, it would still be all right. The nice stewardess would take care of them until their mama and their daddy came, or she would call Gran and Angie and Aunt Sarah and Uncle Henry, and everybody would come tooling out to get them.

"You've got a lot of people to love you and look after you," she said, smiling on them.

They smiled back and were quiet, and presently their flight was called and Sally walked them aboard and saw them seated with coloring books and crayons in hand. She kissed them and went back to the waiting room and stood with her face pressed close to the glass, watching the window by their seats, unable to see their faces and fighting a sudden frantic urge to go and get them off the plane.

Sally stayed at Sarah's until Leslie called to tell them the twins had arrived and to thank her mother once more for what she confidently predicted would be "the best, best Christmas ever." The money had come and they had found an apartment that would do temporarily and she and the children were going straight there to make cocoa and "talk Santa Claus."

"Did you get your things from Denton?" Sally asked.

"Not yet," Leslie said. "Oh, Mama, there's so much to do! And thank you, thank you for what you've done. Merry Christmas! We love you!"

Sally turned from the phone to find Sarah struggling to unknot a popcorn chain and waiting for word from Texas.

"They're all safe and fine?" she asked. "That's good. I guess it's all right about their stuff at Denton. It was mostly junk and no great loss."

"Loss?" Sally said, puzzled. "Was it lost?"

"I thought Les told you," Sarah said. "She went back to get their things out of that old house, and somebody had been there and taken everything. Les suspects the landlord, but he said vandals because what they didn't take they tore up and scattered."

"Everything?" cried Sally. "Not Angie's washing machine! She's still paying Sears for that."

"Oh, my Lord," muttered Sarah. "I forgot that. Mother, don't tell Angie, it'll kill her. Maybe it wasn't stolen."

But it was. After Christmas Leslie decided to tell them, writing Angie a long regretful letter, thanking her again and again for all the months she had enjoyed the convenience of washing their clothes in it and promising to repay her someday. To Sally's surprise the frugal Angie wasted no time in lamentation.

"I got my money's worth out of giving it to them," she said. "Let's not worry about it any more."

They didn't because a new worry assailed them from Texas. Sally knew it was bad news when Henry Parker was waiting at the marina as she docked her boat one raw and windy day in February. He reached for the bow line and secured it before he spoke to her.

"Henry, what are you doing here?" Sally asked, scrambling to the dock. "Anything wrong with Sarah or Hank?"

"No, ma'am, they're fine," he said. And because he didn't know how to dissemble he blurted it out: "Leslie and Hal have been arrested in Houston for possession of marijuana. They called yesterday, and I wired them some money for bail so they could get back to the kids. But they need a lawyer."

Sally went and sat on the bench by the launderette, letting the damp wind from the river whip at her bare head and gloveless hands until Henry took her arm and guided her to his car, which had been warmed by its heater on the trip down from Tallahassee.

She turned a look of mute agony on him, and his chubby face twisted in answering distress.

"I'll tell you all I know," he said. "Maybe it's not as bad as it seemed at first, but I thought I'd better come down here instead of trusting it to the telephone. Sarah would have come, but there was something at Hank's school."

Sally waited numbly.

Leslie had taken the twins to their new kindergarten that morning and come back home to find two narcotics agents with a search warrant turning out drawers and going through their possessions. Hal, awakened by their knock at the door and still drugged with sleep, watched barefoot and bewildered while they rummaged. As Leslie returned they dumped a big box containing crayons, a little tin case of watercolors, coloring books, paper dolls, and puzzles on the floor. From the bottom they brought out a neat brown package containing marijuana.

They arrested Leslie and Hal immediately and took them to jail. Leslie used her one phone call to talk to Henry. Hal called the leader of his band. They were released in time to get the children at school and presumably would be free until the day they had to appear in court, when they could be sentenced to twenty years in jail, fined $5,000, or both.

They needed a lawyer.

Sally had been holding herself stiffly erect and unmoving,

but now she sagged tiredly. "I'd better go there," she said.

Henry cleared his throat and turned and faced her. "I don't mean to try to tell you what to do, Sally, but . . . well, they're going to need money. Maybe a lot of money. The price of a plane ticket . . . well, they might need it for something else a lot worse."

For the first time Sally smiled at her son-in-law. "You're a good somebody, Henry," she said, "and you're right. I'll sit tight and wait to hear what they need."

He remained still, his hands on the steering wheel, not moving to start the car but staring at an oyster boat passing the dock. Sally watched too, trying to summon strength to ask the next question.

"Henry, why did they have marijuana?"

He shook his head. "Why do any of them have it? Kids all over the country are growing it and buying and selling and smoking it. They say it's milder than whiskey and not addictive. I don't suppose it's so bad." He sighed. "But it *is* against the law, and I understand they're rabid about it in Texas."

"Musicians," said Sally wearily. "It's all those musicians they hang around with."

Henry nodded. "Maybe. I don't know. I don't know what it's got to do with playing a horn any more than selling insurance, but then I reckon I'm square."

He turned to face Sally, his face puckered in earnestness.

"There's one more thing. They don't claim they're not guilty. You can let them take their punishment, you know."

She stared at him, aghast. "You mean go to jail?"

"If that's what the sentence is."

"Those kids *in jail!*" Sally was white-faced and shaking. "Henry, you're out of your mind! I'd never let a child of mine spend one night in jail if I could help it. Terrible things happen in jails!"

"I know." Henry nodded. "But, Sally, face it. They are not children any more. They're grown people with children of their own, and maybe they should be responsible for their actions. I don't know. It's up to you."

Sally reached for the door handle. "Thank you, Henry, for coming to tell me and for wiring the bail money. I'll repay you."

Henry leaned across her and opened the door. "Made you

126

mad, didn't I?" he said, grinning. "I didn't mean to. You know you can count me in on anything you decide to do. I've got a little money saved and I can take some leave and go out there, if you want me to."

For the first time since he'd come, Sally thought she might cry. She patted his arm and got out of the car as fast as she could. Henry was the only always-right person she knew that she could abide. Steady, sensible, a pillar of rectitude, and so sweet and kind.

She dredged up a shaky smile and blew him a kiss and hurried toward her own car in the slot behind the launderette.

He watched her get in and start up and followed her down the highway to her office. She turned in and he touched his horn and waved and went on by toward Tallahassee and his law-abiding, pay-the-bills, nice-house-in-a-good-neighborhood, respectable life. If only they were all like him, she thought, she could settle down to a trouble-free and tranquil old age.

The phone was ringing on her desk, and she flung down her purse and her keys and grabbed it.

"Mama." Leslie sounded meek and penitent and far away. "Henry call you?"

"He came to see me," Sally said. "He considered the mess you and Hal have gotten yourselves into serious enough for a trip down here. What on earth do you all mean by fooling around with drugs?"

Shock and pain had given way to cold fury. She wanted to scream and holler and throw things. If I could get my hands on that pair, she was thinking angrily, I would break every bone in their dumb, heedless bodies.

"Mama, listen—" Leslie began.

"Listen, hell!" yelled Sally. "I could kill you and Hal! When have either of you ever listened to anybody? What am I going to tell Angie? Her darling grandchildren breaking the law and going to jail! You know what's right, and you deliberately choose to do what's wrong. I don't think I'm going to help you one damned bit!"

It was something she hadn't even considered and she surprised herself by coming out with it, letting Leslie think she'd given up on them.

"Mama, you don't understand," Leslie said faintly. "Marijuana's not a bad drug. A lot of kids—"

127

"Kids . . . hippies . . . fools!" shouted Sally. "Change the law if you think marijuana's such a boon to mankind. But don't break it unless you're ready to go to jail."

Suddenly she was out of energy and out of fight. Her legs trembled and her back ached. She sat down in the swivel chair and put her head down on the arm holding the telephone to her ear.

"Okay," she said. "What are we going to do?"

Heartened by the "we," Leslie began to tell her. There was a lawyer in Houston who was trying to change the stringent marijuana laws, and he represented a lot of people who ran afoul of them. He would take Leslie and Hal's case and maybe could get them off with probation since they were young and first offenders. But his fee would be $2,000. A fine could be anything and a sentence—Leslie's voice broke—up to twenty years or even life.

"Give me a number where I can reach you, and I'll call you back," Sally said, reaching for a pencil.

She sat a long time, thinking how to raise the money. She had mortgaged everything they owned from time to time, and she was far from certain she could raise enough money fast enough. Loan officers at the bank called Esperance "unimproved and isolated rural property." They'd sing a different tune if there was ever a bridge to the island, Angie said, but there was no bridge, no ferry, and Sally needed $5,000 immediately.

If only she could sell something. The last good sale before Christmas had provided the twins' airplane tickets to Texas, money for an apartment, and that new car sitting out there before the door.

She looked at it with the slow rain falling on its satiny gray hood, turning it to a luminous silver. She had professed not to care about cars as long as she had something that would start, go, and stop. But Angie loved the luxury of what she called "a big car," one with velvety upholstery and a simulated mahogany dash and fat silvery door handles—which, Sally told her, looked like the handles on an expensive coffin.

Angie agreed and had pointed to its length and the easy access of four doors. "Hearse-grand," she called it. After traveling in what she called "a matchbox car," Sally's Volkswagen, she adored the length and breadth of the Buick, the comfort of the cushions, and the new-car fragrance.

"I only hope I'll have a funeral this grand," she had said blissfully as they drove out to give the new vehicle a shakedown cruise.

If she took it right back to the dealer maybe she could get a chunk of her money back, Sally thought. But the Buick dealer she called acted so injured at the idea of refunding her money Sally went to the bank to check more mortgage possibilities. She told Oliver Wilcox she was trying to unload her new car to raise money for "a family emergency." He didn't ask the nature of the emergency, but he took a walk to the bank's parking lot and inspected the car, from its sweet moonstone hood to its delicately curved rump.

"Cars depreciate fast," Oliver said somberly. "If you want me to take it off your hands and relieve you of the problem of finding a buyer, maybe I could do that. I mean personally. Not the bank."

"For five thousand dollars?"

He nodded, looking away. Sally got the idea that she was taxing the bonds of friendship to the limit.

"Sold," she said. "The registration and title papers are in the glove compartment. I'll get them while you get the five thousand and put it in my account. Here's a deposit slip." She ripped one out of her checkbook and handed it to him.

Back at her office, Sally collapsed with relief. She had the money in the bank, faster than she had hoped. Now it remained for the lawyer to be engaged and to start whatever was necessary to save Leslie and Hal.

She slipped her feet out of her shoes and rested her elbows on her desk, chin in hand. She would now have to sell something to get herself some kind of old car to replace the Buick.

She was riffling through a folder, trying to match property to prospects, when the phone rang.

"Mrs. McMillan? This is Andrea Battle. I am calling from Houston. I run the school attended by Harold and Hope Ellis. They are your grandchildren?"

"Yes! Oh, yes!"

"I thought so. I have your check for their tuition with your address and telephone number on it. I'm taking the liberty of calling you, because . . . Mrs. McMillan, did you know that your daughter and son-in-law have been incarcerated by the police?"

Incarcerated. Flossy word for jailed, Sally thought.

"Yes, I have talked with my daughter," she said coolly, as if landing in jail was one of the nice things a daughter did.

"Then you know, I suppose, that the children could be affected? A Miss Sommers from the child welfare division has already been to see me. It's possible they will step in and take custody of Harold and Hope until the court rules on their case. If they are not suitable parents—"

"Suitable parents!" cried Sally. "Of course they're suitable parents! They haven't even been found guilty and the welfare department is after the children?" She couldn't be sure if she shouted out of outrage, self-pity, or annoyance at the superior, schoolmarmish tone of her caller.

Surprisingly, Miss Battle softened. "You're right, Mrs. McMillan. I'm as upset over this as you are. That's why I called. Can't you take the children there?"

"Certainly I can. I will," Sally said. "I'll call their parents right now and arrange to have them fly home tonight or tomorrow. And I thank you for calling."

She checked the number on her pad and dialed what she took to be some bandleader's apartment in Houston in search of Leslie. Hal answered the phone. He sounded vague and heavily casual about their troubles, and Sally told him about the school principal's warning that the children might be taken over by juvenile authorities.

He snorted, clearly not alarmed.

"Hal, I'm scared for them, aren't you? I've got some money to send you all, and I'm going to Delta this afternoon and send tickets to the twins. Can you get them to the airport for that three-o'clock flight they took last time?"

"Well, I suppose," Hal said. "Leslie's not here and I don't know what this is all about. The kids are here and they're okay."

Patiently Sally went over her conversation with Miss Battle, then gave the flight number and hour of the children's departure again. "Got it?" she finished.

"Well, yeah, but the kids are okay here. They've been here since school let out. They're looking at television."

"Hal!" Sally barked at him. "I *know* Bunk and Bunny are all right so far. You told me that. What I'm telling *you* is that the child-welfare-juvenile authorities might decide you and Leslie are 'unsuitable parents' and take the children some-

130

where else to stay. I don't understand how they can—at least not until you're convicted—but Miss Battle assured me that it could happen and we both thought it better to get them out of Houston and safe here with us, just in case. I don't want them upset, do you?"

"Man," said Hal. But it was in a tone of capitulation.

"Ask for the tickets at the Delta counter. I'll be at the airport to meet them."

The arrival of Bunk and Bunny was compensation to Angie for loss of her "big car" and almost made up for the endless dread and foreboding about the fate of Leslie and Hal before an unknown and possibly unfriendly judge.

The children were jubilant to be back on the island but cautious and noncommittal about Texas.

"We didn't like Houston very much, Gran," Bunk would say thoughtfully.

Bunny would flash him a look and temporize. "It was pretty good in some ways."

But they made it plain that they didn't want to go back.

The morning of court Sally lingered at home, dreading to get to the telephone and have to hang around and wait for Leslie's call, which she had promised to make at noon, whether the trial was over or not.

"You want to take a morning walk, Gran?" Bunk asked.

"Go ahead," Angie said. "Bunny and I will clear away. Go with Bunk."

The morning was bright and warm, full of the promise of spring. As they walked through the woods and took the bay road, Sally examined Lucina's skyline and a faint blue tracery of smoke rising above it. Time was, she thought, when I would have waited here for any news of import and they would have signaled me with smoke or fire from that shore. The Spanish and the French explorers and the Indians had not been compelled to sail to Lucina to learn that disaster was about to crush them. The message was written on the sky.

Bunk was watching her face. "You okay, Gran?" he asked.

"Oh, sure," Sally said, determinedly cheerful. "I was thinking about Indians and how they must have sent messages to one another across the Sound."

Bunk appeared relieved, and they talked of Indians and the

131

French who had called the island Hope—Esperance—out of some dream for the new world.

"I hope a lot," said Bunk," "Do you?"

Sally nodded. "A lot."

"I got a wishing place," he confided. "You want to see?"

"Oh, yes!" Sally said, smiling down at him. "I'd like that very much."

He put his hand on hers and said, "Turn around and close your eyes."

Sally obeyed.

"Now take six giant steps," he ordered.

Sally stepped wide six times.

"Now open your eyes," Bunk directed.

Sally stood on the bluff where sailing ships had discharged their ballast a century or more ago. Far below them the waves crashed against rocks foreign to the Florida coast and yet oddly natural and beautiful there. She checked the slope and the coastline for Bunk's "place" and then she saw it—a great slab of slate lodged athwart half a dozen chunky rocks so it made a tilted roof, a little cave. She could see sneaker prints and small hand prints on the white sand floor and, a few feet before it, a rock with a basinlike depression which had caught and held rainwater. After the winter rains the little basin was full— a placid catchment of silver which reflected the morning sky.

Bunk's blue eyes watched her expectantly. "You like it?"

"I love it!" she said.

"You can make a wish if you want to. Just look in the water and say it to yourself."

Sally stepped closer and gazed into the little pool. The wish was on the tip of her mind. It seemed to have been there as long as she could remember. Leslie and Hal, she prayed, let them be safe, let them be happy, let them be good.

She turned to find Bunk had tactfully moved away, fixing his attention on a flock of sea gulls noisily riding the updraft over the bluff.

"I bet I know what you wished for," he said.

"You can't guess," Sally teased him.

"You wished for a flying sandbox," he said. "I always do."

Sally put her arm across his shoulders. "You know, you're right. I believe that's what I always wish for, too."

Word from Texas came at noon, as Leslie had promised. The proceedings had taken fifteen minutes. The officers testified that they had confiscated two pounds of marijuana in an apartment rented by Mr. and Mrs. Ellis. The two young defendants, standing by their attorney, said they were guilty. The attorney said they were first offenders, and the judge said $2,500 and seven years' probation. They were not to leave the state without the permission of the court.

"You can't come home?" Sally asked.

"They want us where they can watch us," Leslie said, laughing tremulously. "Public Enemies One and Two."

It was too late to be extracting a promise in exchange for her help, Sally knew, but she tried anyhow.

"I want you to promise me something," she said. "I helped you all I could, and now I want you and Hal to promise me that you will never again have anything to do with marijuana or any other illegal drug."

"Mama, you *know* we won't!" Leslie cried.

"Promise," commanded Sally.

"I promise," said Leslie.

Later, when she told Angie about it, Sally said ruefully, "I should have made them promise in writing and swear to it before a notary public *before* I sent the money. Then I would have been acting from what they call a position of power."

"It's a poor way to help," said Angie. "Playing swapsie with the recipients. You have to trust to their gratitude and good sense."

SPRING 1977

Leslie's job in Tallahassee ran out the week before Easter, and she came home to Esperance looking much too thin in the clothes they had assembled at Christmas.

"You haven't bought anything new?" Sally asked, as Leslie

changed to cut-off jeans and a sweat shirt and prepared to go down to the beach.

"Clothes, smose," said Leslie. "Who needs them? I've saved every dime I could to go to New Orleans, Mama. I think I know where they are. I have an address on St. Aloysius Street. I'm going to get them and bring them home."

"I'll go with you," Sally said on impulse.

"Can you, Mama? Can you get away?"

"I'll get somebody to keep the generator perking, and then I'll be ready. Let's fly and stay at a good hotel and maybe rent a car, if we have to."

"Let's go tonight," said Leslie.

They arrived in New Orleans after midnight and checked into Howard Johnson's, not the glamorous old St. Charles Hotel Sally had in mind, but at least downtown and close to the courthouse. Lee Lambert had given Leslie the name of a New Orleans attorney and had called him for her.

They were at his office before it opened the next morning.

Sally liked Don Gallé, a swarthy young fellow with melting dark eyes, curly black hair worn to his collar, and a swoopy black mustache that fanned out to his cheeks like blackbird wings.

"Ah, you having trouble with your man?" he murmured to Leslie in a soft Cajun-accented voice.

Leslie, warming to his sympathetic interest, poured out the story of Hal's trick to get the children, the cruel night when she found them at the motel on the Airline Highway and he had knocked her down and run off with them, the refusal of his mother to talk to her over the phone, and his subsequent petition for divorce and custody.

"I think I know where they are now," she said, giving him the address on St. Aloysius Street. "This saxophone player we know likes me better than he likes Hal, and he told me what he knew. He is living with a girl named Gayle Gunner and has my children there too."

"Bad, so bad," young Mr. Gallé murmured musically. "Let us see what is to be done."

He drafted an order requiring Hal to appear with the children at ten o'clock the next morning and to show cause why their mother should not have custody of them. After lunch

134

they would take it to the judge, who had agreed to see them in chambers. Meanwhile, would the ladies be his guests at Tujaque's?

It was a pretty day for a walk through the French Quarter. He gave them the address of the old restaurant opposite the French Market and, looking tenderly at Leslie's suddenly pink cheeks and bright eyes, said, "Stroll. Pass a good time. I will be with you for twelve o'clock sharp."

It had been a surprisingly good lunch in the plain old-fashioned restaurant, and Sally sipped a glass of wine and found herself enjoying the sight of Leslie with the young lawyer. They're flirting, she thought with surprise. How pleasant. Wouldn't it have been nice if Leslie had married such a young man, one who obviously admired and enjoyed her? She remembered with a pang watching Leslie and the children drinking in the *Mister Rogers' Neighborhood* program on television the summer past when Hal was away in Virginia Beach.

"I always watch *Mister Rogers* if I can," Leslie had explained, laughing a little. "I feel so good when he sings that song to me." She sang it:

> "I like you as you are,
> I wouldn't want to change you,
> Or even rearrange you!
> Not by far . . .
> I *like* you as you are!"

She had known then that Hal *didn't* like her as she was. Maybe it was Gallic good manners or professional charm, but this young man seemed to like Leslie as she was.

They walked along together to the judge's chambers, Leslie and Don Gallé chatting animatedly. She's thinking he's Sir Galahad ready to do battle against the infidel, Sally thought contentedly, and maybe he is.

The judge looked like Friar Tuck. He was a youngish fat man with a fringe of fair hair around his bald head and a benign expression back of Ben Franklin glasses.

He read the order twice and then tipped back in his big revolving chair and smiled on Leslie genially. "I can sign this," he said. "No problem about that. And your husband *might* bring your children into court at ten o'clock tomorrow morning, as it specifies. Again"—and he smiled as if he himself liked the idea—"he might take off across the state line with them tonight."

"Oh, Lord!" groaned Sally. "Isn't there anything you can do?"

"Yes, ma'am. I can order the sheriff to bring the little ones back with him and place them in the juvenile home overnight."

"Juvenile home!" Sally and Leslie said it together.

"With children who have done bad things?" Leslie pressed him. "I wouldn't do that to Bunk and Bunny! They're good children. It would be traumatic for them."

"Sometimes it is," the judge said imperturbably. "This is an unhappy kind of case for our courts too, you know. Our laws are not uniform. A judge can grant custody to a mother or a father in one state, and all a parent has to do to subvert it is to grab up the child and cross over into another state. Instant custody. Some of our lawmakers are working to make custody laws uniform, but as of now there are ten thousand children a year who are stolen by one parent or the other.

"Sometimes," he went on—and Sally thought his tone relished the idea—"they are missing for the rest of their lives."

Leslie was crying now, and Don Gallé was handing her a pristine white linen handkerchief. "Isn't there anything I can do to get my children?" Leslie asked desperately.

The judge lifted a pudgy finger. "There's one thing," he said. "One thing. It's called self-help. You can get a detective and find them and get a strong-armed friend to help you snatch them. I haven't heard all the evidence, of course, but I am assuming that you are at least as entitled to your children as your husband is."

"A mother's love," said Gallé delicately.

"Look in the phone book," directed the judge. "In our city, private detectives advertise. If they are specialists in child custody cases, the ad will probably say it."

"Could you recommend a detective?" Sally asked.

The judge was insulted. "Madam, I would not think of doing such a thing! It would not be proper for the court—"

"Mrs. McMillan didn't know that, your honor," Gallé said hastily and motioned to Leslie and Sally that it was time to go.

Sally paid Gallé his $200 fee in the courthouse corridor. He

136

thanked her and held Leslie's hand overlong as they said good-bye.

Back at the hotel they searched the yellow pages for private detectives.

Leslie had been crying again, but she was buoyed up by the search for detectives, and suddenly she let out a whoop. "Look, Mama, here's one named Sam Slade!"

"You mean Raymond Chandler's detective. No, that's Sam Spade. Let me see."

"There it is in the book: 'Sam Slade, private investigator. Domestic Relations and Child Custody a Specialty.' You can't do better than that. I'm calling Della Street immediately!"

"That's Perry Mason," Sally said, absently, rereading the ad. He means child-snatching a specialty, she was thinking. She was beginning to have doubts about forcibly removing the twins from their father's custody. If they didn't want to come, what then?

"Would you take the children if they didn't want to go?"

"You know they'd want to come with us, Mama," Leslie said at the dresser, where she was combing her hair and applying lipstick, preparing to go find Sam Slade. "Can you see Bunk and Bunny ever failing to jump at the chance to go home to Esperance with you?"

In all honesty, Sally couldn't. She got off the bed and put on her shoes and reached for the jacket to her coral suit.

Sam Slade's office was back of a shoe repair store. They had to take a cab to find it, but Sally, paying the driver, made a mental note to ask about bus service for the return trip. They had only begun the search, and they'd need every penny.

The shoe shop was doing a rushing business, with three people back of the counter waiting on customers, but the office at the rear was dark and quiet. Mr. Slade had come to meet them from the plant out back, where commercial-sized stitchers rasped and chugged.

He was a short man, thin and wiry, with sleek Rudolph Valentino hair obviously rooted in a toupee and too dark for his florid skin. He went ahead, turning on a light in the windowless office. It was large and paneled with some kind of dark wood, against which were hung several murky landscapes in oil, each of them cunningly lit by small floodlights attached to their frames.

He caught Sally's glance at the pictures and said, "You like art? You got taste. These are Drysdales. Very good. I gave a thousand apiece for them. Could get twice that now. He's been discovered with a capital 'D.' You know of him, of course."

Sally didn't, but she didn't care to invite a lecture. "Of course," she said, conveying what she hoped was the right amount of reverence.

He motioned them to fat, heavily padded, brocaded velvet chairs and took his place behind a gold-lacquer and glass table which served as a desk. "Renaissance," he said, patting the top with one hand and pushing a bouquet of artificial red roses an inch or two toward them. "French silk," he murmured. "What can I do for you ladies?"

Leslie began to talk but Sally interrupted. "Honey, I think we should be sure we're dealing with the right person. You are the detective, Mr. Slade?"

The wiry little man didn't dignify her question with an answer. He got up and went to a cabinet behind them and pulled out a framed certificate and a newspaper clipping. Wordlessly he dropped them in Sally's hands.

The clipping from the *Times-Picayune* was an interview with Sam Slade, cobbler detective without peer. Some gee-whizzy young female feature writer had been spellbound by his derring-do, his exploits in counterespionage, his solution of crimes insoluble to the New Orleans police, and especially the way he had recovered stolen children and restored them to the arms of grateful mothers and, occasionally, fathers. His shoe repair business was a front, said the story. His last name really was Slade, but he had taken Sam for its obvious literary and commercial advantage.

"Ah," said Sally, impressed.

"Gee," said Leslie, who had been reading over her shoulder.

Mollified, Sam Slade leaned back in his chair and clasped his hands back of his head, causing his toupee to lift and settle in the slight breeze the movement generated.

"Now, ladies, shall we proceed?" he inquired.

Together they told him the story, ending with the information the saxophone player had given Leslie: Hal and the twins were living on St. Aloysius Street with a woman named Gayle Gunner.

"Now, what you want to do is get the children and take them home to Florida with you?" Slade asked.

They nodded.

"See what you mean," he said. "I have an operative—a black man named Treadwell, who was in the CIA. You got any objections to blacks?"

They shook their heads.

"I'll send him out with you in my laundry van. I make reservations on the airline. You snatch the kids. Tread whisks you to the airport. S'all there is to it."

"That's wonderful!" cried Leslie, big-eyed with admiration.

"What if the children resist?" said Sally, pleased that she had found a word to cover what-if-they-hate-us-and-don't-want-to-come?

"A little chloroform," said Slade.

"No!" Leslie gasped.

"No," said Sally. "We couldn't do that."

"Okay, you don't want to play rough," said Slade. "We'll cross that bridge when we come to it. Now, let's see. You all go back to your hotel. I'll call you there in an hour or two. Plan on hitting St. Aloysius Street some time tonight. I'll let you know when. Now, as to my fee, that'll be two hundred and fifty in advance, two hundred and fifty when the caper is completed."

Sally reached for her purse. Outside, the shoe shop was enjoying a lull and the three people back of the counter looked at them curiously and then ostentatiously looked away.

Sally had forgotten to find out about bus service. What the hell, she thought cheerfully. Scotland Yard inspectors may use public transportation, but we're American private eyes!

They were afraid to leave the hotel for dinner, afraid that Slade would call them. They lay on their beds in their slips, waiting and talking about Bunk and Bunny. There was a counseling service called the Bridge which would help her with the children if they were hostile, Leslie said. Sally's heart sank. Of course, they ought to consider it, but she couldn't believe her precious Bunk and Bunny would be "hostile." There had never been anything but loyalty, love, and trust in those two, and she couldn't bear to think it might be otherwise. Did Leslie have reason to believe the twins would be hostile? She closed her eyes and went over things Leslie had said—"It hasn't always been a happy home" . . . "I'm not a good person"—the sometimes heavy drinking, the reference to "my lovers," and Bunny's report that "Mama is mean to us."

Oh, God, she thought wearily, maybe she hasn't been good to them always. What parent is? But she loved them, ah, how she loved the children and their father! And she tried. Stumbling, falling, never enough knowledge or strength for what she had to do, but doing it anyway. Believing in Hal, joining the children in their dreams, certain that someday they would have every good thing.

She opened her eyes and looked at Leslie, who was squinting into the mirror with one eye and trying to apply mascara on the lashes of the other.

"You know Lee Lambert told me that in cases like this the children are often brainwashed, Mama," Leslie said. "Like prisoners of war."

She was silent a moment.

"That's what they are, I guess, prisoners in Hal's war against us."

"Us?" said Sally. "He has no reason to fight me."

"Aw, Mama, I didn't ever let them tell you, but he hates you. He felt so obligated! He never wanted the children to be with you. Angie was all right, I guess. He never said anything against her. But he raised hell every time I let them spend time with you or go on little trips with you. It reached the point where I told the children not to tell him."

"Well, that night," said Sally, looking back. "But you said he was terribly ashamed and apologetic for the way he talked to me that night in the country."

Leslie turned from the mirror. "He wasn't," she said, grinning. "I made that up because I didn't want you to feel bad."

"Didn't he know they'd be with me a lot if you all moved into the cottage last summer?"

"Sure," said Leslie, "but that suited him. He was shucking us and going to Virginia Beach. I don't think he cared where we were then, as long as it wasn't camping out near him, expecting him home at night."

The phone rang.

"How about dinner, ladies?" asked Sam Slade.

"We were thinking about ordering a sandwich from room service," Sally said.

"An atrocity," said the detective. "I have a favorite restaurant out on Lake Pontchartrain. I'd be honored if you'd be my guests."

"Well . . ." Sally said uncertainly, not wanting to go.

"It's settled," said Slade, manfully taking charge. "Meet you in the lobby in how many minutes? I'm already in the neighborhood."

"Ten," said Sally.

The restaurant on stilts out over the water was interesting and unpretentious and the seafood was delicious, but since they subsisted on seafood on the island, Sally would have ordered something French and typically New Orleans if she had had a choice. Slade allowed them no choice but masterfully ordered for them. He also paid, for which she was grateful.

During the meal he assiduously avoided talk of the "caper" they faced, elaborately inspecting the other diners, mostly family groups, and frowning at Sally and Leslie warningly. Back at the hotel he walked into the lobby with them, looked it over thoroughly, and said in a low voice, "Mind if I come up?"

"That's fine," Sally said.

In their room he took the chair at the desk and drew out a pen and a sheet of paper.

"I'll give you the game plan," he said, "after I fill in the background. Your kids are at this address on St. Aloysius. It's the second-floor apartment, rented in the name of Miss Gayle Gunner. Lights, water, and phone are also in her name. The children are not in school. Every morning at ten o'clock they walk down to Audubon Park. They are well-behaved, and my information is that the boy is homesick."

"Oooh!" Leslie squealed, her eyes glowing. "Bunk misses us!"

"Are you sure?" asked Sally, her heart racing. "How can you be sure?"

"I have my sources," the little game rooster said cockily, returning to his sheet of paper. "Now, the game plan. My operative, Tread, will pick you up in the laundry van at four o'clock in the morning. You will notice that the panels bearing the name of my place have been removed and replaced by panels of simulated stained glass. They will permit you to see out without being seen."

Sally and Leslie looked at one another. Real undercover stuff.

"It's important that the van be on the street long enough to collect dew on the windshield so the residents will realize it's been there awhile and won't be suspicious. You may be in for a long wait, so I want you to plan for it. There's an all-night drugstore open on the Airline Highway. I will drive you there and you can shop for a thermos to hold coffee, some sandwiches, and a plastic bucket which you will need for—er, comfort purposes. I want you to get some cloth, preferably black, to make a curtain across the back of the front seat to screen out the light. That is all," he concluded.

"Don't wait for us," Sally said as they reached the drugstore. "We'll take a cab back to the hotel. And . . . thank you, thank you so much!"

Slade clicked his heels and bowed from the waist. "My profession and also my pleasure," he said unctuously.

Sally and Leslie went into the drugstore, giggling and jostling one another in giddy high spirits.

"Bunk is homesick!" whispered Leslie. Sally echoed it ecstatically.

"Bunk is homesick!"

"Sam Slade, or whatever his name is, is the biggest fool I ever saw," Sally said as they hefted plastic buckets, wondering which size—mop, garbage, or paint—would be appropriate for their "comfort." "But I don't care, if he knows his business—and he seems to."

When they came out, to their surprise, Slade's car was still at the curb. He was waiting for them.

"Ladies," he said, "how about a cup of coffee for a . . . nightcap, you might say."

"Fine," said Sally.

"I'd love some," said Leslie.

They climbed into the car and rode to a Dunk 'n Dine. Sally took the thermos bottle out of its wrappings and took it in with them to get it filled. They sat at the counter on stools and Slade ordered coffee, chatting familiarly with the waitress and nodding to two or three of the other coffee drinkers. While they waited he took a bill out of his wallet, tucked it into a napkin, and walked around and handed it to a policeman.

"Explain later," he said out of the corner of his mouth when he sat back down between them.

Sally wouldn't have asked him to explain, assuming it was none of her business, but he volunteered as they walked to the car.

"See that cop?" he said, nodding toward the coffee-shop customers beyond the plate glass. "He's on duty in Audubon Park. He's the one who sees your kids every day. Good source."

"Oh, I want to talk to him," breathed Leslie, stopping in her tracks.

"Why? You'll have them yourself tomorrow," Slade said, taking her by the arm and propelling her toward his car.

Back at the hotel, Sally and Leslie undressed and showered and went to bed but not to sleep. Excitement kept one or the other talking or turning on the light to check the time.

At four A.M., when Detective Treadwell called them from the lobby, they were dressed and ready with black cloth, some plastic scissors and safety pins, sandwiches and thermos neatly packed in a yellow plastic bucket.

Treadwell was a comforting person to have on your side, Sally thought, big, solidly built, and very black. He handed them into the back of the van and helped them hang up the black curtain, which was intended to make the back windows impenetrable.

"Mr. Slade tells us you were with the CIA," Sally said, making conversation.

The big black man chuckled as he started the van. "Ain't he something? He always gets that mixed up. I was a desk sergeant with the New Orleans police."

"Oh?" Sally said, taken aback. "Well, that's good training too, I imagine."

"Not much," said Treadwell briefly.

"Have you been a private investigator long?" Leslie asked uneasily.

"Six months," Treadwell said.

They leaned back on the van's middle seat and touched elbows for reassurance in the simulated-stained-glass twilight. Six months wasn't much experience for the reclamation of Bunk and Bunny to be hanging on. But as the hours went by they began to trust Tread's knowledge more.

He found St. Aloysius Street right away—a slummy thoroughfare at the beginning, gradually improving as it approached a city park. The address they sought was on a block of modest but generally well-kept houses, many of them obviously subdivided to make apartments with private stairways leading to second floors.

"That's the house," said Treadwell, nodding toward a small

143

brown two-story cottage, the telltale outside flight of stairs enclosed along the side with a door opening onto the front porch. "I was there this afternoon."

"Did you see the twins?" Leslie asked eagerly.

"Sure did," said Treadwell. "Said I was a gas man checking a leak, and the boy let me in. Girl was washing her hair. Said their parents were not in."

"Parents!" Leslie sniffed.

"I wanted to be sure the kids were there," Treadwell went on. "But I told them it was dangerous for them to let a stranger like me in. Talked to both of them about it before I left. It *is* dangerous," he added. "They don't know me."

"That was good of you to tell them," Sally said. "But where we're taking them you don't have to worry about strangers. We almost never see one."

"Be good," said Treadwell. "New Orleans getting mean."

"The children," put in Leslie, "how did they look? Did they seem all right?"

"Fine, far as I could tell," Treadwell said. "They mighty pretty children. White-headed, ain't they?"

"Oh, yes," said Leslie. "White gold. Getting darker though, now, I bet."

They thought about the children and the changes that the months might have brought. The street was quiet, the houses dark except for the minute glow of a low-watt night light beyond a window or two. A little breeze stirred around in the moss on a live-oak tree half a block in front of them, and they heard behind them the rattle of an approaching bicycle, links against the chain guard, and the thud of the morning *Times-Picayune* hitting porches. A milk truck went by without stopping. Leslie noted its passage, muttering, "They don't take milk, of course."

An hour passed and nothing stirred except a cat under the fronds of a banana tree. Sally wondered if they should try to sleep and knew they couldn't. She lifted the ridiculous black curtain and asked Tread if he would like a cup of coffee.

"You better drink it yourselves," he said. "I'm used to this. I can keep awake. Or, better, save the coffee and catch a nap if you all can."

Sally put the coffee back and flexed her arms and legs, which were getting stiff.

144

"I'll climb in the back," Leslie offered, "and we can both stretch out."

With a long seat each, they relaxed and were close to dozing when the sky began to lighten and a mockingbird in a pecan tree began singing. Down the street a car door slammed. Somewhere an ambulance or fire-truck siren shrilled. A radio blared and was tuned down.

A vacant lot on their side of the street made the nearest house the one across the street—a neat white bungalow, the boards of its porch glistening under new gray deck paint, its front wall all but obliterated by a row of hanging plastic flower pots in shades of orange and green. Sally, lying on her back with her head pillowed on her arms, was looking at it when the door opened and an old man in undershirt, pants, and bedroom slippers came out.

He stood a moment by the steps, yawning and scratching his stomach. He coughed and cleared his throat and spat into the grass of his yard and picked up the paper, which had landed in a flower box of a particularly livid shade of yellow.

He started to turn toward the door, but something caught his eye and he turned back.

"He sees us," muttered Tread. "He's spotted the van. No," he added, "maybe not. He's going in."

But the old man wasn't going in. He opened the door and put the paper inside and came down the steps across the street.

"Oh, oh," whispered Tread. "Be quiet."

At first the old man walked past the van and to a little vegetable garden on the vacant lot. He took his time, walking down one row and up the other, pinching off a leaf here, checking the state of the earth with a finger now and then. But it was all for show because when he had finished he came straight to the van and put his face close to the gaudy windows, trying to peer beyond the glass.

He said something to himself and started to walk away.

Treadwell came to life. "Said 'niggers.' Did you hear him? This end of the street's white. I better talk to him and explain, or he'll be calling the cops."

"No, wait—" Sally began but the big detective had moved swiftly, catching the old householder mid-street. He spoke to him in a low tone and came back smiling.

"I told him this is a stakeout," he said, "and asked him not to say nothing about it to nobody. He said he'd cooperate."

Stakeout, thought Sally. Is that what I'm doing here? At my time of life, flat on my back in a crazy van thinking about plastic buckets, which I need but wouldn't use to save my life? Stakeout, indeed.

Other residents on the street began to stir, but the brown house where Bunk and Bunny lived still showed no sign of life. There was a small pickup truck parked in front, and in the morning light Leslie was able to make out a big electric amplifier in the back.

"Hal's! He bought it when we were in the house in the country!"

The door of the white house across the street opened and the old man came out. He had put on a shirt and swapped his slippers for shoes, and he went from door to door, stopping at every house on the block.

"He's telling!" cried Leslie. "He's blatting about us!"

"Afraid so," muttered Tread.

Just before the old gentleman reached the brown cottage, a young girl with long fair hair came down the steps.

"Which door did she come out of?" Tread asked quickly. "Did you see?"

Neither woman had been looking, and they peered uncertainly at the girl. Could it be Bunny? Long-legged and tall but the hair was not light enough, the walk not quite familiar.

"It's not your girl?" asked Tread.

"I'm not sure," Leslie said. "Can we get closer?"

He started the van and began moving slowly after the girl, who was walking rapidly now toward the corner.

"If it's your girl you want to take her now?" Tread asked. "Or wait for both of them?"

"Oh, Mama, what should we do?" wailed Leslie. "I don't know! They've never been separated."

"We'll wait," said Sally. "Didn't Mr. Slade say they always go to the park together at ten o'clock?"

"That's the information we have," Tread said.

They were even with the girl now, and both women sighed and sank back in their seats. Not Bunny, not by a long shot. Thin, brown growing-girl legs beneath shorts could fool you. They all look alike, but the face—Bunny's piquant little face with the grave blue eyes—could not be duplicated.

146

"While we're out," said Tread, "I'll call Slade. You all can use the restroom, if you want to."

Sally smiled on him gratefully as she climbed out at the filling station three blocks from the house on St. Aloysius Street. She would also wash her face and hands and comb her hair and buy a few candy bars to chase the drugstore sandwiches which had been smelling pungently too many before-breakfast hours.

When they returned to St. Aloysius Street, their spot had been taken and they had to park around the corner. But the house was in view and Tread judged it to be an advantageous position because the twins would have to pass them on their way to the park.

The busybody neighbor was not in view. Remodelers were apparently at work in the old house on the opposite corner, from the sound of hammer blows coming from it. Restoration, Sally thought, we're in a neighborhood they're restoring, although many of the houses hardly seemed worth the effort. Suddenly the hammer blows ceased and two men and a woman walked down the steps, came out on the sidewalk, and looked toward the van. They were followed by the old man who had pledged his cooperation.

"Good God," whispered Tread. "He's still at it! We wasting our time."

"Oh, please," said Leslie. "Please let's stay a little longer. They may come out yet. It's still early."

"Past dinner time," said Tread, looking at his watch. "They ain't making the park today."

"Maybe they slept late, maybe they'll come in the afternoon," pleaded Leslie.

"Whatever you want to do," said Treadwell.

"Let's try it a while longer," suggested Sally.

They were rewarded by the stair door opening and a young woman coming out. She was tall and trim in a plaid blouse and khaki wraparound skirt. Bare-legged, she wore blue espadrilles on her feet. She paused on the steps to put on sunglasses and check something in her pocketbook, and then she walked to a green Datsun station wagon, unlocked it, and got in and drove off.

"Mama, that's Gayle, I bet!" whispered Leslie, agonized.

"Yes'm, it is," said Tread. "At least she lives there. I waited yesterday till they come home, and she was with the man with the trombone case."

"Do you think she's pretty?" Leslie asked.

"She look very well," said Tread noncommittally.

"Plain. Very plain," said Sally.

Leslie was quiet on the back seat, and Sally wouldn't turn and look at her because she knew she was crying. She still loves that jackass trombone player, Sally thought. She's going to let him break her heart, and there's not a thing anybody can do about it.

The house restorers had gone back indoors, taking their hammers and their curiosity with them. A truck with a camper drew up and a long-haired boy got out and unloaded a bass fiddle and took it up the stairs to Gayle Gunner's apartment.

Now the music will start, Sally thought, but it didn't. The stairway opened again and Hal and Bunk came out.

Leslie scrambled over the back of the seat to sit beside her mother and get a better view.

"Oh, Bunk," she whispered.

Sally reached for her hand, and they clung to one another, unable to speak again or to breathe. An old Ford was parked near the curb, and Hal and Bunk got in it and pulled away.

"Follow them?" asked Tread.

"Please!" whispered Sally.

"Doesn't he look good, Mama?" asked Leslie. "Isn't he a wonderful-looking boy?"

Sally nodded mutely, her throat too tight for speech. The fair head, the solemn face, the set of the shoulders and narrow hips, the long slender feet in sneakers like the ones he wore when she saw him last. Oh, Bunk, she thought. Oh, Bunk, come home.

Treadwell had the van rolling, the old Ford in sight.

"Shopping center down here a ways. That's where he's going," he said. And he guessed correctly. Hal pulled in front of a Delchamps store and parked.

Sally held her breath. If Bunk doesn't go in, she thought, should we go and get him? With him in the van we could rush back to the apartment and get Bunny.

The idea frightened her so she was almost relieved when Bunk followed his father into the store. They waited, tense and motionless. Even the tears in her eyes were paralyzed

148

with the waiting, Sally thought, wonderingly. They did not fall. She didn't dare look at Leslie.

For a while Hal and Bunk were lost beyond the Crisco and Clorox and Pampers-placarded glass of the storefront. Then they saw them through the open door at the checkout stand. They came out together with a small bag each and were in the car and moving in a moment.

Treadwell followed and now Leslie cried brokenly. Sally, crying herself, couldn't comfort her. Bunk and his father were on the porch by the time Tread drew up and parked.

"We could go in," he said. "I couldn't hit the father unless he hit one of you. Three of us . . ." He looked at them in the rearview mirror. "Naw, I reckon not. They big children."

They were considering the next step when Sam Slade came from behind the van, driving a long, low-slung blue convertible with the top down. He wore a baseball cap, to hold his toupee down in the wind, Sally thought. As he pulled up even with the van, he lifted his arm and motioned for Treadwell to follow him, a movie gesture—John Wayne signaling the Marines over the top.

He was waiting around the corner.

"You might as well give it up," he said. "You've blown your cover."

"Okay," said Treadwell.

"Oh, no!" cried Leslie.

Sally thought irrelevantly that it was another funny thing for her to be doing—blowing her cover.

She and Leslie got out of the van and into the convertible with Slade.

"Were we done in by that well-known character, the nosy neighbor?" Sally asked.

"That's my information," said Slade, faithful to detectivese. "Where to, ladies?"

"To our hotel, if you don't mind," said Sally. "I suppose we might as well go on home."

"Mama, I'm not going!" cried Leslie. "We haven't got the children like you promised, Mr. Slade. I'm going to stay until we do!"

"Well, honey," Sally said helplessly, "what else can we do? Hal knows something's going on. He's not going to let them out of the apartment alone, is he, Mr. Slade?"

"That's my view," said the detective. "Not for a certain length of time, probably. Young lady, why don't you keep a low profile for a while? Stay in touch with me and I'll let you know when to return."

"I can't. . . . I can't!" Leslie was sobbing, low racking sobs that shook her thin body and contorted her face, twisting her lips back from her teeth like a person in death throes. "They're here, and if I stay I'll at least get to see them. I'll get a job and a room in the neighborhood. I'll be a cocktail waitress . . . anything!"

Sally put her hand on her shoulder, but Leslie shook it off angrily.

"What do you all care if we don't get them? They're not your children! You don't care if Hal and that . . . that woman keep them! You're glad Hal's left me!"

Suddenly Sally had had enough. She grasped Leslie by the shoulder and said in a low voice, "Don't say one more word! Not a word! We'll talk about it when we get back to our room."

Leslie was glaring at her, her eyes red and streaming, but she waited while Sally thanked Slade, paid him another $100, and told him she'd be in touch, and she followed her mother up to the hotel room, where she collapsed in a sodden heap on one of the beds.

Sally stood over her, angry herself, tired, and aching from the day's fruitless vigil.

"Now listen, Leslie," she said, "you're grown and you can do as you please, stay here or go home. But you are not to act like a little jerk with me. I've spent nearly all the money I brought, and I can't stay longer. You do what you want."

She threw her toilet articles into her overnight bag, clicked it shut, and started for the door. Her face felt stiff and dirty, her hair needed combing, her teeth needed brushing, but she couldn't stay in that room another moment.

Leslie, suitcase in hand, was on the next elevator to the lobby.

"I'm sorry, Mama," she said humbly. Sally, paying the bill, shrugged. Pity, grief, pain, disappointment, and loss were all emotions she was too tired to feel. If she could just hold on, just keep herself from flying to pieces, until she could get back to Esperance.

The first twelve hours they were on the island Leslie slept. Sally found she couldn't sleep any longer than usual, as tired as she was. She got up at dawn and went down to the beach to swim. The water was calm and warm and the rising sun already promised a hot day. She swam parallel to the beach for half an hour and then sat on a towel and waited for the sun to warm and dry her body.

Far out in the Gulf a shrimp boat was a black cutout on a sea of gold against a vermilion sky. An encampment of gulls stood lined up on a little spit of sand that ran out in the water, facing the east, silent and obeisant as white-robed Mohammedans at prayer, their snowy breast feathers stained rose by the morning light. A solitary sandpiper ran along the ocher edging of the last high tide's spent foam, its faint *tileet* cry almost musical.

Sally thought of her mother, who always enjoyed this time of day. She smiled to remember how often Angie quoted James Russell Lowell: "You've gut to git up airly/Ef you want to take in God."

Angie thought God took a hand in the most trivial concerns of His people, and if you did your duty and prayed faithfully things would come right for you. But she also had a thing about God's will which Sally found hard to reconcile. If you didn't get what you prayed and worked for, it was God's will and your duty to accept it. Angie talked a good "acceptance" fight, Sally thought, and then churned and sizzled with indignation and rebellion.

What would you do now, Angie, she asked the morning sky. Fight or accept?

Although at odd moments of the day and night since the twins had been taken she had prayed what Angie called "Oh-God-please-God" prayers, she had not, as her mother sometimes advocated, worn out her knees. She had not yet tried monastic prayer and fasting.

She rubbed reflectively at her wet shoulders with a sandy end of the towel. At the most heavily wooded point on the island, half a mile from the house, her grandfather had once projected a small chapel to be named for his wife, the first of the Sarahs. He had brought an architect all the way from Pensacola, and they had walked over the terrain and sketched a small gray-shingled building which would have clear glass windows looking out to sea on the sides and a modest rose window, circular and symmetrical, with fishes and seashells and marine plants worked out in stained glass over the pulpit.

Nothing had come of the plans. The fortunes of the family, even then, had been feast-and-famine capricious, here today, gone tomorrow, Sally thought.

Now she had an impulse to see Grandpa's chapel site. Stepping into her sneakers and shaking out the beach towel to wrap around her, she climbed the slope and plunged through a thicket of cedar and little gray clumps of rosemary, already loaded with blue flowers. Blackberry vines clawed at her bare ankles, and she had to stop and lift branches of myrtle and yaupon out of her way, skirting an occasional aged and weather-dwarfed pine with heavy twisted branches growing out of its base.

When she was a child she had clambered over these little pines like a monkey on a jungle gym, finding straight horizontal places convenient for seats, loops and whorls in the branches handy for swinging. Now Bunk and Bunny—no, she knew Bunk and Bunny didn't play in the beach pines, not any more.

She parted a green wall of young water oaks and junipers and stood at last on the chapel site. It was still a little clearing, its sand floor as white and even as a housewife's scrubbed kitchen. The tides didn't reach this high, even in hurricane weather, but the wind had etched little ridges and rows in the sand. Coons had embroidered it with their five-fingered baby hand prints, and there was a ribbonlike track where a snake had passed.

One old long-leaf yellow pine stood at the edge of the clearing, its base scarred with the herringbone cut of turpentiners who once worked the island, its top thinned and torn by storms. Still it lived and still it grew, Sally thought, placing her hand flat against the paperlike layers of brown bark, which seemed to glow purple in the early morning light.

She sat down on the sand, her back against the tree, and let the quiet envelop her. The waves on both the Gulf beach and the Sound beach were tranquil this morning, a whisper and a sigh. The wind was a light breath, no more, not enough to make the pines stir and sigh.

She found herself listening and waiting. *They that wait upon the Lord,* she said in her head, *shall renew their strength; they shall mount up with wings as eagles; they shall run, and not be weary . . . walk and not faint.*

She tried to pray, but when she found words they were the

scant uneloquent ones Angie had scorned: "Oh, God . . . please, God."

Nevertheless, she seemed to want to sit on, to keep her eyes closed, her mind empty. When at last she stood, she felt oddly refreshed. "Old tree," she whispered, patting the trunk against which she had leaned, "if you can make it, maybe I can."

Back at the house Leslie still slept, face down. Sally could see beneath the clinging layer of sheet that she slept naked, and she smiled to herself as she closed the door. She always wondered what sleepers in the buff did if their houses caught fire. Even on Esperance it would be unhandy to be left homeless on the beach in your birthday suit. Palmetto fronds, she decided; Leslie could weave a sarong of palmetto fronds.

She poured a cup of coffee, meaning to take it to a chair in the yard, but found herself full of energy, impatient to be doing things.

Angie had another theory—that if you did all you could to make the conditions right for what you wanted, it propelled you closer to your goal. She had an urgent desire to get the house ready for Bunk and Bunny's return.

The porch where they slept in summer was a winter mess, littered with blown leaves and sand and acorns that rattled eerily when the wind rolled them about on a dark night. She had long wanted to enclose the porch and make two additional year-round rooms. She walked around to the side of the house to look at it.

A wall across the middle and a few window sashes would do it—half of it a room with twin beds for Bunny and Say-Say, half bachelor quarters with twin beds for Bunk and Hank.

No, she thought, sipping her coffee and backing up to measure the porch with her eyes, with children you needed extra beds for spend-the-night company. She tried to see how more bed space could be achieved, but the best she could arrive at was room for one double bed and one single bed in each room. That wouldn't do. They'd fight over who got the double bed. Or, in certain perverse moods, they'd fight over who got the single bed. Identical twin beds, she decided, and sleeping bags on the floor, if need be.

She walked around the corner of the house, thinking, Organdy curtains for the girls' room and sailcloth for the boys? Or sailcloth for both? She'd have to talk to Leslie and Sarah and look in the stores. Unbleached domestic ruffles were really what she liked, but who opted for twelve-inch ruffles any more, and where did you get unbleached domestic?

Her eyes fell on the garden, and she walked toward it. Uncleared and unplanted so far this year. It was almost too late. She had missed new potatoes and delicate jadelike green peas. They always had them for Easter. She had not got in the corn and beans which Angie always planted on Good Friday.

She stood at the fence, planning. There were few weeds. The kelp cover took care of that. All she would have to do would be to pull up the dead stalks of last year's okra, corn, and tomatoes and part the blanket of kelp to receive this year's seeds. Because it was late she'd better buy tomato plants, she decided.

A jaybird darted, squawking, to run a cardinal out of the big fig tree. Figs, she thought, surprised, have come along while I was not looking, while I was thinking about something else. It must be time to tie strings to little foil plates and attach them, shining and spinning in the wind, to the fig-tree branches to frighten the birds away.

She put down her coffee cup and went to the kitchen to see if there were any foil plates left from last year. They never bought the frozen foods which supplied other people with plenty of foil plates. It would have melted in the crossing from the store. So they had to buy the plates themselves.

Somewhere she had seen some. The fig tree, an old weatherwise tree that must have been planted in Grandpa Sellars's time, was too close to the kitchen, scraping the roof and blotting out the light from one window. She had complained, but Angie insisted the tree had to be there.

"Fig trees," Angie said sententiously, "need to be near the house. They don't flourish if they don't have human company. They like the sound of talk and laughter. Even tears, if it comes to that."

I guess we've shed enough tears to water you, you old fool, Sally said to the tree, climbing barefoot into its branches with a handful of foil plates. And whindled and caterwauled enough to cure you of eavesdropping.

Her activity in the fig tree awakened Leslie, who came yawning and stretching to the back step, wearing her bathing suit and carrying a coffee cup.

154

"Whatcha doing, Mama?" she asked.

"Collecting stings and gummy stuff on my hide from this old tree," Sally said, trying to scrape a milky substance from one knee and scratching aimlessly at the nettlelike touch of its leaves on her shoulder.

"Better come with me and wash yourself in the Gulf," Leslie suggested.

Sally still wore her bathing suit. It had dried on her. She scrambled out of the tree and stepped into her sneakers. "Come on," she said.

All of them enjoyed swimming, and Leslie was the best swimmer in the family. She capered and plunged in the surf like a young dolphin and cut the waves with strong overhand strokes which carried her out to sea and back while Sally still treaded water close to shore.

"You know, Mama," Leslie said, spurting water out of her mouth and shaking it out of her ears. "I've been thinking what Angie used to tell us to do to get what we wanted. You remember, get the conditions right for receiving it? Didn't she say to do something every day toward your dream?"

Sally nodded, her chin in the water, her eyes savoring the coincidence.

"I've been thinking," Leslie went on. "I'm going to try for a good permanent job, one I can work at all my life, and save money and buy a house so when the twins come back they'll see we have a permanent home and they won't have to move every year or so. Always new schools or no schools, never making longtime friends! I'm going to work for permanence for them, if it kills me. I want them to know the people next door and the grocer and the man at the corner drugstore. We've been so"—she paused, seeking the word—"so fly-by-night. With Hal they'll always live like that."

"What you're planning, Les, would be good for them," Sally offered, turning to float on her back and squinting at the sky. "Sometimes we didn't have much, but you and Sarah always knew you had a home."

"We had a good home," Leslie said loyally. "And strong people to love us. I'm going to try to be like you and Angie, Mama, no more vacillating and fooling around and thinking just of myself and how I hurt. Tomorrow I start job-hunting, and I think I'll go back to church."

155

"Me too," said Sally, catching her resolution.

They swam along together to the beach, pausing on the sand a little while to shake themselves dry in the absence of towels, and then picked their way carefully over the broken shells to the path to the house.

"Mama," Leslie said out of silence, "I'm ashamed of the way I cut up in New Orleans, blaming you. It was bad enough about the children, but seeing that girl . . . I guess I just hadn't really believed that she existed until I saw her. I thought I'd die, and I wanted somebody else to be responsible for it."

She was quiet a moment, looking out to sea. Her blue eyes were filled with sadness.

"I never told anybody before, but Hal has terrible fears sometimes. He comes in, trembling and crying. He always clung to me. Just holding on to me made him feel better, he said. I was the only one who ever had understood him. Now"—her lips trembled—"I guess he clings to *her*. I guess *she* understands him."

Sally put an arm around her as they walked toward the make-shift outdoor shower, jury-rigged by the back door, and turned the faucet. "Always remember the canon rule of a matriarchy," she said, grinning. "And I guess we *are* a matriarchy, aren't we? *Never love the man more than the children!*"

Leslie caught the bus for Tallahassee the next morning, and Sally, having no business to keep her in the office, put a GONE TO LUNCH sign on the door and went to the lumberyard to price materials for the new bedrooms.

1973

"Hippies!" Sally said sadly.

"Hippies?" Angie asked with interest.

"That's what they think they are!" Sally sighed in irritation and disappointment.

She and Angie had been pleased the day Leslie phoned and

said, "Ma, do you want your prodigal daughter and son-in-law to come home?"

"You know I do," said Sally, "but how are you going to get out of the clutches of the law?"

"We went today and talked to the probation officer," Leslie explained. "They're going to transfer our record to Florida. Hal told them we have jobs and a home there. We're pretty sure we can find something. Mama, we're so homesick. I think I'll die if I don't see Bunk and Bunny soon!"

"How are you coming?" Sally asked, wondering if she had air fare.

"We're already at the bus station. We've got enough for tickets to Tally and maybe a hamburger at the New Orleans rest stop."

She sounded downright carefree, and Sally laughed and got the day and hour of their arrival and took Angie and the twins with her to the Tallahassee bus station to meet them.

"Everybody come back here for supper," Sarah said. "We'll have a 'welcome home' party."

But Hal and Leslie did not look partified when they stepped off the bus after the two-day ride. Sally had expected them to be tired and maybe dirty, but she hadn't expected them to be ragged and—well, *peculiar* looking. Hal, always beanpole thin, was now scrawny, and his huge jeans had been ostentatiously patched with pieces of an American flag. His blond hair, always so bright and clean, hung below his shoulders in greasy tendrils, matched by a great golden beard and an oxhorn mustache which, unlike his hair, was rusty looking. He wore a sweater with a torn pocket and a broad-brimmed felt hat with a beaded band around it.

Leslie's weight always fluctuated, and it had fluctuated upward. She looked enormous, Sally thought in amazement. Her long brown hair was pulled into a single plait that hung down the center of her back—a style Angie followed when she prepared for bed at night. The bones of her pretty face were hidden in folds of fat, and her normally slim ankles overflowed heavy Mexican sandals, which she wore on dirty bare feet.

The children were overjoyed to see them, but Sally was so disturbed she didn't want to stay for supper at Sarah's and be around them. She had to get away and try to figure out what had happened to them. She persuaded Angie to push for leaving early by saying she wanted to get across the Sound before dark.

Sarah had not been fooled. Henry was serving the others drinks so she followed her mother into the bathroom. Her smile was knowing. "You're getting the hell out, aren't you?" she asked.

"Oh, Sarah!" wailed Sally. "They look so awful. What's wrong? What happened?"

"Aw, Mother, don't be upset," Sarah said. "They met some flower children and it was catching. You know Les always has caught everything that was going."

"Fat and dirty," Sally said.

"Don't be like that," Sarah rebuked her. "You know at their poorest Leslie always gets her fattest. Bread and peanut butter."

"And beer," said Sally. "I know I smelled beer."

"Well, don't begrudge them a little beer," Sarah said soothingly. "Things apparently have been rough for them. Let us keep them here awhile. We can make room and Henry will help Hal find something to do. Les and I can diet together—I need it too—and maybe make some clothes. The kids always have fun together."

Sally paused in her distress to look at her older daughter. "Sarah, you are fat. Are you . . . ?"

"We-ell, it's a little more than fat," Sarah said. "It's a baby."

"Ah-h," said Sally, sitting on the rim of the tub. "Why didn't you tell us? How soon?"

"Thought I might wait and surprise you by handing the baby to you," said Sarah, grinning. "Five months to go."

"Angie, let's tell Angie!" cried Sally, the worry over Leslie and Hal suddenly pushed aside. "Oh, Sarah, I'm so glad! Let's have a girl this time, want to?"

"That's what Henry's ordered," said Sarah. "It's the only reason we'd want another one, with Hank ten years old."

In the end they stayed for supper and celebrated both the homecoming and the coming baby.

Later, when Sally tugged her mind back to Leslie and Hal, the little space of time made their appearance less shocking to her. Sarah was right. Leslie caught everything that was going. Always had. She had caught the Civil Rights movement when she was in high school and had wanted to run away and meet

Martin Luther King in Selma. Angie persuaded her that Dr. King needed her allowance more. She had been the first member of the family to vote for a black politician, even working for a while in the campaign headquarters of a would-be state senator. She had boycotted the Lucina drugstore, much to Sally's embarrassment since her bill there was past due, staging a one-woman protest march. She carried a placard which said UNFAIR TO BLACK PATRONS until Miss Myra Heath, who assisted Dr. Cawthon, the druggist, made her come in and have a chocolate soda and explained to her that they had been serving blacks at the soda fountain for years.

"It's all standup anyway, Leslie," Miss Myra had said. "Always has been. We don't have room for tables and booths. Nobody cares if blacks are served standing up. It's the sitting down that everybody's scared of."

Leslie felt that she was being conned but she couldn't figure out how. What Miss Myra said was true. It had been the sitting down that white racists raged about—and nobody ever sat down at Lucina Drug. She should have noticed that. She left feeling vaguely wrong and routed, despite her noble effort. She would have found something else to picket but about that time Hal had quit school in Tallahassee and arrived on the scene.

Then—Sally pursued the theme in her mind as she and Angie rode home—they had discovered marijuana. And caught it. Jail. And caught it.

"Hippies," Sally said aloud. "They've caught that now."

It did seem that they had. Hal was no longer interested in classical music and would not try out for the symphony. The pay was practically nonexistent, he pointed out, and they wanted you to rehearse all the time. Jazz bands were giving way to rock and roll and, although he professed to hate it, he joined a group in a nightclub for promised pay, which enabled them to rent an apartment.

They rented a big apartment in what had been a beautiful old house close to town. Sally remembered admiring the house when its original owners lived there. Now it was divided into so many apartments the handsome second-floor balcony, called a belvedere, had been walled up to make kitchens, and wherever there had been a porch there was now a kitchen and a bathroom. Leslie and Hal were lucky in that their apartment was the original living room, dining room, kitchen, servant's room, and bath—lovely big cool rooms with access to the spacious front hall with its marble fireplace, beautiful curving stairway, and parquet floor. Angie, going with Sally to see it and take them some groceries and sheets for a housewarming present, was excited about it.

"It's the prettiest place you've ever lived, honey," she said to Leslie. "Fine, fine rooms. You all must live up to it now by getting some elegant furniture for a change."

"Elegant—*us?*" Hal had said, laughing at her behind his luxuriant haymow beard.

"It *is* too fine for you," Angie agreed. "But, Hal, once in a while everybody needs something that's too fine for them."

They laughed at her as she walked around, planning brocade draperies at the windows and Grandpa Sellars's rosewood commode between them. They had no oriental rugs, unfortunately, but they must all keep their eyes open for garage sales and moving and estate sales. Not in Lucina; people didn't move much in Lucina. They lived with what they had and if, as sometimes happened, they had to die and leave it, it was likely to be plastic and chrome. No, they must look in Tallahassee, said Angie, and she and Sally would watch the papers for sales in Apalachicola, an old town down the coast with nice old houses and an aura of old money.

Sally felt cheered by her mother's enthusiasm, and they walked out the front door feeling optimistic, for a change, about Hal and Leslie's prospects. As they opened one of the handsome beveled plate-glass doors with its brass hardware, they almost stumbled on a body sprawled across the threshold.

Angie screamed but Sally, stepping over what looked like a bundle of dirty rags, knelt and turned it. It was a young man, foreign, Spanish-looking with a Fu Manchu mustache and beard that was thin and dark but oiled and neat-looking despite the dirt-encrusted face beneath it. His eyes were closed and he breathed shallowly, noisily.

"He's sick!" cried Sally as Hal and Leslie and the children rushed out. "Somebody call a doctor."

"Ah, Loco!" Leslie said merrily. "That's Loco. He's staying here with us. Hal, let's get him in."

"Stoned on hash," Hal said admiringly, hefting the inert body to his shoulder.

It was a small burden—Loco was a small man—and Hal carried him as far as the dining room before easing him down in a shadowy corner. Leslie brought a cushion for his head. They smiled on him benignly and saw Sally and Angie to the door again.

"You'll call a doctor?" Angie asked from the steps.

"Never!" Hal laughed. "They'd deport him. I think he's an undesirable alien or something. Undesirable anyhow."

"What?" Sally said sharply, turning around.

"Just kidding," said Hal. "Loco's okay. He'll sleep it off. He really prefers beer to hash if he can get it. Every time anybody leaves the house, old Loco calls, 'Bring *Meeler's!*'"

"Meeler's?" Angie was puzzled.

"Miller's," Hal translated.

They left, but their optimism had long since evaporated. "That corner where they put him," Angie brooded in the car. "That's where the petit-point love seat was to go."

Since they had no petit-point love seat, Sally knew it was merely Angie's way of writing finis to her house-fixing dream.

They did return with things for the apartment: a stove and refrigerator they bought at a house sale, some bedroom furniture for the children, who slept in sleeping bags on the floor, and an occasional load of groceries. But the neighborhood alarmed them. Its small business district had been taken over by macrame and leather shops and places that sold incense and books about Karma and nauseatingly scented candles that smelled of everything but wax. The sidewalks and curbstones were often littered with bodies that weren't dead but almost, and the police patrol made regular trips to pick them up.

The big house next door burned to the ground one night, and Leslie told them the police thought it was done by a motorcycle gang which had chain-whipped one of the tenants and left him to die on the floor. Contrary to their expectations, he had been able to crawl out and tell the police about them. But the cyclists were still around the neighborhood street corners, evil, mean-eyed characters who maimed the strange vacant-eyed young girls who followed them about and were called their "old ladies."

"Leslie, Hal, please move out of this neighborhood," Sally pleaded. "I'm so afraid something will happen to you all—especially the children."

For some reason, maybe because she had put in her oar, Sally decided, they lingered on there. Leslie had an ugly gash on her shoulder which became infected and refused to heal. She fell in the kitchen against a table corner, she said, when Sally brought ointments and fresh dressings for the sore.

Sarah found out about a day camp which would pick up and deliver the children and, relieved to have them out of the neighborhood at least part of the time, Sally provided the fees and took Bunk and Bunny shopping for shorts and sneakers and proper bathing suits to supplant the cut-offs they wore at Esperance.

The twins loved the day camp. It was their only chance at playmates their age in that neighborhood, so Sally, swinging past one day when she was in town, was surprised to find them at home by themselves, playing near the back steps.

"Why aren't you in camp?" Sally asked. "Are you sick or something?"

"Mom couldn't send us," Bunk said carefully. "She had to go to the hospital. Our father took her, and he hasn't come back yet."

"What's the matter with her?" Sally asked the question casually because she didn't want to frighten them.

"I think she tried to kill herself," Bunny said thoughtfully. "Something like that."

"Come with me to Aunt Sarah's," Sally said hastily. "She'll give you lunch and you can play with Hank, and I'll run by the hospital and see how your mommy is."

Hal was nowhere to be seen in the hospital corridors. A nurse told her he had been there but had gone. Sally paced the floor in an agony of anxiety and unreasoning anger. She was furious with Leslie and surprised at herself.

Of all the times when love and pity for her child welled up in her heart, this time, when Leslie might be near death, Sally was hating her with an unreasoning, unjustified hatred. Poor little Leslie, child of trouble, maybe it was all too much for her, she thought one moment.

And the next, How dare she? How dare she do this to me?

By the time the nurse came to tell her Mrs. Ellis was out of danger, Sally found herself half looking for a place to hide. Even in the urgent business of lifesaving it must be obvious to all of them that here was a woman who could hate her dying daughter.

Instead, the nurse smiled at her sympathetically and said they had gotten Leslie in time and pumped out the sleeping pills and she would pull through fine. They were concentrating now on keeping her awake.

"You can see her for a minute," the nurse said, opening the door.

Leslie was gray, mushroom colored. Her lips were bloodless and slack and her eyes kept closing as an aide and an orderly held her between them and relentlessly walked her up and down the limited space of the small room. Her bare feet had trouble with the floor, tripping over themselves, and the short rough hospital gown hiked up to show one thigh and slid off one shoulder.

Sally stopped them at the end of one of their laps to put her arms around Leslie, to kiss her clammy cheek, and, as if they didn't have their own ways of checking vital signs, to lay a hand on her forehead in motherhood's eternal gesture of checking for fever.

"Baby," she whispered. "You gon' be all right?"

"Yes, ma'am," Leslie answered over dry unmanageable lips, trying for a smile which was meant to be reassuring but came out sad and lopsided. "Where's Hal?"

"Around," said Sally. "I'll see if I can get him for you."

She had to go back to the apartment to find Hal. He had gone home and gone to bed.

"Do you know where the children are?" she demanded, accusingly, after she had awakened him.

"Out playing, I guess," he said vaguely.

"I took them to Sarah's," Sally said. "Do you know how Leslie is?"

"Oh!" said Hal, as if he'd just remembered it. "She swallowed some junk last night. This morning. I don't know when. Knocked her out. I had to take her to the hospital for a pump-out. She's okay."

If Sally had been angry with Leslie, she was in a rage at Hal. She wanted to slap him, kick him, shake him till his hay-mow beard jarred loose and smothered him.

"Do you know *why* she did it, Hal? What's so bad that Leslie wants to die?"

"Well, what's so good that she'd want to live?" countered Hal, shrugging.

In the end, Sally saw Leslie and the children home and went

back to Esperance no wiser than she had been and a lot wearier. She didn't tell Angie about it. The old woman had not been feeling well, and Sally knew that in addition to her own hideously contradictory emotions, Angie would suffer something worse. Angie firmly believed that suicide was the unpardonable sin.

SPRING 1977

Leslie thought she had found that lifetime job she had resolved to get. She worked in a defunct restaurant that a man Sarah and Henry knew had bought and was reopening. He didn't have much money, he told her. He was, in fact, squinching along trying to get the place opened, but if she would give him a hand he would pay her something now and make her a partner when the place started flourishing.

The pay was skinny and hard to collect, Leslie found, but she was patient. In her post as his right hand, she knew that the utilities and the restaurant-equipment people and the food suppliers were not getting their money much faster. Pete simply didn't have it. He paid one creditor part of a bill and then borrowed money back from him to pay somebody else.

"He has a good reputation," Leslie reported at Esperance on one of her rare weekends off. "People like him. Henry said he ran a popular place downtown. And when we get going, it'll be great. There isn't a breakfast-and-lunch place that's any good anywhere on that side of town, and there are a lot of factories and warehouses and big trucking lines over there. He gave me a free hand to fix it up. Mama, what do you think about blue checked gingham and red geraniums?"

"Absolutely reliable," Sally said.

Leslie had personally made the curtains and was going to build the flower boxes with the help of an old man who enjoyed the position of retainer and freeloader with the enterprise. He had slept in the restaurant building when it was closed, he told Pete, and he would make himself useful if Pete would let him stay on, sleeping on the floor in the little vestibule leading to the stockroom.

"Pete didn't want him," Leslie said, "but he couldn't bear to put him out. He bought him a cot and one of those cardboard triangles to hang from the ceiling over his bed to assure him harmony with the universe and a good life. I think our stew helps."

Leslie's interest in cooking and her skill had increased since Denton. It came, Sally knew, from necessity, a determination to take whatever she could get her hands on and turn it into something palatable. Fresh vegetables were generally cheaper than most commodities, and she had learned to cook them well. It was her idea to make Pete's Lunchbox famous for its vegetables and its hot breads. They hired a country woman as cook, and her experience lay in that direction.

"No greasy hamburgers, no cardboard-and-glue sandwiches for us," Leslie bragged. "Come by for eggplant Provençal and chicken and dumplings. If you're early enough you can have some of *my* hot biscuits and sausage. I'm breakfast cook, and then I'm hostess and cashier, and if Pete's not there I fence with the creditors."

Leslie had moved into a room in the apartment of a couple she knew who lived not far from the restaurant. Sally was relieved that she was busy and counted it surcease from the constant ache, the waiting and looking for the children. She herself had been happily occupied by helping a carpenter wall in the sleeping porch. It had been a slower job than she expected, but at last it was done: two rooms where there had been one big screened porch.

Sarah and the children came for weekends, Sarah to help make curtains and denim spreads for the boys' room, the children to act as advisers on the decor. Say-Say picked innumerable bouquets of dandelions and bitterweed and arranged them in bottles and cans on the table between her and Bunny's beds. Hank went fishing for the avowed purpose of catching a shark that could be mounted and stuffed and hung in his and Bunk's room.

"I think Leslie's doing better—calmer and easier—don't you?" Sally asked Sarah as they sewed together one afternoon.

Sarah had acquired some reading glasses and hadn't adjusted

to them yet. She peered at her mother owlishly and then pushed the glasses to her forehead.

"I think so," Sarah said, "and then I find her ducking out of the restaurant and hurrying to her room at mailtime, hoping for a letter from the children. She writes them less now than she did when she sat at a typewriter in an office all day. There isn't time at Pete's. But she gets off a lot of postcards and she's worried that she can't send them presents. She wants to, but Pete can't afford to pay her much yet."

Since they now had the address on St. Aloysius Street, Sally and Leslie had been sending letters and little packages to the children direct instead of addressing them in care of the Ellises in Virginia. Sally worried that they were not in school and sent books. She worried that they might not be getting enough to eat—Bunk did seem thinner, didn't he?—and put a few dollars in each letter. The visits of Hank and Say-Say should have helped, but instead they seemed to sharpen her memories of the missing twins.

"Can I play with Bunny's Barbie doll?" Say-Say asked.

Sally was surprised to hear herself saying sharply, "No, you may not!" Immediately she was sorry, and she hugged the little girl and said, "Come on. We'll play together. Would you like to make Barbie a new dress?"

She recognized, to her shame, that it was a precaution against damage or loss to Bunny's doll rather than a desire to play with Say-Say. She found herself jealously guarding the twins' things—the doll-house furnishings Bunny had been working on, the stuffed animals Angie had made for their beds when they were babies, Bunk's fishing tackle, his .22 rifle, the bird feeder he had made out of wire and a piece of driftwood and hung in the oak tree at the edge of the yard, where she could see it from the kitchen window.

On a little shelf by her bed there was a board on which Bunny had painted flowers and hearts and the crooked color-dripping legend I LOVE YOU. On the back she had painted LOVE BUNNY in red letters that descended drunkenly from the upper left-hand corner to the lower right-hand corner. Sally was appalled to find it had become one of her most precious possessions.

She was careful to hide it when Say-Say came so the little girl wouldn't touch it or take it outside.

166

What a fool you are, Sally reprimanded herself. You're becoming like one of those morbid characters who concentrate so hard on the dead they forget the living. She wouldn't have said it to Leslie—in fact, Sarah strongly advised her and Leslie not to get together and talk about the twins, for their own self-preservation—but sometimes she felt as if the twins were so finally and irrevocably gone they were dead to her.

She would mentally yank herself back to the living and plan an outing with Hank and Say-Say. Hank's fourteenth birthday came, and Sally took him to dinner, to a movie, and to shop for the best backpack they could find. The twins' birthday followed and Sally went overboard, sending a check for double the amount of the backpack and a box containing bathing suits, books, and candy.

She wrote a loving letter recalling the day of their birth and dwelling at length on what their brief lives had meant to her and dispatched it, feeling as self-conscious as a girl mailing a love letter. Was everything they sent Bunk and Bunny censored? She didn't know. She had been careful to write only what she didn't mind the Ellises and Hal reading and what she felt they would let through to the children.

Two weeks later, when she looked in her box in the little Lucina post office, she found a letter from New Orleans with her name and address slanted across the envelope in penciled printing. She grabbed it excitedly. Bunk and Bunny, no mistake!

A single sheet read: *Gran, Do not send us anything else. We do not love you. We do not need your money. We will not cash your check. You are on* her *side. Yours truly, Hope and Harold Ellis.*

Sally stumbled blindly on the curb leaving the post office and barely made it to her car before she burst into tears. A few days later the birthday package came back stamped AD-DRESSEE UNKNOWN.

For once Leslie was angry instead of hurt.

Sally had gone up to Sarah's, vowing to herself that she would say nothing about the letter and returned package but would simply comfort herself by being with people whom she loved and, most important now, who loved her.

Right away she showed Sarah the letter.

"Dictated by that jerk, Hal," Sarah said promptly. "Show

it to Les. She'll be here in a little while. She's going to spend the night."

Leslie was furious. "I'm not going to let him get away with it!" she cried. "The bastard, making Bunk and Bunny write you such a letter and then moving! I'm going to call his mother!"

"She'll hang up on you," Sarah predicted.

But Dorinda had not hung up fast enough. They heard Leslie say sweetly, "Dorinda, this is Leslie. How are you? . . . Look, I want you to get a message to Hal. Wait . . . I think you're entitled to hear this. If he doesn't let us know where the children are and *how* they are, I'm going to get the divorce—and *charge him with adultery!*"

Sarah pushed her glasses to her forehead, the better to enjoy the situation. "Right out of *The Scarlet Letter!*" She giggled. "We should tell Les nobody is shocked by adultery any more."

"I bet Dorinda is," Sally said softly.

And she must have been because Leslie was listening intently, waving her hand like a baton in rhythm to Dorinda's babbling and grinning at them triumphantly.

She hung up the phone and began mimicking Dorinda: " 'Oooooh, you can't do that . . . please don't do that! You'll ruin our good name!' She's going to get in touch with Hal and put a little pressure on him."

Sally had gone back to the island and Leslie was back in her room at the apartment of her friends, Asa and Maureen, when she got not one but five phone calls from Hal and the twins.

"I was so happy, so excited, Mama," Leslie said, sitting opposite Sally at her desk in the little office in Lucina. "I started laughing and crying to hear Bunk and Bunny's voices. But, Mama, they were hateful to me. They said why didn't I let them alone, they're happy with their father, and I must be crazy to think there's another woman living with them. Then Hal came on shouting and drunk and said some awful things, so awful I can't bear to tell you!"

Sally smiled faintly. "I don't think it can get much worse."

"He said you were a meddlesome old whore and I was worse, a murderer. He kept shouting, 'You killed my daughter! You killed Dodie!' I started crying so hard I had to hang up, and then he called back. He yelled, 'Why don't you kill yourself, *murderer!*' And Bunk and Bunny yelled, 'Yeah, go on and kill

168

yourself!' They said everybody would be happy if I did."

Leslie was dry-eyed and calm.

"I'm glad you didn't take their advice," Sally said dryly.

Leslie nodded. "There was a time when I would have considered it, but they poured it on too thick. They kept calling back, and all of them shouted obscenities at me. I went to bed, and the next time the phone rang Asa answered it. When I got there Hal said, 'Ah, that's the man you're sleeping with now!' I tried to explain that he and his wife were both there and that I just rented a room from them. And he said, 'Well, I'm glad you're at least honest enough to admit it.' I said, 'Hal, stop hassling me. I know what you're doing. The children are there and you're talking for their benefit.' He laughed and said, 'Ah, you admit you're a whore!' I hung up again and then took the receiver off the hook. Asa and Maureen were tired of hearing the phone ringing anyhow."

Sally was surprised that Leslie was calm and steady and surprised that she herself could hear it all and sit there and take it.

After a time, she decided, things lost their shock value. Obscenities and hateful cruel talk from the twins were so terrible, so unbelievable, she couldn't feel anything at all. She felt drained and, oddly enough, sleepy. Wouldn't it be funny, she thought irrelevantly, if we all did what Bunk did when he was little and found himself outweighed and outmatched? Wouldn't it be funny if we just blacked out? She thought it highly possible that she would black out now.

"What are you going to do?" she asked.

"I'm going back to New Orleans," Leslie said. "Maureen is going with me. Sam Slade called last night and suggested that I come back. He 'has information,' as he puts it, that Bunk is on dope. And, Mama, from the way Bunk acted on the phone the other night, I believe him."

The drowsiness, the numb non-feeling were gone. Sally felt as if an electric shock had traveled through her body. "I can't believe it . . . they wouldn't . . ." she faltered.

"If they wanted to, they could. All Hal's friends do it. It's easy to get. Slade thinks he knows where they moved, and he's going to try something different this time. Lee Lambert got a court order giving me custody. She says a Tallahassee order is worthless in New Orleans, but Hal won't know that

169

and Sam Slade is going to serve it on him. By the time he finds out he's been had, Maureen will have put the children and me on a plane for home."

"Have you enough money?"

Leslie nodded. Sally thought she saw the color rise in her cheeks.

"Pete," she said. "He's broke but he has borrowing power. He went to the bank and got a chunk for me. He's going to be at the airport to get us when the children and I come home. He knows how I feel. He had a little girl once, who died. He and his wife are divorced, but he still grieves for their daughter."

Poor Pete, Sally thought, poor us. Poor everybody. She followed Leslie to the door and saw her off one more time.

1974

That promise she had thought she extracted from Leslie and Hal about never touching drugs again became a bitter joke to Sally.

After a few months in the old house among hippies and bikers, they moved—and then they moved again and again, to a suburban neighborhood, to another seedy apartment in a crumbling old building downtown, and finally to a slightly improved neighborhood on a street with well-kept yards, beautiful old trees, and one of the better city grammar schools within walking distance. In each place they seemed surrounded by the same ragtag crew of friends—Loco, the Spaniard, with his taste for "Meeler's" and a propensity for getting stoned on hash; unemployed musicians; and odd assorted couples who seemed to have loose marital ties, if any.

They all looked dirty to Sally, although she knew for a fact that most of them made a fetish of cleanliness, just as they were fanatical about health foods and exercise and filling their fetid-smelling apartments with houseplants, weird psychedelic posters, and astrological artifacts. Surprisingly, most of them had children, and Leslie spoke lovingly of little ones with names like Fayta, Estir, and Soledad.

Sarah, whose taste in friends ran to chic young women who served as docents at the art museum, took courses at the university, and labored for the Junior League, found most of her sister's friends either wildly funny or completely distasteful.

"Les thinks they're 'far out,' too," Sarah told Sally, "but she's loyal to them. You've heard of the Acid Widow? She takes up with musicians and every time one of them gets busted, as Leslie so poetically puts it, for heroin or something, she gets herself another 'old man.' She's a pretty child, talks with a lisp, and has a little boy who wears his hair in pigtails. She's a religious fanatic. Church of God, I think. I asked her how she reconciled her religious beliefs to so much sleeping around, and she got all wide-eyed and said sweetly, 'Why, Tharah, the good Lord Himthelf made me horny!' "

Sally shuddered. "What does Leslie see in her?"

"Oh, you know Les. Loves evvabody. I can see why she finds it diverting to be in such a crowd. Hal's gone a lot, and she gets lonesome. But I declare I wouldn't want some of them around. One couple sold her a water bed, and they miss it so much they keep coming over to Leslie's to 'sleep' on it."

"Dear God," groaned Sally, shocked.

"Somehow that doesn't shock me as much as the one—Luene, I think—who sits on Les's front steps with her boobs hanging out, nursing her baby. I had to climb over her to get in the front door one day, and I said, 'Do you *have* to be doing that?' Meaning, of course, right there in the public gaze. And she said, 'Oh, yes! We can't afford goat's milk any more.' "

Sally laughed helplessly. "If Hal's working as much as you say, maybe they will move again and make some new friends of a more conventional cut," she said. "You know. Respectable, dull people."

"I didn't say Hal's *working*, Mother," Sarah said. "I said he's gone a lot. He may be working or he may not, but he's gone. Latest thing is that he's hitchhiking to a commune in New Mexico."

"Ah," sighed Sally, "maybe he *will* find himself this time. I never saw a boy with a more mislaid self."

"You can say that again," said Sarah, grinning. But she was immediately sober. "Mother, Les is sick. Bad sick. I don't know if it's alcohol or drugs or if there's something organically wrong. She wants some psychological counseling, she told me the other

171

day, but she's got a thyroid tumor, and I wonder if that could be her trouble. I can't believe Les is nuts, even if she does act that way sometimes."

Sally was already on her feet, headed for the telephone. "I'm going to call a doctor and get Leslie and take her to him. Drugs, drink, a tumor . . . oh, Sarah!" And she began to cry.

But Leslie insisted on going to a free clinic. She had made an appointment, she told her mother, and she did not intend for Sally to spend any more money on her.

Sally should have been relieved, because real estate had been slow and her reserve, never large, was at an all-time low. Still, nobody in their family had ever taken charity. If they couldn't pay their way, they hadn't gone. She considered it not just a blot against the family for Leslie to go to a charity hospital but the beginning of a downward trend for them all. Once you take charity, she thought despairingly, once you let the taxpayers take care of your own, you were done for.

"Superstition, Mother, pure superstition," Sarah said crisply.

"Besides," Leslie, big-eyed and listless, put in, "we've been getting commodities. Flour and meal and welfare beans and dried eggs. Everybody does it. Everybody in our building goes to the food depot once a month."

Sally felt wiped out, robbed, stripped of what she had valued all her life. She sat on the floor beside the waterbed where Leslie lay and looked at her hands: red and rough and calloused from handling the boat and working in the garden and scrubbing and cleaning. Ugly hands, she had always thought, but they can manage, they can *do*. Obviously, they hadn't done enough. Her children were on welfare.

What I lost, she thought tiredly, was not stolen. I threw it away myself. I should have managed better.

Hal left for the commune in New Mexico the day Leslie checked in the hospital for a thyroid operation. The children went home with Sarah, whose own baby was due momentarily.

Looking around the apartment, Sally decided to give it a cleaning.

At the end of the day she surveyed her handiwork. The place looked bare but clean. It smelled of soap and Clorox and Lysol and lye water.

She would bring some flowers and some fruit and a bottle of sherry to welcome Leslie home, she decided, and the minute

172

the girl recovered from the thyroid operation she was going to check out the state's psychiatric services. Anybody who lived the way Leslie had been living must need help.

Leslie was grateful for the cleanup job, pleased with the flowers and fruit and wine, but wan and subdued. She was quietly appreciative of the new nightgowns and housecoat Sarah had brought and happy to have the children home, with new clothes their Aunt Sarah had bought them and new adventures to report. But she seemed draggy and spiritless, and finally she explained why.

"We're going to have to give up this apartment and find something smaller," she said in a low tone so the children couldn't hear her. "I don't think Hal is coming back. I've got to get well and get a job. There's a smaller apartment in the building next door. I think I'll try to get it."

"What makes you think Hal's not coming back?" Sally asked.

"He wrote that he might not," Leslie said, turning her face to the window to hide the fact that she was crying. "He says he has found happiness in New Mexico."

"Oh, for God's sake!" snapped Sally. "He better get back here and 'find happiness' supporting his wife and children! Hal's got to where he talks and thinks in song titles. 'Found happiness'—oh, my God!"

"You don't understand him, Mama, you never have," Leslie said defensively. "He's a good person. What's so bad about wanting to be happy?"

Sally stood up. "I'd better go. I'll talk to you later. We'll go to the shrink as soon as you're able."

Two weeks later Sarah went to the hospital and produced the daintiest prettiest little newborn the family had ever had—a six-pound daughter who was named Sarah for her mother, her grandmother Sally, and her great-great grandmother Sellars, who was the first of them to live on Esperance.

Sally took Hank and the twins to stay on the island with Angie while she and Leslie cooked meals for Henry and made trips back and forth to the hospital to see Sarah and the baby.

"I'm the one who should be sent to the shrink," Sarah told them on one of their visits. "I deliberately set myself up for twelve more years of report cards and P.-T.A."

"Aw, this one is going to be a genius," crooned Leslie, holding the newborn baby. "She's going to make all As and be a comfort and a help to all of us, especially her Aunt Les."

Because Sarah was such a well-worn name in the family, they were running out of diminutives. Sarah deplored "little Sarah," and Sally wouldn't countenance "little Sally." Bunny finally came up with the nickname: "Say-Say."

As soon as Sarah and Say-Say were settled at home, Sally delivered Leslie to the state mental health facility at Fieldcrest. Although she was modern enough to value psychiatric care and mother enough to want Leslie to be well, no matter what, she found that the pleasant, low brick building with its sprawling modern wings, flower beds, and new magazines in the waiting room made her itchy and claustrophobic. Could it be, she thought wryly, that you couldn't trust a medical installation where they had this month's magazines?

They took Leslie off to fill out papers for voluntary admission and Sally waited, looking covertly at the other people who waited also. Were they there with their children? Was their problem drugs, alcohol, wandering husbands or wives? Or just a society that made people think their own happiness was of paramount importance? She leafed through magazines she didn't want to read and thought of Angie's favorite minister, an old man who preached that love was the summum bonum, the greatest good. Would that save us, she wondered, from having to build vast sprawling complexes like this to cure our children? If *we* had enough love, if *they* had enough love, if we all *gave* enough love?

She shook her head tiredly. She was weary of such maunderings and not really good at them. A simpler life was what she wanted and was geared to handle. Fishing, swimming, walking the island, a drink under a tree or by the fire at sundown, a good meal, a book to read—that's what she knew about, that's all she wanted. With an important exception—she wanted the people she loved within reach. There you go, she thought, as bad as Hal and most of his generation, thinking about your own happiness.

A young woman in a pastel pants suit put an end to that. She came out with a clipboard in her hand and invited Sally in to talk to the doctor about what she thought her daughter's difficulty was.

I don't know! Why ask me? Sally wanted to yell distractedly.

174

You be the doctor! Let me alone! But they didn't let her alone. There were two of them, a young man psychiatrist, who was on the staff, they explained, and an older woman, a German psychiatrist, who was visiting for the summer.

"Let's go back," they said again and again. And Sally, feeling naked and exposed and somehow responsible for everything crazy in the whole crazy world, went back.

Bob's death, when Leslie was a baby, seemed significant. Sarah, an older sister to grow up comparing oneself to, was something to think about. Sally had the feeling that nobody should ever have an older sister. Two women, a mother and a grandmother, bringing her up . . . dear God, it sounded sinister! Women-raised children . . . hadn't she read that it was sure to warp? Hal and the premarital pregnancy . . . what had been her attitude toward that? I would have beat my breast and howled in shame and self-pity, Sally admitted to herself (not to the doctors), if I hadn't been told about the pregnancy and the marriage at the exact same instant. The death of Dodie, the trauma of Bunk's narrow escape when he and Bunny were born. The uncertainty, the restless roving, the lack of a permanent home, a permanent job, the marijuana arrest in Texas, the attempted suicide, the welfare food, the thyroid operation, the unusually filthy apartment, Hal's departure.

"Split, did he?" the German doctor asked with a surprising grasp of American argot.

"How do you feel about Mr. Ellis, your daughter's husband?" the young man asked.

"I don't think the way I feel matters, do you?" Sally said. "She loves him, I'm sure. She'll tell you herself. What do you care how I feel?"

"Please say," directed the woman.

"He's attractive looking—or was until he got so skinny and obscured his face with a beard," Sally said. "He's a talented musician, and I think he probably loves Leslie and the children. You understand, to my generation a good husband is one who is faithful to his family and supports them."

"Ah, *ja!*" said the woman, beaming.

"Do you like him?" the male psychiatrist persisted.

Sally was tired and exasperated. How she felt about Hal was her own business, even if she knew, and she wasn't at all sure that she knew. She was disposed to like him because Leslie did, but how could you like somebody who left his sick wife and children to fend for themselves and went off to "find" himself?

"I really don't know," she finally said with as much candor as she could muster.

"Has he ever mistreated your daughter to your knowledge?" the young man asked.

Sally shook her head, wondering as she did if he had. The fall that left an infected cut on Leslie's shoulder which had been so slow to heal, the premature birth of the twins in Washington—she had nothing but feelings about these incidents, and she didn't want to tell these antiseptic strangers about her feelings. Let Leslie talk feelings. She was the patient.

Sally went home to the island wondering if that was really the case. We're all the patients, she decided, when one of us is suffering.

Leslie stayed in the mental health hospital for three weeks—a lovely restful time, she assured her mother and Sarah when they brought a picnic and all the children and spread out on a blanket under a tree for a visit. They had some sort of behavioral therapy which involved wearing a rubber band on her wrist and giving herself a healthy snap with it when she found she was thinking negative, depressing thoughts, feeling guilt and self-pity.

Sally thought better of the treatment when she heard that. It was pure Angie in modern dress: "Don't mope, quit that maundering, stop feeling sorry for yourself, get busy!" The next thing she expected to hear was that these modern therapists were saying wash your hair, take a walk, go to church, everything will be all right.

Whatever the treatment, Leslie seemed greatly improved. Her color was better, her eyes brighter, and she seemed slimmer and neater in her clothes. She had let her gnawed-to-the-quick fingernails grow and was considering putting polish on them.

When Leslie was ready to go home, Sally and Sarah took Angie and the children with them to get her, and on the way Angie left a crabmeat casserole in Leslie's refrigerator and a pan of homemade rolls ready for the oven.

When they got back to the apartment, Sarah walked into

the bedroom to put down her sister's suitcase. They heard her yell, "Hal! You scared me! What are you doing here?"

It was clear what Hal was doing. He was sitting in the middle of the freshly made bed, eating from the crab casserole with a spoon.

SUMMER 1977

Leslie and her friend Maureen came back from New Orleans trying to cheer themselves with good news–bad news jokes. The good news was that Sam Slade had been mistaken about Bunk's involvement with drugs. The bad news was that Hal and the children had moved again.

"I got to talking to Sam in his office," Leslie said, "and it struck me he might have made that up about Bunk. It was just a feeling, but I had it strong. He seems to want to keep the case active, keep us jumping—I don't know. I just felt he was lying. It had me so worried I went and called Don Gallé— you know, the nice lawyer. He took Maureen and me out for a drink, and when I told him about the drug thing he got busy right away. He has a brother on the narcotics squad at the police station, so he called him and told him about us and how scared we were about Bunk and Bunny. He had the St. Aloysius address and knew about the park and the policeman who said Bunk was homesick. Julian Gallé—Don's brother— took a day and a night to check it out, and he was very positive that Bunk had not had the remotest connection with pot when he was at the park. He even checked some kids who played with the twins in that next place they moved to—an apartment on Felicity Street. He says they would have known and would have told him. He's an old neighborhood boy. They didn't think it was true."

Sally let out a long sigh of relief. "I'm so glad you went," she said, "even if you didn't bring them back. What about Sam Slade and the court order?"

"Oh, he had the address on Felicity, and we went tooling over there at eight o'clock in the morning. I thought it might be helpful to get there when Hal was dead asleep and serve him the paper when he was coming up out of one of his comas. He wouldn't be alert enough to question it.

"We found the apartment number, all right, but we didn't have to knock on the door. It was standing open. They had split—maybe the night before. Everything was a mess, but there was no sign of them."

"How do you know they lived there at all?"

Leslie's face crumpled. "This."

She held out a book of O. Henry stories Sally had sent them after writing on the flyleaf: *For Bunk and Bunny. Love, Gran.*

"And this." She drew out of her bag a blouse Sally had made when they were assembling clothes Bunny would take with her to New Orleans last December.

Sally took the two left-behind rejects in her hands. An old book but she had loved it as a child, and when she found this copy in the dusty stock of a secondhand store she had thought of the twins away from home, not in school, needing something to read. The blouse was a cheerful red-and-blue plaid, nothing special. She'd found the material among Angie's sewing things and stitched it up fast one evening. But it had been becoming to Bunny.

Sally held it up and saw the child in it, her fair hair brushing the ruffled collar, her chest swelling under it. Now it had a ripped gap between sleeve and shoulder, a button missing.

She folded it and put it on the table beside her chair. "Maybe they want to divest themselves of all reminders of us," she said. "Did you see anything else?"

Leslie shook her head. "Nothing like that. It's a furnished apartment, and they left it a mess—dishes in the sink, bags of garbage and bottles all around, beds all ratty looking."

"Maybe Gayle Gunner didn't live there with them."

Leslie's face brightened. "I declare, Mama, I hadn't thought of that! A woman wouldn't have left a place so awful, would she?" Then she laughed sheepishly. "I guess I have, though. Plenty of times. You remember them, don't you?"

Sally got up to refill their coffee cups. "Let's remember no error in ourselves," she said. "You're a hard-working tidy-widy type now."

"I sure am," Leslie said, "and I better get on back to the restaurant. Pete will be swamped with work and sorry he lent me money for the trip." She amended that immediately. "No, he won't. He's good where it really counts, even if he is a tightwad sometimes."

Before she collected Maureen, who was sunning on a blanket on the beach, for the trip on to Tallahassee, she said, "Mama, we close the Lunchbox on Saturday and Sunday. Would you mind if I brought Pete down for the weekend?"

"The weekend? Not just for dinner or lunch or something?"

"Well, if that suits you better. He seems kind of lonesome and at loose ends when he's not killing himself working. I thought it might be a nice change for him to get in some swimming and fishing, and I'd like for you to meet him. He's been so good to give me the job—and then time off and money to go to New Orleans."

"Yes, he has," said Sally. "Bring him for all the time he can spare. Let me know when to expect you, and I'll be at the marina waiting."

Pete Gerikitas was the biggest, most cheerful, most relaxed man Sally thought she had ever seen.

She met him and Leslie at the dock, and as she shook his hand she had to tilt her head and look straight up to see his face.

"Bigger than a breadbox and also a Harlem Globetrotter," he said, acknowledging her surprise. "Six feet five and two hundred fifty pounds. Thirty-eight years old."

"Good!" cried Sally, laughing. "I'm very happy when my daughters bring home *big, old* men. I'm always taller and older than anybody we know."

"Sure 'nough?" said Pete. "You look little and young to me."

Laughing, they loaded his and Leslie's overnight bags into the boat, along with extra supplies Sally had bought.

He seemed to enjoy the ride to Esperance, sitting in the bow with Sally and asking questions about everything they passed: the other boats in the harbor, the buoys and the lighthouse, and the island itself. Sally shouted answers over the sound of the motor, and he nodded and smiled, his big swarthy face crinkling, his strong white teeth flashing.

He was eager and prompt to unload the boat himself, carrying the bags and boxes of groceries up the hill to the house. In the kitchen, getting out ice for drinks, Sally said, "He's nice, Leslie. I like him."

"He's off duty and minding his manners today," Leslie said as Pete staggered within earshot with his second load from the boat. "You should see how hard he works his poor hired hands."

Pete smiled down on Leslie, not touching her but standing close in the small crowded kitchen, his eyes so full of approval, so clearly appreciative of her, her looks, her little joke, that Sally turned away, embarrassed to be watching. Mister Rogers all over again, she thought. I like you as you are.

They shelled hot spicy shrimps and ate them with their drinks out under the trees, piling the shells on the sand for the garden. Sally went inside to broil flounders stuffed with crab meat and to make salad and heat the rolls. She couldn't hear what they were saying, but she could hear Leslie's voice and then a mighty, joyful whoop of laughter from Pete. What a wonderful thing a laughing man is, she thought, as she carried the food to the table on the porch and lit the candles.

Pete and Leslie were seldom alone during the whole week-end. They wanted Sally to join them in everything they did, walking over the island, swimming, sunning, or fishing. Pete wanted to see the family burial ground, and Sally went along to tell him about the few graves there under the live-oak trees. Leslie walked past Dodie's small grave without looking at it, and Sally followed her lead, saying nothing about the baby. The new loss was hard enough without dwelling on the old one. They talked about Grandpa and Grandma Sellars and Bob McMillan and an unknown fisherman whose body had washed up on the beach, all buried there. At last they stood before Angie's grave, with its small plain headstone reading:

ANGELINE SELLARS MARLOWE
1892–1976

"I wish I'd known her," Pete said. "Leslie makes her sound like quite a person."

"I was waiting for you to say 'a sweet lady,' " Sally said, smiling up at him. "Then Leslie and I both would have jumped down your throat."

"We sure would have," agreed Leslie. "Angie was so much better than sweet."

"I know," said Pete. "I have a grandmother in Savannah, ninety-two years old, and still the best Greek cook in this country. I'm going to take Leslie to meet her. She's a tough old gal, big for a Greek lady, and mean and funny, like your Angie, I imagine."

Sally looked at Leslie. Meeting the family, she thought. But she saw no signs that there was anything but a jolly working relationship, a thorny friendship, between them. They laughed a lot and insulted one another often, and Sally saw no handholding, no covert kisses. She tactfully closed the door to her bedroom at night but she was wakeful, and although she told herself it was tacky to listen, she did, and she didn't hear either Leslie or Pete stir from their rooms after their lights were out.

Pete announced at breakfast on Saturday that he was chef for Saturday night's dinner, and he and Leslie took the boat and went ashore early in the afternoon to shop for steaks. They toured the small business district of Lucina and the seafood docks at Hammerhead and came back with olive oil, wine, mushrooms, a vast amount of red meat, and, to Sally's chagrin, a gluey package containing squid.

"He's going to cook *that?*" she whispered to Leslie. "I wouldn't touch it with a ten-foot pole!"

"Trust him," said Leslie. "He can cook *anything* and it seems to turn out all right."

Squid marinated in olive oil, vermouth, and bay leaves and oregano out of Angie's little herb patch, then broiled in butter and wine and garnished with lemon and olives, turned out to be the best thing Sally ever tasted.

"And to think," she marveled blissfully as they swatted mosquitoes and ate beefsteak Florentine at a picnic table under the trees, "to think we throw squid back when we catch it in our nets!"

After coffee they picked up crab nets and gigs and lit a lantern and trudged over to the bay side to look for flounders. Pete was unacquainted with the West Florida custom of flounder-gigging at night, and he took to it delightedly, wading barefoot with surprising quietness in the shallow water at the edge of the beach and sending his pole with its sharp metal point into the light-blinded fish with deadly swiftness.

"More, more!" he cried greedily as he threw one shining, wriggling fish after another into the washtub which, fitted into

an inflated inner tube, floated along behind them at the end
of a rope.

"We've got more than we'll eat now," Leslie objected.

"No, no!" cried Pete. "What Sally cooked last night we must
repeat—exactly. And then vary and improvise. We cannot have
too much of this good thing!"

It had been a long time since a man acted so delighted with
her cooking, Sally thought. She found it a heady experience.
The weekend had moved fast and pleasantly, and she found
herself hating to see Leslie depart with this big, hungry, happy
man. He made their old house seem unique, a marvel of comfort and charm. He made the things she did daily seem novel
and full of adventure.

"Come again, Pete," Sally said, shaking his hand at the dock.
"Come often."

"As often as you and your daughter will ask me," he said
seriously.

Leslie asked him as often as their joint operation of the restaurant permitted them to be away together. Sometimes Pete
couldn't come and Leslie came alone. But when he did come
he fell in step with the family, Sarah and Henry and the children, when they were there, as if he'd known them all his
life.

If they were painting or caulking the skiff for shallow-water
fishing in the inlets and lagoons, Pete painted and caulked
with them. If they gathered sea greens for supper he gathered
the most, washed them meticulously, and thought of ways to
serve them besides Sally's standards in salad or boiled with
bacon. If they planned a picnic, Pete checked the larder and
thought of some delicacy he could produce to take along.

In appreciation, the Parkers decided one weekend to take
their boat on the long trip through the inland waterway to
show Pete Tarpon Springs, which his fellow Greeks had made
famous with their sponge-diving industry. He came back, quiet
and bemused by the Greeks he met and the stories he heard
of old triumphs and tragedies, of shipwrecks and festivals and
heroism.

The nights were getting cool now, and Sally lit the fire in
the fireplace after supper. The others were exhausted from
long hours on the water in the sun and wind and went to
bed. Sally, who had stayed behind to show real estate, sat up

late, nursing an after-dinner drink. Pete joined her.

For the first time he spoke of Bunk and Bunny. "The saddest thing in the world, maybe the most evil," he said, turning his glass in his hand and looking into the fire, "is to break up a family. I believe Leslie's children were brainwashed, and that is Old Testament wickedness which will cause the evildoer to burn in hell."

"Do you believe in hell, Pete?" Sally asked.

"Yes!" he said emphatically. "Either here or hereafter. You'll get it if you deserve it, and that man or those people, his parents, have done the worst thing I know of—turned children against their mother."

"In some ways Leslie might have asked for it," Sally said slowly. "She has said it herself, and sometimes I wonder."

"No one, no one turns against his mother!" Pete said. "Sometimes mothers make mistakes, sure. Sometimes they are weak, sometimes wicked. Sometimes they are fools and bores. But you show me a person who turns against his mother, and I'll show you a person without a shred of character."

"Oh, Pete." Sally sighed. "They were the most loving and loyal children in the world, Bunk and Bunny were. They never said a word against either of their parents. Never."

"Brainwashed," said Pete. "They have been brainwashed."

"I have thought and thought about the reason," Sally said after a silence. "I have worried that Leslie did things that she shouldn't. But a grandmother's different, you know. I never had to punish them or scold them or deny them something they wanted. I could love them and enjoy them and indulge them. As far as I can remember, I have never said a cross word to the twins—or to Hank and Say-Say either. It's been pure pleasure for me to do things for them, to have fun with them. And yet Bunk and Bunny have turned against me, too."

She told him about their letter: *We don't love you. We don't need your money. You are on* her *side.*

They were silent for a time. The log on the hearth stirred and fell apart. The wind had switched to the north and blew down the chimney, sending ashes fluttering on the hearth. It was going to be cold tomorrow.

"Time," Pete said gently. "Give 'em time, Sally. They will come around." He stood up and poured them more brandy from Angie's cut-glass decanter on the sideboard.

Sally, holding her glass, laughed shakily. "If they don't come around until after I'm dead, will you promise to run them away from the funeral? I'll have no need for a graveside reconciliation."

"A deal," said Pete, lifting his glass to hers.

Three nights later Leslie, calling over the marine telephone, said she was moving in with Pete.

"Leslie!" cried Sally, as upset to think of all the shortwave eavesdroppers as at the news itself. Automatically she added, "Over."

"Mama, listen," Leslie said. "You like Pete, you know you do. Over."

"I love Pete," Sally said. "But he's too good just to live with. Marry him. Over."

"I can't." Leslie laughed. "I'm not divorced. Over."

The telephone crackled and sputtered. Other voices took over. Sally, banging the cabinet with the palm of her hand, yelled, "Leslie! Leslie!"

The girl's voice came through, trembling with laughter.

"Call you tomorrow, Mama. Over and out."

Sally went off to bed thinking that of all the fool ways for a girl to tell her mother she planned to live in sin, shortwave radio, with everybody on the coast listening in, was the ultimate. But there was something poetic about breaking the news and then saying "Over and out." She plumped up her pillows and fell on them laughing.

1974

Hal came back from New Mexico caught up in a new dream, a new ambition. He was going to take a year off and study guitar.

The two girls and all the children were at Esperance for the weekend, and a radiant Leslie was telling their plans.

"There's this wonderful teacher who came to Tallahassee to work at the university years ago. He's really a composer and he doesn't teach any more, but he met Hal and heard

184

him play and he's absolutely carried away with his talent!"

"I knew it, I knew it!" Angie said triumphantly. "Hal *is* talented."

"So Hal is going to give up trombone and take up guitar and work with Rosho—he's Japanese, I think—for a year."

Angie valued music but she valued a living more. "How are you gon' pay rent and buy groceries?" she asked.

"That's the good part," said Leslie. "We've found this old house in the country which we can get free. It's out on the river in the midst of a whole bunch of land some developers have bought up to turn into a subdivision. We have friends who have been living in a little tenant house on the place, and they say the big old house is vacant now and they talked to the developer and he said we could live there just to keep the place from being burned down until they're ready to start subdividing. He thinks they might use it as an office then."

"I want to see it," said Angie. "Can you have a garden?"

"Ah, a wonderful garden!" said Leslie. "There's lots of land, big trees, a barn, and a beautiful sweep of pasture down to the river, where the biggest, blackest blackberries grow. You'll love it!"

"Until the garden is in, you'll have to eat," Angie said reflectively. "Something besides blackberries."

"We've got that figured out too," Leslie exulted. "Hal is going to collect unemployment. You can get that for weeks and weeks, you know. And by the time it runs out I'll have a job."

Sarah glanced anxiously at her mother. Having them on welfare almost did her in. How would she feel about unemployment?

Sally grinned at her reassuringly. "That's all right," she said. "Hal's entitled to it if he can't find work. And I guess he can't."

Sarah followed her to the kitchen, where she had started making sandwiches for the children to take down to the beach on a picnic.

"Lost again," she said mournfully.

Sally looked up from spreading peanut butter. "You mean Hal? Ah, he's going to find himself for sure this time, if they don't starve first."

Sally and her mother went to see the house in the country and to take Leslie some herb plants and flower seed for her

185

new yard. Fifty years before it had been the comfortable home of a prosperous cattle farmer, but dilapidation had long since taken over. The paint on its walls was a ghostly memory, its underpinnings had sagged, its windows had slipped catawhankers and lost a few panes, its roof leaked, its steps had dropped off, and so had sections of the porch which encircled it, but Sally could see why Leslie loved it. It was the kind of old house that could have made the cover of a magazine devoted to restoration if a millionaire with a regiment of carpenters, plumbers, and electricians had it.

Leslie and Hal probably didn't even own a hammer or a nail and they had no knowledge of how to make the pump in the well go, so they were hauling water from a filling station the day Sally and Angie visited. But an ancient magnolia tree perfumed the air from a corner of the yard, squirrels played chase in an enormous oak opposite it, and the twins were ecstatically introducing Hank to the barn, *their* barn.

Hal boosted Angie onto the stepless porch, and Sally seized a none-too-steady post and swung herself up. There were two big rooms across the front of the house, one already grandly christened the "music room" by Leslie, with a rented piano in it. Both rooms opened onto a hall with a stairway at one end running to the unfinished attic and doors opening to porches and an ell. There were three small rooms on that side and two big light ones—kitchen and dining room. The front rooms and the dining room had fireplaces, and Leslie planned to have a little wood and coal heater in the kitchen where a wood range once stood.

Beautiful big trees encircled the house and barn, and there was still a faint path leading through waist-high weeds in the garden spot to the privy.

"Oh, Angie, I can give you some wormwood plants," Leslie said, her glance calling attention to a little cheese crock filled with blue flowers and aromatic herbs in the center of her scrubbed kitchen table. She was glad to have something to share, and her grandmother knew it.

"Are you sure you have some to transplant?" Angie asked gratefully. "I've never been able to get seed to germinate in that sand, and wormwood is such a great herb to have. Repels fleas and moths, promotes digestion, prevents sickness—and if you can get enough of it you can make your own absinthe!"

"Aw, Angie!" laughed Leslie. "You say that about all herbs."

Angie nodded smugly. "Not the absinthe part. That's the only one I know that makes absinthe. Where did you get your start?"

"It was here," said Leslie. "There's a whole section back there in the garden that looks herby. I wish you would look at it and tell me what I should save. I don't know if the old-time owners who lived here planted herbs or if Auriole and Jason, the couple who lived here before us, did it. They left behind some cute things—that old primitive pine cupboard in the dining room and the Hoover kitchen cabinet out under the tree. It's so dirty I put it out there to scrub with lye water—when we get enough water."

"Did Auriole and Jason leave all the garbage?" asked Sally, looking at the old tires, automobile parts, plastic and paper, tin and glass spread over the back yard.

"They apologized for it," Leslie said, smiling. "Before they left for Canada they went down and told Ree and Ro to tell me they were sorry they didn't have time to clean up. They were in a big hurry. But I don't mind. It's going to be so much fun to get the yard pretty. There's a man who lives up on the highway who has a truck and will haul it all off for me for ten dollars. I'm going to hire him someday."

She looked anxious for a second, and then her face cleared and she said cheerfully, "I want you to meet Ree and Ro. They're characters. They've got the tenant house."

"They've got the names, too," said Angie.

"Aren't they funny?" Leslie giggled. "Ree's real name is Rita and Ro's real name is Roland, but they thought Ree and Ro were cute. She's pregnant, and whatever they have, boy or girl, they're going to call Ray."

"Oh, naturally," laughed Sally. "Ree, Ro, Ray."

After they had inspected the house and assured Leslie that a man with a plow could rid her garden of weeds and lay off the rows she needed for corn and beans and tomatoes, they walked down the hill past a little dirt road that wound through the pasture to a ramshackle tenant house at the edge of the pinewoods. It was the kind of little house Sally's heart went out to—southern saltbox, innocent of paint, its clay and rock chimney reared back a little from the side of the house like a disco dancer not wanting to touch his partner, two rooms

187

and a kitchen and three porches, one of them facing the river.

"Whoo—whooeee!" called Leslie, to warn them of approaching guests. "Ree-ee! Ro-oh! We're coming to see you!"

"Fine," said a masculine voice behind them, and they turned to see a scrawny, bearded young man walking out of the weeds buck naked. He was carrying a roll of toilet paper, but he made no effort to convert it to cover. Nor did he attempt to back into the covering vegetation.

"Ro," said Leslie, gulping, "this is my mother, Mrs. McMillan, my grandmother, Mrs. Marlowe, and you know my nephew, Hank Parker."

"I'm very glad to meet you," said Ro, stepping out into the road and walking along between Angie and Sally with perfect dignity. "Come on down to the house. Ree will brew us some herb tea."

Later, on the way home to Esperance, Angie and Sally had started laughing about it and had laughed so hard Sally had to pull over on the shoulder of the road. "What could you do? What could you say?" cried Angie, wiping her eyes.

Actually they said nothing but walked along the weedy path to the little house, where a pretty girl in a vast nightgown of a dress, made out of some dark cotton so dirty and faded it had no color, came out to meet them. She was barefoot, her hands filled with whole wheat dough.

"I'm baking bread and I have the kitchen so hot you couldn't stand the house," she said. "Let's sit out here. Mrs. Marlowe, you sit where you can lean your back against the wall," she said with gentle hospitality.

They all sat on the floor of the porch, and Ree and Ro disappeared into the house. He emerged in a moment wearing a pair of bib overalls with one gallus hitched over his shoulder, the other hanging down his back. Ree went back to her dough and came out in a few minutes, having washed her hands.

The grown-ups had been afraid to look at one another, afraid of bursting into laughter. The children had handled it by leaping off the porch and running toward the river, whooping and laughing as they ran.

Ree served them weedy-tasting herb tea in cracked cups and Ro walked them down the slope to inspect his garden, a ragged-looking patch of wondrously dark earth, heavily mulched and nurturing deep green rows of elegant-looking vegetables.

Angie, looking uneasily at the one gallus that held up his pants, nonetheless followed down the rows, asking questions and crying out in pleasure at a particularly fine clump of rhubarb.

"I cannot raise it on the island," she said. "And, oh, how I like it in pies!"

"You shall have some the minute I harvest it," said Ro with a courtly bow. "And now would you like some of my cash crop?" He pointed to a dark green stand of plants with finely cut palmate leaves.

"Well, yes," said Angie. "What is it?"

He grinned at her, showing surprisingly white even teeth in the slit between beard and mustache. "Mary Jane," he said. "Sweet Mary Jane."

"Well, now, that's one I'm not acquainted with," admitted Angie. "Does it have another name?"

"It sure does, Angie," said Leslie, walking up and putting an arm around her. "It's marijuana."

They all laughed at Angie's face. She gulped and stared at the fernlike leaves in horror.

"Young man, you ought to be spanked till your sitting-down place is raw!" she said angrily and stalked out of the garden. "You are a lawbreaker and a dangerous one. Girls, let's go!"

Sally and Leslie apologized to Ree, but Angie looked past her into the littered, junk-filled room, sniffed audibly, and walked out to the road. Ree and Ro followed along uneasily.

"Mrs. Marlowe," Ro said, "don't be mad at me. I just grow a little of the weed for my own use. I don't sell it. I don't want to get on the wrong side of Leslie and Hal's folks."

He was so earnest and humble Angie stopped in her tracks and looked at him again, somewhat mollified.

"Roland," she said. "That *is* your name—Roland—isn't it? Well, it's no skin off my nose if you grow, smoke, sell, or eat your dope. But I'm worried about my grandchildren and my great-grandchildren. They call you friend, and we're all known by the company we keep. I don't want them keeping company with lawbreakers and jailbirds. What do you do for a living?"

Hal had come out of the house to meet them, and he answered. "Ro plays drums, Angie. He's the best drummer in Florida."

Angie was clearly softening. "A drummer?"

She turned and walked on, and Sally was relieved to see that she was going to be peaceable.

"Come up after supper and let's have some music for Angie and Mama," Leslie said. "Moonlight tonight. We'll sit on the porch and have a concert. Angie plays piano."

"Okay," said Ro.

"You're coming now?" Hal said, pinning him down.

"Sure," said Ro. "Absolutely. Positively. Probably. I think."

Ro and Ree did not come, and Sally and Angie were relieved because they were ready to start home, but they incorporated Ro's answer into the family's vocabulary, using it every time they had a chance: "Sure. Absolutely. Positively. Probably. I think."

The house in the country seemed a happy place to Sally. Sometimes she recognized that she was caught up in the great American rural dream: Go back to the land and all will be well, even if you do have neighbors as naked and dirty as any wild tribesmen, growing marijuana next to their squash. Somehow the clean air, the river with its sandy bottom, the trees, and the good garden spot would nourish and strengthen the little family and imbue them with the stern, sustaining values of their pioneer predecessors. Upheld by this vision, Sally poured money out—$50 to get the garden plowed and turned, $10 to get the junk hauled off, $30 to a handyman from down the road who remembered that the old house used to have a working toilet and thought he might reconnect the one in one of the small rooms off the hall to a septic tank somewhere in the yard.

He couldn't.

She gave Leslie money to try to get the pump in the well operating and, because they were in the country, she visualized long happy hours with books. She bought the children a set of the *World Book Encyclopedia* which she found for sale at $500.

Ree and Ro had a pig they were raising to butcher when cold weather came, and they invited Hal and Leslie to "buy in."

190

"We'll never be able to use all that meat," Ro explained, although he had tapped the government's supply of free brochures on the killing and curing of hogs.

"Just think, all our own hams and pork chops," Bunk said earnestly. "I can help Ro a lot with that pig. We named him Heathcliff and I already take him our scraps."

"If we have any," giggled Bunny. "Mom cooks a lot of rice, and we almost always eat it right up."

Sally sent Leslie money to buy in on the pig and a sack of pig food besides.

The well pump was an old one and temperamental, even after the attentions of an electrician and a plumber. It would only work a few days and then quit again. The children were pleased to have their baths in the river, but Leslie found housecleaning difficult with only hauled water. Still, she persevered, and the house always seemed neat and attractive to Sally when she came up on an errand and stopped by on her way home.

One day she arrived with some clothes she had bought for the children and found Leslie struggling with a rotary-type mower she had found in the barn.

"I've got to get this grass cut," she said, nodding at the tall weeds in the yard. "Hal's parents are coming. You want to see what the twins are doing?"

Bunk and Bunny had rounded up cardboard and tin signs, painted over what they originally advertised, and were happily lettering WELCOME PA-PA AND 'RINDA.

Bunk stood off, paint brush in hand, looking critically at roses Bunny was adding to embellish the message.

"Beautiful!" cried Sally. "Where are you going to put them?"

"Up on the highway at the turnoff and then all along the road, so they'll know they're on course," said Bunk importantly. "I've got a hammer and some nails and I'm gon' start out early in the morning and get all the signs up. If I did it tonight somebody might steal them."

"You're right," Sally said solemnly. "You can't be too careful." She turned to Leslie. "Where are you going to put them to sleep?"

"Oh, we're giving them our bed," she said. "Hal and I will bunk with the twins. I need to get some things to feed them and some water and . . . Mama, could you lend me a few dollars?"

In the end they went shopping for sheets and towels and groceries and rounded up plastic bottles and milk jugs and filled them with water at the nearest filling station. Sally stayed long enough to help Leslie and the children put the new sheets on the guest bed and convert a little table into a washstand with a plastic dishpan, a milk jug of water, soap, towels, and a slop jar beside it. She and Bunny gathered black-eyed Susans for a bouquet for the guest-room mantel and put together an arrangement of green pine boughs to hide the ashes and soot in the fireplace. She was enjoying the project and would have stayed to help Leslie scrub the kitchen and start preparations for tomorrow's lunch but Hal came back from his guitar lesson in town, and although he said nothing to her, after an answering grunt when she greeted him, she had the uncomfortable feeling that she should be on her way.

The twins hugged and kissed her goodbye and rode to the end of the dirt road with her, again hugging and kissing her and thanking her for her help.

"Have a happy houseparty!" she called gaily, waving at them, her love for them suddenly rising up and making her clear her throat and blink her eyes. "Tell Pa-Pa and 'Rinda hello."

But Dorinda had not come and Hubert came, looked around, and checked into a motel in town.

Sarah had gone out to take a cake her mother-in-law baked for the visitors and had met Leslie and the children coming up from the river with soap and towels.

"He's going to take us out for dinner," Leslie said, nodding toward Hubert's car in the yard. "He's not exactly carried away with our country estate."

"Well, that was good of him," Sally said. "They needed a night out."

"They needed a lot more than that from him," Sarah said. "Encouragement and approval, for one thing. He always belittles anything they do. When they lived in Denton, Dorinda took one look at their house and burst into tears, howling like a banshee. Some of Les's friends at the college and her Head Start social-worker friends had knocked themselves out bringing their furniture over. They had the blank spaces filled up with plants, and a black friend of Leslie's brought fried chicken and sweet-potato pie she made specially. All Dorinda could do was wail, 'To think . . . to think that my child has come to this! You poor, poor things!' "

Hal's unemployment compensation checks ran out but he sat on, practicing the guitar. Leslie found a young fellow who had assembled a hippie building crew and signed on as a carpenter. At first they used her to haul lumber up to the scaffold, but she practiced hammering until she could drive a nail straight and true into a two-by-four. One week she took Bunk with her, and he made himself so useful he collected $20 on payday.

"I'm going to buy myself a twenty-two rifle, Gran," he said. "I been wanting one to hunt with in the woods."

"Doesn't your mother need your money for groceries?" Sally asked.

"Oh, no, ma'am," Leslie said quickly, making a face at Sally. "I'm making plenty, and Bunk worked awfully hard for that rifle. He's going to get it. The game he brings back will be a big help when winter comes."

Sally felt ashamed for having suggested that the boy give up his rifle for groceries. The old bread-and-meat mentality, she thought, in self-reproach. Leslie is much, much wiser than I am.

Leslie's garden, which she and the children had planted with such high hopes, produced a few beans and tomatoes and then Heathcliff, now a big hog, broke out of his pen and moved into it, rooting up everything that grew.

"That's all right," Sally said. "You'll pay him back when hog-killing time comes!"

The twins looked stricken. "Kill Heathcliff?" they cried together.

"I thought that was the original idea," Sally said, perplexed. "Isn't he your winter meat?"

"Not Heathcliff!" cried Bunny. "He's our friend!"

When the time came to kill Heathcliff, Leslie took the twins in to Sarah's so they would miss the traumatic slaughter. And then she herself couldn't bear to accept any of the meat.

Meanwhile, school had opened and Leslie had enrolled the twins in the consolidated county school five miles away. They would meet the school bus at the top of the hill so early in the morning that while daylight time prevailed it was still dark. Worried, Sally bought them flashlights.

The first day on the bus, bigger boys took their flashlights away. Bunk, bruised and bloody from fighting hopelessly to retrieve them, didn't explain why, and for a few days they walked to the bus stop in the dark.

Leslie, walking with them one morning, found out about the missing flashlights and bought them new ones, which they craftily used to get to the waiting place and then carefully hid in the bushes before the bus came.

Life at school must have been torture to the twins, although they said nothing about it except that the other children called them hippies.

"Are we truly hippies, Gran?" Bunny asked anxiously one day.

"I don't know what hippies are exactly," Sally said. "But you are wonderful, beautiful, and smart, and you don't have to worry a minute about what ignorant, ill-mannered children call you."

Shortly after that, Bunk came home with a note from the principal serving notice that he was going to whip him along with some other boys with whom he had been fighting. Bunk displayed a swollen and angry-looking toe, which he'd been nursing since he stumped it on a rock. Knowing it was sore, a boy had stomped on it, he said, and he had struck out at him.

Leslie promptly took the day off from carpentry, put on her only dress, and went to the school.

"Why, Mrs. Ellis, we believe that sparing the rod spoils the child," the principal told her.

"Did you find out why my son fought those boys?" Leslie asked softly.

"Aw, now, Mrs. Ellis, if you start trying to unravel boys' stories of who hit first and all that, you'd never have time for anything else. I make it a practice to whip all the boys—and girls—I catch fighting. No exceptions."

"I want you to look at my son's foot," Leslie persisted. "He has a very sore inflamed toe he's been limping on for a week. That bully knew it and stepped on it on purpose. Harold hit him in anger and pain, and two of the bully's friends jumped in. You're going to whip my son for that?"

"The law says I can, Mrs. Ellis, with proper notice to the parents and in the presence of another teacher."

"I won't have Harold whipped," Leslie said. "It's not fair, and I won't permit it."

"Then you will have to remove him from my school," said the principal.

There was another school, five miles in the other direction and across a county line. Leslie went that day and enrolled the twins there. It was a pretty new school on the edge of a suburban development, and Bunk and Bunny found friends among the other children and fell in love with their teachers. They lost the "hippie" tag because none of the children saw where they lived. The school bus did not pick them up.

"Mama, I've got to have a car!" Leslie told Sally desperately over the phone. "I lied to the principal of that school. I told her we live in her county but we wouldn't use the school bus because it was more convenient for me to bring the children to school. *Then* our old car quit!"

"Oh, honey," said Sally sadly. "The well is almost dry. Could you get anything for a hundred dollars?"

"Yes!" said Leslie. "These people we know who are friends of Ree's and Ro's have an old truck they'll sell for two hundred dollars. I can give them a hundred down and the rest when I make it."

The whole situation upset Sally so she couldn't speak of it to Angie. She wasn't sure Leslie was right to take the children out of the first school, although she saw red at the idea of anybody whipping good, obedient, eager-to-please little Bunk. And to do it unjustly was outrageous. But maybe an unjust principal and an undeserved whipping weren't as bad as the deception of being in a school they weren't entitled to attend and all the pressure of getting there and getting home again when their parents never had a decent car.

Sally closed the office and went to the bank to draw out her last $100 and take it to Leslie. They went together to get the truck, an old, flap-fendered vehicle with holes in its body but apparently a good functioning engine.

"It'll come in handy for my business," Leslie said blithely.

"House building?" Sally asked.

"Uh—no, we finished that house and everybody's out of work, temporarily. But I heard about an apartment-cleaning deal.

When contractors finish an apartment building they hire people to come in and sweep out the apartments and clean the kitchen cupboards and the bathroom fixtures and wash the windows. Easy work, easy pay."

The apartment-cleaning field had already been invaded by the pros, Leslie discovered. They moved in with a crew of black men and power cleaning equipment and could do an entire building while she worked on one apartment. Even so, she got an occasional job and worked at it diligently, until she found a less crowded field—old apartments in a decaying part of town.

"She's working for a slumlord now," Sarah reported to Sally, making a wry face. "I introduced her to a woman who owns about a dozen horrible old apartments where winos and prostitutes and welfare families move in and move out almost daily. Les swears she can clean them, but it's awful work—mattresses they've wet or had bowel movements on, nasty old stoves, roaches and rats."

Sally and Angie went in search of Leslie one day and found her and the children pulling a hideously stained and stinking mattress to the curb from a furnished apartment. She greeted them cheerfully and told the children to take a break.

"Why are they not in school?" Sally asked.

"Thrown out," said Leslie. "A sweet, butter-wouldn't-melt-in-her-mouth, blue-haired old biddy who said she was the 'visiting teacher,' which means truant officer, came to the house and looked us over like we were scum and then pointed out that we didn't live in the right county for the children to go to Lake Briar Wood school. She said we would have to take them out, and I said, 'Where will they go?' She said, 'That's your problem, isn't it, Mrs. Ellis?' So they're helping me—and doing an absolutely fantastic job, aren't you, kids?"

The twins smiled, but Sally thought Bunny's eyes were red and that she had been crying. She fished in her purse for some change and suggested that they go to a nearby store for drinks for everybody.

"Yes, *ma'am!*" chorused the twins and took off running.

"What's Bunny been crying about?" Sally asked.

"Mama, I've been so awful to her," Leslie said. "We do moving too, and they were helping me. There was a twenty-dollar mirror that was too heavy for Bun. I told her it was. But she wanted to be helpful and she grabbed it up anyway and dropped it on the sidewalk and broke it to pieces. I hollered at her and started crying and she's been crying too. It's so awful to make her feel rotten when she's trying so hard to help me. But Mama, twenty dollars! I was counting on it for the light bill."

"Can't the bill wait awhile?" asked Angie. "We're getting some money in a day or two. Your mother persuaded a rich Yankee that he needed a summer cottage on the bay."

"It's been waiting, Angie," Leslie said ruefully. "They cut off the lights days ago."

"Oh, Lordy," moaned Sally. "Then we'd better do something."

The children came back, carrying Cokes for their elders and drinking the ones they bought for themselves.

"Look at 'em," said Angie fondly. "Growing up so fast and changing. They no longer look at all alike. Bunny is getting taller, but Bunk will catch and pass her. Look at his big feet. Come on over here, Acre-Foot," she called to him. "I know a song about you:

> Acre-Foot Johnson toted U.S. Mail,
> In the State of Florida over a mighty rough trail."

A mighty rough trail is right, thought Sally, taking her drink and kissing the sweaty, dirty young faces.

Bunk was beaming at Angie. "Sing the rest of it," he pleaded.

"Let me see," said Angie. "It's an old piney-woods song Will McLean up near Sumatra used to pick and sing. I can't remember it all, but Acre-Foot was a mighty man, all right."

She sang:

> "He stood a little taller than a ti-ti tree,
> Had legs like a pine in the scrub countree.

"I'll try to think of the rest of it and teach it to you when you come to the island next time."

"We could go now!" Bunny said eagerly. "We're not in sch—" She stopped and looked at her mother.

"It's all right," Leslie said. "You can tell family. You can go if your daddy doesn't object. I think he was going to start teaching you all himself as soon as we finished this cleaning job. He's probably waiting at home for you now."

"Oh, boy," said Bunny, rolling her eyes.

"Oh, boy," echoed Bunk, clutching his stomach.

Angie went in and paid the light bill at the power-company office while Sally drove around the block.

"I had to give them a check for another deposit," the old woman said when she got back in the car.

"Ma, we got to stop this—" Sally began, and then she saw the twins' faces in the rearview mirror. They studiously looked out the window as if they were in some private impenetrable world of their own, and Sally hoped for their own protection they had such a retreat. Stop this? she thought. How silly. As long as I live I don't want to stop giving to these two.

The twins spent the weekend on the island and demonstrated to Sally and Angie the gardening skills they had acquired in the country. They pulled weeds and planted daffodils and helped Angie clear away the dead stalks of vegetables and haul them to the compost pile. One afternoon Bunny wanted to putter with doll furniture Angie was helping her make against some glorious future Christmas when she would get a doll house to put it in. Bunk was bored by the project and at loose ends.

"Let's you and me 'stalk the blue-eyed scallop,' Gran," he said, referring to the Euell Gibbons book which had fascinated him since Sally bought him a copy for his birthday.

"Oh, Bunk, I was planning to plant some four-o'clocks," said Sally. "I've had the tubers too long already, and I really want you all to have four-o'clocks to string someday. When I was a little girl they were all around the gallery of the hotel, and when the sun went down their blossoms opened all red and white and yellow and they smelled heavenly. I used to pick them and string them on long grass stalks and wear them for a lei around my neck."

Bunk always listened courteously when she talked, and Sally was grateful to him for hearing her four-o'clock reminiscence. "Did the storm get them?" he asked.

"I suppose," Sally said. "I haven't seem them in years. I remember them so happily, I've always intended for you all to enjoy them too."

"I'll help you," said Bunk. "I'll get the shovel." He was off running toward the toolshed.

Later, when the four-o'clock tubers were in the ground by the chimney corner, where the bushes, when they appeared, would miss some of the stronger winds, Bunk patted the sandy loam in place with the back of the shovel and then squatted down on the ground and finished with his hands.

"Why do you call them four-o'clocks?" he asked.

"Because they bloom at four o'clock," she said.

The sun was low in the west, and its last rays sent a nimbus of coppery light over the little boy. I hope I remember forever how he looks, squatting there, a golden child with earth on his hands and wonder in his eyes, Sally thought.

Hal did teach the children, every so often. Bunny wanted to learn to play the piano, and he started to teach her but found it hard to hear scales when he wanted to be playing himself. Bunk chose the guitar and his father worked with him patiently for a few days, and then they both let it slide. Hal liked best to play them songs to sing and have both children and Leslie join in.

To Sally's surprise the twins themselves elected to read the *World Book*. Bunk, stimulated by Euell Gibbons, was interested in what he called "our natural world," and when he had read all the encyclopedia had to offer about the sea, the forests, the deserts, and the rivers, he decided to start at A and read through Z.

When Sally heard it she relaxed a little about school. She had gone to a teacher in Lucina and asked for the names of books that sixth-graders were studying and then ordered them from a textbook company. There seemed to be a problem about an individual getting them, and Sally was worrying about that when Leslie called with the word that the truck had quit.

"I had to leave it by the roadside and walk home," she said. "Something fell out of the engine and everything just stopped. I went back and picked up this chunk of iron and it was still hot. A man came along and offered to help me, and I asked him if he could put that chunk back in. He laughed his head off. He said it was something called a camshaft and the truck would never run again. But he did promise to tell the next filling station he passed to come and get me and the truck. Nobody came, so I just walked on home. It was only a couple of miles."

At that point Leslie didn't know where the truck had got to. Hal went looking for it but it wasn't where she left it, and even if they had found it, they didn't have towing fees to pay the filling station. So they had given up on the truck.

Sally wondered if the state patrol might find it or, worse, come looking for them.

"I don't think so," Leslie said. "We never registered the title in our name."

It seemed just as well not to pursue the matter, but now Leslie needed more transportation if she was going to work. Sally worried unceasingly about that and about illness and accidents. She knew that country people had not had cars or telephones in days gone by and they weathered everything from diphtheria to snakebite to thunder and lightning. But they weren't her beloved Bunny and Bunk. Sarah would go, if they could reach her, but they would have to walk a mile to borrow a phone and then wait for her to come thirty miles.

Finally Sally drove into Tallahassee and asked Sarah to follow her to the house in the country. She had made up her mind to give Leslie and Hal her car.

"Mama, what will you do?" Sarah asked. And Leslie repeated the question.

"Do without until something breaks," Sally said. "Angie and I have the jeep and the boat, and I can catch the bus back to Lucina and walk anywhere I have to go."

Leslie accepted the car gratefully. Hal was practicing the guitar and did not come out of the "music room."

"How does Hal get to his lessons?" Sally asked.

"Oh, he's hitchhiked since I lost the truck," Leslie said. "He doesn't mind doing that."

Sally thought bitterly that it was decent of him not to mind hitchhiking to a music lesson when he couldn't hitchhike to a job. Why had they not expected him either to get transportation or to move his family where they didn't need transportation? It had been Leslie's problem and, as Leslie's mother and the twins' grandmother, she had had to solve it.

Not having a car in Lucina was really not much of an inconvenience as long as she didn't have real-estate prospects to haul places, Sally decided, and she felt better knowing that Leslie and the twins could get around. She rather enjoyed walking up from the marina to her office and then, before she boarded the *Wild Jelly* for the island, hitting the grocery store, the post office, and, occasionally, the liquor store. The walking was good for her, and, although she had not weighed herself, she knew from the fit of the waistband of her skirt that she was either losing weight or firming up.

She was walking along the main street one rainy morning, enjoying the sight of the rain on the harbor and the feel of it on the poncho she wore over her coat. Christmas was not too far away, and Angie had asked her to stop in the dry-goods store and pick up some wool for a sweater she was knitting for Say-Say. She got the wool and was passing the bank when Oliver Wilcox himself opened the door and called to her.

"Hi, Oliver," she said. "What's on your mind?"

"Come in a minute, Sally," he said. "Do you want some coffee?"

Sally shook off her poncho and left it by the door and followed him to his desk back of the railing. His secretary, old Miss Strong, had poured their coffee and retreated to her desk against the far wall when Oliver said, "Now, Sally, these checks you've been bouncing."

Sally was no stranger to "Returned for Insufficient Funds," but she knew she had none bouncing now. Because her balance was low, she had not written a check in weeks.

"We covered the first four or five, expecting you to come in," Oliver said. "But they kept coming, so my girls, not knowing what else to do, started returning them."

"Let me see them, the ones you paid," Sally said.

Oliver had them in his desk drawer, a tidy little sheaf of demands on the Bank of Lucina for $50, $40, $18.50, and $33. They were cashed at grocery stores, the signature, Sarah M. McMillan, unmistakably Leslie's handwriting imitating her mother's.

Sally sat there looking at them, unable to say anything. She knew Leslie must have been desperate, but suddenly she felt flattened out, defeated, before the onslaught of that family's needs. They'll have my bones and my blood yet, she thought wearily.

She handed the checks back to the banker. "I think I know what happened," she said, standing. "I'll make a deposit today. Thank you for calling me in, Oliver."

"Well, Sally, you know we're your friends. If there's anything we can do . . ."

"Yes," said Sally, "lend me five hundred dollars."

Oliver looked startled, but he reached for a loan form.

"No, make it a thousand," said Sally. "I've got to get some kind of car."

The vitality she had felt walking through the rain was gone. She wished for a car, any kind of car that she might crawl in and die. The walk back to her office seemed interminable, and when she was no more than in the door the phone started ringing.

It was the credit manager of a department store in Tallahassee, where she and Angie had had a charge account for as long as she could remember. "Something is going on here, Sally, that you might not know about," he said. "I looked into it when we noticed an unusual number of returns on your account. Somebody has been buying things at one of our stores and returning them for cash at another. I think"—he coughed apologetically—"we think it is one of your daughters."

"How much?" Sally asked wearily.

"It's two hundred forty-two dollars and fifty-eight cents precisely," he said.

"I'll be in tomorrow," Sally said, "and I thank you for calling me. You'd better close my account."

"Well, temporarily," he said. "Until we know where we stand."

I know where we stand, Sally thought: in the quicksand in Tate's Hell, and we're sinking fast.

She went home early and, to Angie's surprise, went right to bed, huddling under the covers, unable to get warm.

"You're coming down with something," Angie said worriedly. "I'm going to make you a hot lemonade and spike it with bourbon."

Sally drank it to please her mother, but she knew it solved nothing. She had to get into Tallahassee, she had to get out to the country. She had to do something fast.

The next day, feeling shaky and wan, she caught the bus to Tallahassee and called Sarah.

"It's perfectly terrible that that guy will sit up there playing the guitar and put Les through all this," Sarah cried. "She should have left him years ago, but instead she steals from you to feed him. You ought to have your car, Mother, and I'm going to get it for you."

"Can you do that?" Sally asked. "I've got to see the credit manager and . . . I don't know, I'm so tired."

"Go do your errands, Mother," Sarah said. "A boy who works for Henry is here, and I'll take him out to drive your car back. Say-Say enjoys going to Leslie's."

"Well—" Sally caught herself. She was about to say, Give them my love. I want my car but here's my love. Oh, God, I wish I didn't have anything in the world!

She was waiting at Sarah's when she returned without the car. She came up the steps, holding Say-Say's hand and looking pale and big-eyed from shock.

"Mother, Hal ran out on the porch with a shotgun and told us to get off his property!"

"Sarah, he did that to you? He wouldn't do that to you. It must have been what's-his-name, the boy you took to drive."

"He did see him first," Sarah said. "I let him out of the car, and I was collecting Say-Say and her stuff to go in and see them. I got out with Say-Say in my arms and there stood Hal on the porch yelling, 'Goddammit, I'll shoot you!' Mother, I think he might have. You know crazy things like that happen every day. I got back in the car, and we took off!"

"Lend me your car, Sarah, I'm going out there." Sally stood up, feeling her strength flowing back on wings of anger and alarm.

"Mother, take the sheriff with you!"

"Don't need him," Sally said. "He'd just get in the way. I've got to have a talk with Hal."

The sun was going down when she got to the old house, and as she pulled up beside the magnolia tree and parked she thought again what a pleasant old place it must have been before it started shedding its porches and sagging on its pillars. No light shone at any window yet; the electricity is probably off again, she thought.

Then she heard the guitar. She started toward the rock and board steps the children had built, and Bunk and Bunny saw her and came running toward her, screeching delightedly.

"Gran, Gran, we're glad to see you!"

I shouldn't stop, I'll lose my courage if I talk to these two, Sally thought. But she paused because they were hugging her and both talking at once. She listened and smiled and nodded, smoothing Bunk's hair with one hand, cupping the curve of Bunny's cheek with the other.

"Oh, Mama," Leslie called from the porch. "I didn't know you were here. Come in, you're just in time for supper."

"No, thank you," Sally said. "I want to talk to Hal."

"Here I am," Hal said from the door to the "music room." "What do you want to say to me?"

"I understand you have a shotgun," Sally began.

Suddenly Hal yelled at the children, "Get out! Get out! Don't stand there! Get the hell away from here!"

"Come on, children," Leslie said. "We'll go in the kitchen. You can start your supper."

Sally was surprised to see how swiftly they went. She looked after them, troubled. They were too quick, too edgy.

"Now, what about my shotgun?" Hal said, turning to her belligerently.

"It's dangerous, and to wave it around and threaten Sarah was unspeakable. What do you mean, doing such a thing? You could have killed her and Say-Say, not to mention a perfectly strange boy who only came to get my car."

"You can take your shitty car and get off my property!" Hal yelled, pushing his face so close to hers that she breathed fumes of beer—or something stronger.

"Hal, are you drinking?" Sally said.

"It's none of your goddamn business!" he shouted, waving his arms. "Get out of my house!"

It would have been too cheap and easy to say, Since when did it become *your* house? You're nothing but a freeloading squatter, here and in the entire world. But Sally thought it.

She watched him a minute in the fading light. His eyes looked wild and glazed with something, drink or dope. She should go. But she couldn't.

"Don't be silly," she said briskly, sitting down on the floor. "I've been thrown out of better places than this. Sit down and let's talk."

Hal glared at her, and then in the most awful, mincing, ladified tone he mimicked her. " 'I've been thrown out of better places than this.' You have, have you? Well, you can take your

204

middle-class mediocrity and stuff it! I know what you've always wanted. You've always wanted Leslie to have a *little brick ranch house and money in the bank!*" The words came out in a sickening falsetto.

"No, Hal," Sally began, striving for a reasonable, conciliatory tone. "I just want you all to have what you need and to be happy."

"*'I've been thrown out of better places than this!'* " he lisped again in a high voice.

Really impressed him, Sally thought. Aloud she said, "It's just an old expression, Hal. Nothing personal. Sit down."

"I'm going to tell you something, you finagling, manipulating old whore," he began, leaning over to shake his finger in her face.

I won't cry . . . I won't cry . . . I won't cry, Sally said to herself. I'll be damned if I let him make me cry.

"I'm going to have this year to study guitar," Hal went on, "and I mean it. If my wife wants to wait on tables to support me, fine. If she doesn't, she can shove off."

"She's not waiting on tables, Hal," Sally said. "She's not working at all. It's hard to, way out here in the country."

"She's working you," Hal taunted her. "That's best of all!"

"I'll go now," Sally said, standing up.

She stumbled on the makeshift steps and was in the car before she started crying. Leslie and the children were beside her in an instant.

"Mama, I'm sorry," Leslie whispered.

"Gran, you all right?" Bunk asked anxiously, leaning in the car and putting his shoulder next to hers.

"Fine," mumbled Sally starting the car. "See you all later."

Henry gave her a drink, and Say-Say sat in her lap, and Sarah gave her a wet washcloth to mop her face and some powder for her red nose.

"I'll say this for you, Mother, you really took care of everything," Sarah teased from the kitchen door. "Came back without car, shotgun, or a piece of their hide for robbing you!"

Sally made a face at her. "I didn't want Hal to think I was meddling," she said.

The next morning, before she could get herself dressed and head for the bus station, a sheriff's deputy was at the door with a warrant for her arrest for passing worthless checks. A nice old woman, operator of a little grocery store not far from Leslie's, had got back a $20 check and wanted blood. They had tracked Sally down through the Lucina bank, where everybody would know she might be at Sarah's.

"I'll go with you," Sarah said, her face white. "Let me get Henry too. Or a lawyer."

Sally shook her head. "This is Leslie's doing. She'll have to go with me. Lend me your car again."

The deputy was understanding. If she wanted to make the check good and pay the fees involved, well and good. She must just be sure to be at the courthouse before the end of the day.

The whole family was still sleeping when Sally drove back to the old house, and she was craven enough not to want to awaken Hal. She called softly at their bedroom window, and Leslie stirred and answered.

"Put on your clothes and wash your face," Sally directed. "You're coming with me."

"Where, Mama?" Leslie asked, coming out on the porch in an old cotton shift, her hair tumbled, her face rosy from sleep. "Where we going?"

"To jail," Sally said shortly.

"Oh, Mama!" The rosy smiling face crumpled. "The checks!"

"Get dressed and come on," Sally said.

"Are they gon' lock me up?" Leslie faltered.

"No. I don't know. We've got to see the sheriff. I've borrowed money to pay. But hurry, get dressed!"

Leslie emerged in jeans and an old shirt of Hal's, her shoes in her hands. Sally opened the door and said nothing until they were out on the main road.

"You know, Leslie, it's me, not you, they'll lock up for passing worthless checks. Unless I charge you with forgery."

Leslie was pale and silent, her eyes brimming with tears. "Mama, charge me. Charge me with forgery," she said. "I deserve it. I thought you might have lots of money and wouldn't mind. I didn't know you were broke too."

"Why did you do it, Leslie? Just tell me why."

"Food and utilities and gas and . . . oh, Mama, I can't tell you everything! Don't ask me."

206

Sally didn't ask her any more. And as she paid the check, and the fees totaling more than the amount of the check, she wondered why she hadn't asked. Maybe I don't want to know, she thought wearily.

FALL 1977

Sally felt guilty that she had no moral compunctions about Leslie's and Pete's "arrangement." She worried only that Hal would find out about it and use it against Leslie in a divorce suit.

"You were going to charge him with adultery, remember," she said. "Now—"

"Mama, do you know that in many states children can choose which parent they want to live with after they get to be fourteen years old? The twins are fourteen now, so all Hal has to do is pick the right state. He doesn't seem to have ties anywhere. He's free to skip."

They were sitting by the fire in the house on the island. Pete and Leslie tactfully slept in separate rooms when they visited Sally. Pete had gone to bed to read, he said. Sally soon realized it was to give her and Leslie a chance to have a mother-daughter talk.

"What we really came to tell you is that I have filed suit for a no-fault divorce," Leslie said. "Pete and I want to get married as soon as we can."

Sally looked at her, sitting on the hassock close to the hearth, her light hair pulled into a knot on top of her head, her face open and ardent in the firelight. The hunted, frantic look she had worn for so many years seemed to have disappeared.

"I'm glad, honey," she said, reaching for one of Leslie's hands.

"Not just because it would make an honest woman of me?" Leslie asked, grinning.

Sally shook her head. "That will be nice too. It will give

me something to brag about: 'My daughter is married to the finest man.' Instead of: 'Er . . . er, my daughter has a nice *friend*.' You know I love respectability. It makes things so much easier and simpler. But it seems to me that since you've known Pete you've grown up, become steadier and stronger. And happier. Naturally, I would like to see that continue."

"Me too," said Pete from the doorway.

They turned and looked at him, laughing. He came in wearing a short terry-cloth robe, which left yards of his long legs bare, and stopped behind Leslie and kissed the top of her head.

"Sally, I'm so absentminded," he said. "I came down here to ask your daughter's hand in marriage, but I got sleepy and forgot."

"Cad!" said Leslie.

"Just for that I wouldn't marry him," Sally said.

"Okay," said Pete, yawning. "Then I'll marry somebody else. You got any other daughters who need a good man?"

Sally laughed and stood up. "I guess we better get him sewed up before he gets away," she said to Leslie. "So I herewith give my permission and my blessing, Peter Gerikitas. And lacking a bottle of champagne to bust, would you join me in a glass of sherry?"

They sat a long time by the fire, making plans. Lee Lambert, the lawyer, thought the divorce could become final within thirty days if Hal didn't contest it. She had sent a copy of the petition to him in care of his parents. If he didn't respond, Leslie could make an affidavit that she didn't know where he was, and they would advertise in the newspaper for some days.

"The way it looks," Pete said, "we can make it to holy matrimony by Christmas."

"Do you know where you want to be married?" Sally asked.

Pete and Leslie looked at each other. "Here!" they said together.

"Oh, I wish Angie could be here!" Sally said by way of benediction.

Both Sally and Leslie wrote the twins about the suit for divorce, hearing nothing from them. Two months later, when it seemed that the divorce would indeed become final, they sent pictures of the family group at Thanksgiving, which included Pete, in one of their letters.

"He's a towering achievement, isn't he?" gloated Leslie, admiring the way Pete stood heads taller than anybody in the family. "I never thought I'd have such a man in my life, Mother. Do you know that despite his struggle to get the restaurant started he has *good credit?* He pays bills and has Master Charge and has never, never been evicted or had his lights cut off!"

"Aw, go on!" gibed Sally. "You gon' tell me next that he has hospital insurance and a car that runs, sees the dentist twice a year, and *pays* him!"

"It's true," said Leslie, beaming. "He's terribly broke right now, but he's got some kind of odd idea that it's *normal* to do those things." She put down the picture and stared out the window at the deep blue line of the Gulf against the horizon. "What will the children think? I know they'll like him when they meet him, but at this distance—whatever it is—they may hate me for getting married again. They hate me anyway, I guess, but they'll have a reason if I'm the first one to get married."

"Do you think they prefer their father's setup with Gayle Gunner?" Sally asked. "I ask because I don't really know."

"Isn't it funny?" Leslie said sadly. "We thought we knew them so well. We felt so close to them. Now we don't even know where they are, much less how they think or feel."

If anything cast a pall on the wedding it would be the twins—their absence, thinking of them, missing them, grieving for them. Pete's only close relative, his grandmother, was coming from Savannah, and of course Sarah and Henry and their children would be there.

Housecleaning, Sally looked at the rooms she had made for Bunk and Bunny. She and Leslie had given the twins the date of the wedding and offered to send plane fare if they would come. Leslie had written that she wanted them to stand up with her. Just in case they came, Sally was determined the rooms would look pretty for them, and she started casting about for Christmas decorations that would please them.

A small tree in each room, decorated with things they had made, shells with tiny manger scenes, an angel with wings made from angel-wing shells, little coquinas strung like popcorn. She brought out the stuffed animals that had been Bunny's and arranged them on her bed. She put up hooks to hold the fishing tackle that had been Bunk's, and arranged his Euell Gibbons books on the little shelf between the windows.

Every time any of the family talked on the phone, the first question was, "Have you heard from the twins?" And all the time Sally cursed herself for a fool. Hadn't they said, *We don't love you. We don't need you?* Neither she nor Leslie believed they meant it, but they had no evidence to the contrary.

Restlessly, Sally walked over the house to check it for company. Would Pete's grandmother like it? Would she be comfortable here? But all the time her eyes saw the missing children, Bunk sprawled on the floor in front of the fire, reading; Bunny on the window seat making use of the last light of day to check something Angie was teaching her to knit or embroider.

Where are they now? she thought in anguish. Are they hungry? Are they lonely or afraid?

She thought of the clothes Bunk was wearing, the day they saw him in New Orleans. She couldn't be sure, but they looked like clothes she had bought for him a year ago. Did they need new things? Old Acre-Foot, surely he had outgrown his sneakers? His good loafers she had bought him to wear to church were still in the closet, also outgrown by now, but she couldn't bear to give them away.

The house was all right, Sally decided, but she wasn't. She had to get out and walk or she'd be swamped. Angie gone, the twins gone. Angie had talked of dying often since her first heart attack, examining Peter Pan's theory that it would be "an awfully big adventure." Once in the midst of trouble Sally had suggested that it might be a relief to be free of earthly worries and Angie lightly agreed. Then she said, "No, that's the only scary part. I believe in hell, not Dante's fiery furnace but another kind—one where you can see the people you love suffering or in need and you can't get to them to help them. That would be pure hell."

If the twins are suffering or in need, we can't even know about it, much less get to them, Sally thought. I'm already in hell. She stood on the point, looking at Bunk's "place."

The winter winds and rains should have unsettled the big slate slab which made a roof to the little boy's secret spot and filled and covered the stone catch basin in front of it. But it was unchanged except for the sneaker and hand prints. They were gone.

Sally had tied a scarf around her head, but she had forgotten her mittens, and the sharp north wind was chilling her. She knelt by the little pool and was surprised to find that the rock encasing it was warm to the touch. The wind didn't reach it, the sun did.

Make a wish, Bunk had said. And then, *I bet I know what you wished for, you wished for a flying sandbox.*

And I did, Sally thought. It's what we all wish for. Clumsy, earthbound, impotent, we wish to soar. We wish for the impossible, like unending love and luck and happiness. Like, Come home, Bunk and Bunny.

She stood up and turned away. Tears were pure self-indulgence, and she could not take time for them. If she cried she'd feel rotten, and if she felt rotten she wouldn't get the wedding cake baked. She turned down the slope and wiped her eyes fiercely.

Back at the house, she paused by the chimney to check the four-o'clocks. They had bloomed gaily all summer, but frost had done them in weeks ago. The sturdy green plants with their fragrant little carnival-colored cups were black and shriveled. They came back once, Sally thought, but will they come back again? Maybe as long as Bunk's "place" is still there, as long as the four-o'clocks come back, there is hope that Bunk and Bunny will return.

Mrs. Gerikitas was not the colorful old immigrant woman Sally had envisioned from Pete's description of her. She was, as he had said, big for a Greek but then the Greek blood in her had been diluted by generations of intermarriage with Irish and English and Swedes. She was a third-generation American; it was Pete's grandfather, whom she had married, who was straight from Athens. Her knowledge of Greek cookery had been handed down in the family and renewed on trips to visit her husband's family in Greece.

She was very old and very beautiful, her tall body well padded, well corseted, and elegantly covered in a superbly tailored powder-blue suit which exactly matched her eyes. She had, Sally decided, a settled grandeur, unassailable security.

She arrived with Leslie and Pete and the Parkers, walked slowly but without difficulty or help up the hill to the house, and inspected every room and the view from every window before she took off her fur coat and hat.

"It is always important to me to know where I am," she

211

said to Sally. "The prospect here is very beautiful, very peaceful."

"Sometimes it is not so peaceful," Sally admitted, pleased with the old woman. "We have severe storms occasionally. I have never had to leave the island before a storm, but my grandfather did a couple of times—ahead of high water. And of course we lost his hotel."

"Ah," the old woman said, smiling and nodding. "There is spice in a life lived by the Gulf of Mexico, I have always heard. Life without danger is very dull, isn't it?"

Hank and Say-Say were fascinated by Mrs. Gerikitas. The minute they hit the island they usually took off for the beach or the woods. But today they lingered beside the old woman's chair by the fireplace, listening.

"Pete said you would soon be a hundred years old," Hank said. "Did you know General Robert E. Lee?"

"Bobby?" the old lady said promptly. "Of course! He was a friend of my childhood. He fought a duel over me with . . . I forget his name. He was a lovely man!"

Hank thought she might be spoofing before Pete, rolling his eyes in mock despair, said, "Bobby, indeed! Grandmother, nobody ever had the nerve to call Robert E. Lee 'Bobby.' Besides he died before you were born."

"Really?" Mrs. Gerikitas smiled serenely.

"Who won the duel?" asked Hank.

"You know, I can't remember," the old lady said. "I'm sure it was Bobby. He was such a marvelous shot. All that time at West Point. He taught me to shoot, you know."

"He did?" yelped Hank. "Can you still do it? My cousin Bunk has a twenty-two rifle around here somewhere. We could go target shooting."

"Set it up," said Mrs. Gerikitas, accepting a cup of tea from Leslie and patting her arm. "I'm glad Peter has you," she said softly. "That last girl was a decorative disaster."

The wedding was on Christmas afternoon, small, just the family, but Sally was pleased with it and Leslie was ecstatic.

"I feel so bridey, Mama," she whispered, as she prepared to walk out of the bedroom to meet Pete and the minister in front of an improvised altar set before the bay windows and banked with winter-bronzed beach myrtle and red-berried yaupon and lit by tall white tapers. She had wanted to wear white but had been talked into a soft rose wool by Sarah who, to Sally's embarrassment, kept saying, "Try not to act so *virginal*, Les!"

There was champagne enough this time, Sally noted with satisfaction, and turkey sandwiches and wedding cake. The young couple took the *Wild Jelly* and left for Lucina at twilight. They were going somewhere plush for a one-night honeymoon, Leslie confided, "and then back to the restaurant to feed those truck drivers."

Henry had got a new camera for Christmas, and he took dozens of pictures, earmarking a complete set to send to the twins.

Oh, let them like the pictures, Sally prayed soundlessly. Let them see that their mother is happy and be glad.

1975

Sally went to the bank and changed the name on her account, angry and embarrassed that she had to do it. All the girls in Customer Service knew Leslie, and they guessed what had happened. Beyond anger was the fear that Leslie would really need to write a check on her, that the twins would be hurt or sick or Leslie herself would be desperate and not even have that resource, that frail bulwark against calamity. Nevertheless, she burned all her old checks which had Sarah M. McMillan on them and got new ones reading S. M. McMillan and then she took them to her office and locked them in her bottom desk drawer.

Almost as if she had heard Hal say his wife could wait on tables and support him or shove off (and Sally never knew how much of that night's wild babbling Leslie and the children *had* heard), Leslie got a job as a waitress at an old downtown restaurant. They rented by the week a little furnished apartment ten blocks away.

"We're going to keep the house in the country as our weekend place," Leslie reported cheerfully to her mother, as she exhibited their two-room apartment in a decaying old residence. "This is terrible, but we can escape to the country most weekends. The restaurant is closed on Sundays, so I'll be free after work on Saturday night and so will Hal. He has a good job now, playing in a band at a new place that's opening up."

The children showed their grandmother their allotted space in the apartment—and it was space, not rooms. Bunny had a cot in a windowless bit of hall leading to the bathroom. Bunk had a mattress on the floor of a closet under the stairs. There was a kitchen and a glassed-in sleeping porch which served as the master bedroom.

"It's okay," Bunk said. "I'm going to try to get a long extension cord and run a light in there. I don't like the dark much."

Leslie was rushing to get off to the restaurant, and Sally asked if she could take the children to a drive-in for a hamburger and a milkshake.

"They'd love it," Leslie said.

But Hal, who had been in the bathroom for the duration of her visit, emerged in time to say that they could not go. "There's food here for them," he said. "I want them to stay here."

The twins looked stricken but did not protest. They might argue with their mother and Sally, but she had never seen them argue with Hal. She had to approve his control, she told herself. A parent should speak, a child obey. And then she thought, What twaddle! A father has to earn his right to control, to direct, to rule, just as other people do. Hal is no biblical patriarch, no head of the house, good provider, or fountain of wisdom and authority, but a poor boy who never kept a job, never, in fact, did much of anything that he didn't want to do.

She left with a view of the twins standing on the sidewalk, sadly waving after her.

For once Angie was annoyed with Hal when Sally reported the little incident. "I wonder if there *was* food there," she mused. "Did you see anything?"

Sally shook her head. "I didn't look. But Leslie will probably bring home something, if there isn't."

Angie was interested in Leslie's job as a waitress. Unlike Sally, who worried that she was on her feet long hours and

214

then had to walk ten blocks home alone at midnight, Angie gloried in her granddaughter's ability to "do something, do anything" to keep her family afloat.

"Waitresses can make good money if they stick to it and develop a following," she said. "Leslie's smart and strong. Time was, before menfolks seized control of the world and made women think they should be taken care of, the women had power. They were the guardians of the spring, the planters of the orchard, the keepers of the sacred hearth fires."

"Yes, ma'am," Sally said meekly. Angie was a feminist and didn't know it, she thought, amused.

With two jobs in the family, Leslie and Hal might really be able to manage now, she thought. She would not have to worry. The children were in school again. All was going to be well with them at last.

It was a good thing she didn't have the Ellises to worry about, because Angie's health began to be a problem. She slept poorly, ate next to nothing, and finally admitted to Sally that she suffered an occasional bothersome pain in her chest. Dr. West in Lucina saw her and sent her to Tallahassee to the hospital for X-rays and tests.

Sally was at Sarah's, waiting out Angie's hospital sojourn, when the weather, which had been bright and warm, suddenly turned cold.

At noon it was cool enough for Sally to wonder if she should take a sweater with her to wear back from the hospital. By dinnertime a chill wind was blowing, and the temperature had dropped to near freezing. She had supper with Henry and Sarah and the children and was putting on her coat to go back to the hospital when she thought of Leslie.

"I bet she didn't take a coat to the restaurant," she said to Sarah. "I bet she doesn't even have a coat."

"Here," said Sarah. "Take her this old tweed. It's old but my favorite coat in the world, so tell her to take care of it. I want it back." She turned from the closet door. "Tell her to keep it, if she needs it."

It was the time of maximum rush at the restaurant, and Sally didn't plan to linger to speak to Leslie. She merely paused in the vestibule, murmured to the hostess that she was bringing her daughter a coat to wear home, and was about to turn it over to her when Leslie set down a heavy tray she was carrying and rushed over.

"Oh, Mama, thank you!" she said. "Can't you stay for dinner? I'll treat you—at my discount. Please stay."

Sally said she'd had dinner with the Parkers and was on her way to the hospital.

"Give Angie my love. Isn't there something I could send her? A little filet mignon, maybe? They do nice ones here."

Sally said she would get one another day, if Angie wanted it, but she thought the hospital dinner was probably more than Angie could eat now.

"Is she gon' be all right, Mama?" Leslie asked anxiously, following her mother to the door. "Can I do anything for her? I'm off in the mornings. Cold as it is, I guess I'd better try to get some jackets for the twins tomorrow. But I'll go by the hospital."

"She'd love to see you," Sally said. Feeling the proprietor's eyes upon them, she gave Leslie a little push. "Go back, your customers are getting impatient."

"Mama, thank you. I love you!" Leslie said and was gone, coat over her arm.

The next morning, worried that the twins might not have any jackets at all, Sally was at the curb when they came out of the house on their way to school. They were wearing sweaters.

"Come on, I'll give you a ride," she said. "The car's nice and warm."

She went straight to town and bought two puffy nylon and down jackets and was waiting for the children when they came out of school. On the way to the apartment she stopped at a drive-in for hamburgers. The children ate heartily and accepted seconds. She asked how they managed meals with their mother having to leave so early for the restaurant.

"We all cook," Bunk said proudly. "Our father can cook if there's anything in the house. Once in the country when Mom was away looking for a job he cooked us oatmeal for three days."

Bunny moaned dramatically. "Was it yucky! No milk, no sugar, just oatmeal."

216

"You were hungry!" Sally said, stricken. "Why didn't you call me or Aunt Sarah?"

"It was so cold," Bunny said. "Daddy didn't want to get out and walk in that weather to the nearest phone. We just stayed by the fire—or under the covers, when the wood ran out. It wasn't too bad."

"Now our mother brings us goodies from the restaurant when she comes home," Bunk said proudly. "How many kids do you know who have lobster for a midnight snack?"

"How *sumptuous!*" approved Sally automatically, her mind still on the three oatmeal days in the country. "Look, B and B," she said as she stopped to let them out in front of the apartment, "don't ever let things get bad for you all without calling me. Sometimes your daddy is too proud to ask, but you're my grandchildren and I want to look after you when you need it. Call now, remember? And if you can't get me, call Aunt Sarah. She loves you and she is close by."

"Aw, Gran, stop worrying!" cried Bunny, kissing her good-bye.

"We're okay," said Bunk, zipping his new red nylon jacket with glad fingers. "And you're the best grandmother in the whole world!"

Sally took a weak but greatly improved Angie home to the island. For a while she was too concerned about her mother's condition to leave her for more than an hour or two at a time. She went ashore to get supplies once a week and hurried back to Esperance. The days were bright but windy, and Sally kept a small fire on the hearth to take the chill off the house and give Angie something to sit by. Most days Angie moved from her bed to the rocking chair and back again, but one day Sally saw as she approached the dock that Angie was walking on the beach. Her red-sweatered figure, a little stooped and slow, stood out with picture-book clarity against the blinding white sand and the blue-green water. It was a typical view of her mother, Sally thought. All the years of her life she had seen her in many places, involved in many activities, but most typical was this—the bright dominant foreground figure in a seascape. Angie had prowled the beaches since she learned to walk, drawing sustenance from water and shore.

Sally docked the *Wild Jelly* and, leaving the groceries in

the bow, went down the beach to meet her mother. "What are you doing out here, Old Woman of the Sea?" she called.

Angie waved a green branch at her. "Forgot the sweet bay," she said.

"You mean you walked all the way up to the cove?" cried Sally. "Mama, that was too far!"

"Nothing to it," Angie said sturdily, although she had to stop and puff a little before beginning the climb to the house. "I got to thinking about the herbs I haven't dried for winter use, and I remembered there wasn't a bay leaf in the house for the holiday season. So I went by the woods road and came back by the beach."

"Angie, the cove is a mile away. Two miles round trip. That's pretty far for you to be walking."

"Well, send for the native bearers with the litter and hand me my smelling salts!" jeered Angie as she began the climb to the house. "I'm going to put some rosemary to dry, too, this afternoon. The fresh is nice but the dried is stronger." Sally watched her finish the climb to the front steps and went back to get the things out of the boat. She had reached the doorstep when Angie called out, "And another thing, I want you to get the children out here. I need some diggers for sassafras."

" 'Oh, willow, green willow,' " sang Sally, " 'let no one take your thyme.' "

"It's time with an 'i,' not an 'hy,' that I'm afraid of losing," Angie said dryly.

"Are you, Mama?" Sally asked gently, setting down the groceries and turning to her. "Do you think about dying?"

"Now and then," said Angie. "It's high time, when you're past eighty and there's a fellow in your chest at work with a fish scaler. It does come to mind now and then."

"Do you hurt now?" Sally asked, going closer and peering anxiously into her face.

"Not the sharp knifelike pains," Angie said. "Just those light grating whisks with the fish scaler."

"Mama, lie down," urged Sally. "I'll go for the doctor."

"I'll tell you when to go for the doctor," Angie said. "Now I'm thinking about making us a nice oyster stew for supper. While you were gone this afternoon, Bill Gordon put in here with a croker sack full of fine fat oysters, salty ones, fresh-tonged. I got him to open them, and now if you'll just step out to the garden and pull me up a few green onions . . ."

The long golden fall days went by, and Angie, savoring the weather and the flowers which came to the island with autumn, said no more about pain or dying. She spent hours sitting in a deck chair on the point, where she could see both the Gulf and the Sound, and long reaches of beach goldenrod and the little gray clumps of rosemary. Sometimes she had a bit of knitting or needlepoint in her hands, but more often they were empty, lying unaccustomedly idle in her lap.

Seeing her so, Sally worried that they should move into Lucina or up to Tallahassee where her mother would be closer to doctors and hospitals. She took the shortwave radio from the boat to have it checked over and put in reliable condition, and she went by the Marine Patrol office and had a talk with the men on duty, telling them that her mother was a heart patient and asking if they would respond promptly if she called them.

She said nothing of this to Angie except to ask if she would like to spend the winter months on the mainland. "We could see some shows and go to a few concerts and spend a little time with the children," she said.

Angie shook her head. "You go, daughter, if you want to. I like it here. I never seem to get enough of old Esperance."

Sally bought a car, secondhand but newer than most that she'd had, to make sure she had dependable transportation in case Angie needed it. But the old woman seemed to need nothing, and the little Volkswagen sat back of the marina except for short trips to the post office and the grocery store once a week.

Sarah and her two children came often on weekends, occasionally bringing Bunk and Bunny, who had news of great import.

"We moved, Gran, we moved!" Bunny whooped when she got off the boat on which Sarah had hitched them a ride.

"No more black hole for me!" Bunk said. "I got a room with windows!"

They explained that they had only meant to spend a week or two in the cramped little apartment, and a lady named Geneva, a guitar pupil of their father's, knew of this neat house they could get in a nice neighborhood close to their school.

"So Sunday night while our father was away somewhere rehearsing, we helped our mother move," Bunk explained. "Miss Louella let us borrow her station wagon, and we went to the country to get our furniture."

He stopped and looked at his twin, who gulped and looked away.

"It was terrible, Gran," he resumed after a pause. "Somebody got in and stole nearly everything. All our books—our *World Book* even—and all our toys. They didn't get our beds though. We lucked out there."

"Mom said . . . Mom said," faltered Bunny, "no use crying over spilt milk. But Gran, they tore down our barn. It was"—she was crying in earnest now— "it was the best place we ever lived!".

Sally hugged them and looked at Sarah. Oh, the blessed memory of children, she thought. That falling-down old house with no lights or water, no heat, and little food, and because it had a barn and a river it was "the best place we ever lived." She didn't have the heart to lament the loss of $500 worth of encyclopedia she had skimped to buy. At least it had not been a total loss. Because of their front-to-back reading in the books, they were not behind in school.

"Well, you have a good place to live now," she consoled them.

"Super," agreed the twins. Sally realized she had never heard them complain about or criticize any of the many seedy, down-at-the-heel places where they had been quartered for a year or two or a few months. She had no way of being sure what this one was.

She smiled over their gilt heads at Angie, who nodded her approbation. Angie valued loyalty in husbands and wives, but to find children who did not complain or find fault with their parents was the greatest gift of all.

"Your parents have done well by you," she said. "You are nice children."

Christmas was coming, and Sally hurried to do most of the preparations to keep Angie from exerting herself. The Parkers would be there, but Leslie was reluctant to make a commitment.

"Hal will probably have to work Christmas Eve and I will too. So we'll probably just stay at home. The kids are excited over having a big living room with a nice place to put up the Christmas tree—when we get one. Mama, when are you coming to town?"

There was an anxious note in her voice, and Sally made an immediate decision to visit. Angie had a shopping list for her and assured her that she was feeling well enough to be left alone; in fact, she would enjoy it. She had some jazz records Leslie had sent to listen to, and any number of mittens and scarves to finish up for Christmas.

The new place was a compact yellow-brick bungalow of 1930s vintage, ugly but comfortable, Sally thought, as she parked at the door. She knew without going in that beyond the front door, with its three little panes across the top, there would be a living room with narrow yellow oak flooring, a "tapestry" brick fireplace and a pseudo arch into the dining room. There would be counter space and a sink under three high windows in the kitchen, and a glass-enclosed sun parlor which Leslie would undoubtedly call the "music room," a term evoking Tudor mansions and pipe organs. This one would accommodate Hal's trombone, the amplifier, and maybe an electric piano, if he had been able to borrow one. The patch of front lawn was neat, the "foundation" shrubs dejected but resigned ligustrum and pittosporum, which contractors of the 30s must have bought in carload lots, from their prevalance in neighborhoods of that vintage. There would be a fenced back yard and a concrete-floored garage.

But praise the Lord, it has windows and a roof, Sally thought, picking up the basket of jellies and jams Angie had sent, and I bet Leslie is rhapsodic about it.

On the contrary, Leslie seemed subdued and downcast. Hal was still asleep, she said, and she wandered about the house watering the company of disconsolate house plants which she cherished and managed to take with her, no matter how often they moved or how uncongenial the environment for them. They froze in the country and Leslie doggedly watered and petted them back to life. They withered in the darkness of the last city apartment, and she stubbornly lugged them out to whatever patches of light she could find in the sour, shady back yard. Now she had them hanging in windows in intricate macrame contraptions of hairy rope. After she had greeted her mother and got her a cup of coffee, she went back to picking off yellowed leaves and training a trailing tendril of Wandering Jew upward.

"Well, you're all settled," Sally said. "The children seem to like the house, and I know you do."

"Oh, I love it," Leslie said, but without her usual enthusiasm. "Everybody has a room, and we even have a guest room if we can ever get it fixed up. Geneva Jarvis, who lives down the street, knows where we can get a mattress and box springs somebody's not using."

Sally smiled. Leslie always had friends with sources of house furnishings which they seemed glad to share.

"She's the one Hal's teaching guitar?" Sally said.

"Yes, ma'am," Leslie said tiredly. "She's his big fan. A jiggly fat girl who wears thick glasses and calls anything she likes 'groovy.' I shouldn't laugh at her. She got that box of Christmas decorations somewhere—Goodwill, Salvation Army, garage sale, I don't know which—and gave them to the twins. Bunny can't wait to get a tree."

"I should have brought them a pine or cedar from the island," Sally said. "Are you going to buy one?"

Leslie nodded. "If tips are any good tonight, I guess we'll look for one tomorrow."

"Do you want me to take the twins to buy one after school?" Sally asked. "I can do that and still get back to the point before dark, if I hurry."

"Mama, would you?" Leslie seemed near tears. "Hal's off right now and he might do it. But he really doesn't like Christmas much, and he gets depressed when the kids and I start getting excited over a tree and presents."

"Well, I could take them shopping for a little while," Sally said. "If it's all right," she added with a look toward the closed bedroom door.

"If you could"—Leslie gulped—"I sure would appreciate it. I have to go to the restaurant almost the minute they get home from school."

Sally stood up. "Sarah and I are going to have lunch and shop for Hank and Say-Say. Do you want to come with us?"

Leslie looked toward the closed door. "I can't, Mama. I'd love to but I can't."

Sally started toward the car and Leslie followed her. "What's wrong, baby?" she asked, turning to face Leslie.

"I'm pregnant!" Leslie blurted it out and then burst into tears.

Sally opened the car door. "Get in and let's talk a minute," she said, starting the engine. Leslie slumped in the seat, wiping her eyes with the sleeve of her housecoat.

"What are you crying about?" Sally said quickly. "This is good news! You love babies, you know you do. Don't be unhappy about this one."

To the windshield she said soundlessly, Oh, God, where am I going to get the rousing grandmotherly jubilation this calls for?

"I'd be happy," said Leslie, "but Hal's not, not a bit." She managed a weak smile. "He thinks it's one of my dirty tricks."

"We-ell," said Sally, "a lot of men feel that way—until the baby comes. Nobody can resist a little baby, you know that." You and I *say* that, she added to herself, but Hal's been able to resist them up to now.

She drove around the neighborhood, waiting for Leslie's inevitable return to Pollyanna anticipation.

"You feel all right?" she asked.

"Oh, tired," Leslie said, smiling wanly. "But I guess that's mental or something. I'd love a baby, Mama, I really would, but it's kind of the last straw right now. Hal hates babies . . . *and* Christmas!" She brought it out with a sob.

Sally laughed at the exaggeration, stopped the car, and strove for the crisp, no-nonsense approach she often counted on to save Leslie from sogginess.

"Listen," she said, "it doesn't matter a damn whether or not Hal hates babies and Christmas. Both are on the way, and there isn't a thing he can do about it. You just stop crying and let's relax and enjoy! When's the baby due?"

"Seven months," mumbled Leslie. And then, with a flash of her old humor, "Christmas in seven days."

Christmas arrived but the baby did not.

Leslie and the twins drove down to Esperance with Sarah and her two before the school holidays were over. She followed her mother to the kitchen and whispered, "I hope you didn't tell Angie I was pregnant, did you? Because I had . . . had a miscarriage."

"Oh, honey, I'm so sorry!" Sally said. "I did tell Angie to give her something to look forward to. But she can take it, if you can. Are you all right?"

"Fine now," Leslie said. "But I had to take off from work. All that standing and tromping around with trays was too much, the doctor said."

"Go lie on the sofa," Sally said. "I'll bring you a sherry." To herself she said, Don't be a hypocrite and grieve for a little one they never knew, never wanted, couldn't take care of. But she had to stand a minute, looking out at the water and waiting for the lump in her throat to dissipate. A baby, wanted or not, was precious, and its loss as real as any loss.

After lunch Angie went to her room for a nap, and Sarah took the children for a jeep ride to the other end of the island. Leslie helped with the dishes and returned to the sofa, where Sally assumed she too would nap. But when she went in the room to poke the fire, she saw Leslie's eyes were wide open and filled with the most unutterable sadness.

Oh, damn, she thought. She's getting it both ways. If she had the baby it was going to be hell, and now that she's lost it, it's hell.

"You need some cover?" she asked, for something to break the latch of pain on that still face.

"Mama," Leslie whispered, "it wasn't a miscarriage. I had an abortion."

"Oh, no!" gasped Sally, sagging onto the ottoman in front of the fire. "Leslie, how could you?" And then quickly, because she knew her beliefs were archaic and she was being after-the-fact cruel, she said, "Did you have to, honey?"

Leslie nodded. "I thought I did."

Sally stared into the fire. Abortion was considered a great boon to the public weal now. It was being made available to the poor and underprivileged like food stamps and vitamin pills. It was a right, like the vote and public toilets used to be. Young women who could afford it spoke of a trip to a chic abortion clinic the way rich girls used to speak of divorce in Reno—an agreeable way of handling an unpleasant situation.

224

"Was it bad?" she asked.

"Oh, it wasn't all that *murderous* feeling," Leslie said. "They are safe and sanitary now. They gave me something for pain. The physical pain. I don't think they knew about the other kind."

Sally said nothing. She believed abortion to be wrong. She wouldn't have cited religious arguments in support of that feeling any more than she would have joined a Right to Life protest march at the nation's capitol. She simply believed that the whole business of birth was too mysterious, too fraught with wonder and promise to tamper with. She wouldn't have done it. She wouldn't have wanted her daughters to do it. Now one of them had. There was nothing to say.

"Mama, it really isn't murder, you know," Leslie pleaded.

"I don't know," Sally said, standing up. "It's done, anyhow. Let's not talk about it any more. Go to sleep. I think I'll go for a walk."

Outside, the air was cool and the light from the water seemed full of prisms. Sally stood a minute tying a scarf around her head, welcoming the fresh breeze against her face.

Sarah and Say-Say were walking along the edge of the water, picking up shells. They waved, and Sally walked toward them.

"Don't worry about a thing, Mother," Sarah called. "I let them practice *good* before I turned them loose."

"What?" asked Sally dazedly.

"Hank and the twins are driving the jeep. I checked 'em out, and they all know how to steer and to shift. What else is there?"

Sally smiled. "Nothing, so long as they don't run it overboard."

"They won't," Sarah promised. "I did a trial run over the shell roads with them. If they get it stuck in the sand they have to dig out themselves."

"I notice you didn't let them take Say-Say along," Sally said, patting the little girl's Christmas-green cap.

"I'm not that crazy," Sarah admitted.

"I didn't want to go, Gran," Say-Say said. "I'm going to make a forest on the beach."

They stood watching her fill her skirt with twigs from the myrtle bushes and bits of huckleberry and bracken and take them down to the water's edge, where she carefully, one at a time, set the make-believe trees in neat rows in the wet sand.

"Les told you about the abortion, huh, Mother?" Sarah said, studying Sally's face.

Sally nodded.

"Don't feel bad," Sarah said. "It's best. Hal wouldn't have let up on her if she hadn't agreed to do it."

"Yes, well, I guess he hated it too," Sally said listlessly.

"Not much," said Sarah. "He took off for the arms of his new girl friend Geneva."

"Geneva!" gasped Sally. "That's the one who—"

"Who's been so good to them," finished Sarah. "Old Four F—fat, four-eyed, frumpy, fan. I saw her. She an ex-hippie, a religious fanatic. Add another F for fanatic," she said. And then, "Make it old Five F. I could make it six."

"What a horrible thing!" Sally said. "How awful for Leslie!"

"It's killing her," Sarah said. "I think Hal has had his little flings in the past, but Les thought they were in the past. And this abortion thing had her so torn up she needed whatever support he had to offer. Instead, his girl friend, Old Five or Six F, called Leslie and said *he* needed comfort and she had given it to him. She made it her religious duty both to sleep with him and to explain it to Les."

"Religious?" Sally said, baffled. "I can't understand how it's religious."

"A hippie innovation," Sarah said. "I think they started the idea that anything *they* wanted to do was fine and pure and pleasing in God's sight. Les might have gone along with it once, but not—well, Mother, she really feels as you do about abortions, and she's full of guilt and loss over the baby and now over Hal too."

Sally used the old unspecific euphemism when she told Angie about Leslie. "She lost the baby, Mama," she said and was glad she hadn't been more precise because Angie took it hard.

She said nothing, but Sally saw her go to her room and put up something she had been sewing on, and she sat by the fire very quietly for a long time.

"Sometimes I don't understand," she said softly, as if talking to herself. "If I were giving women children I'd pick Leslie for a dozen, she loves them so. I wonder why it's so hard, so very hard?"

I'll never tell you how hard, Sally said to herself, as she gave Angie her hand to pull her out of the chair and start her to bed. "You always think God knows what He's doing, Ma," she said lightly.

"Yes," said Angie and she sighed heavily.

She's got some doubts tonight, Sally thought in surprise. She's not reconciled.

Leslie didn't go back to the restaurant but got a job with a personnel agency.

"She has a flair for it," Henry Parker told Sally. "She enjoys all those job hunters who come in, really believes in them, and does a good job of selling them to people like me."

"Like you?" Sally said.

"I was able to put a receptionist and a clerk-typist to work for her before I got mad," Henry said, grinning.

Sarah laughed. "You'd better explain about your stiff-necked, prissy old secretary."

"Well, it's not nice to describe Mrs. Bolton that way," Henry said, "but she has been around a long time and she's pretty set in her ways. I hired two people Leslie sent me, and when she called with the third I was busy and didn't return her call. The next day I was out of the office and she called a couple of times. The third day she called and left a message with Mrs. Bolton that she was a stripper named Mongo DePravo. She said she was back in town and eager to 'resume a relationship' with me."

"She didn't!" cried Sally, laughing.

"Ask Mrs. Bolton," said Henry. "She hasn't recovered from it yet. She monitors all my phone calls and asks me about Sarah and the children three times a day."

They all laughed, but Sally got back to the point. "You *will* hire somebody from her if you can, won't you, Henry?"

"Sure," he said. "I'd hire Les if I could, just for laughs."

"I wish you would," Sarah said. "You'd let her off to do things. Last week she couldn't get off to take the twins to the dentist, and she called and asked me if I would. I had the car keys in my hand and was half out the door when I thought about

Hal! I went back and called and asked Leslie if he wasn't off and couldn't he do it? She sounded like she might cry. She said he might be rehearsing or asleep or something. I was hateful. I said, 'Well, wake him up.' Now I'm sorry because, of course, the twins didn't get to the dentist."

They all looked depressed, and Henry made a try at recapturing the light mood. "I'd rather talk about Mongo DePravo," he said.

Within a couple of months Leslie had given up her job and was packing to follow Hal to New Orleans. She farmed out their bedding and the few pieces of furniture they had to friends and asked Sarah to look after what was left.

"I'm tired of this," Sarah grumbled. "The old cleanup kid. What do you think we should do with this shelf you gave Bunny for her little doodads?"

Sally had found it somewhere and didn't think much of it at the time she offered it to Bunny, but now she saw it through the girl's eyes—a marvelous thing to hold small collections.

"I'll keep it," she said. "They'll probably come back someday."

"They shouldn't have gone," Sarah said. "They were settled here, Leslie liked her job, kids were in school. Now Hal has uprooted them again."

"Maybe Hal's got a good job this time," Sally offered hopefully.

"He didn't have any place for them to live," Sarah said. "Leslie said they'd find something when she got there. They're staying temporarily at a motel."

"That sounds prosperous."

"Not *that* motel," said Sarah.

Real estate along the coast wasn't selling well enough to justify keeping an office open, Sally decided, and because she worried about Angie's health she didn't spend much time there anyway. If island property became desirable to beach-home seekers, they could always find her at Esperance. There was a water taxi for hire at the marina in Lucina. She arranged to have a marine telephone installed in the kitchen and settled down to get in the spring garden which Angie wanted but couldn't manage alone this year.

Leslie tried calling them, but late spring storms, although benign in nature, made conversation on the phone difficult, and Sally was surprised one day to see the water taxi from Lucina docking with Sarah and her children and Bunk and Bunny aboard.

She rushed to greet them, crying, "Where did you get B and B?"

"I knew you and Angie missed them so I ordered them home by fierce concentration," Sarah said. "You noticed it, didn't you, twinnies? A voice in your head was saying, 'Go home to Aunt Sarah and Uncle Henry! Go home to Gran and Angie!' "

The twins giggled. "That was what you said on the telephone to our mother, Aunt Sarah. She said we were driving the folks we were staying with bonkers, and you said, 'Send them home,' " Bunny said.

" 'Go home to Gran and Angie!' " Bunk repeated in a sepulchral voice. "Catch the bus and go home to Gran and Angie!"

"It's the best thing that's happened in a coon's age," Angie announced from the doorway. "You all rush right in here and help me decide what to do with this old chocolate layer cake I made. It's too fattening for your gran and me."

All the children stayed on the island for weeks, and Sally occasionally worried that their presence was hard on her mother. They were always hungry, sometimes messy, and occasionally they squabbled. But Angie seemed to enjoy them and often joined them on the very outings Sally had planned to get them away from the house and give her a rest.

They played innumerable checker games on rainy days, and then she taught them an old-fashioned card game called setback and beat them at it regularly. They asked the names of birds and flowers, and she pulled out books and showed them identifying pictures. The shells which had ever been a source of pleasure and sometimes income to Angie became an obsession with the children.

They staged competitions, with prizes offered by Angie for the biggest conch shell, the smallest king's crown, the prettiest unbroken pen shell. She got them up early to catch low tide on the mud flats on the Sound side and hitched up her skirt and waded with them to find the fragile sand dollars which they would soak in bleach until they were clean and white and ready to be strung on fine wire or silken cords to make necklaces.

When Angie tired, Sally took them swimming and fishing and taught them to run the boat. They tonged for oysters and seined for shrimp and set crab traps along the pilings that supported the dock. At the other end of the island there was an inlet where the mullet came in at high tide, and Hank and Bunk stretched a net across the slender neck of the inlet and caught two dozen leaping silver fish on their way back to sea. Angie taught them to clean them and fillet them and spread them over chicken wire in the back yard and smoke them. Thereafter, neither boy could leave the house without a plastic bag of smoked mullet tucked in his jeans as iron ration against whatever might befall him during the day.

Leslie sent them postcards showing the French Quarter and marking an art shop where she had a part-time job. They were still staying with their musician friends, and it was lonesome without B and B. They hoped to get an apartment soon.

"I hope Jan and Lefty are missing us," said Bunny. "I tried to help them by taking care of their little baby, but they were mean to me."

"When you live in somebody else's house," said Bunk with a grown-up air, "you have to put up with a lot."

Sarah came to the island to take suntanned and freckled Hank and Say-Say home and to "borrow" their cousins for a few days.

"I thought we might do the dentist and the shoe store while they're with us," Sarah said. "Bunny and I are going to have a 'girl day' on the town. We're going to lunch and to look at dresses and maybe get our hair done!"

Bunny's eyes shone. She could beat Bunk and Hank at some games and she was always eager to join in any project, climb any tree, or fling herself into any scuffle with them. She wore what they wore—sneakers and cut-off jeans and droopy T-shirts—but she loved dresses and beauty-parlor-done hair, and one of Aunt Sarah's "girl days" was a very special treat to her.

Sally saw them off, feeling lonely for them the minute they threw themselves at her and hugged her at the dock. Angie waved goodbye from the front steps and, to Sally's surprise, had undressed and gone to bed when she got back to the house.

"You feel all right?" Sally asked from the door.

"Feel like an orphaned widow woman," said Angie, making a face. "That's pretty bereft, ain't it?"

"The most," said Sally, relieved. "But you do need a rest, I expect. I'll bring your dinner to your bed. What would you like?"

Angie shook her head. "Nothing. I think I'll sleep awhile."

Sally made herself a tomato sandwich, fruit of Angie's garden, poured a glass of iced tea, and went and sat on the back steps. The breeze was from the north, and after the day's heat it was energizing. Blues should be running past the point or out by St. Dominique light tomorrow. Maybe after a good night's rest, Angie would like to ride out and try her hand.

But the next morning Angie looked so exhausted, her face so ashen, Sally knew she wasn't up to a fishing trip.

"I thought you might like to take the boat and some sandwiches and try the blues today," she ventured anyhow.

"No blues," said Angie. "But I bet we'd get a mackerel or two."

"Want to go?" Sally asked.

"I want you to go," Angie said. "Take a good lunch and bring back some of everything that swims. We haven't had a pompano to broil in Lord knows when."

Sally was tempted. After the hectic weeks of having four children around day and night, a few hours on the water by herself would be restful. Fishing itself was secondary to swinging at anchor over some sandbar, listening to the water slapping the boat, feeling its gentle sway under her and the sun bright and warm overhead.

"I don't know," she said uncertainly, looking again at her mother's drawn and gray face.

"Don't stay home on my account," Angie said briskly. "You won't like it here. I'm going to heat up the kitchen baking a pie."

Sally went.

The fishing was disappointing, but the day was beautiful. Fluffy white cumulus clouds piled up against the deep blue sky like silken cushions. The water, always different, blue one day, green the next, and in time of storms sometimes a boiling, angry gray, was the color of a washwoman's bluing rinse today and as placid.

Sally knew where the bluefish ran. If she hadn't known, there were other boats there to show her. But she didn't feel compelled to try for them. Angie had mentioned pompano, and she had a mind to beach the boat on tiny St. Agnes Island across the channel and cast her line in the shallow water close to shore.

St. Agnes was one of a chain of small uninhabited islands, and the National Conservancy meant to keep it that way. The beach was as fine and white as powdered sugar, and Sally nosed the *Wild Jelly* into the shore where she saw an old gray cypress log, half embedded in sand and handy for tying to.

For an hour she waded in the surf and cast for pompano, and then she put her rod back in the boat and gathered driftwood, an occasional silvery piece for keeping, simply because it was beautiful, but mostly chunks of fat pine for the woodbox on Esperance. The years' accumulation of anxiety over money, over the children, over Angie's health seemed to slough off her shoulders and out of her mind. She felt relaxed and sleepy. She took her sandwich and her thermos of coffee up the beach to the shade of a scarred old pine, bundled up her jacket for a pillow, and stretched out there to eat and rest her eyes in the symmetry of tree branches against the sky.

She slept, and when she awakened the sun had vanished, the white clouds were smudged with charcoal, and a gumbo fog was rolling in from the Gulf.

Grabbing her jacket with one hand and the thermos and sandwich wrapping with the other, she raced to the boat. The waves, like the sky, had turned from washday blue to a sullen gray, and the boat wallowed and pitched at anchor. It was to be expected, the caprice of a spring day on the Gulf, and she should have been watching, Sally thought. A cardinal rule on the water was to watch the sky. Instead, she had slept under it.

The fog was thick over the channel, and Sally put on the *Wild Jelly*'s running lights and began to watch the compass. A lifelong familiarity with the coastline and the currents was a mariner's strength, but she didn't trust hers in a fog.

She heard the bong of a channel buoy and righted her course to slightly south of east. Her instinct was to push the throttle ahead and get out of the fog and to the safety of Esperance dock as fast as possible, but experience directed that she take it slowly and keep an eye out for other boats. The fishermen she left trolling for blues would have seen the fog and headed in while she slept. Many of the shrimp boats were equipped with radar and would spot the *Wild Jelly* in time to sound a warning and veer away from her. Shrimp boats without radar would be watchful, dependent as she was upon human eyes straining to penetrate the rapidly thickening grayness, but they would be experienced eyes, trained eyes. The ones she feared most were the sleek, fast, expensive pleasure boats of amateurs, speeding heedlessly toward the marina.

She found an old towel and swabbed the windshield. She fished out a life preserver and put it on, and she listened, first to the sound of the motor, which was blessedly competent and companionable with its regular beat, then to the sound of the water, and then for the sounds of other boats.

Angie would be worried, she thought, and hoped that she, too, had taken a nap. Maybe she was sleeping or reading or listening to music and hadn't noticed the fog. Maybe she was watching her pie in the oven.

She heard a foghorn, and simultaneously a shaft of light as radiant as sunshine cut through the fog and whirled away. Sally felt better. St. Dominique light was alive and well and reaching out to fools like her who were groping their way through the fog. Old-timers lamented the passage of the families who had kept the lighthouses along the coast. They didn't trust the machines which took over from human beings who had lived just to tend the light. But the machine was working today, Sally thought happily. Sensitive to the enclosing fog, its light had come on, and she knew she would be docking at Esperance presently.

The light on the dock burned, an impotent glob of brightness swathed in mist, but the sight of it cheered Sally and she sang as she tied up the *Wild Jelly* and stretched the tension out of her arms and legs on the deck.

" 'Let the lower lights be burning,' " she sang loudly for Angie's benefit. " 'Cast a beam across the wave! Some poor fumbling, stupid sinner you may rescue, you may sa-ave!' " She brought out the last word with noisy vibrato as she reached the steps, finishing with a whoop: "Oh, Angie! Oh, Ma! I'm home!"

The house was quiet. The only light burned in the kitchen, which was fragrant with the aroma of cooking apples, underlaid by the pungent smell of juice which had seeped out of the crust and dripped on the over floor. Burned juice and sugar and butter were a mess to get off the oven, but they had a pleasant, promising smell, Sally thought. The pie itself—golden crust with tawny juice pushing at the slits—cooled on the counter. She tiptoed to Angie's door and looked in. Her bed under its old fringed white counterpane was neat—and empty. She poked her head out the back door and called. Her mother might have stepped out to the garden to get something for her cooking.

The fog, now condensing on the roof, dripped on leaves with a light ticking. There was no other sound.

Sally went to the living room. On the arm of Angie's rocker the little hooded sweater she had been knitting for Bunny was spread out. She had finished it today, Sally noticed. Angie was a fast and enthusiastic knitter. The drop-leaf table by the hearth was open and set for supper. Sally's eyes rested on the centerpiece Angie always managed, even in flowerless seasons. Today she had settled for a little cream pitcher with sage and rosemary. As she looked at the herbs she saw that one place, not two, had been set for supper. Not hungry again, she thought. Ma's felt lousy today. I shouldn't have left her.

Her sneakers were wet and sandy, so Sally stepped out of them and took them to the back door, where they always had a row pinned to a line, drying. She started to hang them up and then changed her mind and put them back on. Angie might have gone to the beach to meet her and wandered away from the dock on one of her tideline errands.

Fog was rolling in, thick and ropy, and at the end of the flight of old cross-tie steps Sally had to lean forward to find her mother's footprints. Angie had not gone to the dock but had turned east along the water's edge. The print of the rubber overshoes she pulled on for gardening or shelling was plain in the wet sand for a hundred yards. And then Sally lost them. The tide was coming in and had obliterated the tracks, but she felt certain Angie was somewhere ahead of her.

She started running.

"Angie! Mama!" she called, but the grayness swallowed the sound and there was no answer except the boom of the waves, the squawk of sea gulls.

Sally alternately jogged and walked for two miles, the wet sand sucking at her feet until her legs hurt. They had once

234

kept cows in a grassy pasture at the end of the island. It was inconceivable that Angie would pick a day when she felt poorly, a day when she could see only a few feet ahead of her, to go and check the manure supply in the old pasture. But Sally went there anyhow, not knowing where else to look.

She climbed the pasture fence and teetered for a moment on the top rail, looking out to sea. A long spit of sand ran out into the water, dividing the Sound from the Gulf. The current, where it swirled past the sandbar, was strong when the tide was running, and they had always warned the children against swimming or shelling there. The sand at the point was soft, almost liquid, and it was easy to bog up in it and lose one's balance, toppling into the swift current.

Sally's eyes swept the point as she turned to check the pasture. She turned back to the water so quickly she almost fell off the fence. There was something out there, something red, drifting in a little eddy where the sandbar curved toward the beach. Sally jumped off the fence and started running.

A jacket lost off a boat, she told herself, an old quilt or some work clothes. But she knew it was Angie. She knew it as she fought for footholds in the soft shifting sand. Angie had put on her favorite red dress that morning.

Angie's eyes were open, her jaw agape in the curious grimace of death.

"Oh, Mama, Mama!" Sally said, kneeling in the water. "Mama, what happened to you?"

An inquisitive sea gull swept low over their heads. The fast-running current moaned faintly as it cut around the bar.

I must go for help . . . go for help, Sally told herself. Get a doctor. Somebody. But still she knelt there, not wanting to leave the suddenly defenseless, suddenly lonely little body in the brave red dress.

The tide took the sand from beneath her knees, and she struggled to her feet and stooped and locked her arms around her mother's chest and pulled her up on the beach.

It seemed a long time before she got back to the house, an eternity before she got the Marine Patrol to answer.

"Leave her, Sally," the radio operator on duty said. "We'll be there as fast as the fog will let us. The sheriff too. I'll call him. He wouldn't want you to move her."

Sally started to agree from exhaustion but then she thought

of Angie, her gray hair loose from its knot flowing with the water, the soaked red dress, the old body alone in the fog, vulnerable to the birds and fishes that would come.

"No!" she shouted into the speaker. "I'm not leaving her there! I'll take the jeep and bring her home."

They protested then and later, when they arrived at Esperance, but not seriously. The doctor who came with them said Angie had died of a heart attack, probably brought on by excessive exertion.

"She shouldn't have walked that distance," Dr. West said sadly. "She shouldn't have been out there in the water. I told her that she was going to have to go back in the hospital. She was stubborn, you know, Sally."

Sally nodded. "I didn't know you wanted her back in the hospital."

He smiled faintly. "She told me not to tell you, because she had no intention of going. She said she was not 'going through all that hospital mess' again, that when her time to die came she wanted it to catch her here on the island."

Sarah and Henry came, bringing all the children, and then somebody brought Leslie, who had caught the bus in New Orleans and spent the night getting to Lucina. They set up a loving conspiracy to keep Sally from being alone. Painfully, she went over every moment of the day, confessing with shame that she had left Angie by herself, knowing that she didn't feel well, and had sailed off for a leisurely time of fishing and beachcombing and sleeping.

"If I just had *been* here!" she cried over and over.

Hank was the one who finally comforted her. "Ha, Gran, Angie tricked you!" he chortled. "She *wanted* you gone."

Sally looked at him in open-mouthed astonishment. She swallowed and stared into space, remembering. "Of course," she said softly. "Of course she did."

They had a graveside service, and one of the big excursion boats which took fishing parties out from Lucina was chartered by Angie's friends to bring the mourners who came from the inland towns nearby and from up and down the coast.

She would have loved to see a big boat docking here once more, Sally thought, watching the *Coastal Queen* drop anchor out in deep water and lower small boats to bring her passengers ashore.

236

They spread the food friends brought on picnic tables under the trees, and when the last boatload of funeral guests had departed, Sally and the girls walked out on the point to watch the *Queen* enter the channel and steam toward the mainland.

"Mama, can I come home for a while?" Leslie asked.

"Well, of course," Sally said, surprised. "If you want to. Not because you think I can't be alone, though."

"Hadn't even thought of that," Leslie admitted sheepishly. "I was thinking of Angie's little rental house. If it's still vacant, maybe the twins and I could stay there. Hal's going to be in Virginia Beach until Labor Day, and the kids and I would rather be here than alone in New Orleans."

"Sure, you would," said Sally. "I'd love to have you come. We'll go now and see what condition the house is in."

1979

Three years had passed since Angie's death, and Sally found she could miss her without pain. But the loss of Bunk and Bunny only four months later was a constant ache to her. She thought of them a thousand times a day, hearing their voices, listening for their call from the bay road, down which they had come so many mornings to spend the day with her.

The fear that they might be hungry or in need was abiding. She never prepared a good meal without thinking of them and seeing them at her table. Sometimes at night she pulled out of a nightmare in which they were lost and alone to hear Bunk's voice saying again, "I *told* her I'd take care of her."

She remembered the old house in the country and Bunny's cry, "It was the best place we ever lived!"

Where were they? Where did they live now?

Once, driving from Tallahassee, she saw a thin blond boy hitchhiking and, because she had promised the family not to pick up hitchhikers, she passed him by. But the instant she did she realized he looked like Bunk. She stomped on the brake and brought the car to a lurching halt.

The young boy was not Bunk but he might have been, Sally thought, and after that, without telling her daughters, she made a practice of picking up all young hitchhikers, male or female.

It might be dangerous, as everybody said, but to her the

real danger was that Bunk and Bunny would try to come home and, unknowing, she would pass them on the road.

Once at twilight, as she walked back from the cottage on the bay side, she met two fair-haired youngsters running up from the beach toward her. Her heart raced and she started running toward them, her arms outstretched. They were youngsters who had swum in from a sailboat anchored offshore.

Her weekly letters to the twins were an outpouring of love. Aware that children don't want to read long letters or preachy letters, she disciplined herself to be brief and amusing. She waxed gossipy about their cousins and the people they knew in Lucina, enclosing clippings from the weekly newspaper and snapshots if she had them. Now and then she tucked a few dollars in her letters, a sop to herself because she thought it might buy them food.

"You're only giving it to Hal," Sarah said glumly, but she didn't protest. She knew her mother had to reach out to them in all the ways she could.

Sally and the girls shopped with agonizing cheerfulness for birthday and Christmas presents and clothes for Easter and school-starting for the twins. Not knowing how much they had grown, they tried to judge by Hank and his friends and then did their shopping at Sears and other chain stores, only hoping that wherever the twins were there'd be a branch at which they could make exchanges.

The letters and the presents no longer came back but there were no answers, no acknowledgments. Mail to Esperance was uncertain. Anybody who came checked her box at the post office in Lucina and started out with whatever there was in it. But sometimes the well-meaning couriers forgot to deliver letters, showing up red-faced weeks later to confess that they'd poked a card or a letter under something in the bow of a boat and forgot it. Sally developed an obsession about the mail. She talked to the postmaster in Lucina and asked that any mail which might conceivably be from Bunk or Bunny be held for her. And then she made nearly daily trips to check in case something was being held there.

She wanted to talk to Leslie about the twins every time they met or talked over the phone, but Sarah warned her against it.

"Mama, she's got a good marriage. Pete's a fine man. But

he's going to get sick and tired of Leslie's fixation about the twins. She goes home, come hell or high water, every day to check for mail from them. She talks about them all the time and has their pictures all around. She won't buy herself a decent dress or even a pair of jeans because she's saving up to try and find them. When you all get together, she's even worse. She has crying jags."

Sally swallowed guiltily. "I do too."

"Well, you can," Sarah said. "But how would you like to be a bridegroom with a crying bride?"

Sally sighed. "You're right, I know. But I don't think I can ever accept this without knowing where they are and how they are. If we could just be sure about that, I think we might begin to recover."

They were silent a while and then she said, "You know, Sarah, there are thousands like us. Ten thousand parents each year lose their children because either the husband or the wife is a sadistic kidnapper instead of a rational human being who is willing to share. That New Orleans judge told us so."

"I don't believe Hal's got the twins chained to the bed or anything," Sarah said. "They could get in touch. That's what Pete and Henry both can't understand. They think there's something seriously wrong with children who can be persuaded by any means to turn on their mother."

"There's nothing wrong with Bunk and Bunny. Or there wasn't. I don't know where the wrong is. That's what is so awful."

In the middle of the night it came to Sally that she could do something. Not trusting the marina telephone, she got up early and went into Lucina to the launderette pay station. Sarah, a later sleeper, mumbled incoherently when she answered, but Sally jerked her awake.

"I'm going to Virginia. Do you want to go with me?"

"Virgin—Mother, have you heard from the twins?"

"No," said Sally, "but I'm going up there, and if they're there I will see for myself how they are. If they aren't, maybe I can find out where they are."

"I'll go with you," Sarah said promptly. "I'll leave Say-Say with Mrs. Parker, and Hank and Henry can take care of each other. Let's take my car."

"Lend me a nightgown, and I'll leave from here right now," Sally said.

"You don't want to ask Les to go?"

"I don't think so," Sally said. "She'll get her hopes up, and it may be bad up there. If they're not with the Ellises she'd be disappointed. And if they are, they might be so hateful to her they'd break her heart."

Sarah was a good traveling companion. She loved to drive, loved to stop and investigate antiques shops, restaurants, and any of the barnlike structures whose signs promised BARGAINS! BARGAINS! BARGAINS! To be on the road with her was relaxing, and Sally found herself enjoying the unaccustomed ease of having somebody else do the driving. She rested her head on the back of the seat and let her mind drift to other days and other perplexities.

"Sarah," she said once, "did you ever ask Leslie why the twins came early? Why, in fact, she didn't know they were twins?"

"Yes, and it wasn't what I'd hoped, something Hal did. Poor Les, she was so upset over Dodie she lived in a kind of nightmare in Virginia. She couldn't bear to go to the doctor, so there was nobody to tell her she was carrying twins. She told me she was so lonely she walked down to the drugstore every day and ate an egg salad sandwich, combining breakfast and lunch, just because the druggist spoke to her. He said, 'Hiya, Ma! How are you?' The only person who spoke to her for days. She developed toxemia, or she'd never have gone to Walter Reed Hospital."

"And then the twins came?"

"Well, pretty soon. They put her in to treat her toxemia and were going to send her home, and the twins started cutting up to get out. Les said she must have thought if she didn't go to the doctor it wouldn't be true, she wouldn't be expecting. Crazy—but she was crazy with grief over Dodie and loneliness."

"Why do you suppose she loved Hal?" Sally asked after a while.

"You know Les, a sucker for sick dogs. He left home and had no place to go when she first fell for him. She never got over the idea that she had to protect him, that he needed her. She still has times of feeling terribly sorry for him—when she isn't ready to put out a contract for his murder!"

The first night out they stopped for supper in an old inn Sarah found by asking at an information center on the highway and then taking a country road through fields and woods. They ate a good dinner and were back in their room undressing for bed when Sally dragged out another question which had haunted her for years.

"Why do you suppose they had that marijuana?"

Sarah was brushing her teeth. She made a *glugh-glugh* sound and came out laughing. "Mama, you didn't know? All this time you've thought Les was peddling the stuff? Boy, I couldn't rest until I found out about *that!* It took me until about a month ago, but I finally pinned her down. It belonged to the band Hal was playing with. They were to have some for their own use, but most of it belonged to the band—and the S.O.B.s didn't come forward with any help whatsoever when Leslie and Hal were—"

"Busted," Sally finished for her.

"That's right, busted," Sarah said. "Only I always thought it was you who was busted."

Sally shrugged. "Financially. But that's almost a perpetual state."

"I guess you didn't know all those checks Les wrote, all that fooling around exchanging things at the store, was to raise money to keep Hal out of jail, did you?"

"It was?" said Sally. "I thought—well, groceries and Christmas. . . . I didn't really know. It was a good bit of money to me, but not much for a family of four."

"That family of four didn't get it. It was Hal, arrested for drunk driving, driving without a license, drunk on the highway, and all manner of things. Les had to get money somehow to pay his fines, and she didn't want to tell you."

I wonder if I would have raised it for him, Sally thought. If I hadn't and he had been compelled to go to jail, to take his punishment, as they say, would it have made a difference? Would he have emerged a more responsible person, one who wouldn't have stolen the children? She went to sleep wondering.

The next day they didn't stop at the more-than-tempting bargain signs but rushed on, out of nervousness at the thought of what they might find in the little Virginia town where the Ellises lived.

"What are you going to do when you get there?" Sarah asked

as they turned off the freeway and took a tree-shaded hilly state road.

"I hadn't thought," Sally admitted. "Let's just drive by and look at the house and—I don't know—think of something. Do you know how to find it?"

"Could I ever forget?" Sarah demanded, laughing. "First place I was ever thrown out of. And of course it's where I learned that my mother is a member of the Communist Party."

Sally laughed. "You should have told them that I'm not one because I don't know what it is exactly, but if I found out and it sounded better than West Florida politics I might join up."

"That would have straightened Dorinda's curls," said Sarah.

Sally was familiar with the address. She had sent hundreds of letters and packages there. But she wasn't prepared for such a closed-face house when they drove down a pretty narrow tree-lined street and finally saw it. Sweeping close to the ground like some modern fortress, with no front windows and a big closed fence, the Ellises' house was set back from the street in the shadow of giant elms. Its side windows were heavily curtained, its shades down, but there was a light on in one of the rooms, and a car in the driveway, suggesting that somebody was at home.

"Do you see any bicycles?" whispered Sally, feeling a tightness in her chest.

"Not a sign," said Sarah.

"Oh, Sis, suppose the twins come out and see us and turn and run?"

"They won't run from you, Mother. Any child can find something wrong with his mother. But the twins will never find anything wrong with you."

Sally swallowed and reached for her bag. Maybe if she combed her hair and put on some lipstick . . .

"I'm going around by the school," Sarah said. "I saw it from the road back here somewhere."

Three teenage girls were walking along the unpaved street they took, and Sally, seeing that one of them was blond, whispered, "Stop, stop! That may be Bunny!"

Sarah stopped beside them. Bunny was not one of them. The three stopped walking and smiled at Sarah inquiringly.

"Can you tell us where Hope Ellis lives?" she asked, not sure if it was a wise question to ask but unable to think of anything else.

"Right over there in that big red-brick house," one of the girls said. "That's where her grandparents live, but Hope's not there now. They went off someplace with their father, she and her twin brother did."

"When?" put in Sally, choking.

"I don't know exactly," the girl said, turning to consult her friends. "Last June, I guess. Are you her mother?"

"No, just a friend," said Sarah quickly, thanking them and driving on.

"Oh, Lord, I don't know what to do!" Sally wailed helplessly. "The Ellises could have told Bunny's friends to say that. They could have warned them that somebody might be asking."

"We'll just watch the house," Sarah suggested. "You know about stakeouts."

"I'm not going through that again," Sally said. "Let's check in at the motel and get something to eat and think about it."

But she couldn't think of anything to do but watch the house, so they came back after supper and parked in the shadow of some overhanging tree branches and watched until eleven o'clock, when the last light went off. Nobody had gone in or come out of the house.

The next morning Sarah slept so soundly Sally didn't have the heart to awaken her. Dressing in the bathroom, she slipped out of the room and went in search of coffee, finding it in the town's one café, a spot near the courthouse where lawyers and businessmen and farmers seemed to gather for breakfast.

Hubert Ellis will walk in, she thought, and he will recognize me and sound an alarm. If the children are here they'll grab them and run. She hastily paid and left the restaurant, taking refuge in Sarah's car, which she had parked in an alley to hide its Florida tag.

The modern house drew her and she went back and stopped as close as she dared to get, hoping the tall hedge and drooping tree branches would hide the car and certainly the driver. Presently one or two children passed, carrying books under their arms, obviously on their way to school. A teen-age girl, walking by herself, got even with the Ellises' front walk and stopped.

Sally sat up straighter, her heart racing. Bunny's friend, she thought, waiting to walk to school with Bunny. But the girl turned and looked behind her, and just then a group of girls caught up with her and they walked along together.

Sally stayed until there were no more schoolchildren passing, and still nobody had come out of the big house. She went back to the motel and found Sarah was up and torn between a mild worry about her mother and hunger for breakfast.

Their waitress in the coffee shop was young and pretty. "Did you go to high school here?" Sally asked impulsively.

She had graduated last year, she said.

"Do you know the Ellis twins?"

"Sure," said the girl. "I don't think they are in town any more, but they were in school when I was—very active. She's in our choir at Park Street Presbyterian."

"They're nice, aren't they?" Sally asked wistfully.

"Who? Oh, you mean the twins? Sure." The girl was gone.

"Now what?" Sarah asked as they paid their check.

"Let's find the church and the post office," Sally said. "You wait in the car and I'll run in."

The postmaster was busy and not inclined to be helpful.

"I'm Mrs. McMillan from Lucina, Florida," Sally said, feeling that she had to be open and aboveboard with a civil servant. "My grandchildren, Harold and Hope Ellis, live here with Mr. and Mrs. Hubert Ellis, their other grandparents. I understand they have moved and I'm a little worried about the mail I've been sending them—packages and letters with checks in them. Do you forward them?"

As a matter of fact, Sally had not sent checks since the first one precipitated that *We don't need your money* letter. She had sent cash, which was not returned, but she had an uneasy feeling that a postal official would not approve of cash in a letter.

"Forward them?" repeated the postmaster, handing down parcels and junk mail to two other people at the counter. "Sure do."

"What is that new address?" Sally asked, taking out a pen and piece of paper.

"Sorry, I couldn't tell you," the postmaster said, reaching for something he dropped on the floor. "Ask Mr. Ellis, he forwards everything."

"Oh, I would," said Sally equably. "But I think they must be out of town themselves. We went by the house."

"He forwards everything," the postmaster repeated. "If you want to find out where he is, ask at the café."

Sally thanked him and came out mumbling. "They've warned the postmaster. You *know* he sees the addresses."

"Well, maybe he doesn't remember," Sarah said. "Now, to the church or the café?"

"Church," said Sally. "I don't care where Hubert is."

Park Street Presbyterian was historic, a bronze sign out front assured them. Built in 1790, it had been attended by Presidents.

"George Washington slept here," cracked Sarah, mounting the wide wooden steps to the white-columned porch and going with Sally into the small spare sanctuary with its stiff white pews and its long clear bubble-paned windows.

"It's a beautiful church," Sally said softly. She slipped into a pew and turned to look over her shoulder at the choir loft. "Bunny sang there. Oh, I wish I could . . . hear her!" Her voice broke.

Sarah sat down across the aisle and they didn't move for a minute or two. The high pulpit, the wide white boards of the walls, the shining brass locks on the doors in the rear of the church, all these were familiar to the twins. And where were the twins now?

"You want to talk to the minister?" Sarah prodded her.

"No," Sally said, sighing and standing up. "It might embarrass the children to have us do that. Let's go . . . straight to the horse's mouth!"

"Dorinda?"

"Dorinda," Sally said firmly.

This time Sarah pulled into the driveway and parked in front of the house, making no effort at concealment. They smoothed their hair and straightened their skirts, braced themselves, and unflinchingly approached the front door.

"What'll we say?" Sally whispered. Before Sarah could give an opinion, the door opened and she herself was saying it: "Dorinda, how are you? Remember me, Sally—?"

"Of course I do, you sweet thing!" cried Dorinda. "And little Sarah, sugar. You all come right in!"

She was wearing a peach-colored satin robe dripping with cream lace and she had a matching peach bow on the crest of her curls, which this morning billowed out in all directions like foam on a riptide. Sally noticed that her makeup was fresh and wished that she herself had remembered lipstick and comb. Dorinda's large eyes, which someone must have once called expressive, widened and rolled to emphasize everything she said.

"Let me kiss you," she said when she got them in the dim hall. "Love you . . . love you!"

Sally tried to smile appreciatively. Sarah bit her lip.

"I do wish Harold and Hope were here," she said, "but the darlings are off to parts unknown with their father. How's Leslie? That adorable girl married again, I hear. Is she happy? Oh, I hope so. I wish her all the happiness!"

She led them to the living room, a big dark room with curtains and the shades they had noticed from the street last night, still drawn. Moving from lamp to lamp, she soon had five of them turned on, revealing rose damask wallpaper, ornate side chairs and sofa upholstered in rose velvet, marble-topped tables, and a bowfront curio cabinet filled with delicate china and bisque figurines.

"This house is a mess!" she said gaily. "I gave up on it this year and went back to my acting. You know I used to think of a Broadway career, before having a baby put an end to all that. You have a baby!" She tapped Sarah on the shoulder. "You know what I mean. The end of everything for a woman."

Sally felt faint. She wasn't up to a lecture on Dorinda's what-might-have-beens.

"But I resumed acting in a small way—the local theater. Hope tried it, too—last winter. A cameo part. Here, let me show you the programs and the picture in the newspaper. Sit . . . sit!"

They sat.

She disappeared down the hall and was back in a moment with a big scrapbook.

"Hope's," she said. "But she won't mind my showing it to you."

For two hours they sat looking at report cards, party paper napkins, church programs, and snapshots.

"This was the first Christmas they were with us," she said, displaying a snapshot of Hal and the twins before an aluminum Christmas tree. They were wearing the clothes Sally bought them for their trip to New Orleans, and their young faces looked strained and unhappy.

"They don't look very jolly in this one," she murmured, handing it back.

246

"Oh, they were a mess then," Dorinda said. "But look at the difference. Here they are last year at our town Christmas pageant with Hal. How do you like Hope in my old formal? It's one I bought when I was much younger and more svelte. Looks adorable on her, don't you think? Her father came for Christmas and waltzed with her in the grand ballroom upstairs over our old theater the night she wore that. Theater's closed now, of course. Young Harold played drums in the dance band—and oh, my, we were proud of them."

"Yes," said Sally, her eyes filling.

"Here, let me read you what Hope wrote about a party I gave when they finished communicants' class and joined our church: 'I didn't know 'Rinda'—they call me 'Rinda, you know—'could give such a beautiful party. You should have seen the table with her best lace cloth, all the candles in the silver holders, and the really elegant party food she made.'"

It was a lengthy account, and Sally found it hard to listen. For some reason she didn't want to believe Bunny had written it. She turned restively on the sofa and Sarah nudged her.

Dorinda's voice lifted eloquently, expressively, with dramatic pauses and occasional warm, happy laughs as she read on.

"Dictated *and* read," Sarah whispered, and this time Sally nudged *her* warningly.

Sally waited for a pause in the reading and broke in desperately, "Dorinda, *where* are the children?"

"I haven't the *faintest* idea!" she said, rolling her eyes heavenward and returning to her reading.

"Dorinda." Sally tried again. "Why don't they answer our letters? Why have they turned on their mother and the rest of us?"

"I haven't listened to a word about any of this distressing contretemps," Dorinda said, showing her dimples in a self-laudatory smile. "I don't like stress. I don't like conflict. I simply refuse to listen."

Sally subsided. Somehow she felt rebuked, as if she shouldn't have raised the subject, as if she should have declined to recognize outrage and loss instead of wading around in it up to her neck.

"I go along my own way, singing if I can," Dorinda said proudly. "I try to be happy, to spread only happiness." She resumed reading.

When she reached the end of the tome, Sally stood up, ready to go.

"Wait, I know you are interested in who their friends are," Dorinda said. "Here are some pictures."

She turned the scrapbook to exhibit group pictures of thirty or forty children, pausing first to see if Sally and Sarah could pick out the twins' faces and then going methodically down each line, naming the child and telling a great deal about his or her parents, their business, where they lived, which church they attended. When she turned a page, Sally rushed in with a question.

"You don't have any idea where they are or if they'll be back here ever?"

"Oh, I'm writing Hal today and urging him to send them back to us," Dorinda said. Then she stopped uneasily.

Trapped, Sally thought. She doesn't know where he is, but she's writing to him today. Ah, it would be mean to trip the trigger on her, as nice as she's being to us. She said nothing, and Dorinda rushed along.

"Hubert and I do hope they come back. They are the most adorable children, and I think they are happy here. It's a sweet little town." She lowered her voice. "Almost no nigras in the high school. No crime. No drugs. They can walk or ride their bicycles anywhere they want to go. We bought them good bicycles for Christmas last year. I'll never forget how happy they were. Hubert and I were resting after Christmas dinner, and they came in from riding around town and knelt down by our bed and said together—you know how they do that sometimes?—'You all are the best grandparents in the whole wide world!'"

I'm going to die, Sally thought. I'm going to break up and scatter bones and blood all over her marble and mahogany.

"You know Hope is going in the U.D.C.," Dorinda confided. "She has four ancestors on our side, and I'm sure your ancestors gave their all to the Confederacy."

Oh, hell, I don't know, Sally thought. What do I care? But aloud she said, "Oh, yes." She thought of Pete's grandmother who called Robert E. Lee "Bobby," and she smiled and was tempted to say, Bunny can use her mother's new husband's grandmother, but she refrained.

"You want to see Hope's room? It's sweet, if I do say it. I'd never show you Harold's, of course." She shuddered.

They followed her down the hall, past several closed doors, to a bright airy room looking out on the back yard. It was furnished in light curly maple, a four-poster bed with a lace tester and spread to match, a three-mirrored dressing table with six small drawers with gleaming brass pulls, a schoolmaster's desk with a shelf of books over it, and a gooseneck rocker with a china doll sitting in it.

"Oh, it's so pretty!" Sarah cried involuntarily. "I wish Say-Say had such a room."

"Hope does seem to enjoy it," Dorinda said. "You see, she has her own bath. . . ." She opened a door.

Poor Leslie, Sally thought, with that privy in the country, with greasy little apartments and sofas in the pads of friends, with awful motels and borrowed beach cottages. Poor Leslie. She walked to the desk and looked at the books. Nothing she had sent was there.

"Do they get our letters and packages, Dorinda?" she asked.

"I promise you they do."

"You know I worry about sending money in the mail," Sally said hesitantly. "They won't cash checks, but if I send money they keep it."

"They wouldn't return it!" Dorinda shook her head as if the idea was inconceivable.

Back in the living room, she said, "Sally, they really love you. I think they have always loved you even more than their parents."

"Then why . . . why?" Sally fought back tears.

"You were on *her* side!" Dorinda said with sudden unexpected vehemence. "They knew you were on *her* side!"

"Well, yes," Sally said slowly. "Why wouldn't I be?"

"Don't ask me," Dorinda said promptly. "I don't know a thing about it. I don't *want* to know a thing about it! If you all will wait a minute till I can get dressed, I'd love to show you our town. We have some very historic buildings, and the founder's grave is right down the street in that picturesque old cemetery."

"No," said Sally. "No, thank you." She was out the front door before Dorinda could answer.

"I think we'd better start back to Florida," Sarah was saying politely. "My mother-in-law is keeping my little girl, and she may be ready to throw in the towel by now. You've been awfully nice, and we do thank you for all you've told us about the twins. We love them and miss them, but it's good to know that they've been safe and well here."

They were out of town before Sally started crying in earnest. "'The best grandparents in the whole wide world!'" she mimicked Dorinda wildly. "Well, don't count on it, 'Rinda, dear! I was the best damned grandmother in the whole wide world not so long ago, and they turned against me, turned on me like I was a snake!"

She was weeping noisily, abandonedly now.

"Where were the *good* grandparents when they were born? When they were sick? When they were hungry? Where were those peachy-dandy Ellises when their mother and father were in jail? Who got 'em out? Did dear 'Rinda and Pa-Pa put shoes on their feet? Pay their dental bills? Get their lights back on?" The more she remembered, the harder she howled.

Sarah, driving, said nothing.

In a mile or two she was hoarse and her rage had dissolved in tears. Sarah handed her a box of Kleenex and patted her knee. "Mother, poor Mother," she said.

"I'm sorry, honey," Sally said after a while.

"S'okay," said Sarah. "You're entitled."

"It's not fair, it's just not fair," Sally whispered.

"You and Angie always told us fair was something you gave, not something to count on receiving," Sarah said.

"Shut up, Sarah. I don't want a replay of my pious prating," Sally said, grinning weakly.

"You're not sorry we came?"

She shook her head. "I guess not. At least we know something."

"You can't have it both ways. You said if you just *knew,* if you could be sure they were all right, you could stand losing them. Les says the same. Now you know and you hate it. Les'll hate it too, I'm afraid."

"Let's get coffee," Sally said, and as Sarah found a drive-in and pulled in the parking lot, she mopped at her face and blew her nose and laughed shakily. "I just keep thinking of Bunk and Bunny and wondering, How dare they? How *dare* they be happy without us?"

They called Leslie the next morning and went to see her at the restaurant before it opened, taking pictures Dorinda had lent them with the specification that they get them copied and return them.

"You went without me!" Leslie cried. "You didn't even tell me you were going! Oh, Mama, oh Sarah, how could you?"

"You would have hated it," Sarah said. "The twins weren't there, and you would have had to sit still and have them described to you and explained to you by that fool Dorinda."

"I guess she's not really such a fool," Sally said thoughtfully. "I cut up a lot about her yesterday, out of jealousy and hurt. But she really was kind and hospitable to us, and if the twins go back there when school starts I believe they'll be all right."

Pete came in and sat in the booth beside Leslie, putting an arm around her. She had the pictures spread out on the table, and her eyes glistened with tears.

"They're so beautiful!" she said chokily.

"Listen to the girl," said Pete. "She calls them beautiful and they look just like her. Vain woman!" He kissed her on the forehead.

"They do," Sally agreed, "except for the coloring. All that bright hair."

"Tell me every single thing," said Leslie. "When did you decide to go? How did the Ellises treat you? Did they tell you where the twins are now?"

Sally and Sarah took turns, cueing each other, interrupting, talking at the same time. Leslie alternately laughed and cried.

Pete got up and unlocked the front door and welcomed the first customers of the day. He brought the coffee pot back to the table where Sally and Sarah and Leslie sat, refilled their cups, and stood a moment listening.

"I want to say something, if you gumshoe girls are finished," he said, grinning at Sarah and Sally. "I'm glad you made that trip to Virginia and learned as much as you could about the children, because it's a good beginning for what I have in mind. The courts and the laws have failed to handle this problem for thousands upon thousands of parents. My lawyer told me so. He told me about an organization of parents who've banded together to help one another recover stolen children and, long range, are working to get custody laws uniform."

"Long range!" sniffed Leslie, wiping her eyes. "I want my children now."

"I know," said Pete, laying a hand on her shoulder. "And

251

if I have anything to say about it, you're going to get them back soon. Just be patient a little longer, baby."

Sally looked up at his usually merry face. It was solemn with concern and love. She swallowed hard.

I don't know, she thought. I really don't know. What if they don't want to come back? I thought if I just *knew* they were all right I could bear it. Leslie thought that too. Now she's having a hard time. I know, because I am too. Knowing is sometimes harder than it's cracked up to be.

In the face of Pete's pledge to get the children back, and soon, she didn't want to raise the old stumbling blocks. She didn't want to say, We've had detectives and lawyers and court orders—to what avail? She didn't want to say that ugly word, brain-washed, and yet older, tougher people than Bunk and Bunny had been successfully subjected to that.

Pete read her mind. "If they've been brain-washed, we'll get professional help on that. Don't worry, we're going to be moving now. You girls with your trip to Virginia make me see how slow I've been to act."

Sally and Sarah stood up to go. Leslie followed them outside and stood by the car.

"I do thank you," she said softly. "I guess it hurts to know that they've been happy and all right without me, but it's better than worrying and not knowing. You all were wonderful to go and find out. I'm sorry I cried."

"Welcome to the club," Sally said, hugging her briefly. "I bawled. I hollered and yelled and cussed and cried. But that was yesterday. Today I feel pretty good, and you are going to feel better soon."

Leslie turned away and then quickly turned back. "I already do," she said clearly. "Pete and I are going to have a baby!"

Sally stumbled getting out of the car. Sarah almost beat her in reaching Leslie's side. They hugged her and asked all the old questions, and Leslie smiled and answered, and after a while they left.

Sally slumped down in the seat. A baby, she thought, and her heart lifted. Another baby. It would not take the place of the missing children. You don't replace children. And yet . . . oh, it's good, it's good.

She smiled at Sarah and Sarah smiled back.